**She awkwardly lifted Will onto her shoulder.**

The baby snuggled up next to her neck like his brother had. She shut her eyes for a moment. Casey paused, watching her. There was something in her expression—more than discomfort…pain.

"No pressure, if you'd rather not," Casey said. "It would just help me out, is all."

"I thought you didn't like me," she said, her eyes opening again, and she fixed him with a direct look that made him shift uncomfortably.

"I don't like what you stand for, Ember Reed, but Will seems to settle right down when you're holding him, and babies are like dogs that way. They smell bad people. And like I said, I'm a bit desperate right now. You help me with the boys, and I'll go out of my way to help you find the information you need to make your choice about buying this place. Fair is fair. I'm as good as my word."

**Patricia Johns** writes from Alberta, Canada. She has her Hon. BA in English literature and currently writes for Harlequin's Love Inspired and Heartwarming lines. You can find her at patriciajohnsromance.com.

Award-winning author **Stephanie Dees** lives in small-town Alabama with her pastor husband and two youngest children. A Southern girl through and through, she loves sweet tea, SEC football, corn on the cob and air-conditioning. For further information, please visit her website at stephaniedees.com.

# Her Cowboy's Twin Blessings

Patricia Johns

&

# The Cowboy's Twin Surprise

Stephanie Dees

LOVE INSPIRED

INSPIRATIONAL ROMANCE

## LOVE INSPIRED®
INSPIRATIONAL ROMANCE

ISBN-13: 978-1-335-46128-5

Her Cowboy's Twin Blessings and The Cowboy's Twin Surprise

Copyright © 2021 by Harlequin Books S.A.

Her Cowboy's Twin Blessings
First published in 2018. This edition published in 2021.
Copyright © 2018 by Patricia Johns

The Cowboy's Twin Surprise
First published in 2019. This edition published in 2021.
Copyright © 2019 by Stephanie Newton

This edition published by arrangement with Harlequin Books S.A.

For questions and comments about the quality of this book,
please contact us at CustomerService@Harlequin.com.

Love Inspired
22 Adelaide St. West, 40th Floor
Toronto, Ontario M5H 4E3, Canada
www.Harlequin.com

**Printed in U.S.A.**

# CONTENTS

# HER COWBOY'S
# TWIN BLESSINGS

## Patricia Johns

To my husband, the love of my life.

And it came to pass, when the people heard the sound of the trumpet, and the people shouted with a great shout, that the wall fell down flat… and they took the city.

—*Joshua* 6:20

# Chapter One

Casey Courtright crossed his arms and chewed the side of his cheek as he looked down at the sleeping newborns. They were in matching cradles in the middle of the sitting room. He felt a wash of tenderness as he watched those little chests rise and fall. He'd had the infants in his house for a week now, and they were growing fast—as was Casey's attachment to them. When he'd agreed to be his cousin's babies' guardian, he'd never suspected to be called upon to take custody! A tragic house fire changed all that… But even with these precious additions to his household, he was pretty sure he could keep his life on track. He had plans—rather immediate ones, actually.

Casey shot the old ranch hand a grateful smile. "I appreciate the babysitting, Bert. My niece should be here to take over in an hour. I've got the bottles ready in the fridge. Diapers are here." He nudged a box with his boot. "Wyatt there tends to wake up first. If you feed him real quick, you can be ready for when Will wakes up. It's a handful with two."

"Sir, I'll be fine," Bert replied, rubbing a hand over

the coarse stubble on his chin. "My wife and I raised five of our own, and we're on our eighth grandchild. Granted, twins'll be a new one for me, but I'm pretty sure I can figure it out for an hour."

"All right, then. Thanks. I'll see you."

If only Casey felt that sure of himself with those two babies. He glanced over his shoulder once more as he headed through the kitchen to the side door. He'd worked here at Vern Acres Ranch for the last fifteen years, ever since his father was forced to sell the family spread. There wasn't much money left over from that sale after debts were paid, and Casey had gone looking for ranching work on someone else's land. That brought him here—Vern Acres. Mr. Vern ran a tight ship, and Casey had climbed in the ranks, finally landing as ranch manager. It was a respected position, but Casey would never feel quite settled until he had his own land again.

Last Sunday in church, the pastor had talked about circling those Jericho walls. God said to march, and they just kept on marching—but seven days of circling those massive, impenetrable walls was a long time. Well, Casey had been circling these walls for fifteen years, looking for an opening, and just before those babies arrived, Casey had seen the cracks start.

Mr. Vern was selling the ranch, and Casey had a down payment saved up and had arranged for a mortgage just large enough to cover what this land was worth. Not a penny more, mind you, but Casey was a man of faith, and he didn't think he'd need that extra penny. He'd been praying for this chance ever since the Courtright land went to Reed Land Holdings, and when he told his dad that he had a chance at getting this ranch, old Frank Courtright had added his prayers to the effort. This morning, Casey was going on up to the main house to tender his offer to Mr. Vern himself.

The drive from the manager's house, where Casey lived, up to the main house took only about five minutes, and Casey's truck bumped over the gravel road in a cheerful rhythm. Spring had come to this corner of Montana. Everything had sprouted—from the grass in the ditches lining to the road to the pasture, lush with tender new growth. Golden sunlight shone through the windshield and warmed up the cab.

This was it—this was the day! And the bright sunlight sparkling off the last of the morning frost on those long, nodding grasses felt like a gift from above. He'd tell the boys about this day when they were old enough to understand—the day the Courtrights got land again. He'd have a ranch to leave to those kids, and they'd be raised right with horseback riding, chores and a personal pride in the land under their feet. And if he could find the right woman, maybe he could even give them a mom.

Casey crested a hill, and the main house came into view. It was a low, wide ranch house with a porch that curved around the side. The backyard was fenced off, with a garden and a shade tree. And beyond the house in the distance, the snowcapped Rocky Mountains loomed in all their glory.

Casey pulled his truck up next to the boss's and turned off the engine. He sat for a moment, raising his heart to his Maker.

*Bless this, Lord*, he prayed. *This land would be the world to me, if You saw fit to give this Your blessing.*

Then he pushed open the door and hopped out. No time like the present.

The side screen door was propped open with a brick, and Casey could hear the sound of voices as he approached. Mr. Vern's laugh boomed out, and then Casey heard another laugh—softer, more musical. Was a woman in there?

Casey knocked on the door as a formality, then pushed it open as he always did and stepped inside. His eyes took a moment to adjust to the dimmer light of the kitchen. Mr. Vern stood with his arms crossed over his chest, his belly sticking out in front of him. He had a bristling white mustache that covered his lips so that you never could be sure what that mouth was doing unless he was laughing out loud or bellowing an order across a field.

"Morning, Casey," Mr. Vern said. "Good timing. This here is Ember."

Casey turned to make the introduction, and he was met with a tall, lithe blonde woman—bright blue eyes and a smile turning up the corners of her mouth. She was stunning—skin like cream and her lips shining with the lightest touch of gloss. He shook her hand and her grip was firm and confident.

"Pleasure," Casey said with a smile. "You a friend of the boss?"

"Not exactly," Mr. Vern cut in. "She's considering putting an offer down on my ranch, and I need you to give her a tour of the place."

"An offer—" The words stuck in his throat. "Right. Not a problem."

This was his job, after all. He was ranch manager, and he'd be the one who knew the ins and outs of this place. It just came as a shock to hear he had competition already.

"Her car is out front," Mr. Vern added. "She hit that big pothole just before the turn." Mr. Vern exchanged a look with Casey. No one who knew these roads made that mistake. That pothole formed every winter. "Looks like a bent axle to me. She's going to be in town for a bit while she gets that fixed. The tow truck is on its way."

"Great." Obviously, this wasn't the time for Casey's business with Mr. Vern, and already he could feel his opportunity slipping away. Of course, Mr. Vern would be cheery about all of this—the sale of this ranch was going to fund his retirement.

"After you give her the tour, I'd like you to give her a ride back into Victory," his boss said, then turned to the young woman. "The land is beautiful. I have a feeling you're going to fall in love with the place."

Casey smiled tightly. "What was your name again?"

"Ember," she said. "Ember Reed."

"Wait—" Casey's heart thudded to a stop and then hammered fast to catch up. "Reed... Not as in Reed Land Holdings?"

Ember's cheeks flushed. "Yes, actually. But I'm not acquiring land for my father's business. This is a personal purchase."

"Right." As if that even mattered. That wealthy family was the money behind the faceless corporate giant that had been gobbling up the land in the county for years. "Sir, could I have a word?"

Mr. Vern's smile faltered. "Sure. Ember, why don't you go on outside and check out the view. Casey will be right with you."

Ember hitched a purse up onto her shoulder and headed out the side door. The screen slammed behind her, and Casey watched her look around for a moment before walking away from the door, affording him some privacy. For good measure, Casey swung the door shut.

"Reed Land Holdings," Casey said hollowly.

"I need to sell, Casey. You know that."

"Yeah, but to *them*?" Casey clenched his teeth. "You've seen what they've been doing to this county! We used to be family ranches, shoulder to shoulder, until that soulless giant came through and started buying us out. They own sixty percent of the ranch land out here, and you want to turn that into sixty-five?"

"Linda's care isn't cheap," Mr. Vern replied. "And the place she's in has been going downhill. I need to get her into a better care home."

Mr. Vern's wife, Linda, was suffering from early-onset Alzheimer's, and Casey could sympathize with his boss's sense of urgency here.

"Sir, I was coming up here to make you an offer, myself," Casey said, pulling the folded papers from his pocket. "I've talked to the credit union about a mortgage, and with the money I've saved and the bit that my dad gave me from the sale of his land, I've got enough to make an offer."

"Oh?" Mr. Vern reached for the papers and scanned them. He nodded twice, then shot Casey an apologetic look. "It's a fair offer, Casey. And I appreciate it. If all things were equal, I'd rather sell to you, but Miss Reed says that if she likes what she sees, she can offer twenty percent more than this."

Casey accepted his papers back, emotion closing off his throat.

"I know how this seems," Mr. Vern went on. "I know what your family lost, and I'm not some heartless cad. You know that. But with Linda's cost of care going up,

I need every penny I can get. This is my chance to re-tire, spend what time I can with my wife and set things up for my kids to inherit a little something when my time comes. I'm not young anymore. You might as well know that I'm in a lot of debt. Reed Land Holdings did a number on my profits, too. They've hurt everyone."

"But you're selling to them—"

"I'm *not* selling to them," Mr. Vern retorted. "I'm willing to sell to that young lady out there. Like she said, this a personal purchase for her. Nothing to do with her father at all."

"Funded by him, no doubt," Casey shot back.

"Who am I to judge where someone gets their money?" Mr. Vern shook his head. "Everyone gets it from somewhere, and I don't care if I'm paid by a bank or a checking account. I've got my own worries, Casey. You have to appreciate that. She's not adding this to her father's stash of land—this is for her."

"Her—" Casey hooked a thumb toward the closed door. "That little blonde with the city heels on her boots and the clothes that look like money. She's going to ranch this land herself?"

Mr. Vern shrugged weakly. "Whatever she chooses to do with it is her concern. I've got Linda to worry about, Casey. I'm sorry."

And Casey couldn't argue that point. Mr. Vern loved his wife, and he'd do what he had to in order to get her the care she needed. Casey heaved a sigh.

"I was going to show her around myself, but my old knee is really sore this morning. I need you to show her around," Mr. Vern went on quietly. "I know it's a lot to ask right now, but I also know the kind of man you are. I wouldn't trust this to anyone else, Casey. Besides, she mentioned needing a manager around here. I could make it a stipulation of the sale that you stay employed."

Mr. Vern was trying to help—Casey could see that much—but he didn't have any intention of working for a Reed. Ever.

"I'll do my job, sir," he replied tightly. "You can count on me for that."

He headed for the door. Fifteen years was a long time to work this land, circling those fields and cattle like his own personal Jericho walls. Fifteen years was a long time to pray for God to set things right for his family once again.

It looked like he'd be praying for a little while longer.

Ember turned as the door opened, and that tall, lanky cowboy came back outside. The screen swung slowly shut behind him as he strode into the sunlight and re-placed a cowboy hat on his head. He wore a thick vest over his shirt, but his sleeves were rolled up his fore-arms, revealing solid muscle, and those brown eyes locked on to her somberly—none too glad to see her now that he knew who she was, apparently. He was good-looking in a way she didn't see too often in the city. He wasn't clean-cut by a long shot, but he carried himself with an easygoing confidence.

"Miss Reed, I was asked to show you around," he said. "I'm Casey Courtright, by the way. Ranch man-ager."

Ember nodded. "Pleasure to meet you. Call me Ember, though."

She turned back to drink in the cattle-dotted hills. It didn't matter which way a person stood on this land, there was a magnificent view from every angle—

nothing like her home in Billings. She owned a small apartment in the city—a gift from her father when she graduated with her master's degree in family counseling. And she loved that little apartment. This land, though—this was a chance at something much bigger... Her mark on the world at long last.

She could see a modern silver barn, a web of roads leading away from it. But farther south, there was a red barn, brilliant against an emerald background of pasture, and it kept drawing her eye. If she did buy this land, that barn would stay. She'd have no use for the other one, though.

"You're not a country woman, are you?" Casey said, interrupting her reverie.

"Why do you say that?" she asked, casting him a guarded look.

"Your clothes. Those shoes—" Then he nodded in the direction of the picturesque little barn. "The way you look all wistful when you look at barns."

She smiled, then shook her head. "No, I'm from Billings."

"So what plans do you have for the ranch?" he asked.

"I'm not even sure this is the right ranch," she said, and she noticed the tall cowboy stilled at those words. He raised an eyebrow.

"What do you mean, the right one?" he asked.

"My family had a homestead around here somewhere, and I want to buy the land they used to live on back in the eighteen hundreds."

"Oh." He hooked his thumbs into his belt loops, then shrugged. "And how will you know if you've found the right land?"

"There are some descriptions in old journals. Some

names of creeks and rivers… Before I put down an official offer on this place, I need to confirm it's the right
property."

"Does Mr. Vern know that?"

"I'm not hiding anything."

From the view that spilled out in front of her, she
very well might fall in love with the place as Mr. Vern
hoped. But it wasn't the view she was passionate about
purchasing, nor would loving the place stop her from
walking away. She wanted the land where her ancestors struggled through long winters, where they hunted
to keep their growing family fed, where they chopped
down trees for their very own log house and barn. Ember's mother had told her stories about the old days
when men had to guard their cattle against wolves, and
when wagons clattered over trails on their yearly trip to
Victory, the closest town they had. Those stories had
inspired her, made her feel like she was part of something bigger than herself, something more meaningful.

"You must have people who can look into this stuff
for you," Casey said.

"People?" Ember turned to face him. "Oh!" She
laughed. "We should probably clear that up right now.
Yes, I'm Alistair Reed's daughter, but I'm illegitimate.
I don't exactly have the full weight of the Reed legacy
behind me. My father helped me get my education and
get a start. That's it. I'm not quite the heiress you're
taking me for."

"Ah." He eyed her skeptically. "What's your education in?"

"Family counseling." And yes, she noted the irony
that she, a dirty little secret for so long, would want to

devote her life to helping other families be more functional than hers had been.

"And what do you want the land for?" he asked.

"I want to open a family counseling center—a resort-style environment where families can get away from the pressure of their everyday lives, enjoy some outdoor activities together and talk out their issues." She smiled, wanting him to see and understand her vision.

"So if you bought this place, you wouldn't run the ranch," he clarified.

"No. I'm not a rancher. I'm a therapist."

"Gotcha." Casey chewed the side of his cheek. Was he worried about his own job? Likely. Who wasn't in this current economic climate? She hadn't grown up rich, and she'd only recently come into any kind of money, so she wasn't unfeeling when it came to these issues.

"Casey—may I call you Casey?"

"Might as well," he replied.

"Casey, obviously, I don't even know if I'll buy this place, but if I do, I'll need a manager for the land. I wouldn't be running a full ranching operation, but there'd be horses, some cattle—"

"What would you do with the cattle?" he interjected.

"Do with them?" she said. "Raise them, I suppose. Cattle are very soothing. I think a lot of my clients would benefit with some time in nature."

"So…" Casey squinted. "You'd just feed them? And…keep them?"

"I suppose, yes."

"So your vision is to have fields full of elderly cattle?" He eyed her with a veiled expression on his face, and she was relatively certain he was mocking her.

"I'm not a complete fool," she retorted. "I know where the meat on my plate comes from, but I'm not looking to run a cattle ranch. I suppose those are all decisions I'd have to make later on."

"Fair enough."

"What I was trying to say," she said, "is that if I buy this place, I'll need a manager, and I understand that the prospect of losing a job is a daunting one. You wouldn't need to worry about that."

"I'll land on my feet," he replied tersely. "No need to worry about me."

"Okay." That definitely didn't sound like gratitude for job security. In fact, he sounded like he had no interest in working for her at all. "Is there a reason you don't like me?"

"Let's just say that this county has been hit hard by your father's corporation," he replied.

"My father's corporation provides a lot of good jobs to this county," she shot back.

"Your father's corporation pushed my family out of our ranch," he snapped. "And yeah, the Reed ranches provide jobs—jobs I don't want. I want my land back. But that's not happening, is it? You're an outsider— don't think you know people around here or how we think."

Ember swallowed. "I'm sorry about that. I didn't know."

"Yeah?" He shook his head. "Great. Thanks."

His tone dripped sarcasm, and some anger simmered deep inside. She might not know him or the people around here, but he didn't know a thing about her, either!

"Hey—my mother was the housekeeper in the Reed

house," she said. "I wasn't raised in some mansion. My mother gave me the Reed last name on my birth certificate, but my father didn't publicly acknowledge me until I was twenty! We lived in a basement apartment and wore secondhand clothes. My mom worked *hard* in order to provide for us. I'm no spoiled heiress."

"I'm glad to hear it," he replied curtly. "But you're still crossing lines you know nothing about around here. There's such a thing as family pride. We don't want to work for someone else. We want land that's connected to us…land we can pass down."

"And in that, we can finally agree," Ember replied with a tight smile. "I want what you want—land connected to my family. And for the record, the family connection is on my mother's side, not my father's."

Casey met her gaze for a moment. Then his cell phone rang and he dug it out of his front pocket.

"Yeah…" he said, picking up the call and turning away from her.

This ruggedly handsome man didn't like her, but there was more to the anger and frustration he was showing—she could sense it. If he were a client, she'd ask him how all this made him feel. And he likely wouldn't answer. She knew Casey Courtright's type— stubborn, reticent, silent. They were the hardest kind of man to get to open up—the kind that clammed up during appeals to talk inside a therapist's office, but became more relaxed and responsive during outdoor activities like horseback riding or long hikes. Or work.

She eyed Casey as he talked on his phone, his tone low. Yes, Casey Courtright would be the kind of man who valued his work higher than anything else. And she was threatening to change it. Was that his problem with her?

Casey hung up the phone and turned back toward her. "That was one of my ranch hands. He's got to head out to check on a herd, so I need to take over for him." Casey nodded toward his truck. "I can't start the tour until I take care of this, I'm afraid. Care to come along?"

"Take over what?" she asked, her interest piqued.

"Childcare," he replied with a small smile. "I'm the new guardian of twin baby boys, and one of my ranch hands was staying with them, but it looks like he'll have to report back to work."

Baby boys…that hit her right in the heart. She'd had her own baby boy and held him in her arms for one long night, and her memories of him made her heart ache. She sucked in a ragged breath. Casey wasn't the only one to pour himself into his work. She did the same. This trip to discover her family's land was the closest she'd come to anything like a vacation in ages. She was out here until her car was fixed, and she had a mission to discover whether this was the land her family had settled or not. Now was not the time to delve into her own personal issues.

"So you're—" she began.

"Heading back to my place," he said. "It's five minutes down the road." He paused, regarding her with a thoughtful look on his face.

"What?" she asked with a small smile.

"You and I might be able to help each other, Ember. You're obviously going to need some time on this property to figure out if it's the right place. And I need some help with those babies."

"I'm no nanny," she said with a short laugh.

"I'm not asking you to be. I can show you around this ranch properly, but my availability is going to be hit-and-miss. We run a really efficient operation here without a lot of extra employees hanging around, and I'm in a unique situation being a new guardian of these babies. Everything is in a knot right now. Seeing this ranch is going to take you more than one day, and if I'm going to give you a proper tour, I'd need to scrounge up a ranch hand to babysit while I take you around, and I can't always spare the man. My niece helps out, but she's got school and a part-time job of her own, so I can't really count on her. But if you were here on the ranch so you'd be available when I manage to get everything lined up, and if I had some extra help with the babies in the meantime, we could both have our needs met."

"I'm not a long-term solution," she countered.

"I'm not looking for one. My aunt is coming in two weeks to help me out full-time. All I need is a bit of help until then. Plus, your car is in the shop for a week at least, isn't it?"

Ember licked her lips and looked away. He was right—if she was going to get the time on this property that she needed to make an informed purchase, she'd have to make some kind of arrangement to stay. This setup made the most sense. But it didn't take that aching part of her heart into account. Baby boys…she wasn't ready to reopen that wound. Not yet, and not with an audience.

Ember looked back at the house, over at her wrecked car and up into the face of that rugged cowboy. His expression didn't betray any of his feelings, and he raised an eyebrow at her.

"What do you say? You can think about it, if you

want. But I've got to head back to the house. Coming or staying?"

This wasn't about old wounds and sad regrets. And she couldn't avoid babies forever. As much as she hated being pushed into a corner like this, she had a priceless opportunity to look at this land with the attention to detail she required. Could she set aside her personal issues long enough to make her dreams for her future work come true? She sucked in a breath, her limited options circling her mind.

"I'm coming," she said.

Somehow, Ember needed a fresh start…and this land held a promise of just that.

# Chapter Two

Casey looked over at the woman beside him in the passenger seat as he bumped over that familiar gravel road. She looked relaxed enough, unless he noticed her hands—white knuckled in her lap. Was it him? Was she nervous about driving down some isolated ranch road with a guy she didn't know? He didn't like the idea of anyone being truly afraid of him. She was the competition—here to slap down more money than he had any access to—but she was also a woman out of her element and alone, and that made him soften toward her a little bit.

"You okay?" he asked.

"Of course."

"Because you're white knuckling it there." He shot her a half smile.

"Oh…" She breathed out an uncomfortable laugh. "Sorry."

She released her grip, stretched her fingers out and laid her hands flat against the tops of her legs.

This drive back down the road wasn't quite the celebration the drive up to the house had been. Was this it, then? Mr. Vern would sell to this city slicker, and Casey's dreams of owning a ranch would have to be put on hold yet again? Yes, there was always the chance that another property would land on the market, but would the timing ever be right again? Those babies were going to cost money to raise, and he'd be chipping into that down payment he'd squirreled away in no time. Plus, he knew he couldn't do this alone indefinitely. His aunt would come help full-time for a while, but she'd never take the place of a real mom. He hoped to get married and bring his wife back to his own land…not another man's.

"So how much have you researched about this ranch so far?" Casey asked.

"The maps I could find online and in local records were limited," she replied. "But my great-great-grandmother wrote a journal where she talked about some specific landmarks. If I could find the actual site of the old house, there's something I know to look for. My great-great-great grandfather put a single red brick in the front of the fireplace. It was something they brought from across the country—a touchstone of sorts. I don't know if I'll be able to find it, though. Plus, I'm waiting to hear back from some local historical societies."

Casey glanced toward her again. "And if you don't find the landmarks?"

"I don't have unlimited resources, so this purchase has to be the right one. If this isn't the land I think it is, then I'm not buying it. There are cheaper ways to open therapy centers."

Hope surged up inside of Casey's chest. Maybe Ember Reed was just a temporary inconvenience on the Vern ranch. Maybe this wasn't the spot her family had settled after all, she'd go on her way and he could buy this land fair and square. He had plans for raising a family here, too—an honest, hardworking family who would raise cattle and ranch like the generations of Courtrights before him. Casey knew this ranch like the back of his hand. It wasn't a huge operation, but he'd been running it well, and the chance to be a landowner once more… it was enough to make him hope in that dangerous way that meant his heart was already set on it.

He had an attachment to this land already, too. He'd imagined himself living up in the big house, hiring another manager and being the owner who called the shots…and in his mind, that felt really good! He'd be able to bring his dad back to live with him, and his old man could live his last years on Courtright land.

So, yeah—if it didn't make things harder on Mr. Vern and his sick wife, Casey would like to see this land come to him. He was praying that God would provide for them all.

"That's my place ahead," Casey said as he turned into the drive that led up to the ranch manager's house. It was within sight of the ranch hands' bunkhouse just down another gravel road. The ranch manager's house was a small one-bedroom bungalow, and as he parked and pushed open the truck door, he could already hear the babies' plaintive wails, and he felt that wave of anxiety he always did at the sound of their cries.

Ember hopped out, too, and she followed him around the truck toward the side door of the house. Casey pulled open the door and held it for Ember, letting her step inside ahead of him. Bert stood in the kitchen with Wyatt in his arms, a bottle in one hand and a panicked look on his face.

"They woke up at the same time, boss," Bert said.

"I'll get Will," Casey said, heading through to the sitting room, and he scooped up the baby, settling him into the crook of his arm. The baby kept up his wailing, and Casey headed back to the kitchen, turning on the hot tap on his way past the sink.

"Ember, would you grab the bottle in the fridge?" he said.

Ember did as he'd asked and handed it over. Casey stuck it under the hot tap until the count of twenty, then shook it up and tested it against his hand. Warm. Perfect. He popped the nipple into Will's mouth, and there was blessed silence as both babies slurped back the milk.

"I'm Bert," the old ranch hand said, nodding to Ember.

"This is Ember Reed," Casey said. "She's—" how much to say? "—she's a special guest of Mr. Vern's. I'm showing her around."

"Pleasure." Bert smiled. "But I've got to head out. I still have work to do out there. Mind if I just pass this little guy over?"

Ember's eyes widened, and she was about to answer when Bert deftly eased the baby into her arms. Bert stood there, still holding the bottle until Ember had the baby in a comfortable position and took the bottle from his hands.

"Thanks, Bert," Casey said. "Much appreciated."

"Yup. Not a problem." Bert took his hat off the top of the fridge, dropped it onto his head and headed out the side door.

Casey looked over at Ember, and he saw a stunned look on her face. She wasn't looking at the baby, even though Wyatt was slurping back that bottle in record time. What was with her? This was a baby, not a hand grenade.

"Bert there is one of the ranch hands," Casey said. "He's worked here for thirty years, and he's good at his job. He's one of the guys who'll be out of work if this isn't a full-scale ranch anymore."

Wyatt finished with his bottle, and Ember put it down on the kitchen table, then took a moment to get the little guy up on her shoulder, patting his back in a slow rhythm. Wyatt snuggled into her neck, and Ember sighed, tipping her cheek against his downy head.

"He likes you," Casey said.

She didn't answer, but she smiled wanly and continued her gentle patting of the baby's back. Then Will finished with his bottle, and Casey popped the nipple out of his mouth and put the infant up onto his shoulder, too.

"I'm not trying to put people out of work," Ember said.

"I'm just pointing out the reality of things," Casey replied. "Mr. Vern asked me to show you around, and I'm going to do that. But I'm not going to sugarcoat anything, either. You'll get a real tour of the place— see what this ranch is, the people whose livelihoods depend on it. You need to understand the whole picture, not just what you could turn this place into if you swept it clean."

"You're one of those guys who doesn't believe in talking about his feelings, aren't you?" she asked with a small smile turning up her lips.

"What have I just been doing?" he asked. "I thought I was pretty clear about my feelings here. I talk. But I generally do it around a campfire on a cattle drive— away from civilization, like a real man."

"And ironically enough, that's the experience I want to provide to men from the city," she said. "Because you're right—sitting in a counselor's office with a tissue box in front of his wife isn't the most inviting atmosphere for a man to open up."

"The real work on a cattle drive makes a difference in how much we'll open up, too, you know," he said. "Responsibility, exhaustion, pushing yourself to the limit. You can't simulate that in some counseling setting with a bonfire."

Casey's cell phone rang, and Casey had to adjust the infant in the crook of his arm as he dug the handset out of his pocket. He glanced at the number—it was his niece who was supposed to arrive any minute, and his heart sank. No one called at the last minute to say there was no problem… Will squirmed and Casey rocked him back and forth as he hit the talk button.

"Hi, Nicole," Casey said, after picking up. "Where are you?"

"I'm sick, Uncle Casey…" Yep, exactly what he'd been scared to hear. "I think it's the flu. I'm so sorry."

He sighed. "It's okay, kiddo." He glanced over at Ember once more. Had she made her decision yet about sticking around for a little while? "Don't even worry about it. Feel better, okay?" After a goodbye, he hung up the call.

Ember's phone rang just then, and he sighed. He'd have to wait to get an answer from her. As she talked in low tones, Casey looked down into Will's tiny face.

"You're wet, aren't you, little guy?" he murmured. The babies were always wet after a bottle—it was one of those constants he could depend upon. He glanced over at Ember, and she stood there with the baby up on her shoulder, her gaze directed down at the floor as she listened to whoever was on the other line.

Casey kicked the new diaper box across the kitchen floor toward the living room. This was the routine. He kept a towel laid out on the couch, and he'd been using that as a changing station. It was a rough setup, but it seemed to work out okay.

He laid Will on the couch cushion and sat on the couch next to him to do the honors.

"That was the mechanic," Ember said, coming into the room.

"Oh, yeah?" Casey set to work on the sodden diaper, then reached for a new one. He was getting pretty good at this, but two babies went through a phenomenal number of diapers a day. He rolled up the soiled diaper, then lifted the little legs to pop a new one underneath the baby's tiny rump.

"It'll be over a week before my car will be fixed," she said. "There are other cars ahead of mine, and—" She sucked in a breath. "How would it work if I stayed on this ranch for a few days?"

"I'd talk to Mr. Vern, explain the situation and see if he'd be okay with you staying up at the big house," Casey said. "You wouldn't have to worry about inappropriately close quarters here at my place, but you'd be close enough to make everything relatively convenient. I can pick you up and bring you back here no problem."

He fiddled with the snaps on Will's sleeper—they were so easy to accidentally snap together one snap off-center so that he'd have to start all over again...

"What about your niece?" she asked.

"She's got the flu, but even if she didn't, the kid's fifteen. She's supposed to be in school, not minding children."

Ember eyed him. "And just to be clear…" She let it hang.

"I just want a hand. I'll find people to babysit when I give you the tours and all that, but I need another person—another set of hands until my aunt can get here. You can see how much work they are. We could both benefit, if you're game. What do you say?"

Ember looked down at the baby in her arms and wrinkled her nose. "This little guy dirtied his diaper."

Casey chuckled. "Let's trade. Will here is clean."

Casey took Wyatt from her arms, and Ember awkwardly lifted Will up onto her shoulder. The baby snuggled up next to her neck like his brother had. She shut her eyes for a moment. Casey paused, watching her. There was something in her expression—more than discomfort…pain.

"No pressure, if you'd rather not," Casey said. "It would just help me out, is all."

"I thought you didn't like me," she said, her eyes opening again, and she fixed him with a direct look that made him shift uncomfortably.

"I don't like Bert, either, but who can be picky?" he said, shooting her a teasing smile. "I'm joking. I don't like what you stand for, Ember Reed, but Will seems to settle right down when you're holding him, and babies are like dogs that way. They smell bad people. And like I said, I'm a bit desperate right now. You help me with the boys, and I'll go out of my way to help you find the information you need to make your choice about buying this place. Fair is fair. I'm as good as my word."

"Okay," she said with a nod.

He felt a wave of relief. At least he'd have a hand here for a few days, and that was a bigger boost to his peace of mind than she seemed to realize. "I'll talk to Mr. Vern, then."

She smiled wanly. "I'm not good with kids—the childcare side, I mean. I should at least warn you."

"It's just diapers and bottles," Casey said, grabbing another fresh diaper and the bucket of wipes. "I only started on this a week ago, and I've gotten pretty good at it. You'll catch on."

And here was hoping that when he'd done his duty and shown her the ranch, she'd decide not to buy the place. But that was in God's hands—the hardest place to leave it.

When Casey was finished with the diaper, they traded babies again. She was getting better at this—easing one baby into his arms and taking the other baby into her own. Ember looked down at the tiny boy in her arms. Wyatt. The baby was wide-awake, those deep brown eyes searching in that cross-eyed, newborn kind of way. She lifted him closer to her face, inhaling the soft scent of his wispy hair.

She'd held her own newborn son in her arms ten years ago, and she'd breathed in the scent of him. She hadn't named him. That wasn't her role, but she knew the name the adoptive family had chosen—Steven. She would always remember how he'd felt in her arms, how her heart had stilled just having him so close... After spending one tearful night cradling him, feeding him with a bottle of formula lest she grow too attached, she'd passed him over to his new mom and her heart had broken. The sound of his cry as they took him away had slid so deep into her soul that she dreamed of it at night even now, and woke up with achingly empty arms.

It had been for the best—that was what she told herself. But she wasn't so sure anymore. Ember sucked in a stabilizing breath.

"How did you end up with these babies?" she asked.

"My cousin and his wife had asked me to be their guardian should anything happen," Casey said. "I thought it was nothing more than a gesture, because I'm single. I'm a ranch manager. I don't have time for kids, right? But then there was this horrible fire, and they managed to get the boys out, but Neil and Sandra didn't make it. That left the kids with me." He cleared his throat, blinked a couple of times.

"Will you keep them?" Ember asked hesitantly.

"Keep them?" Casey repeated, casting her a questioning look. "Yeah, of course. I'm the closest family they've got. What else would I do?"

"Some might let them be adopted by another family," she said.

"Yeah, some might." Casey finished with the sleeper's snaps, noticed he'd done them up wrong and whipped them all open again to start fresh. "And honestly, it did occur to me. But—I don't know. I can't bring myself to do it."

Ember nodded. She'd felt nearly the same way…but she hadn't seen any other choice. She remembered how helpless she'd felt at the prospect of single motherhood and losing the support her father offered if she didn't cooperate and give the baby up…

"How will you do this?" Ember asked. "Raise them on your own, I mean."

"How does any parent raise their kids?" Casey picked up the baby and put him onto his shoulder, then headed through to the kitchen. The water turned on, and he raised his voice to be heard. "I figure I'll just wing it. Isn't that what the rest do?"

Ember chuckled at that. "I'm more of a planner, myself."

"Well, I've got a few plans," Casey said, coming back into the room as he awkwardly dried his hands on a paper towel while balancing the baby on his shoulder. "My aunt has agreed to watch the kids for me during the days. I'll pay her, of course. And I've been advised by a nice lady in social services that I should have them sleep on their backs without blankets, and that I should be feeding them once every three hours." He lifted his watch on his wrist. "And counting, right?"

He was strangely optimistic, this cowboy, and she regarded him in silence for a moment.

"Now, I've got some maps of this land," Casey said. "I don't know if it's anything you haven't seen yet—"

"That would be great," Ember said. "You never know."

Casey turned away from her and headed for a cupboard in the corner. He opened the door with a squeak, and a roll of paper fell out. He used the toe of his boot to lift it, and grabbed it with his free hand. He passed it back toward her. "That might be one. Hold on…"

He rummaged a bit, handed back three more rolls of paper, then closed the cupboard and readjusted the baby on his shoulder again.

"Will, you're going to have to sit in that little chair of yours."

Ember watched as Casey pulled out a wire-framed bouncy chair from beside the couch, then arranged the baby in it. Little Will turned his head to the side and stared at a patch of sunlight on the wall. Then Casey pulled out a second bouncy chair, and relief welled up inside her at the thought of putting Wyatt down.

She was already dreading this—the baby minding. These tiny boys brought up feelings she wasn't ready to deal with. Or rather, feelings she'd been trying to deal with rather unsuccessfully. It was supposed to get easier over time—that was what they said—but it hadn't.

"Here we go, Wyatt," she murmured, bending to put the baby into the chair next to his brother, but as she tried to put him down, Wyatt's little face screwed up into a look of displeasure and he opened his mouth in a plaintive wail.

"Or not." She stood back up and the crying stopped. She looked into Wyatt's little face, and he peered back at her. "You sure?"

"Guess he likes you, too," Casey said. "Never mind. I'll open these up."

Ember's heart sped up as she looked from the baby to his guardian, and then back again. This was not a good plan, but what was she going to do? She'd already agreed to this, and if she backed out, she'd only cement her reputation as the heartless city girl who'd come to ruin everyone's lives.

Casey opened one of the rolls and revealed a map. "So what are you looking for, exactly?"

"The journal mentions Milk River and some creeks that ran off it."

"Milk River runs for over seven hundred miles," he said, glancing back at her. "We only have about fifty miles of Milk River on this ranch."

She nodded. "I think it might be the right fifty, though. The creeks were named after local wildlife—Beaver Creek, Muskrat Creek and Goose Creek."

Casey looked closer, chewing on the side of his cheek. "This here is Milk River." He pointed with one calloused finger, following a line along the map. "There are a couple of creeks, but they're not named. Not officially." He rerolled the map, then picked up another one. He scanned it, rolled it up again and picked up the third. "Here we go. That's Milk River again—"

Ember leaned closer to look. The line of the river meandered down the map, and there were about fifteen little lines snaking off. The darker of the lines had names, and cocking her head to one side, she could read them.

"Allan Creek. Wallace Creek. Burns Creek. Trot's Creek…" She sighed. Then there were the lighter lines that had no names. She'd seen this map already online. Back in the city, she'd been looking for mention of the Beaver, Muskrat and Goose creeks, but no one seemed to have record of them. Maybe those names hadn't stuck.

"Milk River goes up into Canada, you know," he said. "I don't have the maps for that."

Then her eye landed on one creek name she hadn't seen before that brought a hopeful smile to her lips. "Look at that one!" She pointed. "Harper Creek!"

"That's familiar?" Casey asked with a frown.

"My mother's last name was Harper. That's the family name."

"Hmm." He nodded. "Okay."

"What's the matter?" Wyatt was getting heavy in her arm, and she shifted him to a new position.

"There are a lot of Harpers around here," he said. "They might be relatives of yours, though."

She'd never heard of them, if they were. It might be nothing more than a coincidence. Or a creek named much more recently—a random moniker slapped onto a tiny creek in honor of some locals.

"We aren't Canadian. My mother always said that the family had settled exactly fifty miles from the mountains, and they'd been another forty miles from Victory. That's right here. This land. Give or take."

Casey nodded slowly. "Approximately, yes."

"I know it's a very rough estimate, but since this land came up for sale, I wanted to check it out," she said.

"Well, we'll have a look," Casey said, but his expression was grim.

"You don't want me to buy this land, I know," she said.

"You're right," he agreed. "I don't. This is prime ranching land, and cattle fuel this community. It's our way of life, and I've worked this herd for fifteen years now. There's something to be said for consistency. Also, there's honor in feeding America's families, and the beef we raise is top quality. That matters to me. To see this place turn into some therapy center— No offense, ma'am, but from my way of thinking, it would be a crying shame. The city folk might need their therapy and their chance to enjoy the wide outdoors, but we ranchers need pasture under our boots and cattle to drive. So what you're suggesting isn't going to help us at all. Again, no offense."

"None taken," she murmured.

"But that doesn't mean I won't treat you honestly," Casey said.

"Can I be sure of that?" she asked.

"I'm a rancher, Miss Reed," Casey said, his voice a low growl. "But I'm also a Christian. That one sits a little heavier. I believe in right and wrong, and I stand with the truth. So if I find out that this is the land you've been looking for, then I'll tell you honestly, because I want God's blessing more than I want my way. And God's never yet blessed a lie."

Ember regarded him thoughtfully.

"Are you a Christian, Miss Reed?" he asked.

"Yes," she said.

"Then a handshake should be enough, wouldn't you say?" he asked, holding out one hand toward her.

Ember took his rough hand in hers, and she felt the gentle pressure of those strong fingers. It was a muscular hand—veined and broad—and she realized anew just how attractive this stubborn cowboy was. She tugged her fingers free.

"Could you take the baby back?" she asked, slightly breathlessly.

Casey did as she asked and she slid the infant into Casey's arms. Wyatt didn't complain this time, and she exhaled a shaky sigh.

This was the right land—she could feel it. Everything had fallen into place in that way that God had where she could sense His fingerprints on all of it. From the sale of the swampland, down to this ranch popping up for sale just at the same time she'd pinpointed an approximate location of the Harper homestead.

Ember had felt drawn here, but looking at that lanky cowboy and the babies he was honor bound to care for, she couldn't help but wonder if this was God's doing for other reasons entirely—like forcing her to face her own issues. Ember wanted to belong somewhere—be someone other than the illegitimate child of a wealthy man. She wanted a connection so solid that her paternity wouldn't be the most defining factor in her lineage any longer.

The sooner she could investigate this land and decide on her next move, the better.

# Chapter Three

Mr. Vern, as it turned out, was perfectly happy to have Ember stay with him if she was helping out his ranch manager. Those babies had sunk into his heart, too, it seemed.

"They need loving," Mr. Vern said. "That's all. Just loving. But there's two of them, and Casey's got a big job. So I think we all appreciate you being willing to snuggle some babies. It'll take a village with those boys."

A village was the precise thing she hadn't had on her side when she'd been pregnant with her son. If there'd been a village for her, she might have been able to keep her little boy, but she didn't have any support. When she'd told her father about her pregnancy, he'd recommended an abortion, but said that if she insisted on having the baby, she'd have to give it up for adoption. He wasn't interested in supporting her for the long term. He'd agreed to pay for her education, but his one stipulation to his support had been that she *act like a Reed* and not embarrass the family. Raising a baby on her own without a husband apparently violated that clause. Set aside the fact that she'd been fathered in an affair…but Alistair was the one with the money and she wasn't in a position to argue with him about his morals. It had seemed hopeless then…

Ember lay between crisp sheets that night, listening to the soft sounds of a strange house, and she lifted her heart in prayer. She'd been so sure when she'd come out here—confident, excited. But somehow, she'd gone from completely in control to feeling entirely out of her depth.

*Lord, I need Your help,* she prayed. *I don't know how I got myself into this, but here I am…*

Only God knew how she'd been struggling with memories of her own son lately. She'd naively thought that giving him up would allow her to move forward with her life. And in some ways, she had, but lately, memories of that traumatic day were coming back like punches to the gut. So she lay in bed *not* asking for God to help her sort out her emotions right now, because she knew better than to ask for that! A woman didn't hop over her feelings; she waded through them. And wading would have to wait until she was finished with this task at hand. As ironic as it was for a therapist, she wanted God to help her put a lid on her feelings. For now, at least.

Ember slept remarkably well that night. Maybe it was the exhaustion from the adventures of her day, but she didn't even stir until she awoke to the distant aroma of brewing coffee. Ember rubbed a hand over her face and reached for her watch, checking the time. It was just after six, and outside, the sky was awash in pink. She pushed back the covers and reached for her clothes. She'd come with a bag packed and had intended to stay in a local hotel for a few days, so she had a few necessities with her. Ten minutes later, she'd washed up, put on a little makeup and made herself presentable before leaving the bedroom for the kitchen.

Mr. Vern stood in front of the stove, a bowl of whisked eggs in one hand as he flung a pat of butter into a sizzling pan.

"Good morning," he said without turning.

"Good morning." She headed for the coffeepot. There were two mugs waiting, and she filled one. "Is this for me?"

"Sure is," Mr. Vern said. "I'm just whipping up some eggs now, too."

"You're up early," she said.

"I've already been out to check on some cattle," he said with a low laugh. "I saw Casey down there, and he said to tell you that he's got a ride planned toward Milk River today. He thought you might be interested."

"Oh!" Ember brightened. "Yes, I am."

"He says he's planning on leaving about seven," Mr. Vern said. "You'll want to eat hearty before then. Have you ridden before?"

"No," she confessed.

"Hmm." Mr. Vern glanced back at her, a look in his eye like he was sizing her up. "It's a good way to take a look at the land, but…"

"I'll be fine," she reassured him. "I'm assuming I'm in good hands with Casey Courtright?"

"The best." Mr. Vern poured the egg mixture into the pan. "In fact, you'd do well to keep him on, Miss Reed. He knows this land better than I do at this point."

"He's already said that he's not interested in working for me," she admitted.

"Has he now?" Ember couldn't see the older man's face, but his tone sounded displeased. "That's just pride. Give him time."

Time for what? She didn't want to be saddled down with an employee who didn't want to be here. But this wasn't the time to discuss that.

After breakfast, Mr. Vern drove her down the sloping gravel road, his radio playing a jangly gospel tune. Mr. Vern wore a dusty trucker's hat, and he chewed on a toothpick as he drove.

"So left, we've got the cattle barns—you can see them, right? The big modern silver ones. Those are used for some calving, injured animals and the like. For the most part, the cattle spend their days in the field. I'll bring you down there later if Casey hasn't got the time."

The older man followed the road right, heading away from the cattle barns and toward that picturesque red barn bathed in golden morning sunlight.

"There's four hundred acres in total—that includes the forest as well as the pasture. I know you're not interested in raising cattle, but the property includes about two hundred head that we've raised for market. So you'd have at least one market run. Casey would be able to fill you in on the finer details there, of course."

"Where are we going?" Ember asked.

"To the horse barn," Mr. Vern said. "We've got twenty-two horses at present. Our ranch hands use them when they check on herds and that sort of thing. Now, there are three horses that belong to Casey personally, and another two that I'm not willing to part with. But the other seventeen are included in the sale."

"Are they good for trail rides?" she asked.

"About five are gentle enough for newbies, but the

others need a more experienced hand," he admitted. "I can sell off the others first, if you want. Just to save you the trouble later."

"We'd have to talk about that," she agreed with a nod.

"Some ranches like to use quads for checking the herd, but I've stuck to the tried and true. We've got a paddock, and since you mention trail riding, we've got some good trails, too." They rattled over a pothole, and Mr. Vern shot her a grin. "If you do buy this land, miss, you're going to need a solid truck. I'm a Ford man, myself."

Ember could see the wisdom in those words. Her car had already shown that it would be jolted right apart on some of these roads. But as they crested a hill, her to-do list melted away at the sight.

Green field rolled out beneath them, fence posts running like lines of neat stitches across the verdant plains. Some horses were grazing—one tiny foal trailing close to its mother. The red barn stood out in comforting contrast to the rest of the scene, and Ember felt all that tension seep out of her body. They eased down the road toward the red barn, and as the truck came to a stop out front, a door opened and Casey looked out. He was dressed in a pair of jeans, a button-down shirt and a padded vest. He pushed his cowboy hat back on his head and raised a gloved hand in a wave.

"Have a good day," Mr. Vern said. "If you have any questions, Casey's the one to ask. Like I said, stubborn lout or not, that man is worth keeping around. Mark my words."

Ember thanked him and hopped out of the truck. Casey waited for her at the door, holding it open for her. His dark gaze followed her as she approached, and she felt heat rise in her cheeks. It was different out here—on a ranch, away from the city. Everything seemed more basic, more pared down. And when a man's gaze followed her like that, it was harder to ignore.

"Good morning," he said. "Bert's with the babies, so we've got some time."

"Is he getting paid for that?" Ember asked, stepping past Casey's broad chest and into the warm, fragrant barn. Dust motes danced in the air in front of her, and her nose tickled. High windows let in squares of morning sunlight, and it took a moment for her eyes to adjust.

"Of course," Casey said, slamming the door shut. "He's getting overtime. Most expensive childcare ever. I asked if his wife might be interested, but she's got her hands full with her elderly mother, so..."

Casey led the way down the center of the barn. Most of the stalls were empty. He paused at one stall and held a hand out toward a horse's velvet nose. The horse nudged his hand and nickered.

"How much riding experience do you have?" Casey asked, glancing back at her. Again, that dark look trained on her face in that way that made her feel slightly self-conscious.

"None," she admitted.

"Okay, so not Captain, then," he said, moving on. "Captain is fast and strong, but he needs an experienced rider."

"That's not me," she agreed. "Can't we drive?"

"Drive?" Casey turned toward her again, his eyebrows raised. "Not where I'm headed. Why—you scared of horses or something?"

"No, I just thought—" She didn't know what she was thinking. She'd rather feel more in control.

"You don't have to come along, you know," Casey said. "I'm going to check a gate latch out toward Milk River. You said you were interested in that area—"

"No, I want to come along," she interrupted. "I'm fine. Let's do this."

"I'll let you ride Patience here. She's gentle."

That sounded a little better, and Ember watched as Casey led a brown mare from her stall and stroked her glossy neck.

"Good morning, girl," Casey murmured. "You up for a ride today?"

Ember leaned against a rail as she watched Casey saddle the horse. He worked quickly, all the while talking softly to the animal.

"Mr. Vern mentioned that five of the horses would be suited for trail rides with clients," Ember said.

"Patience isn't included in the sale. She's mine," Casey said when he'd finished. "I bought her myself about ten years ago."

"Oh." Ember nodded quickly. "Of course. Sorry, I didn't mean to be presumptuous."

"Never mind. Come around front. You can pet her and introduce yourself."

Ember circled around to the front of the horse and looked up into those gentle, liquid eyes.

"Hello," Ember said softly.

"Now, let me help you mount," Casey said. "Here. Foot in this stirrup. Can you reach? Hold on." He grabbed a wooden box and put it down next to the horse. "Stand on this. Now, foot in the stirrup."

Ember did as he instructed.

"Hand on the pommel— There," Casey coached. "Now, up and swing that leg over."

It wasn't exactly graceful, but a moment later, Ember was settled in the saddle, and Casey gave her a quick look over.

"Good. We're ready," he said, walking over to the far, rolling door. He pushed it open and whistled sharply. A tall, proud horse trotted up, already saddled, and Casey caught the reins. He took a rifle from a corner and slung the strap for it over his back, then put his boot in the stirrup.

Ember gave her horse a little kick in the sides, and nothing happened, save a slightly annoyed shuffle from the horse. Was she supposed to kick harder?

Casey swung up into his saddle effortlessly, and he turned to shoot her a smile. "You ready?"

"How do I get the horse to start moving?" she asked, heat rising in her cheeks. At least she'd warned him that she had no experience.

"Oh, you don't," Casey said with a low laugh. "Patience is my horse, and she'll do what I tell her. You just hold on."

So Ember was literally just along for the ride here… Great.

Casey made a clucking sound with his mouth, and Patience plodded forward toward him. The sensation was a strange one—feeling the movement of the muscles of this empathetic animal, and Ember sucked in a breath.

"I told you that I'd be giving you an honest tour of this ranch," Casey said over his shoulder. "And I'm making good on that."

*She's most definitely a city slicker*, Casey thought as he stole one last look over his shoulder. A dose of reality might go a long way into showing her exactly what she was getting into here. This was a functioning ranch—a thing of beauty, in Casey's humble opinion. But also rugged, wild and not so easily tamed for her purposes. Shutting down the cattle operation wouldn't change that.

Wolves and coyotes didn't respect lines on a map. Those boundaries had to be patrolled by men who know how to shoot. There were a hundred things she hadn't even thought of yet, he was sure.

And yet, while she might be clueless, that woman was beautiful, too. He could tell that he was softening toward her. There was something about the way her emotions played out in her sparkling blue eyes... He tried to push the thought back. If he met her in any other situation, he'd want to talk to her, get to know her better...figure out if there was a boyfriend in the mix.

Casey leaned down and pulled on the latch to the gate, swinging it open. Ember rode through first—or maybe he should say Patience did, carrying Ember with her—and then Casey rode out, slamming the gate shut behind him. The latch dropped back into place with a satisfying rattle.

"I'm going to take you through the trails," Casey said. "On the other side is pasture, and that's the fence I need to take a look at."

"Where's the river?" she asked.

"You'll see it from the fence." Far down below—but it would give her an idea, at least. "This way." He clucked his tongue, and Patience picked up her pace, catching up with him.

They rode along the gravel road for several minutes, a chilled breeze slipping comfortably past. Casey had always enjoyed this ride—he came out and fixed damaged parts of the fence each spring. But this year was different than the others. Wyatt and Will had brought a certain grounding to his life that he hadn't had before. Everything seemed to matter more in the light of his responsibility toward them.

"You're doing okay," Casey said, glancing over at Ember next to him. She was still sitting rather tensely in the saddle, and she looked over at him.

"Relax," he said. "Let your joints move. You're not going to fall off. You're fine."

"Easier said than done," she observed with a breathy laugh, but he could see her attempt at relaxing her position. "Oh, that is better."

"You've got to trust the horse," he said. "She's not going to listen to you anyway."

Ember smiled ruefully. "You should know that I don't go with the flow very well."

"Yeah, I guessed that," he replied.

"I like things planned. I like to know what's coming."

"Then a ranch isn't good for you," he cautioned.

"Trying to talk me out of this again?" she retorted.

"Maybe," he agreed. "But mostly, I'm just pointing out the obvious. You say you want to take advantage of the great outdoors, but you can't plan so much when it comes to land and weather. Storms come, seasons change. You can't sweat it. You just…wait."

"But you're still prepared," she countered.

"I'll give you that," he agreed, then nodded ahead. "Up there—that's where we enter the trails."

It was nothing more than an opening in a tree line, and Casey pulled the reins, guiding his mount toward it.

"That's it?" Ember sounded less sure of herself now, and when Casey looked over at her, he caught the uncertainty in those blue eyes, too. "How wide are these trails?"

"Wide?" Casey laughed. "Wide enough for a horse, but watch the branches. They can slap you in the face if you don't pay attention."

This would be a lot easier if Miss Ember Reed was a little less attractive. There was something about her that made him want to act the protector. The male side of him wanted to guide her through all of this and make it easy for her. Except she wasn't just a woman out of her depth, and she certainly wasn't a romantic option—she was his direct competition. So he'd better tamp down those chivalrous instincts if he knew what was good for him.

Casey plunged into the foliage first, and he glanced back to see Patience and Ember coming up behind. He ducked his head under a twig and dug his heels into his horse's sides. The woods were cooler than out in the direct sunlight, and the twitter of birds silenced for a moment, and then started up again in a hesitant chatter.

"It's beautiful, isn't it?" he said.

"Yeah…"

He looked back again and saw her gaze moving around them. "How safe is it in here?"

"Safe?" Casey chuckled. "Why do you think I brought a gun?"

"Har har." She shot him a mildly amused look. "You said you'd deal straight with me, and I'm asking as a potential buyer here. How safe are these woods?"

"I wasn't joking," he replied. "This is a hungry time of year for everything—including wolves. Nothing is risk-free out here. But I'm sure you'd have your clients sign a form that saves you from lawsuits."

Ember fell silent, and Casey allowed his horse to pick his path over roots as they made their way through the familiar maze of trails. They weren't all visible anymore—some hadn't been used in years. But a trained eye like Casey's could spot them still. He felt a twinge of guilt. He'd decided to give her an honest tour of this ranch, but it wasn't fair to scare her unduly, either. He wasn't that kind of man.

"You're safe with me, though," he added grudgingly. "I'm a good shot."

"That's why I want to hire you if I do buy this land," she said.

Hire him… Yeah, that wouldn't work well. Not if she'd bought this land out from under his boots and turned it into some city folk feelings center. Not a chance.

He didn't answer her—he'd turned her down once already, and he wasn't about to turn the next week or two into some lengthy argument about his reasoning, either. He'd made his choice, and that was that. But there was something about that woman behind him—city slicker though she was—that made him want to open up more, talk, just to hear her say something in reply. He wouldn't give in to it, though.

They rode in silence for a few more minutes, and then the dense green of trees began to brighten, and in the distance, Casey could make out the glitter of sunlight.

"We're almost out," Casey said, mostly just as an excuse to say something to her.

"Good," she said. "It's a bit eerie in here."

Casey's horse picked up his pace as they got nearer to the tree line, and a moment later, they erupted into sunlight. He reined in his horse, and Ember came out next to him. She looked ready to say something, but then she saw what he'd been waiting to show her.

Grassy hills rolled out beneath them, some rocky piles jutting up from the grass here and there. This used to be plowed land back when people first settled, and those groups of rocks had been made by picking them out of the soil and tossing them, one by one, into those piles. A creek cut between two hills, and to the east there was a marshland with reeds and birds rising up in mesmerizing clouds. The morning sunlight splashed over the scene, and Ember's eyes glistened.

"Oh, my…" she breathed.

"You see that rise over there?" Casey pointed ahead, and Ember followed his finger. "That's where the fence is."

"This is beautiful land," she murmured.

"It's beautiful, but it's rugged," he said. "When we bring the cattle this way to graze, we need cowboys on duty with guns."

Casey clicked his tongue, and they started down the incline at an easy pace.

"Mr. Vern told me last night why he needs to sell this land," Ember said. "He told me about it, but do you know?"

"Of course I do. His wife is suffering from Alzheimer's, and he's used up his insurance. He wants to keep her in a quality care center."

"So even if I don't end up buying this land, someone will," Ember said. "Mr. Vern needs to sell. I'm not the bad guy here, Casey."

Casey eyed her for a moment, wondering how much

to say. "I didn't call you bad," he said. "I just said I don't agree with what you stand for."

"Like what, exactly?" she demanded. "Therapy? You might not need someone to talk things out with, but some people do. There's no shame in having some professional help in sorting out difficulties."

"There are plenty of places to get therapy. This is ranching land," he said.

"And it could be set to other uses, too," she said. "And it very well might, depending on who buys it."

She was making a good point. Except she hadn't hit on the reason why he was taking this so personally. It wasn't only about therapy and changing good ranch land into something so unsuited to this place. This wasn't just about a stubborn man and his ideals. This was personal.

"If you don't buy this ranch, I will," he said, his voice low.

Ember blinked at him in surprise. "What?"

"You heard me," Casey said. "I can't afford to pay what you can—and that's why you've got Mr. Vern's priority. The money matters. He needs to get as much as he can for this land. But if you decide against this ranch, I've got an offer on the table behind yours."

"You want to buy it—" she said weakly.

"Yeah." And *want* was a wimpy word. He longed to buy this land on a bone-deep level. He loved every square acre of this place, and if he was going to be raising kids, he couldn't think of a finer place to do it.

"If this is the site of my family's homestead, though—" she began.

"Then you'll buy it," he confirmed. "And I'll understand your attachment to the dirt under your feet. It'll be a connection to generations past—I'm not unfeeling here. But if you don't buy this ranch, then I will, and I'll raise those boys here, teach them about hard work and perseverance. I could have a story here, too—moving into the future."

Casey urged his horse a little faster, pulling out ahead of her. He didn't want her to see the emotion in his eyes. This mattered to him just as much as it mattered to her, and he wasn't going to just walk away from a chance at owning this land himself.

"So I *am* the bad guy," she called from behind him. "To you, at least."

Casey turned in his saddle and met her gaze. "From my perspective, you're just another Reed. You're playing in a different league. You've got money behind you that I couldn't even hope for. And unless you change your mind about this place, there's no doubt that you'll have your way. Reeds always do."

She dealt in feelings and relationships—let her sort that one out.

But Casey was also a Christian, and he stood by his word. They had an agreement, and they'd shaken on it. She'd help him, and he'd give her an honest introduction to Vern Acres.

Fair was fair.

## Chapter Four

Ember sucked in a wavering breath as Casey urged his horse forward again. Her heart hammered in her chest as this new information rattled around inside her. Casey wanted this land, too… It sure explained his chilliness toward her, but it complicated their professional balance, as well. He was just supposed to be a tour guide, not someone with a personal investment in stopping her plan.

Her horse started forward, too, picking up her pace as she plodded along behind Casey's down the rocky slope. He wanted a future here, and she craved a connection to the past—but their dreams were mutually exclusive. The only thing tipping the scales in her favor was that she had more money to give to make her dream come true. She could sympathize with a man who didn't come with the same financial backing she did, because she hadn't always had these opportunities, either, and she had no idea how long they'd last.

Ember's relationship to her father was a fragile one—even if it satisfied a part of her that had always longed to know her dad. Alistair Reed had expectations of his own, and a family pride that she threatened to tarnish by her very existence. Her father's wife, Birdie, had been furious when she found out about Ember. Birdie saw Ember as a threat to her marriage, even though Ember hadn't been the menace—her mother had been, and that affair had ended years ago. But Birdie would take any excuse to drive Ember away and sever the financial cord. Ember wondered what role her stepmother had played in the pressure for Ember to give up her child. Had Birdie been banking on Ember choosing her baby?

That thought clamped down on her heart. *I should have chosen my son. I should have told my father that I was keeping him, and that I'd find a way...*

Again—at the least opportune time—she was thinking about her child. But this wasn't the time or the place to delve into all of that. When she'd made a decision about this land and gone back home, then she could use her last week of leave from work to do some real soulsearching. She could promise herself that much. But not in front of Casey Courtright—the man who wanted to buy this ranch, too.

Patience caught up to Casey once more and Ember felt the heat rise in her cheeks when he looked over at her.

"I couldn't hang back if I wanted to," she said.

He smiled faintly, then shrugged. "We had to face that eventually. Better to lay it out straight."

The horses fell into pace together, and Ember let her gaze move over the countryside. Copses of trees and rock piles broke up the pasture. She breathed out a sigh, wondering if there was a more beautiful place anywhere on God's green earth. If this was the land her family had settled, then she understood why they'd been willing to battle the elements, the wild animals and even unsavory neighbors just to make this land their home.

The thought of neighbors reminded Ember of another problem she faced—the prejudice people around here had against her family name. Would she face pushback from the community? It was possible, but it didn't seem entirely fair. Maybe Reed Land Holdings didn't have many fans out here, but her father was more than just a company. He was a human being.

"Did you ever meet my father?" Ember asked.

"Nope, never did. He sent lawyers to do his dirty work," Casey replied.

Of course. That actually stood to reason. And perhaps it made him easier to hate, too. She'd had her own prejudices against him when she'd first learned that he was her father.

"He's not a bad man," Ember said. "He supports a lot of state charities. Everyone seems to like him."

"Everyone?" Casey raised an eyebrow.

"Except people out here, maybe," she conceded. "But I do understand. When my mother told me who my father was, I wasn't thrilled, either. He has the image of being very aloof and cold, but he's not like that deep down."

"When did your mother tell you about him?" he asked.

"I was seventeen, and she had stage four lung cancer," Ember replied softly. "She wanted me to know who my father was before she left me alone in the world. I knew my father's last name was Reed, since my mother had given me his name, but she'd never told me who he was. She'd been the housekeeper on the Reed estate back then, and when she got pregnant with me, she quit and went away. My father had a family, after all. Anyway, it turned out that he'd known about me all those years, but he'd never reached out to meet me."

"I'm sure he provided financially," Casey countered.

"Not much," she replied. "He helped Mom out a bit, but not enough that I ever saw any. It got sucked up in rent and food and the like. We pinched pennies."

"And you're standing by him being such a good guy," Casey said dryly.

"People change, Casey. And my dad softened up when his youngest son died in Afghanistan. He didn't want to waste any more time when it came to his kids, including me. He rearranged his priorities."

"And the rest of his family?" Casey eyed her from beneath the brim of his hat.

"Were less excited," she said with a dry laugh. "His wife can't stand me. His other kids see me as a drain on their inheritance. My father paid for my education and then gave me this piece of swamp in Florida. None of his other kids wanted it, but then I managed to sell it for a decent amount of money—and that's what I've got behind me right now. So I doubt I'll have anything else coming my way from my father, if his wife and kids can help it. I have enough to buy this land and start up my therapy center. But after that, I'd better start making a profit, because I'm not swimming in endless privilege like you assume. Still, I didn't want to meet my father for his money. It was never about that for me."

Casey was silent, and she couldn't help but wonder how much he was judging her now.

"Are you close to him?" Casey asked as they dropped down into a small valley, and then climbed back upward toward the ridge and faint line of fencing.

"Uh—" That was a loaded question. "I'm glad to finally know my father."

"That doesn't answer me," he replied.

"He's doing his best to make up for not being in my life in my childhood."

"Not by giving you equal consideration with his other children," Casey countered.

"No, that's true, but what I really want from my father isn't financial. I want—" Her voice trembled, and she paused, swallowed. This was getting too personal too quickly. "It doesn't matter what I want. He's not the monster that you seem to think. He's a man who made a big mistake by cheating on his wife, and he's had to make that up to his family, too. He works hard, he's very smart and he has a really strong sense of family pride."

"So strong that he gave you a piece of swampland in Florida that no one wanted," Casey countered. "But if you want a connection to him so badly, why sell the land he gave you? Why come here?" Casey asked.

"Because my mother was the only family I had for seventeen years, and my pride for her isn't dimmed because of my father's money or her past mistake," she shot back. "I have family pride, too, and the stories I heard growing up were all from the Harper side. I might have a wealthy father, but I'm my mother's daughter."

Casey nodded slowly. "Good answer, Miss Reed."

Had she just earned a little bit of his respect, there? "My point is, my father has his own challenges to deal with, and I'm not some prissy heiress. We're all just people, doing our best. Including my dad."

"Hmm." Casey cast her an indecipherable look. "I like you better as the proud daughter of a housekeeper."

"Well, I'm more complicated than that," she retorted. Chances were, he was more complicated than he was letting on, too, but she wasn't expecting him to open up.

Casey chuckled softly. "All right, all right."

"Everyone makes mistakes, Casey."

Everyone, including her. And mistakes couldn't be undone. That was the problem with too many of them—they were so final. Would her son resent her decision, too? Would she ever be able to admit why she gave him up? At the age of twenty, everything seemed a whole lot more dire than it did now. But then, she now had an education, a career, a home... Things *were* more dire back then.

They came up the last of the incline, a few pebbles clattering down the hill behind them, and Casey reined his horse in. He dismounted, in one smooth motion, then came around his horse toward her.

"You aren't what I expected," he said quietly.

She smiled slightly and sighed. No one ever was. She'd learned that when she counseled families. Under all the mistakes and external shells lay soft, vulnerable human beings.

"You want to dismount, or stay where you are?" he asked after a moment of silence.

Her muscles were already strained and sore from the position they'd been holding the last little while. Getting down and walking around for a bit sounded good, but she looked at the ground uncertainly. It was a long drop, and there was no handy wooden box out here.

"I don't know..." she said.

"Come on." He held a hand aloft. "I'll help you down."

"But how will I get back up again?" she asked with a breathy laugh.

"I'll get you up there." He eyed her, squinting slightly in the sunlight, and her heart sped up just a little bit. She looked around them, her gaze moving over the rolling hills, the rocky stretches…feeling just how alone they were out here.

"How do I do this?" she asked at last.

"Take your other foot out of the stirrup, and stand up on this leg." She felt his hand tap her ankle. "Patience can take it. She's fine. So all your weight—this leg."

Ember did as he said and swung her leg back over the saddle. It was a long way down, and as she started her descent, her stomach leaped to her throat. She landed in a strong pair of arms before her boot hit the ground, and the air squeezed out of her lungs.

Casey was stronger than she'd thought, because he supported the full weight of her while she got her feet back underneath her, and boosted her back into balance. For a moment, she felt his strong chest against her back, and the steady pounding of his heart thudded slow and steady. Then she was upright again, and he stepped away.

"That wasn't graceful," she breathed.

"Not at all," he said with a short laugh, and when she turned, he raised his hands. "Hey, who says you have to be graceful all the time, huh?"

Casey went to his saddlebag and pulled out a hammer, a plastic bag of what appeared to be nails and a pair of work gloves.

"Look, I don't mean to insult your father," Casey said and cleared his throat. "There have been some pretty serious consequences to his success around here, so I'm not going to pretend I like what he's done, but I can understand that he's your dad, and you're going to have a different experience of him."

"Thank you."

"Still, you've got to understand that while your father got richer, a lot of us lost our family's legacies. So." He shrugged, then turned away. "I'm going to fix the latch on the gate."

Casey headed past the horses and down another incline toward the fence. Most of it was barbed wire, but in the center was a tall wooden gate that swung loose in the wind, the hinges creaking. Ember watched as he worked on the broken latch for a few minutes. He was silent, but in the wide outdoors, constant speaking didn't seem necessary. It was companionable, and she realized that she liked Casey's company. Casey finished with the gate, then tested it a couple of times before ambling back to his horse to replace the tools in his saddlebag.

"Where's Milk River?" she asked.

"Come here." Casey went to the fence again and waited while she made her way down the rocky terrain. He pulled off his work gloves, then nudged his hat up higher on his forehead as she reached his side. He smelled musky and warm, and even a few inches away from him she was aware of just how tall he was. "See down there—" He leaned a little closer so that she could follow his pointing arm. "Past the trees, there's a glittery patch—"

Ember looked the direction he pointed, and she spotted the glitter he was referring to.

"I see it."

"That's water. The trees grow by the bank, and it's dug its way down pretty deep over the years, so the banks are steep and high over there. But that's Milk River."

Somehow, it seemed less impressive than she'd built it up to be in her head, and she let out a pent-up breath. "Oh."

Casey paused, tensed, his gaze still locked in the same place. He didn't move, and Ember looked up at him hesitantly.

"What's wrong?" she asked.

"I'm staring at a wolf right now." His voice was calm—too calm for her comfort—and he slowly turned, scanning the landscape. "I only see one right now. The others might be hiding, or it could be a lone scout. Either way, we're moving out."

Ember squinted, looking in the direction he was, and then she saw it—a tuft of gray on the other side of that glitter of water. It stood tall and motionless, then turned and paced a couple of times before stopping and staring in their direction once more.

Casey pointed to her horse. "Let's go. Saddle up."

Ember headed for her horse, lifted her leg to get one foot in the stirrup and felt strong hands around her waist propelling her upward. With a gasp of surprise, she fumbled but managed to get her leg up over the saddle and turned to see Casey already moving toward his own horse, looking over his shoulder in the direction of the wolf.

"It's pretty far away," Ember said, trying to keep the tremor out of her voice.

"Let's keep it that way," Casey replied, and he pulled his gun off his back and reached into his saddlebag, coming out with two shells. "You go first." He slapped Patience's rump. "Go home, Patience."

The horse didn't need to be told twice, and Ember lowered herself over the saddle as they headed up to the tree line once more.

"Lord, protect us," she whispered, but when she glanced back, she saw Casey with a rifle in one hand and his dark gaze scanning the landscape. If anything was going to come at them, she had a feeling she was in good hands.

Casey urged his horse faster as they approached the tree line. He looked back, surveying the countryside from his higher vantage point, but the wolf had disappeared, and he couldn't see any more movement. Still, wolves blended into their environments rather easily, and he wouldn't feel right until he had Ember back on the other side of the woods where wolves didn't dare approach.

It was one thing to be looking out for himself and another ranch hand who knew how to deal with these things, and quite another to have a completely green city girl on his hands. One day he'd get married, but in his mind's eye, his wife would be just as good a shot as he was. This land required respect and a steady trigger finger. That was a lesson he'd be teaching the boys when they got old enough to hold their own guns…

Ember put an arm up, pushing some twigs away from her face as Patience carried her into the forest. He took one last look behind them before he followed her into the woods.

"Are we in any danger?" Ember asked, looking over her shoulder at him.

"I wasn't about to stick around and give the wolves any ideas," Casey replied. "We can shoot them if they harass us or the cattle, but they're endangered, too, so I'm not about to start taking potshots at wolves if I don't have to."

She turned back to face forward, and he was struck by the shine to her blond waves that fell over her shoulder and down her back. A twig was caught in her hair, and Casey had the urge to pluck it out, but he wasn't close enough. She was a beautiful woman, but also vulnerable. A country woman wouldn't be quite so reliant on him for safety and common sense out here, and he felt the weight of that responsibility.

They rode in silence through the woods until they emerged on the other side into the scattered shade at the forest edge.

"The wolves never come this close to a human settlement," Casey said. "Not in daylight."

"Shouldn't you be able to do more about the wolves?" Ember asked.

"Yeah, if you buy this place, the wolves are your problem, too," Casey said with a rueful smile. "But they're an important part of the ecosystem out here.

"Like I said before, it's not about your convenience out here. It's about finding a way to live alongside nature safely."

"I get it."

Did she? He wasn't so certain.

Casey let his eyes roam over the patchwork of fields and those gently snaking roads that made their way between them. He'd driven every single one of those roads, and he knew these fields—the kinds of grass that grew in them, the drainage when the snow melted, the state of the fences that surrounded them—like the back of his hand. If only he'd known his boss as well.

He understood that things had deteriorated quickly for Mrs. Vern, but his boss had kept that private for a long time, too. He hadn't opened up, shared a bit, given Casey any indication that he should be scraping some money together to make an offer that could compete with what a Reed brought to the table.

Everyone looked out for themselves, it seemed. Even Christians. Even country folk. Everyone kept their personal business close to the vest and tried to sort out their own situation.

*Casey, people might like you a whole lot, but they like their own hide more*, his father used to tell him. Funny how it took a couple of decades for wisdom to grow deep.

When they got back to the barn, he dismounted, then helped Ember down from Patience's back. She rubbed her legs and stretched—definitely not used to the exertion of horseback riding, and he turned his attention to unsaddling the horses and turning them out to pasture for the rest of the day.

"Mr. Vern invited us up for lunch at the house," Casey said, then paused. "Hold on—" He reached behind her back and plucked that twig out of her hair. It took a moment to untangle it, and her hair felt silky in his calloused hands. He held the twig up as proof that he'd had an excuse to touch her.

She smiled feebly. "I'm not scared off, Casey."

"I'm not trying to scare you," he replied, feeling mildly offended that she'd think so. "You saw the wolf, didn't you?"

She eyed him for a moment. "You're a ranch manager here. What would make working for me so different?"

"First of all, you wouldn't be ranching," he retorted.

"Fine. But I have a feeling that even if I were intent on raising cattle, you'd still have a problem with working for me."

Casey headed for the door, pushed it open and waited for Ember to leave the barn ahead of him. "My family had a ranch, and we'd been on that land for three generations. Reed Land Holdings ran us out of business, then bought the ranch when we couldn't hang on any longer."

Ember stepped outside into the spring chill, then turned back to look at him, some combination of uncertainty and compassion swimming in those blue eyes.

"When was this?"

"Fifteen years ago. I got a job here and worked my way up—not because I have a passion for ranching someone else's land, but because I had no other choice. And now I've got the boys to raise, and no land of my own to do it on."

"What happened to your father's ranch had nothing to do with me, you know."

"It's your family," he said.

"But not *me*." She met his gaze almost defiantly.

"It's your family's money," he said. "And forgive me for being picky about that detail, but it amounts to the same thing. I get that you aren't some spoiled rich girl in the deepest sense, but you're a part of the machine, and you're looking to take a running ranch and turn it into something completely different. There will be ripples. This will affect a lot more than you think."

"And a good number of those ripples might be positive," she said with a shake of her head. "Turning this place into a therapy center isn't about me and my career. This is about something I owe to God."

"What's that?" he asked, softening his tone.

"I promised I'd do everything I could to strengthen families. If He helped me to get the education I needed, I'd take every penny that came from my tarnished family and put it back into building other people back up. I'm sorry this isn't about cattle, Casey. Maybe you'd approve if I cared more about cows. But I am going to build something important here. This is about people."

She carried on toward the truck, leaving Casey to catch up this time, and he shook his head. They'd never see eye to eye on this, but she was convinced that she was doing something good and moral. There was no one more stubborn than a do-gooder. He picked up his pace and met her at the vehicle.

"Let's go," he said, hopping into the driver's side. She got in next to him, and as she buckled up her seat belt, he turned the key and snapped his own strap into place.

When they got to the house, Mr. Vern was waiting. He met them with a cordial nod and stepped back as they came into the kitchen.

"So what did you think of what you've seen so far?" Mr. Vern asked as Ember took off her jacket and hung it on a hook. The smell of tomato soup and toasted BLTs met them.

"It's a beautiful area," Ember said. "Breathtaking, really."

"That it is," Mr. Vern agreed. "And that's only a tiny taste."

The old cowboy pulled a pot of soup off the stove. Sandwiches already waited on the table, cut diagonally and stacked on a plate. Mr. Vern ladled soup into a bowl and brought it to the table, then headed back to the stove. He moved slowly, purposefully.

"Have a seat," Mr. Vern said.

It wasn't Casey's place to be served by the boss, but Ember sat down in a chair and looked hungrily at the spread before them.

"Let me finish that up, sir," Casey said.

"Nonsense. Sit down, Casey. How was your ride?"

"It was cut short," Ember said. "There was a wolf eyeing us."

"Linda always hated them," Mr. Vern said, coming back to the table with the last two bowls in his hands. Some soup slopped over the side of one bowl as he placed them on the table, and Casey dropped a napkin over the spill. "Before they passed the law protecting wolves, we had a whole herd of migrating elk that moved through in the fall. We had a decent income from hunters coming to hunt on our land, and we offered a guide service. But not anymore. The herd isn't so big anymore, and they move through fast. The wolves make sure of that."

Ember frowned slightly, looking over at Mr. Vern with questions in her eyes. Casey's mind wasn't on the wolves, though. They were an old problem. He was wondering how the babies were doing. Funny how he'd started to worry about them when he was gone.

"Let's pray," Mr. Vern said, bowing his head. "For this food we are about to eat, make us truly thankful."

He raised his head, nudged the plate of sandwiches toward Ember, then picked up his spoon. The older man's hand trembled, and he put the spoon back down.

"Everything all right, sir?" Casey asked.

"Fine," he growled, and Casey eyed him a moment longer. That was a lie, but maybe he didn't want to talk in front of Ember. Casey nodded, then took a mouthful of soup, watching his boss from the corner of his eye. After a beat or two, Mr. Vern sighed.

"I got a call from the care home," he said, his voice tight. "Linda had a bad morning. They couldn't calm her down. They needed my permission to sedate her."

"What was she upset about?" Ember asked.

"Don't know," Mr. Vern replied. "Something about getting dressed. She didn't want to be touched." He sucked in a wavering breath. "I'd have her here with me, but she kept wandering off, and the last time I found her, she was by herself in three feet of snow wearing nothing but her pajamas and holding a cookie sheet."

Silence descended around the table.

"When we were kids, we used to sled on cookie sheets," Mr. Vern said, then cleared his throat. "Maybe she saw the snow and in her mind... Anyway."

Mr. Vern picked up his spoon again and took a mouthful of soup. Casey and Ember followed his lead, but Casey's stomach no longer wanted the sustenance. He could see the pain in the older man's eyes. And he knew that it was more than just his wife's problems that morning. The bills were climbing, and as his boss had told him earlier, he was in debt.

"I'm a licensed therapist," Ember said after a moment. "If you wanted to talk about it—"

"No," Mr. Vern said with a bitter laugh. "I appreciate the offer, young lady, but I don't need to be asked how I feel. I know how I feel, and I don't want to talk about it. I'll go visit my wife. She'll be sedated, but I think there will be a part of her that will know I'm there."

Ember fell into silence, and Casey met her gaze for a moment. She needed to understand that people out here were different. Tougher, maybe, and more self-sufficient. She was right that everyone had their personal issues, but not everyone wanted to talk about it. Sometimes, a man just needed enough dirt under his boots to soak up the pain.

"I'm sorry—" Mr. Vern stood up. "I hope you'll understand if I head down to the city now. It's a long drive, and I need to see Linda for myself—know that she's okay. You stay and eat. Just lock up on your way out, if you don't mind, Casey."

Casey pushed back his chair. "Absolutely, sir. Do what you need to do."

That kind of love was a precious thing, and while the price was this kind of heartbreak at the end of that love story, it made a life deeper and more meaningful for the years of devotion.

Casey had two little babies waiting for him back at his house, boys he'd determined to raise, and he wondered if they'd creep into his heart like that... become his meaning for all the hard work. Because that was what a family was, wasn't it? And he was doing his best—taking care of the babies, trying to arrange things so that he could give them the best childhood possible. He'd be their dad—or at the very least he'd be the only dad they'd remember. Still, he couldn't help but wonder how long it would take before they truly felt like his.

# Chapter Five

They finished eating after Mr. Vern left, then wrapped up the leftover food and put it in the fridge. Mr. Vern would be hungry eventually, and Ember wondered if there was any way she could help this man in his time of need. Except he didn't want her help—that seemed to be a theme out here. Even Casey didn't seem to want her well-intentioned offering of a job. Would it be so miserable to work with her for a little while until he sorted out something better? She didn't want to turn his life upside down. She was trying to be reasonable here.

Before they left to go back to Casey's house, Ember made some phone calls to two different local historical societies. She'd asked them to look into the records to see who owned this plot of land going back as far as possible. So far, they had owners going back seventy-five years, but back in 1981, there was a big flood that had damaged a lot of the antique records. She'd hoped that coming out here might give her access to records that weren't readily available online, but that didn't look likely right now.

"Any news?" Casey asked her when she hung up after her last call.

"No," she admitted with a sigh. "But I'm not giving up quite yet."

"Didn't think you would." He smiled ruefully. "Let's get back to the house."

Once at the ranch manager's house, Bert left for his own shift at work, leaving Ember and Casey alone with the infants. Ember ruminated over her challenge to find some evidence about who settled this land while she focused on the tasks at hand: diapers, bottles, sleeping. Casey put in a load of laundry, and Ember set to washing a sink load of baby bottles. She'd known it wouldn't be easy to track her family's holdings, but it seemed like every time she had an idea, she hit another roadblock.

And while she agonized over her own problems, that old rancher was off visiting his ailing wife. She felt a pang at her own selfishness. Was that the Reed in her?

"I feel for Mr. Vern," Ember said, raising her voice a little so that Casey could hear her in the other room.

"Me, too," Casey said, and he ambled over to the doorway of the kitchen. "This is a tough time for him."

"How long have he and his wife been married?" she asked.

"I don't know. Since they were about 18, I think. He told me once that he met her in high school."

"That's sweet… I come across couples who have been together since high school in my practice. It used to be a regular occurrence. Not anymore."

"You mean marriages lasting that long?" Casey asked.

"Marriages that started that young that last so long,"

she amended. "But when it lasts, there is a really beautiful bond that only comes with time together."

"But the ones you're seeing are coming for therapy," Casey pointed out.

"I never said it had to be marriage counseling," she said, shooting him a rueful smile over her shoulder. "The last couple I met with who had been together that long were working through grief over the loss of—" She swallowed, biting off the words.

"Loss of what?" Casey prodded.

"Family land," she finished, and a wash of guilt came over her. Land could mean something to various different people, but only one person could actually own it. It didn't matter who won this—someone else would lose.

Even in adoption, in order for Pastor Mitchell and his wife to adopt her son, she'd had to give him up. And they'd been trying for a decade to get pregnant, they told her. Nothing had worked. The wife—Sue—had told Ember a little bit about her struggle. She said that all she'd ever wanted was a big family...

Ember's mind continued to wander as she plunged her rubber-gloved hands into the hot, sudsy water. In order for Ember to gain some feeling of connection to her biological father, she'd had to tear into a perfectly happy family. Birdie hated Ember because she'd only found out about her husband's affair when Ember showed up after her mother's death. Then Alistair had been forced to confess it all to his wife and kids. So in order for Ember to have a relationship with her dad, her half siblings had to learn the ugly truth that their father had cheated on their mother. In order for anyone to take a step forward, it felt like there was a cost to be paid by someone else. Hardly fair, but the way the world worked—only one person could "win" at a time.

Back then, when her mother died, Ember hadn't been thinking clearly enough to consider consequences—the consequences of meeting her father...and of other things. She'd hated facing life on her own, and she'd had one surefire way to numb everything—parties.

So that fateful night during her second year of college, Ember sneaked out to a party, as she'd done so many times in the past. The next morning, she'd woken up in a confused fog on a strange couch, and missing some rather important articles of clothing. Had she done what she feared she'd done?

And she'd felt a flood of shame. Was this what she wanted for the rest of her life? A blur of alcohol and parties...flunking out of college, because she was too hungover to pay attention in class? Was this all she had to look forward to?

Ember had pulled together what she could find of her belongings and headed back to her dorm room. Sitting on the edge of her bed, her head spinning and her stomach churning from the drinking she'd done the night before, she realized that she wanted more...she wanted to be better. Not to impress her father, or punish him—but for herself! She wanted to turn her life around and belong to the one Father she could count on to never stop loving her. And she longed for forgiveness for whatever it was she'd done the night before that left her feeling so soiled and empty. Sitting on the edge of that dorm bed, she'd bowed her head and given her life—as muddled as it was—over to Jesus.

"...if You still want it," she'd whispered.

Unknown to her in that moment, she was already

pregnant. Her change of heart—her desire to be something better—had all come one night too late.

Behind her, one of the babies woke from his sleep, a hiccuping wail piercing the quiet. Ember pulled herself out of her memories and looked over her shoulder. Casey stood by the couch, a laundry basket filled with onesies, sleepers and tiny socks, and he dropped a onesie on top of a pile of folded laundry then headed for the cradle. Just then, the other baby let out a whimper.

"You want to give me a hand?" Casey asked, and Ember dried off.

"Sure." She went to the other cradle and looked down into the scrunched little face. Will waved one tiny fist in the air, his lips quivering and tears welling in his eyes. She bent down and scooped him up, propping him up onto her shoulder. At a few weeks old, he was already bigger than her son had been the last time she'd seen him.

But Will didn't settle. He sucked in great, heaving breaths and wailed with all his might. She tried changing his position, patting his back, rocking...and nothing seemed to work. Both babies cried their hearts out and Ember met Casey's gaze with a panicked look of her own.

"What's the matter with them?" she asked helplessly.

"This happens sometimes," Casey said, raising his voice above the babies' cries.

"What do you do?" she asked, looking down into that red, tear-streaked face of the tiny boy in her arms. She rocked back and forth, swinging her weight from one foot to the other in an instinctive sway. The cries paused for a moment, then started up again, as if the rocking had only been a mild surprise.

"Maybe they miss their mother," Casey said, and Ember froze.

She swallowed, then adjusted Will up onto her shoulder once more so she had an excuse to turn away. Tears pricked her eyes, and she tried to swallow the lump that rose in her throat when she remembered that heart-wrenching cry that had erupted from her own son as his adoptive mother walked away with him.

*It's for the best*, everyone said. She'd bestowed the gift of life by giving birth to him, and by placing him for adoption she was giving him a family that could provide him more than she could. But what if her baby boy had sobbed his little heart out while strangers tried to comfort him? What if that guttural, heartbroken wail had been her son's only way to call for his mother?

And she'd never come.

This was why she shouldn't be caring for infants—these memories that kept sweeping up and threatening to knock her down. She sucked in a wavering breath as she realized that Will was starting to settle. The baby's cries were softer now, and as she swayed back and forth, his eyes were drifting shut. But Wyatt still wailed from Casey's arms.

"Whatever you're doing, it's working," Casey said with a grin. Then he hesitated. "You okay?"

"Yep." She nodded quickly, keeping up that swaying as her throat thickened with repressed emotion.

"I have a theory," Casey said. Then he nodded to a La-Z-Boy chair in the corner. "Go sit down there—it rocks."

Ember sank into the chair. Will's howls had fully subsided now, and he buried his wet little face into her neck. He sucked in deep, trembling sighs. If this child was crying in hopes of calling his mama, how long would it be before he forgot her? How long before his tiny heart stopped yearning for the mother who would never come?

Casey eased the wailing Wyatt into her arms on the other side of her chest, and Wyatt sobbed out his grief. Will started to whimper again, and then Casey put a big hand on the back of the chair and started to rock it for her.

"Talk to them," he ordered.

"Uh—" Ember looked down at the frustrated babies and swallowed against the tightness in her throat. "Boys, I want you to stop now. Okay? I want you to be good boys and be quiet for me."

Wyatt blinked up at her in mild confusion, but the crying stopped.

"All right, then," she said quietly. "That's good. Let's not cry just now, okay? Because we're okay. We're going to get through this. It's a feeling, and while feelings are very, very strong, they pass. They aren't forever."

Her words were meant as a reminder for herself— this overwhelming grief she'd been battling, the guilt at the thought that she'd made the wrong choice, or made her choice for the wrong reasons... It wasn't forever. She could wade through it, and she would feel happiness and contentment again. Eventually.

Feelings were not permanent. Feelings did not define her. She might feel like a failure at times, or like she was unworthy after what she'd done, but that was not a fact. The fact was that she had a God who loved her despite her mistakes, and her identity was in Him.

The babies settled into quiet, softly hiccuping as their breathing slowed. Casey kept the chair rocking with his strong arm, and she was struck again by the size of him. Standing over her like that, she could feel his strength and his gentleness contained in that muscular physique—the last thing she wanted to be reminded of just now.

Her emotions were in enough of a muddle without adding a handsome cowboy into the mix, but when she glanced up at him, she saw a wistful look on his face.

"A woman's touch," he murmured.

"Maybe they just tired out," she said.

"Nah, they've gone for way longer than that," he replied with a soft laugh, and his brown eyes sparkled, then faded. He straightened, and Ember took over the rocking of the chair for herself.

The babies were quiet now, their eyes closed, wet lashes brushing their pink cheeks.

"Feelings don't last forever," she whispered against their wispy hair. "You just have to wait them out, and they go away eventually."

One day, they wouldn't remember their mother anymore and they wouldn't yearn for her smell or her voice or her touch… One day, even memories would fade, as she knew would have happened with her own little boy. Her son—named by another woman—would have forgotten her entirely.

It was the mother who couldn't forget.

Casey looked down at the woman in his armchair. Ember leaned her head back, her golden hair tumbling around her shoulders. The babies' eyes had shut, and they slept facing each other as Ember rocked them. She had a hand on each little rump, but her attention seemed like it had wandered away as she looked toward the window and the afternoon sunlight outside. Whenever she held a baby, she seemed to do that—slip mentally away.

It shouldn't matter. The babies were soothed, and it looked like those boys needed the feminine touch—the one thing he couldn't provide. But he'd have to—sooner rather than later. He needed a woman in this with him—a wife to stand by him and help him raise these kids. Maybe a mom in the mix would make this feel more like a proper family.

"Thanks for this," he said, and he sank into the couch opposite her. The room was cozily warm, and he exhaled a tired sigh.

Ember looked over at him and smiled weakly. "No problem."

They were quiet for a couple of beats, and then Ember asked, "How long have you known Mr. Vern? You two seem pretty close."

"Most of my life," Casey said. "He and my dad were friends, and when we lost the ranch, Mr. Vern offered me a job. I've been working here ever since."

"That's why he trusts you so much."

"I'm good at my job because I was raised on a ranch and I was bidding on cattle at the auction by the time I was twelve. My dad showed me the ropes—I know how to run a ranch. So, yeah, he trusts me."

She eyed him for a moment. "But you're not happy here."

Happy wasn't something he'd been worrying about lately. He'd had a job to do, and land to buy. His happiness was going to come later—at least that was what he told himself.

"It's been a place holder," Casey admitted. "I want to

own a ranch, not just run one for someone else. There's something about having your stake in a place—makes a difference. And it isn't that I'm not happy here, because I do love this land. I'm just not happy being only a manager."

She nodded. "I get that."

"You're perceptive," he said, then added with a teasing smile, "for a city girl."

"You aren't so mysterious as you think," she replied with a smile. "It was how you acted in the house—kind of tense and coiled. You're different on horseback."

"Isn't everybody?" he quipped. "But I'm not the only one who isn't happy until I'm my own boss. You're the same way, from what I can see."

She angled her head to the side in acceptance of that. "Actually, I'm just trying to make the most of this before my father cuts me loose."

"You've mentioned that before. Do you think he will?" Casey asked with a frown.

"I know he will," she replied. "His other kids can count on his continued support and an inheritance eventually. He gave me an education and a little money. I'm grateful for it—it's my step up—and I'm not going to squander it. Because after this, I'm sure there won't be any more."

"You're smart," Casey said with a slow nod.

"I am." She smiled ruefully. "But this isn't about money. I'd trade it all in for an actual relationship with my father."

"You aren't what I expected," he admitted.

"Under it all, everyone is surprisingly human," she replied. "That is the one thing I've learned in my years as a therapist."

"So if you aren't terribly close to your family, who are you close to?" Casey asked.

"The money complicated things," she said. "My old friends from high school fell away when I went to college. That happens, of course. And then the friends I made in college got a little jealous when I had privileged problems, like how to make sure I could make enough money off a property sale in order to invest in a new business venture. That sort of thing."

"Their hearts bled for you," he said with a low laugh.

"Something like that." Will moaned in his sleep and Ember patted his back absently. "I'm in a bit of a no-man's-land right now. Even you can't quite decide what you think of me."

Casey had to admit that was true. She was beautiful, insightful, but still stubborn when it came to her own point of view. She'd been on his mind lately, both as his competition, but also as... Dare he think of her as a woman? She was surprisingly human, but it didn't change that she was going to alter the landscape of this ranching country—or that she'd be doing it on the land where he'd hoped to settle down and raise a family.

"Well, in the moment, you're helping me out of a tough spot, so I'm inclined to like you." He shot her a teasing smile. "You want some coffee?"

"Sure."

He pushed himself to his feet and headed into the kitchen. He pulled the plug on the sink full of soapy water on his way past, glancing at the row of freshly washed baby bottles. He'd wanted a woman's touch around here, but he had to admit that it stung when the babies seemed to prefer Ember to him when they wanted comforting.

But whatever. It was help, and he couldn't be picky.

Casey grabbed a coffee filter and the tin of coffee grounds from a cupboard and set to work measuring and filling the coffee maker with water. His hands did the work without any thought, and his mind spun ahead.

"Mind if I ask you a question…professionally?" he asked.

"You mean as a therapist?" she said.

He winced, then turned around. "Yes."

"Shoot."

"When do I tell the boys about their parents? I mean, their death was pretty grisly, and I'd hate to scare little boys. The thought— I don't know. How do I do that?"

"Never hide what happened," she replied. "But there's no need to go into detail. You can tell them a little more as they get older. But I'd recommend starting out with a picture of their parents in the home. Point to it, and tell them that is their first mommy and daddy. If they know from the start that they're adopted and why, there are no big, shocking conversations to have later on."

"Makes sense. I guess I'm a little afraid of being told I'm not their real dad when I tell them to do something."

"Oh, kids come up with all sorts of stuff, even if you are the biological parent," she replied. "Don't be afraid of something they might say later. Besides, if you are always very open about their parents, they won't feel like they're betraying you later when they want to learn more about them."

"Yeah…" He nodded, then sauntered back into the living room. Ember looked down at the sleeping babies, then up at him.

"Help me get them into their cribs?" she said.

"Sure." Casey bent and picked up Will first, freeing up Ember so she could get to her feet. He laid the baby in his cradle and looked down at the little guy. "I guess I'm afraid that they'd be right."

"About what?" she asked, laying Wyatt in the other cradle next to his brother.

"That I'm not their real dad." He looked up at Ember uneasily.

"Because they don't feel like yours yet," she supplied.

He was silent—was that a terrible thing to admit to?

"Casey, I'm going to tell you something," she said, stepping closer and putting a hand on his arm. "I've heard biological parents say the same thing. Childbirth is traumatic. They expect to feel this rush of unblemished love when they look at their baby, but that child is purple, squished and, frankly, a little ugly. They're in shock from the pain, the blood loss, from meeting their child for the first time... And when they get home from the hospital, they are sleep deprived and overwhelmed. They don't feel what they expected to feel. It isn't all picture-perfect and rosy. It's exhausting and scary and a massive change."

"Okay..." he said slowly.

"My point is, you lost your cousin when you became legal guardian of these boys. That's traumatic. You're busy, trying to adjust your life to two infants, and have no idea what your future with them will look like. This wasn't planned. This wasn't anyone's ideal, including yours. And that's okay."

"Is it? I think those boys deserve to be someone's ideal," he said.

"You'll get there."

"I want to."

"You will." She met his gaze evenly, and she seemed convinced of that, at least.

"Yeah." That was all true. Frankly, it was downright scary at the moment. He'd gone from bachelor to single parent of two overnight.

"Stop expecting perfection." She let her hand on his arm drop.

"That's it?" He eyed her.

"That's it." Ember shrugged. "None of us are perfect, Casey. Stop expecting it of yourself. You'll adjust. You'll figure it out. You'll be a good dad."

"What makes you so sure?"

"You cared enough to ask." She shot him a smile, and for the first time she looked relaxed, and that smile lit her features. She went from awfully pretty to stunning, and he swallowed. Ember pulled her hair away from her face with a swipe of her fingers, and he tried not to notice how appealing she was when she relaxed like that.

"Okay," he said feebly.

"That right there—" She waggled a finger at him. "That was therapy."

He rolled his eyes. "Hardly. That was advice."

"Yeah, well, it was advice from a professional, and if you don't get that reassurance, you might worry for nothing, or beat yourself up when you should really be cutting yourself a little slack. Sometimes it helps to have someone else point out that you're doing okay." She eyed him, waiting.

"And this is the gift of therapy that you want to bring the people of this county," he said with a wry smile.

"It isn't such a terrible thing, is it?" She smiled again, her blue gaze meeting his.

"You relax when you're solving other people's problems," he said instead. She did more than relax—she came to life. Not that he'd put it that way out loud.

She blinked, and some of that self-confidence fell away. The smile slipped, the sparkle in her eyes dimmed. He hadn't meant to do that, exactly, and he regretted it. He was just meaning to point out what was obvious to him—she seemed to blossom when sorting out other people's garbage.

"It did…uh…help, though," he offered after a beat of silence.

"You hate that a little bit," she said, a rueful smile curving her lips again.

"Nah…" He chuckled, then shrugged. "I'm a man. I'd rather rub dirt on it and walk it off, but that doesn't always work."

"I daresay it never works," she countered.

"You walk long enough and you forget," he replied with a lift of his shoulders.

"You don't forget, though." The smile evaporated and sadness misted her eyes. She compressed her lips into a line and swallowed. "They tell you that you will—but that's a lie."

Those words were coming from a deeper, more private place inside her, he could tell, and he tried to catch her eye again, but she turned away and headed back into the kitchen, where the coffeepot was burbling away. She grabbed a mug and poured herself a cup prematurely, the drips of coffee hissing on the heater below before she replaced the pot.

"Ember?" he said. "You okay?"

She turned back toward him, recomposed. "I'm

fine." She lifted the mug in a salute. "You rub dirt, and I drink coffee."

"You want to talk about it?"

"Not really. It's—" She shook her head. "It's old. I'm fine."

Fair enough. But when he'd seen that pain in her eyes, it made him want to fix it somehow. Maybe that was just the man in him. But he had a feeling that she wouldn't let him, anyway.

# Chapter Six

Ember got up early the next morning. Casey had offered to drive her to church with him, and she'd accepted the offer. From what Casey told her, this was the only congregation a comfortable driving distance from the ranch, and most of the Christians in the area attended one of two services in a little country church that wasn't big enough for everyone at one time.

But Ember hadn't agreed to go to church just to see the local parish. She felt like she needed some grounding after her last week. Worship was healing.

Ember heard the rumble of Casey's pickup truck outside the house, and she grabbed her purse, slipped on a pair of strappy heels and went out to meet him. The chill spring air made her shiver as it met her bare legs. She hurried to the passenger side and Casey leaned over and pushed the door open for her.

"Good morning," he said as she hopped up into the cab and the welcome jet of heat.

"Morning." She smiled at him and looked into the back seat. Both babies were sleeping, their soothers rising and falling in a syncopated rhythm. She pulled on her seat belt as Casey started forward again.

They fell into a companionable silence as Casey drove out to the gravel road and turned onto it.

"You seem like an old hand at this," Ember said. "The car seats, the soothers…"

"Oh, that took forty-five minutes," Casey said with a low laugh. "But I had no faith in my ability to do this quickly, so I started early."

Ember chuckled. "You seem to just…roll with these things, though. It's admirable."

"Then I fake it well." He shot her a rueful smile. "I'm pretty overwhelmed here. In fact, I considered not taking the babies to church at all today, but I don't want to start that. I doubt it'll get easier as they get bigger, so it's probably better to just jump in."

Ember smiled. He didn't seem to realize that his attitude was rare. Not a lot of men would just launch themselves into childcare the way he had.

"What about you?" Casey pulled down the visor as he turned onto the highway and the morning sun glistened into their eyes.

"What about me?" she asked, adjusting her visor, too.

"Do you want kids one day?"

Ember sucked in a breath. She was asked this from time to time, and the answer was never easy.

"No," she admitted. "I don't."

"Okay." He nodded, then leaned back in his seat. "I get it. Not everybody wants kids. I always thought I'd be a dad, but after I was married. Not before! This took me by surprise."

"I think babies are wonderful," Ember said. "Don't get me wrong there! I had a tough time after my mom died, and I had to grow up really fast. When I made that promise to God that if He helped me to get my education, I'd put all of myself into helping others with my career, I took that vow really seriously. I know that I could do that and have a family, but…" How could she explain this without saying too much?

"God doesn't call us all to the same life," Casey concluded.

"Yes, and maybe we aren't all suited to the same things. I do feel called to help others through therapy. I know I can make a difference there."

"I get it."

"Most people tell me I'll change my mind. But you know when you've stepped into stride with God's will. You can feel it."

"It isn't anyone's place to change your mind, Ember," he said. "From what I know of you, you're a woman who's thought things through."

"I have. I've been through a lot, but those experiences help me to understand what others are going through in their rough patches. My clients don't need to feel as alone as I did."

God was the God of second chances. But Ember didn't see motherhood as something in the past—it was very much in the present. She would always be a mother, even if she couldn't raise her son. But having more children felt like a betrayal to the son she gave away. What made them worthier of her time than he was? No, she'd had a child and she was a mother. But that was enough. The rest of her life would be spent in the service of other families—helping them stay together. With great mistakes came great penance.

The church was a half-hour drive from the ranch, and it sat on the crest of a hill in a pool of golden morning sunlight. The church property was squeezed between two fields, young green wheat rippling in the breeze on either side. It was beautiful, and from their vantage point, she could see the pickup trucks turning into the church property and parallel parking along the fence.

"I have to say," Casey observed. "You have a gift for reassuring people. One conversation with you, and I felt a whole lot better."

"That's about as close as I'm going to get to you telling me you approve of my profession, isn't it?" she asked with a low laugh.

"Yup." But he shot her a grin. "You're a good woman, Ember. I'm glad I've gotten to know you a bit...properly."

They turned into the parking area in front of the church. Casey parallel parked next to another truck and turned off the engine. He sucked in a deep breath, then glanced over his shoulder at the babies.

"Am I crazy to think I can do this, Ember?" Casey asked softly.

"No, you're daring," she replied. "And there's a difference."

Casey smiled, then nodded. "All right, then. Here's the plan. We each carry a baby, I'll take the diaper bag and we see how we all fare through church."

The next few minutes were spent getting the babies out of the truck and wrapped in blankets against the chilly morning air. People stopped to say hi and peek into the blankets to get a better look at the babies, so their progress to the church was relatively slow. When they finally got inside and got seated, Ember adjusted Will in her arms, then glanced over at Casey.

"I think you'll be okay," she said. "There are several women who would be more than happy to hold babies for you."

"Yeah… I hadn't thought of that, exactly," he said.

"Mr. Vern said you've got a village," she noted. "I'm inclined to agree."

"It might take a village," Casey said, and for a moment his gaze warmed and enveloped her. "But we three guys here need more than a village. We need a mom in the family."

Her heart clenched in her chest, and for just a moment, she had an image in her mind of what it might be like to be that mom. A handsome husband, two adorable boys, living out in the Montana wilds… But she pushed it back. No, that wasn't for her—he hadn't even hinted at that! He needed a wife and a mom for these boys, and he'd find a woman worthy of them all.

To save her from answering, a lady at the front began to play the first chords of a hymn, and everyone started to settle and put their attention into the service that was about to begin. A family… That thought tugged at a part of her that she'd thought was dormant. She didn't want to be the mother to other children. She didn't deserve it…so why was she feeling that yearning when she looked over at Casey and the babies?

*Lord, provide Casey with the wife he wants so badly*, she prayed silently. *And don't let me want what isn't for me…*

It couldn't be her, but that didn't mean he didn't deserve someone really wonderful. So did Will and Wyatt. They all deserved a woman far less broken than she was.

\* \* \*

The service went smoothly enough. The babies slept through most of it, waking up for bottles once. Sitting in that pew next to Ember was an oddly endearing experience. She was petite next to him. Her personality made her seem bigger than she was, and looking down at her, watching her smooth one ivory hand over Will's downy head, he'd felt his heart swell. She was beautiful and gentle, and while she seemed to try to hold herself back somehow with the babies, there were moments like that one in church when he could see the tenderness in her gentle touch. But she'd made it clear that she didn't want to be a mom.

What should that little detail even matter? She was a Reed come to buy the ranch out from under him, but in a little country church with babies in their arms, those facts felt cloudy and distant. He'd convinced himself that his trip to church would be more of his promised tour of the area, not a quiet moment as the sermon washed over them, her shoulder pressed warmly up against his as the babies slumbered in their arms.

The pastor spoke about new beginnings. He and his wife were moving on to a new church shortly, and there would be a proper farewell service midweek. Today, however, they'd have a big potluck in the church basement, and everyone would have a chance to say how much they appreciated this pastoral family.

Except when the service ended and Casey turned his phone back on, there was a text waiting for him from Bert. There was a new calf to be bottle-fed that had been rejected by its mother. Casey would have to go over to make the final call on whether or not the calf would need a vet. A ranch didn't stop running on Sundays, and Casey couldn't leave all the work to the remaining workers. Bert said his wife had a respite worker with her elderly mother at the moment, and she could watch the babies for a few minutes if Casey would just say the word, so Casey answered the text in the affirmative, grateful for the offer.

"Ember, I've got to head back. There's a calf that needs tending. Bert's wife can stay with the babies for a few minutes. Did you…want to come with me and see the barn? Or stay longer here at church? Should be a good potluck…"

"I'll come," she said, and he felt a funny wave of comfort at those words. He shouldn't be getting attached—she was certainly not a permanent fixture in his life. If anything, she'd be the one to push him out of this little church he loved so well and into another county with another ranch to be managed.

And yet having her at his side was strangely comforting. He'd need to get his head on straight with that.

The sky was overcast as they stepped outside. Two hours had made all the difference, and now the day looked gray and chilly. The cloud cover hung low, and Casey was confident they'd have rain before the day was through. Good. The land needed it. There were vast fields of crops and pasture depending on spring showers, and he'd never been one to be depressed by rain. Rain meant farming success, and the promise of a downpour always cheered him right up.

They got the babies back into their car seats and within a few minutes they were heading down the highway again, back toward the ranch.

"Does Mr. Vern normally attend that church?" Ember asked.

"Yeah, normally," he said. "He must be wanting some time to himself, what with all the hard stuff with Linda lately."

"He came back late last night. It was past midnight." She looked out the window, and her face was shielded from his view. "I was already in bed, but I wasn't sleeping. I think he wanted to be alone anyway. He made it pretty clear before that he didn't want to talk about it."

"It's a tough time for him," Casey said.

"I know." She glanced back and cast him a small smile. "And not every man likes to talk. That's okay. I can slide into work mode pretty easily, and I don't take it personally. It's the therapist in me that wants to help. That's all."

Work mode. Yesterday, that talk they'd had that had made him feel so much better about raising two boys on his own had felt more personal. She had her own pain, too, and she'd been opening up to him little by little. It didn't feel like a professional divide between them. But maybe that was just him not used to therapists and the like. This mess of feelings—that was all part of the job for her.

"So how do you separate that out?" he asked. "The work mode versus, I don't know, like, real human connections."

"When I'm working, people come to me for my unbiased perspective," she replied.

"Like I did," he clarified.

"I suppose."

"And when it's more personal?" He glanced over at her, and he realized he cared about this answer a whole lot.

"They want my bias," she said with a small smile, and he couldn't help but smile back.

"Okay." Casey turned onto the road leading up to the barn. Professional—that was what this was, and he had to remember that. Even if having this woman so close the last couple of days was starting to make those lines feel blurred. It was the childcare—that was the great equalizer, it seemed. Add to that, she was beautiful in the most disarming way...

Casey stopped at his house, where Bert's wife, Fiona, was already waiting. She happily took over with the boys and waved Casey back out of the house.

"The sooner you sort things out, the sooner you'll be back," she said with a good-natured smile. "Don't worry about me. I'm happy to snuggle some babies."

Casey got back into the truck where Ember was waiting, and the gravel crunched under his tires as he turned again out onto the road that led down toward the cow barn.

"I haven't given you a tour of the cow barn yet," Casey said as he steered around a pothole and stepped on the gas.

"That's true..." She glanced over at him. "Not that it will matter much for my purposes."

Casey was silent for a moment, but something had occurred to him...something he could choose to conceal. That would be more convenient for his own goals. Still, he'd promised honesty. "There might be some better-preserved records in Cascade County," he said. "I knew a guy who was researching his ancestry, and he found some information that way. No promise that they'll have what you're looking for, but it's something."

She brightened. "Thanks, Casey. I'll try that tomorrow morning. I can send some emails and make a few calls. Sunday should be rest…technically."

"Yeah, not for a cowboy." He shot her a smile.

"What happened with the calf?" she asked after a beat of silence.

"I'm not sure. We've got an orphaned calf is all I know."

She was more relaxed out here in the truck, away from everyone else. She seemed different alone with him, and he wondered if she shared his affinity for quiet and for the fresh afternoon air coming in through the partially opened window. Was it petty of him to hope that her search in Cascade would end up in his favor? He was supposed to be on the side of truth, not just on his own side.

They drove in silence the rest of the way, and Casey pulled to a stop outside the barn then put the truck into Park. They both got out, and Casey glanced up at the sky. A chilly wind was blowing, and the clouds were moving at a pretty good rate overhead. Maybe that rain would come faster than he'd thought.

"So this barn was built about twelve years ago," Casey said as he came around the truck and met her on the other side. "The original barn that was in this location was storm damaged from a particularly nasty winter, and Mr. Vern took the opportunity to completely replace it that summer. It was pretty costly, but it was going to be worth it in the long run."

Ember looked at the barn, then around herself at the surrounding land. There was more he could tell her, but he decided against it. She wasn't interested in cow barns, and he knew it. She wanted to find her connection to her own family history, and a barn wasn't part of that. Besides, they were here for a calf.

"Let's head in," he said.

He matched his pace to Ember's, slowing down a bit as they headed toward the barn. She was little compared to him, and that floral scent from the truck still whispered close by. He pulled open the barn door and she stepped in ahead of him.

The long, low barn was the place where sick cattle came to be treated or separated from the herd for whatever reason. This was also the makeshift nursery for motherless calves. Casey led the way past an aisle of supplies neatly stacked on shelves, and down to a section of stalls that were set aside for the calves. The ranch hand Greg Stein was crouched in the nearest stall next to a tiny calf covered in a blanket.

"Hey, Mr. Courtright," Greg said, rising to his feet. "I found it in the south field—the mother had twins and abandoned this one. We tried to reintroduce them, but she wouldn't take it back. Bert said to wait for you."

"How bad is it?" Casey asked, moving into the stall next to the cowboy and squatting down to take a closer look.

"Hard to tell. I was just cleaning it off and was going to try to warm it up," Greg replied. He seemed to take notice of Ember just then, because he added, "Ma'am."

"This is Ember Reed," Casey said, unwilling to give more explanation than that. "Ember, this is Greg Stein, one of our ranch hands who's been here for about four years now."

"Pleasure, ma'am." Greg leaned over and shook her hand. "We're working half-crew, so if you don't mind, I'll get back out to my duties, sir."

"Absolutely. I'll take it from here," Casey said, and he watched as the young man headed back out. Casey angled his head, inviting Ember into the stall.

"Poor thing," Ember said, sinking down to her haunches next to the calf.

"I'm going to go grab a new blanket and get some calf formula to get this little guy started," Casey said, standing back up.

"Can I help?" She looked up, clear gaze meeting his. He hadn't expected that. He'd figured she'd want to stand back and watch.

"Uh—" He shrugged, then smiled tentatively. "Yeah, if you want to. Why don't you use that blanket and wipe the calf down. The mother didn't clean him off properly, and he's cold."

Without another word, Ember turned to do as he'd asked, rubbing the blanket over the calf's head and shoulders, murmuring reassuringly as she worked. Her movements were confident and gentle, and if Casey didn't know differently, he'd have thought she'd worked with cattle all her life.

"Thanks," he murmured, more to himself than to her. He watched her for a moment longer before he pulled his mind back to the task at hand and headed down the aisle of supplies to fetch a clean bottle and some formula powder to mix up. That calf would be hungry and weak, and it needed strength if it was going to pull through this.

When he returned with a new blanket and the freshly mixed bottle, he found the calf clean. He handed Ember the new blanket.

"We need to keep him warm," Casey said. "So just cover him up to keep his body heat in."

Ember settled the blanket over the calf, and Casey handed her the bottle. "You want to do the honors? Same idea as in the house, just bigger."

Ember chuckled and took the bottle of formula. The calf could smell milk and nuzzled toward the nipple. Casey leaned down, grabbing the end of the bottle to get it up at the right angle for the calf to drink. Except when he knelt down to help Ember, he found his face right next to hers, the warmth of her cheek emanating against his rough stubble. She smelled sweet, and he had to physically stop himself from putting an arm around her in that position—it would only feel natural. But that wasn't his place, and while she didn't seem to notice how close he was, he stayed motionless for a moment while the calf got its rhythm.

"You have it?" he asked, his voice low, and she nodded, so he pulled back, cool air rushing between them once more. "You're a natural."

"It's just a helpless little thing," she said.

Yeah, so were the twins back at the house, but she hadn't engaged with them like this—wholeheartedly. So what was the difference?

Milk foamed around the calf's slurping mouth and dripped down its chin.

"You're a person who connects with animals, then," he said.

"I always liked the idea of a hobby farm," she said, then glanced up at him. "And I know that probably sets your teeth on edge."

"A little," he admitted with a low laugh.

"You never did tell me what drew you to this line of work," she said, her eyes still on the calf as it drank.

"I was born on a ranch," he said. "I told you that. It's what I know."

"Yeah, but plenty of country boys end up in the city," she replied.

He shrugged. "True. I like it. I—" He wasn't sure he had the words to encompass what this meant to him. "It's like it's a part of me somehow. When I'm on horse-back, everything else melts away. When I look at a herd, I'm already looking ahead to what needs to be done… but it's more than that. Cattle are soothing. A contented herd almost purrs."

Ember looked up at him; her expression softened. "And you're willing to work another man's land in order to work with cattle."

"Yeah. It's not the ideal, but it's better than nothing, isn't it?"

"But you won't work for me."

Casey let out a soft laugh. "No, ma'am, I won't."

She smiled ruefully and dropped her gaze. "I like that."

"That I won't work for you?" He squinted at her, unsure what to make of this woman.

"No, you refusing to work for me is annoying, because from what I can see, you're the best around, and I want only the best," she said. "What I like is being called 'ma'am.'"

"Aren't you called 'doc' or anything like that at work?" he asked.

"It's not the same. 'Ma'am' is…based on nothing more than the fact that I'm a woman. It's…reassuring somehow."

"That's country manners," he replied.

She was silent, and Casey sank down onto an upturned bucket, watching as the calf drained the last of the bottle. Ember pulled the nipple out of the calf's grasping mouth and passed it over.

"So what drew you to therapy?" he said.

"I want to help." She smoothed a hand over the calf's head. "After I started college I hit a really rough patch. I struggled with depression, and there was a therapist on campus who helped me through it all. I was young, scared, heartbroken, orphaned—"

"You had a father."

"I had a biological father, not someone who loved me like Mom had." She sighed. "That therapist helped me to straighten it all out in my head. If it hadn't been for her, I would have partied away my life, looking for comfort in all the wrong places. She's the one who said that faith could be a safe place in all the chaos. I was angry at God then, and she wasn't even a Christian therapist. She was just helping me find my footing again, and that one comment she made stuck. I thought about it for a week or two, and one morning after a rough night, her words seemed exceptionally true and I gave my heart to God. I needed to look higher. And when I'd made it out of my own hard time, I realized that I wanted to do that for other people—help them sort it all out and point them higher."

"I can't imagine how hard that must have been," Casey said quietly. "You were pretty young."

"It was tough." She nodded. "But even in our darkest valleys, there is always something brighter on the other side. There has to be, or how could we keep going? Sometimes we just need another person to believe it strongly enough that we get swept along in their current of hope."

"I guess that's faith," he said. "Believing, even though you've been marching around those walls for what feels like an eternity."

"I guess it is." She smiled up at him.

Except Ember was the one standing between him and the one thing he'd been longing for—independence, land of his own. She was vulnerable, beautiful, and just as impossible to get around as stone walls. So why did he have to feel this strange mixture of emotions when he was with her? She was part of the problem, and he just couldn't bring himself to resent her anymore. But whether or not he found her likable, beautiful, or endearing in her own way, she'd walk away with this ranch if she wanted it.

Absolutely nothing was simple with Ember.

## Chapter Seven

Ember watched as Casey settled the calf with another, older calf. They curled up together in new hay, and Ember and Casey leaned against the rails, watching them.

"The calf will be okay, won't it?" Ember asked.

"The odds are pretty good," Casey said. "A belly full of milk goes a long way."

Funny how attached she could get to a calf in half an hour. But the little guy looked like he was settling in comfortably in the hay, and she sent up a silent prayer that he'd thrive. It was tough to picture now. He was so small, so dependent.

"That's a hard start without a mother," she said softly.

"Oh, but he'll get attention and bottles full of milk. He'll be part of a rotation of bottle-fed calves, so the ranch hands will come by every three hours and give him another bottle."

"So this is normal," she said.

"There's always three or four," Casey said. "Come on. Let's let the little guy rest."

Ember could see why Casey loved this ranch so

much. It was more than charm—the place had a certain amount of heart to it. And almost all of the employees would be left out of work if she fulfilled her goal. Change was never easy, and a success for one person always meant a failure for another…or for a whole ranch worth of employees.

That thought sat heavily for Ember as they drove back to Casey's house.

Casey breathed out a long sigh as he turned off the truck, and Ember eyed him curiously. He looked worn and tired, but also eager.

"You've missed the babies," she said.

He looked over at her, lifted his cowboy hat off his head and ran his fingers through his hair. "I guess I have."

The first few fat drops of rain started to fall, each landing on the windshield with a wet thwack, and Ember leaned forward to look up at the darkening sky.

"Let's get in there before the skies open, shall we?" he said.

"Excellent idea," she said with a grin, and they both pushed open their doors.

Ember had farther to run than Casey did, but he waited for her at his side of the truck all the same. Then they made the dash to the side door together. He turned the knob and pushed open the door, then stood back to let her inside first. As they erupted into the house, there was a flash of lightning and the rain came down in sheets. Ember shivered and Casey swung the door shut. It was then that she heard the reedy wails of the babies crying in unison.

"You're back," Bert said, coming into the kitchen with a baby propped up on his shoulder and a panicked look on his lined face. "They just won't settle. Fiona's finishing with Wyatt's diaper, but—"

Fiona came into the kitchen at that moment with Wyatt in her arms. She looked less stressed than her husband, and she held Wyatt close to her cheek, making a soft shushing sound next to him that didn't seem to be helping much.

"Thanks for standing in," Casey said, taking Will from Bert's arms. "Much appreciated."

Fiona handed Wyatt over, and the older couple exchanged a look of unmitigated relief.

"I'm glad you're back," Fiona said, putting a gentle hand on Ember's shoulder as she tried to adjust the wailing infant in her arms. "Too much change, I'll warrant. They just need a quiet evening with their daddy. Will's settling down already."

And he was—Will's cries had softened into whimpers, and as Casey swung the baby from side to side, he seemed to be winding down.

"Thanks again," Casey said, raising his voice over the babies' sobs. "I'm really grateful. My aunt will be here to help me out middle of next week, so there's an end in sight for you, Bert."

"It's not a problem," Bert said with a grin, but all the same, he put a hand in the center of his wife's back and propelled her forward toward the door. "Have a good night!"

When Bert and Fiona had left, Ember's attention turned to Wyatt, who hadn't calmed in the least. She jiggled him a couple of times, her heart filling with misgiving.

"Just rock him," Casey said, still swinging Will in that perfect arc that seemed to be working for the baby.

"I am!" Ember jiggled Wyatt a few more times, then started rocking back and forth, but Wyatt wasn't having it. And in Ember's heart, she saw a tiny calf without a mother, and deeper down still was the memory of her own tiny boy, who had cried for her so desperately as another woman took him away.

"He wants his *mother*—that isn't me," she said, tears rising up inside her.

"Well, she isn't an option anymore, is she?" Casey shot back. "She's gone! So hold that baby like you mean it!"

Like she meant it. She'd been holding herself back whenever she cradled either baby, and she'd been repressing all those instincts on purpose. She was trying to stem the flood of memories of her own little boy, and the harder she tried, the more vivid he was in her heart.

She'd never named him, had let his adoptive parents have the honor—that was supposed to make it easier. But it hadn't been. They hadn't let her be a part of anything…and nothing of her had gone with her son to his new home, nothing but his memories that would have faded eventually, and she couldn't help but wonder if a part deep inside him would always be wounded, wondering why his mother gave him up.

"No—" Ember's voice quivered as she swallowed back tears, but Casey's arms were already full, and she couldn't very well just put the sobbing baby into the cradle and walk away. He needed something, and she wasn't enough—she couldn't be.

"Ember, just—" Casey didn't seem to know how to put it into words, but Ember knew what it would take to quiet this child—it would take her whole heart.

So with a prayer for strength, she pulled Wyatt

in close against her cheek, shut her eyes to the room around her and rocked him with all the love that had lain dormant in her heart this long, long decade. She rocked him the way she wished she could have rocked her own little boy, soothing away that anguished cry as they'd walked away with him, cooing over him as if his tiny heart hadn't been searching for her in that swarm of strangers.

And as she rocked, her tears flowed, and Wyatt calmed. He sucked in a few ragged breaths and snuggled against her neck. That was what he'd needed—for her to open herself up, empty herself out.

"Ember…" Casey's voice was low and concerned, and she opened her eyes to find him looking into her face. He put a hand out and touched her cheek with the back of one finger.

"Sorry," she whispered. "It's—" She swallowed.

"What happened to you?" he whispered. "And don't tell me it's nothing, because I'm no fool."

Ember had never told anyone else about her son. He'd been her heavy secret, and giving him up had been her deepest heartbreak. She looked down at Wyatt, now stilled and soothed in her arms, then back up at Casey.

Casey stepped closer still and pushed her hair away from her face, wiping a tear off her cheekbone with the same movement. Those brown eyes were locked on hers, and she sucked in a ragged breath.

"I gave up a baby boy for adoption ten years ago, and it's been hard lately," she admitted softly. It sounded so…ordinary.

"So that's why…" He nodded a couple of times. Had she not hidden her pain as successfully as she thought?

"I've been trying to just set it aside for now," she

said, wiping a tear from her cheek with the flat of her palm. "I'm sorry. I didn't want to do this. I knew I'd have to deal with it, but I wanted to wait until I was back home…and alone. So… I'm sorry. I'm not supposed to be melting down here—"

"Hey, it's okay." He met her gaze tenderly. "You weren't ready to give him up, were you?"

"I thought I was." Ember licked her lips and looked down at little Wyatt, whose eyes had drooped shut. Her arms were already feeling tired, and she looked up at Casey helplessly.

"Come sit," Casey said. "It'll be more comfortable."

Ember followed Casey into the living room, and they sank down into the couch, side by side. For a few beats they sat in silence, and then Casey said quietly, "So what happened?"

"You don't have to do this," she said, her voice raspy with unshed tears.

"I'm asking as… I don't know…a friend, I guess."

Ember looked over at Casey. "Are we friends?" she asked hesitantly.

"I thought so. We seem to have gotten there. Aren't we?"

Ember let the silence flood around her once more, and then she sucked in a breath. "I was seventeen when my mother died, and I didn't know how to grieve. I was stuck being angry—I was so mad that my mother had left me. It wasn't her fault, but I wasn't ready to be alone without her yet…" Ember's voice trembled, and she cleared her throat. "So instead of feeling it all, I tried to avoid it. While she was dying, I was busy running away from the heartbreak I wasn't ready to feel. I drank. I partied. I did whatever I could to numb the pain."

"And your father?" Casey prodded.

"My father told me that if I didn't straighten up, I'd never see another penny from him. I don't blame him. Obviously, I was out of control." Ember looked down at the slumbering infant, then smoothed his hair with her fingertips. "So I pulled myself together enough to pass muster. I started college—my dad got me in— and I tried to just put my childhood behind me. I actually thought that was possible! I'd kept up the partying through college, and one night... I don't remember anything from the party, but the next morning, I was pretty sure I did some things I regretted. Some friends took pictures, and I was—" She looked away, feeling the heat rise in her cheeks, even after all this time. "It doesn't matter. Suffice it to say, while I didn't know it yet, I'd conceived my son that night, and I had no idea who the father was."

"How old were you?" he asked.

"Twenty. Old enough to know better," she said, then shook her head. "I had to tell my father, and he suggested—rather strongly—that I give the baby up for adoption. I wasn't in any position to be properly supporting myself, much less a child. I had no idea who the father was, so I couldn't get help from him. I was halfway through my first degree, and if I dropped out and raised my son on my own, I'd have been a poor, single mom, just like my own mother. I was scared, and I thought that if I could only adjust my thinking and know from the start that I was giving the baby up that I wouldn't get attached."

"Did it work?" he asked softly.

"I thought so... I chose a family—a pastor and his wife who were childless. They were good people, and I knew they'd love him and raise him well. I brought them to doctor's appointments and everything. But then when he was born, it felt different," she said, and the memory of her little boy's squished, red face rose up in her heart so forcefully that it felt like a punch. "His adoptive mother talked to me a little bit. She said they were naming him Steven. And that name was all wrong… my son wasn't a Steven, but I had no say. I forced myself to sign the papers, thinking that if I just got over that hurdle, it wouldn't hurt so badly. Then she asked if she could hold him. I tried to be strong, and I said yes. She took him from my arms." Ember closed her eyes, steadying her breath. "I'll never forget that cry… I dream of it still."

She felt Casey's hand close over hers, and she looked over at him to find his eyes misted with tears.

"They say it'll get easier, that you'll go on with your life… Except it never got easier for me." She shook her head faintly. "I can't call my son Steven. I still haven't named him in my heart, but he isn't a Steven. He's just my baby."

And her heart still ached for him, as did her arms. She wouldn't be complete again, because he was gone, and he was no longer a baby, either. Time had swept him away along with that adoptive family.

"I'm sorry," Casey murmured, and his grip on her hand tightened. It was comforting, and she was glad for the contact with him, rooting her to the present.

"Ironically, I thought that searching out this property would be a welcome distraction from it all." She smiled bitterly.

"And then I show up with the twins." He finished the thought for her.

She didn't answer, but they both knew it was true.

"Is this why you don't want children of your own?" Casey asked.

"Yes." She nodded, her control coming back. "I didn't pray about it—not in earnest—before I gave my son up. I just closed my eyes and did it, and it was the biggest mistake of my life, trying to please a father who never really loved me in order to keep my financial security. Adoption is a good and right decision for so many people, but not for me."

Ember looked over at the big cowboy, wondering what he was thinking just then, but he didn't say anything, just looked down at her hand in his.

"You don't stop being a mother when you give your child away," she went on, hoping he could understand this. "I carry him in my heart, and I pray for him constantly. He has a birth mother who loves him more than he'll ever know."

"You should forgive yourself," Casey said quietly.

"Have you given up a child?" she asked, meeting his gaze painfully.

"No." He swallowed.

"It isn't about forgiving myself," she said softly. "It's about living with myself. Two different things."

"Is it?" Casey shook his head. "It might feel different to you, but I'm pretty sure they're the same thing."

"You can't understand," she said.

"I can try." He released her hand and put his arm up across the couch, his rough hand close to her face, and she wished she could lean into him, feel his calloused palm against her cheek. Comfort… But longing for physical comfort could be a dangerous thing, and she'd learned that lesson young.

"When I gave up my son, I knew I couldn't ever be a mother to another child. Adopted or biological—how could I tell my son I gave him away, but I kept another child? No, I knew when I gave him up that I was closing the door on future motherhood, and I'd focus my life on the good I could do for others."

"Penance?" he asked quietly.

"Of sorts," she agreed.

"I'm sorry if I made all of this that much harder," Casey said, looking down at the infant in his arms. "If I'd known what you were going through, I obviously would never have asked you to help me with the babies—"

"But you didn't know." She shook her head. "I'm fine, Casey. I really am."

And ultimately, Ember *was* fine. She was educated, she had a career, an avenue where she could help others through their difficult times, and she was that much more sympathetic to the shortcomings of her patients because she had been in their shoes and made choices that she'd later regretted, too. Her past weakness made her a better therapist today.

"Do you need to stop this? Helping with the babies, I mean," Casey asked.

"I can't avoid infants forever," she replied. "You need help, and my mission here hasn't changed. I know I had a bit of a meltdown today, but I'm really okay. I promise."

"For the record, it sounds to me like you were young and confused, and did what you thought was the right thing for you and your baby," Casey said. He leaned forward and used the back of one finger to brush a tendril of hair away from her cheek, his touch lingering there. She let her eyes flutter shut and leaned her cheek against his warm hand. But when she opened her eyes and looked into his face, she saw no judgment there. His voice was low and warm. "It was forgivable, Ember."

And while she knew that anything was forgivable in a contrite heart, forgiveness wouldn't erase the consequences of her actions. Forgiveness wouldn't return the child she'd given away. This wasn't about absolution so much as grief. And a mother never stopped being a mother to her child.

"Thanks," she said with a sad smile. "But I'm okay."

And she was. She was sad, she was living with deep regret and she had more hard-won wisdom than any other thirty-year-old woman she knew. But she was okay, because she was still in God's hands.

Outside, the rain continued to fall, puddles forming on the gravel road and the patchy grass beside it. While she wished she could just lean into Casey's strong arms and rest there awhile, she knew better. No man could fix this. Even a sweet man like Casey with those dark, gentle eyes and that stubborn streak that kept him good. He'd be an excellent father to these little boys. God was providing for these tiny orphans, and she could see that plainly.

But Casey Courtright wasn't the answer to her prayers or her tears in the dark. Right now, all she could do was carry on. There would be light ahead eventually.

## Chapter Eight

That night, Ember crawled into bed with the two heavy quilts on top of her, and she dreamed of her son as she so often did. She heard his infant cries and her dream-self was determined to find him. She would not hold herself back—not this time! She went down a hallway, opening door after door; she kept searching and searching, his cry so close. But whenever she tried to call out, her voice wouldn't respond, and the baby's sobs seemed to come from every direction at once. She woke up sweating and gasping for breath.

"Steven…" she choked out. He wasn't Steven to her…but it was the name he'd be called throughout his life. He wasn't a tiny infant anymore—he'd be a ten-year-old now, a tall boy with his own opinions.

Did he look like her? If she were to see him again, would she see her own features in his? But that was a dangerous line of thought, because she *wouldn't* see him again. She had agreed to stay away. Unless he searched her out when he was an adult, that had been their last goodbye. Not every adopted child wanted to meet his birth mother. She might still yearn for him, but that didn't mean he wouldn't be perfectly happy and fulfilled in the life he'd been given.

Ember swung her legs over the edge of her bed and sat there for a few minutes, pulling herself out of the dream and reaching out in prayer.

"Father, take the dreams away," she murmured. "And wherever he is, protect my son. Bless him. Provide for him. Pull close to him and let him feel loved."

The nightmares had been getting worse lately, and caring for Casey's charges wasn't helping matters. This visit to Vern Acres wasn't supposed to be such a drawn-out affair, either. She should be finished with this task already. Finding her family's land and starting up her own enterprise on it was going to fill her heart and squeeze out that aching sense of loss. Life *had* to move on.

She'd meant to wait until Monday morning, but last night she'd found the Cascade County Historical Society and had gone ahead and sent them an email. She'd gotten an automated reply saying that someone would be in touch at their earliest convenience, and she was hopeful that there might be some sort of information that could guide her. *Something.*

But everything seemed to be spinning out of her control, including her ability to keep her personal issues private. She pulled a quilt over her legs again, shivering against the night air. Her mind went back to yesterday when she'd said far too much. She hadn't meant to speak to him about her son. She kept telling herself it was only the timing—she'd kind of melted down in front of him, after all, and he'd deserved an explanation. But it was more than that. Casey was warm, strong, resolute and oddly comforting. She'd told him because she'd *wanted* to. What did that mean?

She'd kept her secret locked away these last ten years, opening her heart for no one. And having revealed her deepest regret left her feeling vulnerable in a whole new way.

Ember shivered, tugging the quilts back up over her shoulders. It was time to refocus her priorities. When the sun rose, she would see how close she could get to Harper Creek and see what was out there. She might be hoping for proof that wouldn't even exist anymore, but at least she'd be able to see it all firsthand. She had to get moving on this—or she'd lose herself here.

And she fell back into a fitful slumber.

That morning, Ember awoke feeling less than rested. It had been a rough night, and the thought of helping with the infants this morning was too much to face. She could fall in love with those baby boys a little too easily.

When she ambled into the kitchen that morning, Mr. Vern had just come back in from his early chores. He poured himself a mug of coffee, and another for Ember.

"So how much of the ranch have you managed to see?" Mr. Vern asked as they sipped their brew together.

"I've seen a few fields, both barns, some silos—" Ember swallowed a scalding sip. "What I really want to see is Milk River, though."

"It's a ways out," Mr. Vern said. "You mind if I ask why seeing it is so important?"

"My great-great-grandmother's journal mentioned the names of some creeks off the river in the area of their homestead. Those old names don't exist anymore, but there is a Harper Creek. My family name is Harper.

I'm wondering if it's possible that my family settled by that creek. I know it's a long shot."

"How would you even know if you did find the right land?" Mr. Vern asked.

"My great-great-great-grandfather brought a single red brick from New York State when they came out to settle here in Montana. He built it into the front of their fireplace as a reminder of where they came from. I don't know if anything would even remain of an original structure, but if it did…"

"You're right. It's a very long shot. And I hate to be the bearer of bad news, but there is also this…" Mr. Vern rose from the table and sauntered out of the room. He came back a moment later with a map that he unfolded and stretched over the tabletop.

"This is an older map," Mr. Vern said, "and you'll see Harper Creek isn't on it. That creek was renamed for a mayor in the seventies."

Ember sighed. Another dead end. Except she still wanted to see it…get close enough. Who knew? Maybe she'd recognize something there on a heart level. That was crazy, and she knew it, but when her mother used to tell her those family stories, she used to think that if she could just stand on the soil that her family had homesteaded, she'd feel them there…their memories, the family connection. She was a grown woman now and wasn't the superstitious type, but still…

"—but if you want to see Milk River, get an idea of the area," Mr. Vern went on, "there's a service road that will take you all the way up there. It brings you a little east of this area you were looking at on the map, but it's something."

"Really?" Ember looked at the older man in interest. "How far is the drive?"

"An hour, maybe less," Mr. Vern said, leaning back over the map. "There—this road here. You follow it up past the cow barn, and it circles east, so it's not quite in the same direction you're wanting to go, but it does bring you right close to Milk River here—" he jabbed a finger at the map "—and you can get a good look. That's as close as you get without going on horseback."

"That sounds doable!" Ember grinned. She wasn't sure what she hoped to see…or feel. But she needed to at least lay her eyes on the river, get close enough to touch it.

"I can't take you today, myself. I'm going back to the nursing home to see my wife. They're saying that she needs to be transferred to a different facility that can give her more services." He sighed. "I could get Casey to give you a ride."

Casey—no, he was turning out to be a little *too* comforting lately.

"No, no." Ember shook her head quickly. "Casey's a busy man, and I don't need him to chauffeur me everywhere. If it's just a matter of following a service road, I'm perfectly capable of doing that."

"Your GPS won't work on those service roads," Mr. Vern warned.

"Understood."

"And there's no cell service out there."

Ember shot him a grin. "I'll survive. It's just a road. Would you be able to lend me a vehicle so I could drive up there and take a look?"

"Can you drive stick?" Mr. Vern asked, raising an eyebrow.

"Sure can."

"Then you can take the red truck." He went to a wooden board covered in hooks and key rings, and pulled down a set of keys. "You sure you don't want that chauffeur? Casey would be happy to take you up there, I'm certain."

"I'd rather do it alone," she said.

"Suit yourself. Don't wander too far from your vehicle, and keep a sharp eye out. The wolves are hungry this time of year. They tend to leave people alone, but I'd still keep pretty close to the truck, regardless."

"I'll be fine," she said with a smile. "I appreciate this, Mr. Vern. I want to get closer to the river. I don't know what I expect to see, but—"

"Understood. Drive safe. I won't be here this morning, so when you get back, if you could just put the keys on top of the sun visor, I'd be much obliged." Mr. Vern gave her a nod, and Ember felt a weight lift off her shoulders.

Freedom, at last. She'd been praying all this time that God would show her what she needed to see out here on Vern Ranch. Maybe this was the land she was meant to buy, and maybe it wasn't. But it was hard to listen for God's voice when always surrounded by people. If God was going to show her something, she had a feeling He'd do it when she was alone and listening.

She was so ready for some solitude that she felt like skipping at the thought of getting out on the road by herself.

*Guide me, Lord*, she prayed. *Help me to know if this land is my family's or not.*

Casey spent the morning checking on some new calves out in the south field. The cows hid their babies, so they could be hard to find sometimes, but there were nine new calves in the herd as of this morning—at least that he could see. Ember hadn't come to take care of the babies today. She'd called him to let him know that she was taking a drive south to see the river, and Casey didn't have much say in that. She had the boss's permission and seemed intent on going.

"You sure?" he'd asked. "It's pretty rugged out there."

"I'm positive, Casey. I'm just letting you know where I'll be." There'd been a finality in her tone that told him she wasn't interested in being mollycoddled.

One of the homeschooled girls from church came for the morning to do some babysitting, for which Casey was eternally grateful, and he'd headed off for his work-day, doing his best not to worry about Ember.

She'd drive on down to the river, check things out and drive back. There wasn't much to it. He'd called twice to check on her—he was the manager on this ranch, after all, and her safety was his business—but there was no cell service out there, so it was no surprise that she hadn't picked up. Except, she'd been gone now for five hours, and Casey couldn't help that stab of worry.

His cell phone rang, and Casey dug it out of his pocket, glanced at the number and picked up the call.

"Mr. Vern," Casey said, punching the speaker button and dropping the phone to his lap. "What can I do for you?"

"Have you heard from Miss Reed yet?" the older man asked. "I just got back, and I don't see the truck. Is she still out there?"

"It looks like," Casey said. "I'm starting to get concerned. She might have had a flat or something. I was thinking of going out there to check on her."

"That's a good idea," Mr. Vern agreed. "If you'd drive on out and get tabs on her, I'd feel better."

"Will do, sir. I'll head in that direction now."

Casey pulled to the side of the road and dialed his house number. The babysitter picked up, her voice hushed.

"Are they sleeping?" Casey asked.

"Yes, finally," the girl replied. "Diapers changed, and they're due for a bottle soon, but I don't want to wake them up. What do you think, Mr. Courtright?"

"Wake them up one at a time to feed them," he said. "Or you'll have two hungry babies at once."

"Okay, I'll do that," she answered.

"I'm going to be a bit later than I thought, Jane. Are you okay to stay another hour or two?"

"Sure thing," she responded. "It's no problem. I'll just call my parents and tell them."

"Thanks," he said. "I'll be back as soon as I can."

Casey pulled a U-turn and headed back down the service road in the direction of the cow barn. It was a good forty-minute drive to the river if he stepped on it, so he had time to think. Normally, he liked the solitude, but today, he found himself frustrated and antsy. Having Ember on this ranch was turning into a real irritant. He couldn't seem to stop thinking about her. She wasn't quite so self-sufficient as she seemed to think, and whether she liked it or not, he was worried about her. He wanted to keep her safe.

Last night, she'd opened up, and it was only having infants in their arms that had stopped him from pulling her close. It would have been instinct—and not the kind of instinct he had with every other woman in his life. Ember was different. She was tugging at his defenses in the most infuriating way, because while she was the one standing between him and his life's goal of owning his own land, he also found himself drawn to her.

"You're an idiot," he muttered to himself.

Ember's emotional situation was her business…but he did care, even though he knew he shouldn't. In fact, he cared too much.

Ember's story about the baby she'd been talked into giving up… That had stuck in his heart like a shard of glass. He couldn't quite forget it. If Ember hadn't lost her own mother so young, she might have had someone on her side who could have given her better advice. Or if her mother agreed that adoption was the best choice, maybe she would have been able to help her make her peace with it all. A little support might have gone a long way.

Casey had lost his mother young, too. He'd been fifteen, and she'd drowned in a boating accident one summer. So he knew what it felt like to be motherless when he still needed a mom. The difference for him was that he'd still had his father. They'd pulled tight and moved forward together.

If this land truly had belonged to Ember's family, he knew what that would mean to her. But this land would mean the world to him and his dad, too. Will and Wyatt might grow up right here. Casey had grown up on a family ranch, and there was no experience that could compare. That was something he might be able to give these boys—a decent childhood.

For the next forty minutes, Casey drove down that long, straight road, dust billowing up behind him. Finally, ahead at the side of the road where it took a sharp turn, Casey could see the red truck. He slowed down as he approached, unsure if he should be relieved or not, because it was empty. His truck rumbled to a stop behind the other vehicle and he turned off the engine. Outside, all was silent and still. Casey got out of his truck, and a brisk wind whipped around him.

"Ember!" he called.

The wind whisked his voice away, and he grabbed a rifle from the rack at the back of his cab and slammed the door shut. Where was she?

He hooked a boot up on his truck's bumper and stood up straight, getting a higher view over the terrain. From that vantage point, he could make out the slope of the land going down toward the river. He looked in both directions.

Harper Creek was west from here, and Casey shaded his eyes as he looked in that direction. He could make out some movement down by the water farther down the river. A flash of purple, and relief flooded over him. She was fine. He'd been worried for nothing—and that forty-minute drive was for nothing, too. He had work of his own to do and a teen babysitter doing overtime so that he could come out here and make sure she was okay. He should be piping mad.

What did it say that he was this glad to see her again when fetching her was such a wild inconvenience?

## Chapter Nine

Ember sank lower on her haunches, holding her breath as the beaver swam silently closer, dark shining eyes looking at her above the water.

The narrow creek that led off the river had been dammed up by the animals, and she'd been watching them for some time now.

Beaver Creek—that had been one of the creeks, hadn't it? There was no saying this was the same creek because beavers could certainly move locations, but she couldn't help but wonder…

She was looking for proof, and she likely would never find it. But what would be proof enough for her to buy this land? How much did she need to be certain of the purchase in her own heart, even if not in her head?

"Ember!"

Ember startled. The beavers all disappeared with soft plops as they skirted beneath the water, and she twisted to look behind her. She knew that voice, and then Casey was marching through the brush toward her, a gun over one shoulder and his eyes blazing in annoyance.

"Casey—" She pushed herself to her feet.

"What are you doing out here?" He stopped to scan the brush and trees, that glittering gaze coming back to land on her.

"What am I doing?" Her own annoyance was rising now. "I'm looking at the land I'd like to buy. I'm trying to get a closer look at Milk River. That is why I'm on this ranch to begin with, isn't it?"

"No, that much is understood," he retorted. "The part I have trouble with is that you've been gone for almost six hours now."

"I drove up the road farther, came back, looked around on both sides of the river and discovered the beavers here. I've been…busy."

"You should have let me drive you," he said. "You crossed the river?" He closed his eyes, seeming to be looking for some calm.

Let him drive her? No, that was the exact thing she'd been avoiding. Instead, she'd had time alone—a precious, silent commune with her Maker. And she'd had some time to pull herself back together. Being thrust into the company of strangers as she navigated newborn babies, a ranch and her own ambitions left very little time for her to sort out her own feelings. She was the kind of person who needed solitude for that.

"I didn't want company," she replied honestly. "I needed to be alone for a while."

Casey's annoyance seemed to slip, and he dropped his gaze, glaring down at his boots for a few beats before he looked to the side, his dark gaze moving over the trees and toward the burbling creek. She'd offended him, and that wasn't her intention, either. It wasn't his fault she'd been a weepy mess.

"I'm embarrassed, Casey," she said tightly, "if I have

to spell it out for you. I said too much last night. None of that was your business, and I—I should have kept my mouth shut and I'm regretting that."

"Regretting having opened up," he clarified, that intense gaze snapping back to her face once more.

"Yes."

"Thanks." His tone was dry.

"You think last night was appropriate?" she asked with a short laugh. "Because it wasn't! You asked me a question professionally, and I… I totally crossed lines there. My history, my personal issues—none of those matter. They're mine to deal with. So I should be apologizing to you—"

"You aren't my therapist!" he shot back, cutting off her words. "Do you see a counseling office out here?"

"Isn't that the point?" she retorted. "To have an inviting environment? Apparently, it works rather well on me, too."

"You aren't my therapist, Ember," he repeated. This time, his voice was a low rumble. "Let's keep that clear. I don't need a therapist, nor do I want one. When I talk to you—if I open up—it isn't about professional boundaries."

"You asked me as a professional," she countered.

"Okay, I did—" He shook his head. "*Once.* I phrased it badly. What can I say? I'm telling you now that you can let all those boundaries go around me. You aren't my therapist and never will be. Neither will you ever be my boss. I think I've been clear about that one, too. Things between us aren't 'professional' because I haven't hired you and you haven't hired me. You opened up because you felt safe enough to do it. So quit running away up your ivory tower."

"I'm not running away," she responded, turning back toward the creek. "I'm taking care of my own business."

"Well, your safety is *my* business," he shot back. "And I had to drive forty minutes to come find you because Mr. Vern was worried."

"Mr. Vern was?" She looked back at Casey over her shoulder, and his cheeks flushed slightly. She felt the smile tickle her lips. "It wasn't Mr. Vern who was worried, was it? It was you."

"It was both of us. You have no gun," he said. "And you're a bit far from the truck, aren't you?"

Ember looked toward her vehicle and realized it was hidden behind trees. She sighed. "I may have strayed a little far. But I'm obviously fine."

"Obviously," he said dryly. "And that couldn't possibly have changed at any moment."

"So maybe I should be glad you found me," she admitted.

Ember turned back toward the creek and squatted back down. The beavers had disappeared—all was silent except for the twitter of birds and the rush of water from Milk River a few yards off. She scanned the dam—a bulging tangle of sticks and branches that seemed to hold together by a will of their own.

"There is a story in that old journal about beavers damming up a creek and turning the garden into a marsh." Ember sighed. "They had to move the garden. It was easier than moving the beavers. But the potato crop was ruined. They nearly starved that winter."

Twigs cracked under Casey's boots as he came up to her side. "This land might be beautiful, but it's not easy. It never has been."

"I don't need it to be. My family survived because

they learned as they went," Ember said. "My great-great-great-grandfather did everything from building their log house to trapping meat to feed the family. That winter when they didn't have enough food, he fed the family on rabbits and deer. When they lost their cow to wolves, they trapped beaver and traded their pelts for another cow the next summer, and then built a new barn right next to the house so they could protect it better."

She'd been raised on those stories—the tales of ancestors from long ago who had passed down their grit and determination to the generations that would come after. If they could survive blinding blizzards that lasted for days…if they could keep their family warm by burning cow dung and stopping up the cracks in their house with mud and hay…if they could break up that hard prairie earth and make it grow vegetables…then what about the rest of them? What could they survive?

"Those journals are priceless," he said.

"They are. They tell us what we're capable of. They homesteaded on the prairies before it was tame. And they made it."

Casey was silent for a moment. "Your mom sounds like she was pretty tough, too."

"She was." Ember smiled sadly. "But she was pragmatic, too. She always told me not to make her mistakes—never get pregnant before I was ready. She worked her fingers to the bone to provide for me, but she also reminded me that my great-great-great-grandmother who survived so much on the Montana prairies died in childbirth having her ninth baby. She was only forty-three."

"Was that a warning?" Casey asked.

"Yes," she replied, her mind going back to her mother's earnest face—tired and lined from long hours at work. They used to talk together late at night when Mom got back from her cleaning shift at the high-rise office building and after Ember had finished her homework. They'd sit in the kitchen together, eating a quick dinner, and that was when Mom was the most honest, when she had the least energy to keep things bright for Ember's sake.

"Mom always said that we can survive nearly anything for a while, but eventually life catches up. She didn't want me to be foolhardy."

"Like coming out here on your own?" he asked with a small smile.

"I was thinking about my son—what she would have advised if she'd been around," she replied softly. Ember glanced over at Casey, gauging his interest, worried that he might be judging her. His dark eyes were pinned on her, but she saw sympathy there, nothing else.

"Would she have suggested you raise him on your own?" Casey asked.

"I didn't think so at the time," Ember said, her throat thickening with rising emotion. "I thought she'd say the same thing my dad was saying—that the best thing I could do would be to give him a life with someone else. I wasn't ready to be a mom yet. She always told me not to make her mistake—to wait until I was ready. She said it was harder than I needed to know, and she wanted better for me. So when I found out I was pregnant—" Ember could hear the hoarseness in her own voice, and she took a beat to swallow. "She would have been really disappointed in me."

"And your father knew that." Casey's voice hardened.

"I don't think so," she replied with a sigh. "He just

had no intention of supporting a single mother. He wanted me to make something of myself. It seemed like the smart choice."

"If you had it to do over again?" he asked, and a breeze picked up, chilly, wet air winding through the woods, and Ember wrapped her arms around her body and found herself stepping instinctively closer to Casey just as he did the same. He didn't retreat, though, and instead put his warm palms on her upper arms.

"I'd keep my son," she said, her voice nearly choked. "I'd do whatever it took."

"Why don't you hate your father for putting you in that position?" Casey asked, shaking his head.

"Because it wasn't his fault. My choices were on me. I was an adult and I could have told my father to get out of my life and leave me alone. I could have done what my mother did and worked my heart out to provide for my child."

But she'd believed what everyone told her—life didn't have to be that hard. Life could be sweet and simple. She could get another chance to build a life she was proud of, and this mistake could all just melt into the past. They were wrong, of course, but she'd believed what she'd wanted to believe.

"Twenty isn't all that grown up," Casey said gruffly, and he moved a tendril of hair away from her eyes. She looked up at him, her breath catching in her throat. Those dark eyes were entrancing, and she should look away, break this moment, but she didn't want to. She'd been so afraid to let her secret out for fear of being judged for it, that to have this man understand... But he was being too lenient on her.

"What were you doing at twenty?" she asked softly.

"I was a cattleman."

"See?" she murmured. "Quite grown-up."

"I sure thought so," he said with a rueful smile. "I'd imagine you did, too. But I wasn't. I was outspoken and I thought I knew it all... But no, I wasn't grown-up, and I would live to be proved wrong on a whole lot."

"Me, too," she said, and another finger of cold wind worked its way between them. She shivered, and Casey tugged her just a little bit closer, so close that his lips hovered over hers. He wrapped his arms around her securely, and his eyes locked on hers.

"What are you doing?" she whispered.

"I don't know," he murmured back.

"I thought I was the bad guy..."

"I forgot," he said ruefully, and his gaze flickered upward, just for a moment, and then he froze, the moment evaporating around them. He slowly pulled his arms from her waist, and those dark, direct eyes were locked on something behind her.

"What?" she breathed, whipping around, and she saw a wolf several paces ahead of them on a rise, crouched down and teeth bared. The animal was huge—so much bigger than she'd imagined them to be. This was no "dog," but a feral beast who was looking at them as its next meal. Her heart hammered hard in her throat, and she sent up a wordless, panicked prayer for help.

Casey's eyes never left the wolf, and he didn't even seem to hurry as he pulled the gun from the strap that held it on his shoulder and reached into a pocket, coming out with two red-tipped shells. He cracked the shotgun open and dropped the shells into place.

"Don't move, Ember," he murmured, his voice low and quiet. "Don't...move..."

\* \* \*

Casey snapped the gun closed, aiming it over Ember's shoulder—directly at the wolf. Ember was trembling, her breath coming in ragged gasps as she stared at the massive, shaggy predator. Its fur hung heavy and patchy, still thin from a long, cold winter. This wolf was hungry, and for a split second, Casey felt the entire forest slow down to a crawl.

The wind shifted a tendril of Ember's hair as if in slow motion, and Casey felt the barrel of the gun snap together into the loaded position in his palm. His muscles knew the movements, so he didn't even need to think about them.

He locked eyes with the wolf, watching as its golden gaze narrowed almost imperceptibly. Then the wolf's shoulder twitched.

"Drop—" Casey ordered, his voice hollow, and Ember obediently crouched down just as Casey pulled the trigger. There was a deafening bang and the wolf dropped where it stood, the huge, shaggy beast slumping to the ground.

Casey let out a pent-up breath, then quickly surveyed the trees around them. He had another shell in that gun, and if there were more wolves—

Ember tried to stagger to her feet, but she pitched to the side on her way up, her hands going to her ears protectively. That was why he'd told her to duck—he could have made the shot past her, but the sound of the gunshot right by her ear would have deafened her. Casey raced out a hand to catch her and managed only to graze the soft material of her jacket before she stumbled away.

He let her go. Casey's eyes were scanning the woods, the river, the trees—looking for more hungry eyes and shaggy gray coats. Because where there was one wolf, there were always more.

"Ember—" he barked, and as he spun in her direction, he saw her walking unsteadily toward the creek. Then she lost her footing and plunged into the icy water. Casey darted forward and caught her outstretched arm as she sank down with a cry.

He grabbed her under one arm and hauled her back onto dry land, but as she came out, she cried out again and nearly collapsed as her weight hit one foot. She'd hurt herself—that was plain as day, and his heart pounded in his ears even as he spun back around to keep up his surveillance.

"Let's get back to the truck," he snapped. He didn't mean to sound as harsh as his voice came out. He *did* care about the fear written all over her face, and the gasp of pain as he dragged her forward, forcing her to keep walking, even though her knee buckled underneath her. But they didn't have time to linger. The wolves spotted weakness and it piqued their instinct to attack. They needed to get back to a vehicle fast.

Ember tried to limp after him, but she wasn't going to be fast enough. There was a blur of gray across the river, and another one beyond that. He had one shell loaded, and it wasn't going to be enough to take on a pack of hungry wolves.

"God protect us!" he whispered aloud, then swept an arm underneath Ember's legs and whipped her up into his strong grasp.

Staggering forward, he hurried through the marshy undergrowth up to firmer ground, but as he ran he could hear the howls of wolves behind them. They only had seconds—if that!—and he knew it. Running away only encouraged these predators.

His breath was like fire in his chest as he dashed as fast as he could run up the rocky incline toward the trucks. He could make out the blaze of their paint through the trees—so close, yet so far, and then as if by instinct alone, he dropped Ember to the ground, stepped in front of her and spread his arms wide, bellowing his loudest roar.

Two wolves stopped in their tracks only a few yards away from them, low growls coming from deep in their throats.

"Father, save us—" Ember whispered, and his own heart echoed her prayer with every beat.

"Hey!" Casey shouted. "Back off! Hey!"

The wolves took a tentative step back, and Casey whipped the gun from where it hung on his shoulder, pointed it at the closest wolf and pulled the trigger. With a thunderous bang, the animal dropped dead, and the other turned and sprinted into the forest.

There was still no time to waste—Casey put an arm around Ember's waist and hauled her forward as they scrambled the last few yards to the truck. Casey pulled open the passenger-side door and shoved Ember inside first. She cried out in pain—again something he noticed and definitely cared about, but he still didn't have time to soften his approach. Then he headed around to the driver's side, keeping his eyes peeled for more movement in the trees.

He was out of shells—at least loaded shells—and he was vulnerable out there. The pack might just cut their losses, but wolves were smart, too. They grieved a loss to their pack, and they avenged it.

The driver's-side door opened as Ember pushed it for him, and he jumped into the cab, slamming the door shut behind him. He was breathing hard, and he turned the key, the engine rumbling to life.

"You okay?" He turned toward Ember and she looked as white as paper, her lips trembling. "You aren't... Ember, you're hurt—"

"My ankle—it twisted when I fell in the water, and—" She squeezed her eyes shut. Casey had no idea how bad the injury was, but by the look of her, she needed some medical attention—the sooner the better.

"I'm going to drive us a few miles away from here, and then I'm going to take a look at that ankle," he said. "I'm going to need to get out of the truck to help you, and I'd rather not do that with wolves at my back."

She nodded mutely, her eyes still shut, and Casey slammed the truck into Reverse, turned around and then started down the road once more the way he'd come, leaving the red truck behind them. He'd send a couple of guys out tomorrow to pick up the truck—with a warning to stay clear of the trees.

The truck bounced over a bump, and he grimaced in sympathy as Ember gasped in pain.

"I'm sorry," he said. "I'm being careful—I promise."

"I'm okay—" she breathed.

"Liar," he retorted. "But you will be. Don't worry. I've got you."

As he drove toward the welcoming expanse of open field, he was filled with relief. Wolves would have a hard time ambushing him from pasture, and the more minutes that ticked by, and the closer they got to the settlement, the safer they were. Once the trees were about five minutes behind them, Casey let up on the gas and pulled to the side of the road.

He had a first-aid kit in the truck—every ranch vehicle had one—and he grabbed it from behind the seat before he jumped out and headed around to her. He opened her door and put a hand on her knee.

"Okay, I'm going to lift your foot out of the truck, and we're going to get your shoe off," he said.

Ember nodded, and Casey put a supportive hand under her shoe as he brought her leg out so he could see how bad it was. Her jeans were wet through, as was her shoe. She was already shivering with cold. He pulled a knife out of his belt, slicing through the laces of her shoe in one flick of his wrist, and he pulled the shoe off, then rolled off her sodden sock.

"I'm going to owe you for those laces," he said wryly, his fingers moving expertly over the puffy, swollen flesh of her ankle. Her skin was damp and chilled, but there was heat pulsing from deeper in her flesh. "Move your toes."

She winced but she managed to move her big toe, so it wasn't a break. But it was a very bad sprain, and the pain must be excruciating. He dropped the first-aid kit in her lap so that he could keep a hand under that foot. If he let go, she'd probably pass out from the pain.

"I need you to get out the tensor bandage," he said. "I don't think it's broken, but it'll hurt a whole lot less once I get this wrapped."

Ember fumbled with the zipper, but opened the kit and handed him the bandage roll. He worked quickly, starting at her pale toes and moving up her already bruising foot. He wrapped tightly, keeping her ankle supported until he'd finished the job. Then he gently put her foot down on the floor of the truck.

"There," he said.

"Thank you." Her voice was soft, and when he looked up at her, he found blue eyes fixed on him with a look of overwhelming gratitude. "You saved my life, Casey."

"Oh, hey…" He wasn't sure how to answer her, so he shrugged. "And my own, right?"

She smiled, then shook her head. "Play it off all you want, Casey Courtright, but you just faced down a pack of wolves for me today."

*And I'd do it again in a heartbeat*, he realized ruefully.

"Next time you want to come out here, wait for me and let me give you the ride," he said gruffly and slammed her door shut, heading around to the driver's side once more. When he pulled himself back into the driver's seat, he leaned over and grabbed her seat belt, pulled the belt out long and clicked it into place before he let go. The emergency was past, and the last thing he needed was another one.

"I'm sorry," she said. "You're right—that was my fault. I was stupid and naive, and—"

"Hey, it's over," he said, clicking his own seat belt into place. He looked over at her, her blond waves tumbling down over her shoulders, the color so pale that it almost matched the whiteness of her skin. Her lips were pale, too, the only color in her face right now that of her glittering blue eyes that were misting with unshed tears.

Casey reached over and caught her hand in his. He lifted her fingers to his lips and kissed them, keeping his lips against her skin longer than he needed to. It helped stabilize him a little bit. He'd almost lost her today, and his heart was still catching up with that. "I'm just glad you're okay."

He lowered her hand and put the truck back into Drive. Then he pulled back onto the gravel road, his heartbeat still not quite slowing down to normal.

There were dangers out here that Ember hadn't even thought of. And she wanted to let the land go wild and bring a bunch of city folk onto the property! Maybe after they risked life and limb they'd walk away from here with a little bit of perspective, he thought bitterly, her idea of a therapy center sounding crazier than ever.

And her idea to come out here alone was even crazier.

He was angry, he realized, because it was easier than processing the rest of his pounding emotions. And his anger wasn't about the land being ranched anymore, or even about her father—in this moment, it was about her safety.

If she'd gone out there and gotten herself killed, he'd have lost something that was only just awakening in his heart. What it was, he couldn't say, but he knew he'd carry that loss with him for the rest of his life.

"Let's get you back to my place, and we'll get you dried off and warmed up. That'll help matters, too. Just make sure you bring me with you the next time you go exploring," he said, glancing over at her.

"I will."

"Promise me," he pressed. This mattered. It was her safety on the line.

"I promise." And those blue eyes met his and his heart stuttered in his chest. Whatever he was feeling for her was a very bad idea. He just wished he had a choice in the matter.

# *Chapter Ten*

An hour later, Ember sat in the La-Z-Boy chair, pulled up next to the wood-burning stove in Casey's living room. Orange flames glowed behind the glass, and heat pumped pleasantly against her aching foot. Her jeans were still damp, but warm now, and steadily drying. The fear and pain from her recent adventure were melting away as she sat in that chair.

*Thank You for protecting us*, she prayed in her heart. *I could have died out there. If Casey had been a few minutes later, or if the wolves hadn't stopped when he confronted them... Father, You protected us!*

The babies were sleeping in the matching cradles, and from the kitchen, she could hear Casey clattering away putting together a sandwich for her. That stubborn cowboy was still taking care of her, and she felt so grateful for it all that she could almost cry.

It was only now sinking in how close she'd come to meeting her Maker. The memory of those white fangs bared, the fur standing up on end, the sparkling, hungry eyes... A shudder ran down her spine. If Casey hadn't swept her up in his arms the way he had and carried her most of the way to the truck, if he hadn't faced the wolves himself, roaring back at them as if he could take on a pack of wolves with his own ferocious desire to protect her—

Casey had saved her life, and he'd proved today what he was made of. He was a brave, good man who would lay it all on the line for a stranger who was going to buy this land out from under him.

*Can I do it?* Ember leaned her head back against the chair and breathed out a sigh. Unless she was certain this land was the site of the Harper homestead, she couldn't go through with buying it. One ranch was as good as another for her professional purposes. There would be other options. Unless this was the Harper land, the place where all those family stories had taken place—then she would have a claim on this land and she wouldn't be able to walk away.

She'd gotten an email back from the Cascade County Historical Society and found it on her phone when they returned to the ranch. While they didn't have any information for her directly, they did have a website with scanned early photos from the area. Most were undated and about half had some names attached. But if she wanted to go through the website, she might find some familiar people, or images of landmarks her ancestor had described. For what it was worth…

She'd asked God to show her something out there at Milk River, and she'd seen the rugged beauty of nature and felt a strange connection to this land…right up until they'd been hunted by a pack of hungry wolves. What did it mean? Was this land for her, or was God showing her how foolhardy she was being over this? She wished the message were clear!

"Is the aspirin helping?" Casey asked, coming back into the room with a fat sandwich on a plate.

"It took the edge off the pain," she said. "Thanks."

Casey handed her the sandwich, and she adjusted herself in her chair, sitting up a little taller so she could eat.

"Aren't you going to have one?" she asked. The sandwich—turkey, lettuce, tomato and cheese—was sliced diagonally in half, and she took half then handed him the plate. "Come on. We were in that adventure together."

Casey accepted the plate with a small smile. "All right. I do make one good sandwich."

He raised his half in a sort of salute and took a bite. Ember took a bite, too, her teeth sinking into soft white bread with a tangy crunch of pickle. It was delicious, and she finished half of it before pausing to look up. She found his eyes locked on her, his expression oddly grim.

"You're a surprise," she said, meeting his gaze.

"Yeah? How so?"

"I've never had a man pick me up and run me to safety before," she said.

"A guy does what he has to do," he said, a smile flickering at his lips. "Getting you into my arms wasn't such a hardship."

"You're flirting," she said with a low laugh.

"Cut me some slack. We could have died out there."

"What would you have done if the wolves hadn't backed down?" she asked.

"Died?" He laughed softly. "You aren't supposed to run—that piques their instinct to chase. But I had to get you closer to the truck. When I turned on them,

I did what you're supposed to do—face them, make noise, look big."

"And shoot," she added.

"If you can. I had one shell left—we got out of there alive because of God. I didn't have enough time to reload."

Ember believed that, too. Their prayers had been answered, but she'd still watched that man stare death in the face in order to protect her. If he'd left her behind, he could have gotten to safety much more easily—but somehow she knew that had never been an option for him.

Casey put a hand on her wrapped ankle. "How much does it hurt?"

She shrugged weakly. "It'll heal."

"I guess you got a real, up close view of this land today," he said.

"It's not what I thought." She heaved a sigh. "I figured I could handle it—whatever dangers might lurk on this land. I didn't expect…that."

"Yeah, well…there are ways to deal with the dangers, but they never actually go away. We're just careful. We know what dangers lurk, and we're prepared. I know it's overwhelming right now, and telling you that you could still do this goes directly against my best interests at the moment, but it's the truth. You could learn all of this, too—figure out how to really be prepared."

"You think I could actually turn this land into my therapy center?" she asked dubiously.

"I'm saying you could survive it," he said with a short laugh.

Casey pulled a stool up and sat down, his hand still resting protectively on her ankle.

"I didn't expect you to say that," she said softly.

"I'm an honest guy," he said, and she saw the sadness in his gaze as he said it.

"I'm not buying this land unless I'm sure it's the Harper homestead," she said quietly. "I'm no country woman. I don't know how to deal with all the dangers of land this wild. It would be foolhardy for me to even try without a really good reason—"

"I'm not trying to scare you," he said earnestly. "I need you to know that."

"Those wolves—that was scare enough," she replied with a rueful shake of her head. "I'm not blaming you, Casey. You can't help it if you were right."

Casey's phone buzzed in his pocket and he froze. He pressed his lips together into a line, then rose to his feet, pulling the phone from his pocket. Whatever he'd been about to say, he'd decided against it.

"Hey, Bert," Casey said into his phone, and he walked a few steps away. "Yeah. Okay... Where?"

Ember finished her sandwich, and as she chewed the last bite, she leaned forward to gingerly touch her bandaged ankle. It was a bad sprain, but the tight bandage was helping to support her joint. Casey was a good emergency medic, and if he could soften up toward her, he'd be a good manager of what remained of the ranch if she did buy the place. She was fast realizing that there would be few others she could possibly trust the way she trusted this man, and if she did open her therapy center here, she would feel safer, more confident, maybe even happier with him at her side.

Except he'd been clear that she'd never be his boss. If she bought this land then he wouldn't be staying. Whatever they were starting to feel between them—it couldn't last.

"I'll be there soon," Casey said, then hung up the call. He looked over at her, his expression conflicted.

"What's going on?" she asked.

"There's a cow having trouble delivering in the south pasture. The cowboys doing patrol don't have the equipment with them to help the cow, so I'll have to head on out there. I don't want to just leave you like this, and the babies—" He glanced toward the sleeping infants in the cradles.

Ember gingerly lifted her foot to the ground. She could stand up if she put her weight on the good leg only.

"It's a sprained ankle. I'm not exactly out of commission," she said.

"Hold on a second." Casey disappeared up the stairs, and she could hear his footfalls overhead. There was a rustle against the floor, a thump, and then his steps came back down the stairs once more. He emerged into the living room holding a single crutch.

"You just had that hanging around?" she asked with a soft laugh.

"What can I say—I'm ready for emergencies. It's part of the job."

"That will help enormously." She accepted the crutch, and he held out a hand, helping her to stand on her good foot. Then he adjusted the crutch for her height.

"There you go." He sounded satisfied, and with the crutch's support, she did feel a lot more mobile. "Would you watch the babies while I go take care of this?"

"Sure."

"Are you sure you'll be okay? I know this is really hard for you, and I don't want to add to it. I probably never should have asked for you to help out with the babies to begin with, but—"

"Casey." She put a hand on his arm. "I'll be fine."

Casey looked down at her—and she was struck again by just how big this man was. Tall, broad, strong, and those dark eyes were fixed on her with an expression so complex she couldn't read it. But she didn't need to read his thoughts to know what kind of man he was. All she knew was that in this room with him, she felt warmer and safer than she had in her life.

"If I'd lost you out there—" He clamped his mouth shut, as if biting off the words.

"But you didn't," she said.

"I'm just saying—" He didn't want to say it, whatever it was. She could tell by the battle on his face. "I've known you a week. This is a strange circumstance— what with the babies and now the wolves... We're not exactly in an ordinary situation here."

"I agree," she said softly, but his eyes were still locked on hers.

"So why does this feel like more?" he asked, his voice a low rumble.

It *did* feel like more. It felt like something deep and undeniable was developing between them, despite the fact that she could never be a mother to his sons, and he could never support her as she fulfilled her promises to God. They were stuck, but her heart kept stretching anyway. Her stubborn, stubborn heart that wouldn't let go, even when it was for the best.

Like with her own son that her heart yearned to- ward, even in her sleep. She'd given him up. He had another family. He wouldn't even remember her! But her heart wouldn't stop and she dreamed of his infant cries anyway.

"Go and do your job. I have it under control here," she said with more surety than she felt.

She glanced toward the babies, still sleeping deeply. Will's tongue was stuck out, and Wyatt was sucking rhythmically on a soother.

"I'm going to regret this," he said with a sigh. Then he dipped his head down and caught her lips with his. His lips were soft and warm, and they moved over hers with confidence. Her eyes fluttered shut, and she felt like the room evaporated around them, and all that was left was him and her and the whisper of his breath against her face. He slid his arms around her waist, tugging her closer against him. Then his hand moved up to her cheek as he pulled back and looked down into her eyes.

For the first time since this whole drama with the wolves had unfolded, she felt a rush of comfort, as if in this tall cowboy's arms, she'd come home.

"How inappropriate was that?" he murmured.

"Wildly," she breathed.

"Thought so. I'll kick myself for it later, but I couldn't leave the house without doing that just once—" He swallowed, closed his eyes for a moment, then stepped away from her. Cool air rushed between them, and Ember wished she could close that distance once more and just rest her cheek against his broad chest.

"I'll be back," he said and turned toward the kitchen and the door. She stood there, her lips still warm from his kiss and her heart hammering in her chest. All she wanted to do was run after him and have him do that all over again, but she couldn't run—and even if she could, she didn't dare. She knew as well as he did that there was no future between them...only these frustrating emotions.

Will squirmed in his sleep and let out a whimper. Ember used the crutch to hop over to the cradle, and she looked down at the sleeping baby. This was hard—opening up her heart for the sake of a defenseless baby, and then closing it up again for her own sake. It was like tearing open a wound every time she did it.

Ember couldn't be a mother to these children, no matter how sweet or deserving they might be. It would tear her heart out to do it. She'd shut the door on motherhood for good reason. She'd deemed her education and career important enough to hand her son to another woman. If it had been important enough once, it would have to be enough now.

Ember pulled the stool closer, sat down to give herself some proper balance and bent over the cradle to pick up the infant. Will snuggled against her chest, squirming to try to get closer. She sighed, leaning her cheek against the baby's downy head.

This ranch was a place of strangely deep emotion, and she couldn't help but wonder if that was because of some familial tie to the place calling her home.

Or was she only fooling herself? Because this ranch had ties to other families, too, and her emotions were tugging her toward one man right now—a man who needed a mother for his twins. She couldn't be that mother. She *could* be tough, strong, empathetic and staunchly determined to shepherd other people through their darkest times. She could be like the other women from the Harper family, standing tall and persevering. God had something He wanted her to do, and she'd felt His hand in bringing her to Vern Acres. He would pay her back for everything she'd given up. She just had to hold on.

\* \* \*

Casey tightened the saddle strap and led Soldier out of the barn. The only way to check out the situation in the south pasture was on horseback. He was going through the motions, but his mind wasn't on the job ahead of him. It was still back at the house with Ember—and that kiss.

It was dumb. He shouldn't have caved in to his desires like that. She was no country woman, and she had no desire to buy some land and raise cattle with him. He wanted to show those boys what hard work looked like, and how the day in, day out chores contributed to an industry that fed a nation. He wanted to raise those boys to say *Yes, sir* and *No, ma'am*. He wanted them to ride herd, earn the respect of the other men and stand by their word. He'd raise those kids right—just like he'd been raised, and like his dad before him.

Boys grew into men over time, regardless of where they did the growing, but life on a ranch did the best job of instilling time-honored values, in Casey's humble opinion. And Ember might like being called "ma'am," but she didn't understand the lifestyle that created those country manners. It wasn't just about using the words; it was about a sense of respect for women, a desire to live honestly and the humbleness that came from hard work. It started before dawn, and it ended when it ended— regardless of how many hours a man had been at it, or if the sun had already set.

Add to that, Ember didn't want to be a mother to any other children... Maybe that should have come first. They wanted different things, valued different things. Kissing her—he had no right to be crossing those lines with her.

And yet he wasn't sorry, and that frustrated him. He should feel bad about that—except that kiss had been honest. What he felt for her might be dumb as a bag of rocks, but that was how he felt when he looked at her. She was beautiful, wounded, more vulnerable than she liked to admit, and when he was next to her, all he could think about was if she was comfortable, and what she was thinking...

Casey put his foot into the stirrup and swung up into the saddle. He made a clucking sound with his mouth and pulled on the reins, guiding Soldier out of the barn.

Horseback was where he did his best thinking, so maybe this ride would do him good.

"Lord," he murmured aloud. "Take away whatever I'm feeling for her. I know she's all wrong for me. I don't even need help in seeing that. Just—take it away. Give me that peace that passes understanding."

God had always answered that prayer for him in the past. If something wasn't meant for him, he asked God to remove the desire for it. Like a woman he was interested in who wasn't a believer, or even some fancy truck he knew he couldn't actually afford. He'd pray for that peace, and he'd get it. Every time.

Except with Ember. He'd been praying for peace for days now, and God had gone silent.

Casey rode the rest of the way, the scenery passing him by without him giving it much notice as his mind gnawed over the problem. *He* was the problem—that was clear enough. Ember had come for one reason—to buy this ranch—and he'd been the one to overstep, pull her into his arms and kiss her. Given a chance to think that one over, she'd have every reason to be angry with him.

"Hey, boss!" Bert called as Casey rode up to where

the old cowboy stood. The sun was lowering in the sky, shadows stretching long and languid. Cattle dotted the grassy field, grazing and chewing their cud. Casey spotted a few new calves since he'd last been out this way. He swung down from his horse and pulled the tools he'd brought with him out from the side bags. Then he patted the horse's rump, letting Soldier go graze with the cattle. They were close by Milk River, and Casey could see the glitter of the water from here. A creek snaked between two hills, copses of trees thrusting up from the banks.

"Right there." Bert nodded toward the cow. She was pacing, her head down as a ripple of contraction moved over her bulky middle. Her udder was leaking a steady drip of milk, and a pair of hooves poked out from beneath the tail. The baby was in the birth canal, but the mother looked exhausted. "Been like that for the last hour. No progression. I've tried getting in there to pull, but she won't let me close."

The cow shook her head, ear tags rattling, then hung her nose down again as another contraction hit.

"We're gonna have to get in there," Casey said. "That calf has to come out."

"Agreed," Bert replied. "But it'll take us both. I'll go around front and keep 'er occupied, and you see if you can get a hold of those hooves."

Bert and Casey had worked together on births for years now, and they had a well-oiled system. Cows had an instinct to go give birth alone, and they didn't welcome intervention, either, but this cow just might be tired enough to allow them to give a hand.

Casey had brought the calving chains with him—a device that settled over the cow's hips and attached to the hooves that were protruding. It gave the cowboy some leverage as he pulled the calf steadily out of the mother with every contraction. Closer to the barn, they'd put the cow in the head gate to keep her from getting spooked and trampling them, but he'd just have to be light on his feet tonight. Because there was no head gate available, and if this cow didn't get assistance, they'd lose them both.

"There've been wolves out—past the barn, on the east part of Milk River," Casey said, and Bert instinctively looked in that direction.

"How brave were they?" Bert asked.

"I shot two."

Bert's eyebrows went up, and he chewed the side of his cheek. "We'd better have a man with a gun patrolling tonight, or we'll lose the new calves."

"My thoughts, too," Casey agreed. "You ready?"

They moved toward the cow, and it took a few steps away from them. They approached again, and she did the same, moving steadily toward the river.

"Oh, no, you don't—" Casey got in front of the cow, cutting her off so she couldn't make more trouble for herself by getting too close to the water, and this time the cow stumbled to a stop as another contraction took over. For the next forty minutes, they assisted the cow in the delivery of the calf. It was a big male, and when it dropped to the ground, it didn't start breathing until Bert rubbed its chest with a handful of grass and Casey tickled its nostrils with another long stem. Finally, it pulled in a breath and they left the mother to clean up the baby.

They backed away to give the cow some space to bond with its calf, and Casey's boot hit something unexpectedly hard. Casey was on top of a small knoll, but instead of his boot connecting with dirt and grass, he'd hit sharp rock. He looked down, used the toe of his boot to work the soil away from the rock, and he frowned. That wasn't loose rubble. He kicked more, and Bert watched him curiously.

"What's the problem?" Bert asked.

"This—what is it?"

Bert came over and bent down, using his gnarled hands to pull weeds and soil away, then brushed the rocks clean.

"Looks like it's got some mortar between these rocks," Bert said, and between the two of them, they uncovered enough of the structure to recognize it. "That there's a chimney. Or what's left of it."

"Yeah. Looks like—"

Casey's heart sank. He'd sensed it the minute his boot hit it. There had been a cabin here, or a home-stead, a long time ago. He looked around—it was an ideal spot, high enough to avoid flooding from the river and near a stretch of open plains. This had been a home once upon a time—possibly the homestead that Ember was searching for.

"You okay?" Bert asked, his lined face creasing with worry. "You look like you got bit by something."

"Help me dig down a bit. I want to see something…"

Bert gave him a funny look, but he complied, and they dug together for another couple of minutes. There wasn't much left in one piece, but as they uncovered more of the structure, at first he thought it was a chim-ney, and then he realized it was a hearth. Rock had been mortared together with some real skill, but then his gloved fingers hit something that felt different.

"What's that?" Bert asked when Casey brushed the soil away from it.

"A brick," he said hollowly.

"Huh."

A single brick mortared in with the rest of the rock. Ember had mentioned that…

"I know what this is," Casey said.

"Yeah?"

Casey slowly shook his head. "It's the end of my hopes for this place," he admitted, his chest constricting as the reality settled in.

He was an honest man, though, and a Christian. He wouldn't live a lie, and he'd given Ember his word that he'd help her find out the truth about this land. He'd just hoped that the truth would be more favorable to his position. How was it possible that this woman from the city with a rich daddy and a broken heart was the one with the rightful moral claim to this place?

This ranch wasn't rightfully his, either, but he'd been working this land long enough that he could have made it his, started out some new memories and put down his roots. He could have raised the boys here, and if he'd been able to see through his offer, his roots would have settled all the way down to the bedrock.

"Boss?" Bert pulled Casey out of his reverie. "You okay?"

"Yeah, Bert," he sighed. "But things are going to change around here."

"How so?" the older man asked with a frown.

"Miss Reed is going to buy this ranch."

"I figured that was why she was here," Bert said. "I'm sure she'll need a manager yet. And I'm due to retire here pretty soon. Fiona keeps asking me to hang up my spurs. We might not be rich, but we'll be okay."

"I'm not working for her," Casey said, his voice a growl.

"I know you're not crazy about the Reeds as a whole, but—"

"No, I can't work for her…" Casey sighed. "I'm feeling things for her that I shouldn't, and working with that woman isn't a possibility. I need a mother for those boys, and she's not it."

And there it was—the flood of certainty he'd been looking for on his ride over here, the knowledge he'd been avoiding when he was busy kissing the beautiful blonde in his living room. Ember Reed couldn't be the mother his boys needed. She couldn't be the wife to raise these kids with him. And while he could make his peace with her family background, he couldn't raise those boys at a therapy center. They needed land, cattle, chores and responsibility. He wanted to give them a proper ranch childhood…

There would have to be another woman to be the wife and mother they needed so badly. But it would have to wait until his heart had healed from this one…

Whatever he'd been hoping for—he needed to let those dreams go. Just because a man wanted something so badly he could taste it, that didn't mean it was part of God's plan. These weren't his walls. They'd been hers all along.

"Soldier," he called softly, and his horse nickered and sauntered in his direction. "Let's go, boy."

It was time to go back and face reality. He wouldn't be forgetting about that little detail again.

## *Chapter Eleven*

The sun was setting outside the window. Ember held Wyatt in her arms, the baby looking at the glowing, partially blackened door of the woodstove in that cross-eyed new infant kind of way. Ember cradled the baby in one arm and used the crutch to sink back down onto the stool.

"Hey, you…" she said softly, and Wyatt lifted his head away from her shoulder, then let it drop down again. He had grown in the last week—she could tell by the way he fit in her arms. "How are you, little guy?"

Wyatt blinked up at her, big brown eyes fixed on her face searchingly. She smiled and smoothed a hand over his downy head. So small, so sweet…so easy to fall in love with.

"You deserve better than me, Wyatt," she said softly. "You remember that. You and your brother deserve only the best, and one day you'll have a mom of your very own."

Her throat tightened at that thought. One day, there would be a woman who'd be able to open her heart to these boys. She wouldn't be all emotionally battered like Ember was. She'd be whole and pure, and she'd be filled with good advice and endless hugs. She'd be the woman that Casey needed.

Ember sucked in a breath, trying to push back that stab of pain at the thought. She knew this little family of three deserved better, so why did it hurt so much to imagine what that better woman might be like? These boys needed a mom who could kiss away their pain, get them into line when they misbehaved and love their dad with all her heart. She'd be the center of that home, her love binding them all together.

"You deserve better, Wyatt," she whispered softly.

She'd missed out on all of this with her son—the snuggles, the diapers, the bottles. She'd given it away for the promise of a better future, believing that another woman would be better for her son, too.

It only occurred to her later that her father's advice that she give her baby up might have been coming from *his* experience. He'd known about Ember, had supported them with sporadic financial gifts and had otherwise stayed out of her life. He'd never seen her.

Hadn't that hurt him as a father? Hadn't there been some paternal part of him that had wondered about his little girl, worried about her, even? Because Ember thought about her son constantly, worried that he wouldn't know how much she'd loved him, that it would affect him later in life. She'd longed to see him again, just to know he was okay.

But her father seemed quite happy with how his life had gone without Ember there to complicate matters. He had a family already, wealth, respect in his community. He'd swept Ember aside like the mistake she had been.

The sound of boots on the step outside pulled Ember

out of her thoughts. She looked down at Wyatt, those big eyes still searching around him, taking in his little world. The door opened, and Casey came in, Bert on his heels.

"Hi," Ember said, forcing a smile. "How's the calf?"

"Fine and healthy," Casey replied, and those warm eyes met hers in a way that made her heart speed up just a little. Did he do that on purpose? "I brought Bert along to stay with the boys while I drop you back off at the house."

Bert could have dropped her off on his way home for the evening, but it seemed that Casey wanted the honor, and she felt a flood of warmth at the thought. She'd missed him, too, as inconvenient as that was. But opening her heart to her grief over her son also meant opening it up to everything else she might be feeling, and she wasn't able to simply push her emotions down.

"Let me just wash my hands," Bert said, heading for the kitchen sink, and Ember looked over at Casey. His dark eyes met hers, and she saw a strange mix of emotion there—so different from the tender longing in his eyes a few hours before when he'd kissed her. Had something changed? Or had he simply had time to think about it?

"How's the foot?" Casey asked quietly, coming up closer to keep his words private.

"Manageable," she said with a small smile.

"Could you ride?" he asked.

Ember eyed him uncertainly. "Right now?"

"No—tomorrow, maybe."

"Let's see how it feels tomorrow," she replied. "But I can guarantee you I won't be putting much weight on it."

Casey didn't say anything else, and when Bert dried

his hands, Ember passed the baby over to his confident arms. Her heart tugged a little as she let the infant go. She was already attached to these little boys—how easily that happened. Bert gathered Wyatt up onto his shoulder.

"He's had his bottle and I changed his diaper half an hour ago. But normally after that bottle—" Ember began. Then she smiled sheepishly. "Sorry."

"Nothing to be sorry about," Bert replied. "And Will?"

"He's had his bottle, his diaper is changed and he's been out like a light since." So he'd wake up soon and want some entertaining.

"Sounds good," Bert said, then nodded to Casey. "Take your time, boss."

Ember got her jacket, and when Casey opened the door, she eyed the three steps with trepidation.

"Grab your crutch," Casey said, and when she did, he scooped her up into his arms. He smelled warm and musky, and her breath caught in her throat as he effortlessly carried her down the stairs, then put her down lightly once more.

"Now you're just showing off," she said with a low laugh as she caught her balance once more.

"Easier that way," he said with a wink, then pulled the house door shut behind him. "So how did it go with the boys?"

"Fine."

"I meant, how are *you*?" he said, his gaze catching hers.

"Better than I was before. There is something to be said for just feeling your grief. It has less power that way."

"So they say." He looked away from her, scanning the scene for a moment, then bringing his gaze back to lock on to hers. "I could see us being in each other's lives, if you stuck around."

"But not as your therapist, and not as your boss," she said. She hopped over to the truck, and Casey pulled open the passenger-side door. She turned toward him, and he stood there looking down into her face, his eyes locking on to hers in that tender way again. His broad chest emanated heat in the cool evening, and she had to hold herself back from leaning into those strong arms.

"But I could be your friend," he said quietly.

"You're assuming I'm staying here," she said, sadness welling up inside her. "If I found the evidence I needed, I would. But I'm not buying this land without it. This isn't only about me and my feelings. My plans would affect a lot of other people…" Who was she fooling? She wasn't even thinking about the ranch hands who would be out of work or the wider community that wanted this to stay ranching land. "It would affect *you*, Casey. I don't like the thought of that."

Casey ran a finger down her cheek. Whatever it was about Casey that was so comforting and appealing, she'd have to sort out when she could be alone again. And while she couldn't just turn off whatever she was feeling, maybe she could wade through it and get to thinking rationally again.

"Hmm…" He didn't say anything else in response. Did he not believe her? Did he think she didn't care how he'd be affected?

"Casey, I'm serious—"

"I know you are," he said, and there was a flash of pain in those dark eyes. Then he dropped his gaze and pressed his lips together. "That's why I said I could be your friend. You're a good woman. I might think you're crazy, but you're deep-down good."

She smiled at that. "Crazy, am I?"

"I stand by that." He smiled ruefully. "I actually don't think I could stay away from you entirely. But I will stop kissing you in moments like this."

Ember felt a sink of disappointment at that. She didn't want him to turn off his feelings—even though it was best for both of them. But what did she expect? This wouldn't work between them, and she wasn't fooling herself about that.

"Okay," she said.

He pulled in another breath, then nodded. "Okay." He smiled into her eyes. "You want a hand up?"

"Sure." Casey put his hands on her waist and boosted her up into the passenger seat of the truck, and her stomach rippled at the sensation of his touch. He handed the crutch up to her, and then he slammed the door shut, leaving her in momentary silence as he circled around to the other side. She adjusted the crutch to fit more easily down by her feet and leaned her head back.

She'd pored over those grainy photos on her phone's internet browser while Casey had been gone, and there weren't any family photos that fit the descriptions from those journals. There were some unidentified pictures of wildly bearded men or somber women standing alone... but what did that help her? They could be anyone. It seemed there was no way to be certain whether this was her family's land or not. Maybe that was for the best. She didn't need to disrupt things here any longer. As soon as her car was ready at the shop, she'd leave Vern Acres and let Casey put his offer down on the ranch.

He deserved it—he'd worked this land and maybe he was right that this county didn't need any more Reed influence.

Casey opened the driver's-side door and hopped up into the seat.

"So why do you want me to be able to ride?" Ember asked, glancing over at him.

"I want to show you something." He put the key in the ignition and the truck rumbled to life. "And we can only get there on horseback. That's one of the many complications of this place."

"What do you want to show me?" she asked, shooting him a curious look.

"You'll have to wait and see it yourself," he said with a small smile. "Words won't do it justice."

"And my ankle?" she said.

"I'll wait until it heals up enough to get you onto a horse."

Ember couldn't help the curiosity that bubbled up inside her, but when she looked over at Casey, his expression was resolute. She wasn't going to get anything out of him.

"Did you find something?" she pressed.

They pulled out onto that now-familiar gravel road and headed up toward the main house. Casey was obstinately silent, and she couldn't help but wonder if he'd stumbled across that proof she'd been searching for. Excitement simmered up within her.

Was this old ranch her home after all?

## *Chapter Twelve*

That night, Casey sat in the kitchen, an untouched mug of tea on the table in front of him. His Bible lay open on the tabletop where he'd been rereading the story of Joshua and those walls.

"I'm sorry, Lord," he prayed. "I shouldn't have kissed her. That wasn't right—it doesn't matter what I feel for her. She's not mine to kiss."

He looked over at the cradles where the babies were sleeping peacefully. He was a dad now. He'd struggled with how he would handle all of this, but it had started to settle inside him. These boys were his responsibility, his God-given obligation. They were also his blessing and his joy. They needed him, and maybe he needed them just as much. Caring for these little guys was hard work—he couldn't deny that—but he'd fallen in love with them in the process.

"Make me a good father," he prayed, his voice choked. "Give me the wisdom I'm going to need to raise these boys right. Give me strength, and tenderness, and insight… Make me into the father that these kids need. And please, Lord, take away whatever it is that I'm feeling for Ember. There is only so much a man can handle at one time, and I'm pretty sure I'm reaching my limit here…"

Once he showed Ember his discovery, she'd finalize her offer—and he'd need to figure out where he and the boys would go. Surely, God had something in mind for them. He'd given Casey a family, hadn't He? If that wasn't God moving in His own mysterious ways…

But Casey did need a woman in his life—a mother for those boys. He needed someone to stand by him, raise kids with him, wrestle with the hard stuff. He needed a woman who could help him teach those boys the country manners and the Christian morals. He needed a partner.

So what was he doing letting himself fall for Ember Reed? It was dumb—there was no way around it—but he also felt a little helpless when it came to his feelings for her. When he looked at Ember, a part of his heart he'd never known existed woke up.

Casey didn't sleep well that night. Telling Ember about that stone hearth with the single brick worked in that was by the river wouldn't be easy, because it would be a sort of goodbye to all of his hopes for this land, too. But at least he'd have some time alone with Ember and he could show her what she needed to see…alone, without an audience.

The next morning, he went to do his rounds after the ranch hands had completed the early chores. Bert stayed with the babies, and Casey called his aunt, just to make sure she was feeling well enough to start helping him out on a full-time basis the next week as they'd agreed. There were two baby boys who needed nurturing and love while he was working to provide for them, and his wayward heart was not the top priority. Those boys were.

When he'd done his rounds, Casey headed on up to the main house. He parked his truck and stood outside for a moment, the cool morning air soothing his mood. The sun hadn't risen very high in the sky, but the warm rays felt good on his shoulders. The curtain flicked, and he saw Ember standing by the kitchen window. She wore a gray sweater, her hair tumbling down around her shoulders, and those direct blue eyes followed him with a mildly curious expression.

"I can't put it off, Lord," he prayed under his breath. "Guide me."

Sometimes God expected His children to hand deliver a blessing to someone else. If only that particular blessing wasn't the one he'd been praying for, himself.

Casey headed to the side door and knocked once before opening it. Mr. Vern was seated at the table with his ledgers open as he worked through the ranch's monthly finances, and he glanced up as Casey came inside.

"Good morning," Mr. Vern said. "How's the herd?"

"Twelve new calves last night," Casey said. "All healthy."

"Good, good." Mr. Vern nodded, turning his attention back down to the ledger. "I'm just trying to get these accounts sorted out. I need to write a check for the nursing home."

"No problem, sir. I'm here to see if Ember's well enough to ride," Casey said, turning toward Ember. She stood by the counter, her bandaged foot gingerly touching the floor, but obviously not holding her weight. She took a sip from a mug.

"That depends on how much will be expected from me," she said.

"I'll get you in and out of the saddle," Casey said, and he had to admit, he was looking forward to any excuse to be close to her again.

"If that's the case, let's go." She put her mug down on the counter and turned to Mr. Vern.

"Thank you for breakfast, Mr. Vern."

The older man looked up with a distracted smile. "Not a problem." He pursed his lips. "Are you any closer to a decision on this place?"

"It's beautiful land, sir," Ember said. "But unless I can find some solid proof that the Harpers homesteaded here, I'm not going to put in an offer."

Mr. Vern nodded slowly. "All right, then. Thanks for being honest."

And he sank back down into his ledgers again. Casey looked at his boss for a moment, his heart going out to him. The financial pressure was heavy this time of year, and with his wife's medical care getting more expensive, Casey could only imagine the weight of those worries. But it would be over soon enough, and Mr. Vern would have his sale.

Casey helped Ember limp down the steps and into the waiting truck. He turned the key and the engine rumbled to life. Then he looked over at her. God worked things together for good—not just for a collective good, but for an individual's good, too. For a man with a heart that kept loving when it shouldn't, for two tiny boys whose parents were dead and for this woman who'd been through too much in her lifetime. God worked things together for good—Casey had to hold on to that.

Casey pulled out of the drive and headed down the

gravel road toward the red horse barn. He felt better with Ember by his side, even knowing that he was about to give her the keys to this place, figuratively speaking. What was it about Ember Reed that did this to him?

"How is your ankle on the bumps?" he asked. "Because on a horse, it'll be even worse."

"It's not too bad," she said. "It wasn't as bad of a sprain as I thought—or maybe it was the ice compress Mr. Vern gave me last night that fixed it right up. I expected to see all sorts of black-and-blue on my foot, but it's only a little bruised."

Casey was thankful to God for the small blessings—it could have been a whole lot worse. They fell into silence for a few more minutes as he circled around toward the barn. When they arrived, he pulled to a stop and leaned forward to look at the corral.

"I think this will be worth it for you," he said.

"Casey, I'm not a country woman," Ember said with a low laugh. "It might be easier to just tell me about whatever it is you think I need to see… Besides, I'm not sure I'm going to pursue this sale. I was praying about this pretty seriously out there by the river, and in response, I was attacked by wolves and sprained my ankle."

"Maybe that wasn't a response to your prayer," Casey replied.

"And maybe it was. I don't need to be shown any more rugged territory to convince me that I'm in over my head, Casey. You've already accomplished that."

"This isn't about proving that you don't belong here," he said with a shake of his head. "This is…just for you."

Casey got out of the vehicle and circled around to help her down from the passenger side of the truck.

She was warm in his arms as he helped her down, and he went ahead to open the door for her into the barn.

Casey had the horses saddled and ready, so all he had to do was help Ember up into the saddle. Once she was settled he looked up at her, drinking in this beautiful woman with the aching heart. She was lovely, interesting, tender, smart—the whole package. But she wasn't for him. He could be a part of answering her prayers, though, and today he'd get to see the look on her face when she saw the foundation of her family's homestead.

Those weren't his walls—they were hers.

He just prayed that while God was working out Ember's good, that He would remember Casey, too. Because he'd marched so long that every single part of him was deeply tired. Especially his heart.

Ember's ankle was a little sore as Patience started to move, following Casey's large stallion, but she wouldn't complain. She could tell that Casey wanted to show her something important, and the curiosity if she waited longer would be more agonizing than the ride, in her opinion. There was a throbbing place in her heart that wished she could find some proof that this had been the Harpers' land, but maybe Casey had found a hint that would mean something to her... Because it wasn't just about her therapy center—it was about coming home.

The day was bright and warm, and she could feel summer coming in that fragrant wind. She sucked in a chestful of spring air as Casey led them out of the corral and then through the gate.

"Are we going through the woods again?" Ember asked.

"No, we're heading across a pasture. It's through open fields," he replied. "It was when I was dealing with that difficult calving that I saw something you'll be interested in."

"And that's all you'll say?" she asked with a rueful smile.

"Yup." He grinned back at her.

"Are you sure this ranch won't kill me yet?" she asked with a low laugh.

"Not entirely," he replied, then chuckled. "I told you that ranch life wasn't what you were expecting. There is no living peaceably with nature. You live peaceably in spite of it, and you'd better know what you're doing."

"For every story in that old journal about catching crayfish in the creek and running around outside or befriending some animal, there was another story about someone just about dying," Ember said, her mind going back over those well-worn stories told and retold by her mother.

"Oh, yeah? Like who?" Casey said.

"Oh, like Bernard—that was the oldest son in the family. He went hunting with his father, and they shot an elk. He went up to finish it off and he got a hoof to the head. They had to carry him back to the house and bandage him up. He was unconscious for a week. They sent for a doctor from town who said he'd die. But he didn't. He eventually woke up. He was never the same, though. Walked with a limp, even though his leg hadn't been hurt, and he slurred his words. A brain injury, I'd imagine. They didn't have an explanation for it back then."

Ember sighed. Was she crazy to want this rugged, unforgiving patch of land? But even with the risks involved, if this was Harper land, then she did! She wanted to come home to those stories and the ancestors who battled the elements to make a life in these wild Montana plains.

"So why did your ancestors choose to come out here to homestead?" Casey asked.

"No idea," she admitted. "That was never mentioned. They just did. But I think it must have been a sense of adventure. Pa—that's what the journal called the father of the family—was the adventurous sort. He was the kind of man who could build a log cabin by himself with an ox and a hatchet. He was a big man—stood head and shoulders taller than anyone else—and he hardly ever talked. Mam adored him and did all the chatter for him. And she…trusted him to keep them all alive, I suppose."

The horses plodded comfortably forward, and Ember adjusted herself in the saddle, trying to find a better position for her ankle. She bent down to rub a hand over the tensor bandage. She was trusting Casey to keep her alive, too, so she felt like she could understand Mam a little better now. With the right man to rely on, a woman could face more than she ever thought possible.

"You sore?" Casey asked.

"Yeah." She winced. "I'll be okay."

"You want to stop and rest?" he asked, and there was concern in his voice. "I knew it was too early to take you on horseback."

"No, I'm fine," she said, forcing a smile. "I want to see—whatever it is you've got to show me. My car will be ready soon, and I have a feeling I've come close to outstaying my welcome with Mr. Vern, so if you have something to show me, I guess I'd better see it now."

Casey nodded, but the smile slipped from his face. "Yeah, of course."

"I doubt you want me around here getting in your

way any longer than necessary, either," she said, trying to sound more jovial than she felt.

"I don't know about that," Casey said. "I've been getting used to you around here."

She smiled sadly at that. She'd been getting used to him, too. Maybe even more than that… It was hard not to lean into him, trust him. It was hard not to get comfortable in those arms.

Was that what she was looking for in her family land—a man of her own to stand by her side and fend off the wolves? If she was, she needed to stop that fantasy right now and see this ranch for what it was.

"I have patients who are waiting for me in Billings," she said. "I have a whole life waiting for me."

"I know," he said.

What was he thinking? She wished she knew, but his expression was granite and he rode facing straight ahead, his hat low and shielding his face from both the sun and her scrutiny.

"So tell me some family story of yours," she said.

"Is it going to say something about me?" he asked, shooting her a rueful smile.

"Very likely," she retorted. "But I told you mine, so you tell me yours."

Casey was silent for a moment, then said, "Okay… So when my grandfather was a teenager, he was in love with a girl from a rich ranching family. His dad wasn't rich—he worked his land with nothing to spare. Anyway, so Grandpa decided to try to see the girl by sneaking onto her property and throwing rocks at her window to get her attention. He threw a rock too hard and it broke the windowpane. Her father let the dogs out, and they chased him all the way home."

"Did he marry her?" Ember asked with a smile.

"He went back the next day to pay for the window and apologize to her father in person. Her father yelled at him a bit, and the girl just stood there and watched. Grandpa said that's when he knew he could never marry her—a woman who just stood there and let someone else come down on him like that. Either she didn't have the gumption to stand up to her father—or she didn't love Grandpa enough to fight for him. Whichever it was, she wasn't the one for him."

"Who did he marry?"

"The girl at the ranch next door. They'd been friends for years, and she might not have been fancy, Grandpa said, but she once shot a wolf that was attacking his dog. He said a woman with an eye like that and steady trigger finger—he wanted her on his side in life."

Ember laughed softly. "I like that one."

"So what does it say about me?" Casey looked over at her, flicking his hat up higher on his forehead as he met her gaze.

"It says your family values ability over a pretty face," Ember said. And if that were the case, then whatever he felt for her would evaporate soon enough, because Ember didn't have that steady trigger finger. Maybe that was for the best.

Casey didn't answer, and they rode on in silence for a few more minutes, the horses plodding along at their own pace. Ember let her mind wander and she looked around at the mountains in the distance, the gently undulating hills and the crystal-clear sky that stretched over them.

There was a scattering of cows grazing and chewing their cud, and Ember smiled as she saw a calf drinking milk from its mother. The cow's eyes followed her

as she rode past—that look both protective and doe-
eyed all at once.

"Milk River is just over there—you can see the trees
that line the bank."

"I see it." There was a faint sparkle of water that she
could just make out through the foliage.

"This is where we'll dismount," Casey said, reining
in his horse and swinging down from the saddle in one
continuous movement. He made it look easy, and she
looked down at the ground, which suddenly looked very
far below her, and licked her lips nervously.

"I'll help you," Casey said. He held up a hand. "Take
your sprained foot out of the stirrup and stand up on
your good leg. You're going to swing it over just like
you're coming down on your own."

"No, that's going to hurt—"

"Trust me," he interrupted her. "I'm not some kind
of monster. Your foot will never hit the ground. I've
got you."

Ember did as he'd instructed and put all of her weight
on her good foot in the stirrup, then eased her injured
foot out of the other stirrup and swung it around. The
momentum kept her moving, and her stomach lurched
as she started down to the ground. Before she'd gotten far, though, she felt Casey's strong arm scoop underneath her, and she landed solidly in his arms. She
let out pent-up breath and looked up to find those dark
eyes pinned to hers. Casey smiled slightly, then lowered her to the ground.

"There," he said.

"Thank you…" It hardly seemed like words enough
to encompass how she felt about all the little things this
big cowboy had been doing for her over the last week.

"Can you walk a bit?" he asked.

"Yes, I can hobble around," she said with a low laugh. "It's not graceful, but it's a lot better than it was."

Casey scooped her hand up in his warm palm. "Lean on me if it's easier," he said. "What I want to show you is just over here."

A young cow let out a moo and sauntered away from them as they made their way over lush grass. Casey tucked her hand into the crook of his arm, and he slowed his pace for her as she limped along. She could hear the sound of running water, even though she couldn't see the river from this vantage point. A cool breeze lifted her hair away from her face, and she looked around, wondering what he could possibly want to show her out here.

"Is it the herd?" she asked, looking up at him quizzically. "I don't get it—"

"Come on," he said with a shake of his head. "I wouldn't drag you all the way out here to see cattle. Give me more credit than that."

"Maybe you just wanted to get me alone for a bit," she said with a teasing smile.

Casey arched an eyebrow, then shrugged noncommittally. "I *did* want to get you alone. But it's more than that. Over here."

Casey led the way to a rocky area that looked scuffed, like it had been dug up a little recently. And when her gaze fell on those patterns of the exposed rock, she stopped short. It was a perfect rectangle—about the size of a packing box.

"What is it?" she asked breathlessly, looking up at Casey, and her heart sped up in her chest. She had a feeling she knew what it was, but she wanted him to say it.

"A fireplace hearth," he said. He pulled a trowel from his jacket pocket, sank down to his haunches and started to dig around the outside.

"A home—there was a house right here—" Ember

looked around before her gaze came back to Casey, who dug steadily around the rocks, exposing mortar and more rock as he dug. "Casey—did you know about this before?"

"I had no idea," he said. "Even Mr. Vern didn't know about it. There aren't any stories about houses by the river…not that Mr. Vern ever mentioned. But there's more."

His trowel scraped raspily over rock, and then he tapped something that made a slightly different sound, and she bent down to get a better look. It was a single red brick. Her breath caught in her chest, and she stared at Casey, the words still formulating in her mind.

Ember let out a low laugh and shook her head. "This is it. You've found it—the homestead. The brick! Who else would have done that? The house was by the river, they said—walking distance to fetch fresh water. And behind them were the open plains where the wolves roamed at night and the buffalo would wander past in massive herds… This is it!"

Casey rose to his feet, the trowel still in his hand, and she moved toward him, looking up into his eyes uncertainly.

"This is your proof," he said quietly.

"And you showed it to me—" Ember shook her head slowly. "You showed it to me, knowing what it meant— for you."

Casey's dark gaze met hers, and he reached up, touched her cheek with the pad of his thumb. "I told you that you could trust me."

Ember put her arms around his neck. She'd meant to simply go up on her tiptoes to hug him, but with her injured ankle, tiptoes weren't a possibility, so he came down to her, instead, and she found his face so close to hers, and she did the one thing she knew she shouldn't— she closed her eyes and touched her lips to his.

Casey gathered her up in his arms and kissed her back, the lowing of the cattle surfing the warm prairie wind that circled around them. This was Harper land, and she could feel it in her heart. But Casey showing her… That had been a bigger gesture than she could even comprehend right now. Her heart soared with excitement, and when Casey released her, she felt heat rush to her cheeks.

"I'm sorry," she said, hobbling back. "I shouldn't have—"

"Hey." Casey caught her hand in his, stopping her retreat. "It's okay. That was honest."

And it was. She met his eyes once more and found that warm gaze enveloping her.

"I have my proof," she said. "This is it—the land where all those stories took place. It's like my very own holy land."

"It's yours," he said quietly.

"Pa and Mam must have chosen this place, and I can see why. They had no idea how many children they'd have, or how they'd make it each winter, but they managed." She looked around once more at the swell of the field and the jagged peaks beyond. Despite today's modern world, it was still so rugged, so vast. Even knowing this land was settled, she felt like a speck on the landscape.

"But what about you, Casey?" she asked quietly.

"I don't know what to say," he said, his eyes filled with sadness. "Fair is fair."

## Chapter Thirteen

Ember went with Casey to church Wednesday evening for the farewell service. They sat in the back of the little country chapel, the babies sleeping in their arms as they had the week before.

"Would you like me to take the baby for a bit?" an older woman asked Ember with a smile.

Ember hesitated, then looked down into the dozy face of the tiny boy. He opened his mouth in a yawn, and she smiled down at him.

"Actually, I'd rather hold him," she said. "But thanks."

The woman moved off and Ember allowed herself the brief luxury of leaning into Casey's strong shoulder and enjoying Wyatt's sleepy warmth in her arms. She'd come to care for these babies more than any of them knew. They'd sunk into her heart, no matter how hard she tried to protect herself, and when she went back to the city again she'd miss them deeply.

Ember looked up at the stained-glass windows, her gaze following the pictures backlit by early evening sunlight. The first pane showed the Virgin Mary sitting with her son on her lap, and she sparkled with bright colors and obvious joy. The next pane showed her bowed by the foot of the cross, her heart breaking in a way only a mother could understand. And the last pane showed Mary in her iconic blue robe standing before the empty tomb, and those bright, glittering colors of wonder and happiness were back.

Mary was the mother every Christian woman looked to…the mother who had endured the deepest of all heartbreak, all for the sake of her son. Ember tore her eyes from the stained-glass windows. Sometimes, motherhood meant enduring untold pain like Mary had. Mary might not have said goodbye to her boy in infancy, but she'd had to relinquish him eventually, and it would have torn her heart in two.

Casey's little finger touched the side of Ember's hand, pulling her attention back to him. The movement was gentle, purposeful. She looked over at him, her heart swelling with sadness. His face was clean-shaven for church, and he smelled of the musky aftershave he must have used. His shirt was crisp and open at the neck, revealing his tanned skin. He caught her eye, and he slipped his hand over hers, warming hers. She wished she could freeze time, and she could avoid all the changes that were coming.

She'd miss Casey and the babies, and she realized that she'd worry about them a little bit, too. Would Casey's aunt understand Wyatt's need for snuggles after his bottle, or Will's curiosity and the way he liked to look around the room? When the infants cried for their mother, as Ember was convinced they still did, would Casey's aunt know why those little hearts were breaking?

But these babies weren't Ember's business—not officially. Casey would raise them, and he'd find appropriate childcare for them. He would find a job somewhere, and another ranch would benefit from his expertise… And she'd begin the process of setting up her own therapy center here on her family's land. Life would go on, and Ember's hopes and goals would be achieved.

So why wasn't she feeling happier about that? It was hard to feel the full impact of that joy because she'd be both putting a good number of men out of work, and moving forward in her goals without Casey Courtright in her life, and until a week ago, that would have meant nothing to her.

He shouldn't matter! But he did. He'd proved himself to be invaluable—he'd saved her life! He'd shown her the very spot where her family had built their homestead… He'd been her answer to prayer. He'd caught her when she was injured, carried her when she was weak and kissed her so tenderly that she'd melted under his touch. And yet he couldn't be her answer to *every* prayer.

Sure, just tell her heart that—it hadn't caught up.

This was a goodbye service for the current pastor—his last sermon to be preached in this church. Another pastor would come and lead this country parish, and the sentiment of goodbyes seemed appropriate this week.

The pastor's sermon wound up, and he sat down. The pianist went to her place at the old piano and began the prelude to the last hymn. The service was over.

"You okay?" Casey whispered as he picked up the worn hymnal and flipped it open.

Ember nodded. "I'll have to be."

"Do you want to head out early?" He leaned down to keep his words private.

Ember's heart was too full to stand there listening to those sweet old hymns and still be able to keep her emotions under control. She glanced around—the other parishioners had risen to their feet and the first swell of singing began.

"Let's go," she agreed softly, and Casey dropped her hand. Casey waited for Ember in the aisle, and then they slipped out the back door, leaving the service behind them as they headed for the freedom of sunshine.

Ember's ankle was still sore, but much better than before. They paused in the rosy wash of lowering sun and Casey got the car seats out of the truck.

"It might be easier if we can put them down," he said.

They got the babies settled into their seats, and then Casey nodded toward the fence line that cut off church property from a neighboring field.

"Let's go over there," he said.

Ember nodded. The babies were still fast asleep, and they ambled across the grass together. Casey put the car seats down on the grass by the fence, angling them so that the boys' faces stayed shaded. Across the grass, the piano could still be heard, the chords seeping out of the church and into nature. Toward the west, pink and red washed over the sky, the sun large on the horizon.

"You haven't put your offer in on the ranch yet," Casey said, breaking the quiet.

"Not yet," she admitted.

"Are you going to?" he asked.

Ember nodded. "Yes, I am. I just couldn't bring myself to do it yesterday. I don't know why…"

"It'll change this," he said, his voice low and hollow. "Us. It'll end whatever we're doing here."

"And what are we doing?" she asked, turning toward him. "We've crossed all professional lines, you know."

Casey looked down at her, then shrugged helplessly. "I don't know about you, but I've been falling for you something fierce."

Tears misted Ember's eyes and she shook her head. "We can't do this—"

"I think it's already done."

Ember put her hand on the rough wooden fence, and he slid a warm palm on top of hers. He was so confident, so comforting, and she tipped her head over onto his shoulder and heaved a sigh.

"Why won't you work for me, Casey?" she pleaded softly.

"I can't do it." His voice was low and filled with pain.

"And why not?" She lifted her head and looked up at him. "Are you just that stubborn?"

"I have a couple of good reasons," he said, still not looking at her. He was staring out into the rippling field of young, green wheat. "The first is that I'm a rancher, not some city-slicker babysitter."

"That's harsh, but fine," she said. "And the second reason?"

"I fell in love with you." He finally looked over at her, those dark eyes drilling into hers, and he sighed. "Against all my better judgment, might I add."

"You…" she breathed. "You love me?"

"I didn't say it was logical or right," he replied with a shake of his head. "But yes."

And it suddenly all fell into place for her. She could see it come together, and this missing piece explained it all—her misery, her inability to embrace the blessings she had because they didn't include the tall, protective cowboy in the picture.

"I love you, too," she said, the words catching in her throat, and Casey turned and pulled her into his arms, his lips covering hers with a kiss of longing and anguish. He kissed her long and slow, and when he pulled back, she saw tears glistening in his eyes.

"Isn't there some way we could make this work?" he pleaded. "Some loophole here that will let us live happily together in spite of it all?"

She wished that there were... If she had a couple in therapy facing the challenges they were facing, would she see a solution that they were missing out on? But no—not every relationship was salvageable. Not every couple who loved each other could make it last for a lifetime. There were heartbreaking times when love just wasn't enough.

Ember shook her head and put a hand in the center of his chest, pushing herself back out of his arms.

"No," she whispered. "There isn't."

Casey put a hand over her fingers in the center of his chest, but she tugged them free, and his heart ached as she stepped back. She licked her lips and looked down at her feet, then limped another step back. Ember Reed was so stubborn, yet so vulnerable. He longed to hold her again, but she didn't want his touch, and he let his hand fall to his side.

"What makes you so sure?" he demanded. He needed a reminder of all the reasons why they wouldn't work because right now, he couldn't remember a single good reason why he shouldn't gather her up in his arms and simply claim her as his.

"We want different things, Casey," she said, her chin trembling ever so little. "I want my therapy center, and that goes against everything you want in life! It goes against your vision for this county, everything you value and respect—"

"Then run a ranch with me," he said. "There's honor in feeding the nation, in raising cattle—"

"And there is honor in helping families to reconnect!" she interrupted him. "It's what I do, Casey. It's not going away!"

"I'm not saying there isn't honor in what you do," he said feebly.

"Also, you need a mother for those babies."

Those words landed more heavily than anything else, and he looked down at the sleeping boys in their car seats, their long lashes brushing chubby cheeks. Will was opening and closing one little fist as he slumbered, and Wyatt heaved one tiny, shuddering sigh. Those boys needed a mother... He needed a woman to parent with him. She was right there. But he'd been watching her blossom with the babies over the last couple of days, and he shook his head.

"Ember, you *could* love them..."

"I daresay I already do," she said, wiping a tear from her cheek. "But I can't do it, Casey. I can't be a mother to another child. Don't you understand what I did when I gave up my little boy? I shut the door on motherhood—"

"And maybe that was a mistake!" he countered.

"Mistake or not, it was a choice I made!" she shot back. "And don't say I was too young to make it, because at the age of twenty I could have joined the army or gotten married! I was plenty old enough to make a life-altering decision. I know you want to think the best of me, Casey, but I had nine months to think it through. And yes, I regret it—deeply. But that's the choice I made, and I can't just back out on it. I can't stand in as mother to your boys, because I wouldn't be a good one, Casey. They deserve better than what I can offer."

"You could be—" he began.

"No!" Tears shone in her eyes and she shook her head vehemently. "Because every single time I look at those babies, I think of my own! I can do it for a few days. I can put my heart aside for a little while, but for the rest of my life? I *am* a mother, Casey, but I'm not a good one."

"But you love me," he said, his voice almost a growl.

"I love you," she said with a teary nod. "But it isn't enough."

The church doors opened and the first few people came outside, chatting voices floating over the grass-scented breeze toward them. They weren't alone anymore, and Casey straightened, then shot Ember one more miserable look.

"So what now?" he asked softly.

"I'll submit my offer in the morning."

Casey nodded, a lump shutting off his throat.

"And if you changed your mind and agreed to work for me—"

"No, Ember." No matter how much he longed to change his mind right now, he knew he'd only regret it. He couldn't be her manager, her protector, her source of advice. He couldn't work for her, next to her, feeling as he did and knowing it was hopeless. It would be torture, and he'd get hardened and meaner…or he'd weaken in his own moral resolves. He didn't want to be that man.

"Then I'll go back to Mr. Vern's house and I'll pack up," she said with a quiver in her voice. "I got a text from the auto shop before the service started. My car is done. I'll pick it up in the morning, after I've talked to Mr. Vern. I can finish up the sale from Billings. I've seen what I needed to see, thanks to you, Casey."

"Will I see you before you go?" he asked softly.

"If you want to—" she met his gaze, then pressed her lips together as if trying to hold back tears "—if you don't think it would be hard for nothing…"

"It wouldn't be for nothing," he said curtly. "It would be for a proper goodbye."

"Okay."

More people were flooding out of the church now, and a few were looking over at them in curiosity. This was a small community, and gossip would fly around the rural community like wildfire. Casey sighed.

"Let me drive you back to the ranch, then," he said.

It would be a difficult drive, sitting next to the woman he loved but couldn't be with.

She'd buy the ranch, and Casey would have to build his life somewhere else. Just not next to her, because he couldn't endure any more heartbreak.

## *Chapter Fourteen*

Ember hadn't slept much the night before. She'd lain awake listening to the sound of wind outside, the soft moan that echoed her own heartbreak. Falling for Casey had been a bad idea, but it hadn't been a choice. There was something about Casey that filled a part of her heart that she hadn't peeked into before. He'd opened his heart to her, too, and that made this all the harder. If a few vital things had been different, she'd have married him.

"Did I really just think that?" she murmured. Morning had dawned clear and unforgiving. She stood in front of a small mirror, checking her makeup. Some concealer under her eyes and some powder seemed to cover most of the evidence of last night's tears, but she still felt puffy.

Loving Casey wasn't going to just go away because they knew it wouldn't work. She realized that. And now, instead of grieving for her son, she was grieving for her son, the man she'd fallen in love with and the tiny babies who had stolen her heart. Vern Ranch would never be the same for her again, because every single inch of this place had Casey's fingerprints on it.

"But it's still mine," she reminded herself. "Or it will be…"

Feelings passed. They didn't last forever. Eventually, she would be able to put this all behind her. Harper women carried on, even when it hurt.

So Ember went out into the kitchen, where Mr. Vern had just returned from his morning inspection of his land, and she handed him her official offer. Mr. Vern took the papers from her hand, scanned them and then shook her hand with enthusiasm.

"I'm thrilled, I have to say!" Mr. Vern enthused. "I wasn't sure you'd find what you were looking for on this land."

"Casey was the one who found the ruins of my family's homestead," Ember said. "So we have him to thank."

"Really now?" Mr. Vern nodded slowly. "And what about hiring him on as your manager?"

"He's been very clear about that," she admitted. "I'd love to have him work for me, but he's not interested."

"Ah." The smile slipped from his lined face, and then he shook his head. "All the same, I'm very happy to be selling this ranch to you, Miss Reed. These acres have been good to me, and I wish you only the best in your future endeavors here." The older man tapped the sheaf of papers he held in his hands. "I suppose we'll leave it up to the lawyers now, but I anticipate this being smooth and uncomplicated."

"I'm sure it will be." She forced a smile. There were no issues financially, at least. "I got a text yesterday saying that my car is fixed. I was wondering if you'd be willing to give me a ride into town to pick it up? I'll stay at a hotel tonight, and I'll be back in the morning to sign any more papers the lawyers send us."

"You wouldn't rather Casey give you that ride?" Mr. Vern asked. "You two seemed to have a special friendship."

"No." She swallowed quickly and dropped her gaze. "He's busy, and I'd rather not bother him."

"Ah." Mr. Vern looked at her a little more closely. "He's a good man, you know. Honest, stable, reliable."

"I know." Ember looked up sadly. "He's a very good man. But still, sir, I'd rather just go get my car this morning, if it's all the same to you. But if you're busy, I'm sure I can get a taxi from Victory to come out here—"

"No, no!" Mr. Vern said with a shake of his head. "A taxi... Of course I will drive you myself. I only thought—which doesn't matter. Obviously, I thought wrong. Let's get going now. I'll drop you off on the way to see my lawyer."

Ember smiled. "That sounds perfect. I do appreciate your hospitality, Mr. Vern. You've been very kind to host me the last week and a half."

"It was my pleasure, ma'am," Mr. Vern said, and he gave her a nod, his eyes sparkling.

Mr. Vern drove Ember into Victory. It was a forty-minute drive, and when they reached the auto shop, Ember thanked Mr. Vern for the ride, then went into the mechanic's office to pay her bill and pick up her car. It would feel good to be self-sufficient again with her own vehicle, and as she paid with her credit card, the realization that she was about to own all four hundred and two acres of the Vern ranch was just settling into her mind.

It wouldn't be the Vern ranch anymore. It would be the Harper Family Therapy Center. She'd already decided on the name when her dream for the place took root—professional enough to make the purpose for her therapy center evident, but with the personal addition of her mother's last name, too. The Harper women were strong—they were survivors. And that was the spirit she hoped to instill in the guests at her new, rural practice. She might have her father's last name, but she'd been raised by a single mother. Her mother's spirit was what guided her in her ambitions and hopes, not the Reed money.

Ember was hungry, and she decided to stop and get some breakfast at a diner before she went to find a hotel.

The streets of Victory were narrow, and there only appeared to be two or three stoplights in the entire town. Main Street was lined by clapboard-fronted buildings, and the parking spots in front of stores were all filled with dusty pickup trucks. Her car felt tiny compared to all the other vehicles. Over that last week she'd started to enjoy riding around in a pickup, high above the road. She just might take Mr. Vern's advice and get a shiny new Ford—not that it would stay shiny for long on these roads.

Pop's Diner was on the corner, and Ember pulled into a parking spot between a pickup truck and a U-Haul truck. She got out of her car and headed into the diner.

There weren't many patrons this morning—a scattering of men in blue jeans and trucker hats, and a family over by the window. The mother was facing in Ember's direction; the father and a boy were sitting with their backs to her. There was something about that family that drew her attention more than the others—the mother's face. She wasn't just gentle and laughing at something with a sparkle in her eyes… She was familiar. Ember *knew* her.

"You can just take a seat anywhere," the waitress said with a smile on her way past with a pot of coffee in each hand. "I'll take your order in a minute, hon."

"Sure. Thanks," Ember said distantly, and it was then that the woman lifted her gaze and saw Ember. She froze, the laughter slipping from her face. Ember watched the emotions clamber over the other woman's features—shock, fear, uncertainty. No, seeing Ember was not good news—not to Sue Mitchell.

Sue looked toward her husband, murmured something, and then both husband and son turned and looked at her. The boy—he was the one who had Ember's attention. He had a rumple of curly brown hair and big dark eyes. He looked at her with mild curiosity—obviously not knowing who she was—then turned back to his plate.

"Who's that, Mom?" Ember heard him say, his voice floating over the din of the restaurant.

Sue got up from their table and came across the dining room toward Ember. She glanced back at her family once, and her husband's gaze was locked on them, his expression filled with trepidation. What they thought, Ember had no idea. Did they think she'd followed them or something?

"Ember?" Sue said quietly when she reached her. "What are you doing here?"

"I could ask you the same thing," Ember said, dragging her gaze back to the woman in front of her. "I just put an offer down on a piece of land out here. What are you doing in Victory?"

"You're…" Sue swallowed. "You're moving out here, then?"

"Yes." Ember looked back toward the table. The boy was putting his attention into his food, and Ember's heart sped up, all of this hammering home into her brain. "Is that Steven?"

"Yes." Sue took Ember's arm and tugged her farther away from the table, closer to the door. "He doesn't know who you are, Ember. We didn't tell him your name. He knows he's adopted, but we said we'd tell him more when he got older."

"I'm not here to find you," Ember said, pulling her arm out of the other woman's grasp. "I had no idea you were even located out here."

Her gaze whipped back to the table. Even though she'd suspected from the moment she saw Sue, the confirmation still bowled her over. That was him? That was her boy?

"We're just moving into town," Sue said. "You might as well know that my husband is the new pastor for Victory Country Church. It's out in the country, about half an hour from town."

"You're the new pastoral family—" Ember breathed.

"Yes." Tears rose in Sue's eyes. "Ember, I know that when we adopted Steven, we agreed to no contact. I know you didn't want to see us—it would have been harder, you said. So I never got the chance to properly thank you for the gift you gave us in that little boy. He's our treasure. And he's such a sweet kid! He's smart and kind…"

Ember looked toward the table again. The pastor was dropping some bills onto the table, and Steven was standing up.

"Is he happy, though?" Ember asked suddenly, her throat tightening with emotion. "Is he…? Did he miss me very much? I've been worrying about how hard it must have been at first—I know, it was ten years ago, but in some ways it feels like yesterday still."

"He's very happy," Sue replied.

"But that first night—the first few weeks…" Ember could hear the pleading in her own voice. Didn't Sue understand the misery that Ember had carried with her after that day?

"I stayed up with him all night that first night," Sue said softly. "And Ted stayed up all night the next night. We just held him and talked to him and sang to him. We wanted him to feel awash in love. We knew it would be hard on him, too, so we did our best to make sure he knew that he was as loved as humanly possible in our home. I promise you that. The third night, he slept, and when he woke up we both got up with him because we just wanted to look at him…"

Tears welled in Ember's eyes. They'd loved him as hard as they could—that helped, somehow.

Sue looked back at her approaching husband and son. "I'm going to introduce you, but we haven't told him yet—"

"Yes, you already said," Ember acknowledged. "Don't worry. I don't want to upset him, either."

Sue nodded, and as Ted and Steven approached, Sue pasted a smile on her face.

"Ted, you remember Ember, don't you? Steven, this is an old friend of ours—Ember Reed."

Steven looked up at her, clear eyes meeting hers. "Hi," he said and held out a hand to shake hers.

Ember took his fingers in her own and tried to drink

in every detail of his rounded, boyish face. He looked like her a little bit—in the eyes, she thought. He didn't have her blond hair, but he had her cheekbones and fair complexion.

"Hi, Steven," Ember said, swallowing back her own emotion. "I haven't seen you in—in a long time."

"I don't remember you," he said, frowning slightly and tugging his hand back.

"You wouldn't," Ember said. "You were pretty tiny. But it's great to meet you now—all grown-up."

"Almost grown-up," he corrected her, and Ember laughed softly.

"Almost." She glanced toward his parents—the couple who had raised and loved him in her absence. She had so much she wanted to say to her son, but now was not the time. Her emotions weren't his problem, and she wouldn't make them a burden for him. "What grade are you in?"

"Five," he said. "Almost in grade six."

"Do you like school?" she asked.

"I'm starting a new one." He grimaced. "I don't like that."

"Well, Steven and I are going to go get that truck started," Ted said, reaching out to shake Ember's hand. Then he stopped short and opened his arms in a hug. He pulled her in close, patted her back a few times, then released her. "Ember, thank you. It's good to see you again."

Steven looked up at his dad questioningly, and then the pair walked out of the diner toward the U-Haul, father's arm around son's shoulder.

"So he's doing well?" Ember asked, her voice shaking slightly as she followed the back of her son's retreating form. *Her son.* That was him. She felt a wash of pride. He'd turned out well.

"He's doing great," Sue confirmed. "He's healthy and strong. He's always been popular at school, too, so I'm not worried about this new school at all. He's nervous, but he'll do great."

Ember nodded quickly, and she looked over at Sue, her eyes brimming with tears. "Thank you for being his mom," she whispered.

"Thank you for giving me the honor," Sue said, and she wrapped her arms around Ember. The women clung to each other for a moment. Then Sue released her and stepped back. "If you're going to be in the area, Ted and I had better have a talk with Steven about you."

"I won't get in the way," Ember said quickly.

"But he'll want to know you, too," Sue replied. "He's been asking more about you lately, and it just seems— the timing seems providential, is all."

"A little," Ember agreed with a misty smile.

"Here—" Sue dug into her purse and pulled out a card. "That's my cell phone number. Call me if you want to. I guess you know where to find us. But give us a few weeks to have some talks with Steven first, if you don't mind."

"That's fine." Ember nodded quickly. "Thanks. This is my card."

Ember pulled out her own and passed it over. Sue scanned it, her eyebrows rising. "Therapist?"

"I got that degree, and then some," Ember said.

"I'm happy for you, Ember." A smile radiated over Sue's face. "Really happy. You've done well for yourself. I hope all your dreams come true."

"I'm not sure I deserve them—" The words were out

before Ember could think better of them, and she felt heat rush to her face. She was saying too much.

"Deserve them?" Sue shook her head slowly. "Ember, you gave us the most personal, painful gift that anyone could give. You made it possible for me to be a mom. You *chose* me—and for that I will owe you my life. Being Steven's mom—he's my world. That sacrifice doesn't make you weak, Ember. It makes you *strong*! You deserve happiness—the whole package. All of it! I don't want to overstep here, but I'm going to be praying that God gives you all of your heart's desires. Every last one!"

"Will he hate me?" Ember asked uneasily.

"Our Steven?" Sue shook her head. "He doesn't know your name, but he knows that while his birth mom wasn't in a place to be able to raise him, she loved him with her whole heart. So she made the hardest choice in the world and made our dreams come true instead of her own. He knows that his adoption was wrapped in love from the very start, and that his birth mom is our hero."

A tear slipped down Ember's cheek.

"Mom!" Steven's voice sounded faintly from outside, and Ember's heart leaped at the sound. Through the glass door, Ember could see Steven hanging out the window of the U-Haul.

Sue waved and smiled, then turned back to Ember. "I'd better go."

Ember wiped the tear from her cheek. "Yes—they're waiting."

"We'll be in touch, I'm sure," Sue said, and with one last little flutter of her fingers in a wave, she walked from the diner and outside into the sunlight. Ember watched as she hopped up in the U-Haul truck and gave her son a kiss on his cheek.

Her son was loved, cherished even. And he was okay.

In her heart, instead of a newborn's frantic wails, she thought she could hear a lullaby sung by a brand-new mom and dad who had never left her baby alone, not even for a minute. God had answered all of Ember's prayers for her tiny boy through the love of adoptive parents.

Sue had loved Steven, opened her heart to him and anticipated all his needs. Even now—she was willing to give Steven a chance to get to know his biological mom…and why? Because he would need it.

Back on the Vern ranch, there were two baby boys who needed love. And maybe, just maybe, their mother had sent up one last prayer of her own, much like Ember's. Was it possible to open her heart to those little boys and become the mom they needed so desperately? Could *she* be the answer to their mother's heart-deep prayer like Sue had been for hers?

Ember felt something inside of her lift, and a new yearning took root in her heart. She was a mother—she always would be—but a mother's heart grew with each child she loved. Maybe there was a chance that Ember could be a mother again.

She wasn't ready to pray for that new yearning. She'd only just recognized it deep under all that pain. But maybe one day God would fulfill that wish, too.

But it wouldn't be with Casey, much as she loved him. Even if she could accept his babies and be a mother to them, he couldn't accept her career or her dreams for the future. It wouldn't work. Not this time.

She'd just have to trust her heart to God.

* * *

Casey poured two mugs of coffee and nudged one in Bert's direction across the kitchen table. Outside, the sun had set, but there was still a smudge of crimson along the horizon. Casey's heart was heavy. Ember had left that morning, taking her bags with her, and she hadn't said goodbye.

"So Mr. Vern sold the place, did he?" Bert asked, taking a sip of coffee.

"He accepted Ember's offer this morning." Casey sighed.

"I'm sorry you lost out on your chance to own this ranch, Casey. I know how much it meant to you," Bert said.

"Yeah. Well." What else was there to say?

"And that Miss Reed," Bert went on. "There was something between you, wasn't there?"

"It wouldn't last," Casey said. "She has her own issues around motherhood and she can't be an adoptive mom to these boys. Obviously, that wouldn't work between us."

"Obviously," Bert agreed. "Was that all?"

Casey smiled bitterly. "Whatever I feel for her, it isn't enough, Bert. She and I want different things. I want to raise these boys on a ranch with cattle drives and morning chores. She wants to set up some therapy center..."

"What's wrong with a therapy center?" Bert asked. "It's something to help the families around here."

"Families need to work!" Casey shot back. "They need employment and self-respect. I'm not saying this center wouldn't be beneficial for the city folk who never get out into the open air, but for us? For the locals?"

Bert was silent. One of the babies started to whimper

and Casey scraped his chair back and handed a prepared bottle to the old ranch hand. "Care to take a baby?"

"Sure."

Casey went over to Will, who had woken up, big eyes blinking and his little mouth opening and shutting as he searched for milk.

"Hey, buddy," Casey said softly, scooping him out of his cradle. "You hungry?"

Will let out a little frustrated cry, and Casey handed him to Bert, who expertly tucked the infant into the crook of his arm and popped a bottle into his mouth. Will slurped away immediately.

Then Casey went and picked up Wyatt. It was better to wake this sleeping baby and feed them both at the same time, or he'd be up every hour overnight feeding one baby at a time. Wyatt blinked his eyes open as Casey lifted him from his cradle and put him up onto his shoulder as he came back to the table.

"Fiona and I went to a therapist for the better part of a year," Bert said after a moment, his eyes still pinned on the baby in his arms, slurping away on the bottle.

"You—" Casey cleared his throat. "Seriously?"

"It was after our daughter was killed in that car accident. We just couldn't… It was too big of a loss, and we weren't talking to each other because we didn't want to make it worse, I guess, and it was just eating us up."

"I didn't realize that," Casey said quietly, and he adjusted Wyatt in his arms and offered the baby his bottle.

"Therapists just help you talk about stuff," Bert said. "I wasn't any good at that. And if I hadn't learned how, I wouldn't have stayed married real long. So you could say that therapist saved our marriage."

Casey eyed the big cowboy, who still refused to look up. "Cowboys don't talk much, Bert. We ride."

"Well, maybe we should talk more," the older man replied. "Maybe *you* should talk more."

"Me?" Casey asked in surprise.

"What are you wanting to give those boys on a ranch?"

"A country upbringing," he retorted. "You know what I'm talking about."

"Yeah, well, spell it out for me," Bert replied.

"I want them to learn perseverance, fortitude, morals, how to stick with something even when the weather's against them," Casey said. "All the stuff you learn when you're raised on a ranch with chores and 4-H. It's a priceless childhood."

"And what about communication?" Bert asked. "Because that's mighty important once these tykes grow up and get married. What about flexibility? What about softness?"

"I'll throw that in, too, I guess. Or I'll try," Casey replied with a rueful smile. "What are you getting at, Bert? I'm not married yet. I don't have a woman to bring in the feminine stuff for me."

"You're so focused on the upbringing you had, Casey, that you're forgetting you had a mother who raised you with lessons of her own outside what you got from your father. Perseverance is important, but so is flexibility. I grew up watching my dad stay the course, and I never stopped to think that the course could change if you needed it to. Bending isn't weakness, Casey. It's making room for another person in your life."

"And you think—" Casey started.

"I think you love her," Bert finished for him. "And don't even bother arguing that, because I know it's true."

"I'm not arguing," Casey said with a sigh. "But, Bert, ranching is in my blood!"

"And that woman is in your heart," Bert replied. "You want to raise those boys alone and teach them to be rock-hard cowboys? You can do it. Or you can raise them with a woman you love—a woman worth bending for—and you can teach them how to be successful in more than just their work. Because a home life matters, too. No cowboy is fully content coming back to an empty house. Those boys need to learn how to fill their hearts as well as their barns."

Casey looked down at Wyatt's face as he drank the last of the bottle. He put the bottle on the table, then tipped Wyatt up onto his shoulder to burp him. His mind was spinning.

"You know how long I've wanted to own my own ranch, Bert?" Casey asked, his voice tight.

"Yup," Bert replied. "But life is long, and you've got a lot more years ahead of you than you do behind you. There will be other ranches, and who knows what the future holds? But will there be another woman who makes you feel like she does?"

"The pastor preached about Jericho's walls," Casey said. "They marched and they marched until they must have felt like they were going crazy. I've been marching, too—circling my own Jericho walls. After all that marching—to just give up—"

"There's faith in God to answer our prayers," Bert said, "and then there's faith in God when He gives us the unexpected. Maybe you prayed for land, but God saw fit to give you a lifelong love instead."

A lifelong love… It may very well be! Casey didn't see any easy way to stop loving her, but she didn't want what he could offer—and she didn't want to be a part of this little family. It was very likely a lifelong love, and he'd be measuring women against her for the rest of his life, but it didn't change those basic facts.

"It's not going to work out, Bert," Casey said gruffly.

Bert nodded. "Okay. Sorry to pry. I'll keep my peace."

But it got Casey to thinking…maybe there was more than one way to raise a kid right, and more than one way to find a heart-deep satisfaction in life. It had always been about the land before, but what if he had to choose between the dirt beneath his boots and the woman in his arms?

What if he'd been circling his Jericho walls and God had wanted to show him another way? What if God had other plans for his life that didn't include a ranch to run? Would he have faith enough to follow?

## Chapter Fifteen

Ember printed off the documents her lawyer sent her on the printer in the hotel office. She thanked the manager and left him a tip for his trouble. She spent the next hour reading over the contract, making sure she understood exactly what she was signing with her lawyer on the phone explaining the details. And when she was ready, she got in her car and followed her GPS to Vern Acres.

As she drove up to the main house, her heart was in her throat, and not because she was buying this ranch, either. Somehow, that personal achievement had paled in comparison to her feelings for Casey. She'd promised that she'd say goodbye, but this parting would be a difficult one.

Would he even be here? She'd called ahead and told Mr. Vern that she was coming. He'd asked if he could tell Casey, and she'd agreed. Would he want to see her? Or would he rather avoid her altogether? She wasn't sure she'd blame him if he didn't come…

Ember parked her car and got out. The warm air ruffled through her hair, and she looked around, soaking up the view. The trees, the looming jagged mountain peaks… One day soon this view would just be home. She started toward the house and the side door opened. It wasn't Mr. Vern who came out, but Casey.

He'd come! Her breath caught in her throat as he stepped outside and headed toward her. That dark gaze locked on to hers, and he closed the distance between them and wrapped his arms around her, not saying a word. His lips came down over hers, so warm and strong and confident. She closed her eyes and sank into his embrace…but this wouldn't make their goodbye any easier. She reluctantly pulled back.

"No…" she said, her eyes brimming with tears. "Don't toy with me, Casey. We've been through this—"

"I know." He stepped back, his eyes still locked on hers pleadingly. "I'm sorry. I just— I'll stop doing that when I see you in town or whatever. I promise."

It was true—she'd see him around. Even if he didn't work for her, maybe he'd work in the area. Ember looked down at the pages in her hands.

"The final papers?" Casey asked.

"Yeah…" She sucked in a breath. "Casey, I saw my son."

He blinked at her, then squinted. "What?"

"The new pastor of the church and his wife—the Mitchells. That's the couple who adopted my son ten years ago. And I saw them in Pop's Diner."

"You're kidding!" Casey shook his head. "That must have been… Are you okay after that? Are you— I mean—" He didn't seem to know how to put it all into words, but she could feel the depth of his concern.

"I'm okay," she said. "It was so wonderful to see him. He's tall for his age, I think. He's got this headful of curly brown hair—it's so cute. And the big brown eyes. He's beautiful. And he's happy. That was my biggest worry, that he'd be empty and searching because of what I did, but he's not. He's a happy kid. He's definitely loved."

"That's awesome," Casey said, and he reached a hand out and ran a finger down her cheek. "I'm glad you got that."

"It changed things—" Ember wasn't sure if it was even fair to bring this up. They'd already gone over why they'd never work as a couple, but she was still so overflowing from the experience that she felt she had to talk to someone, and there was no one but Casey who she wanted to share this with.

"Changed what?" he murmured, stepping closer.

"I prayed every day for my son," she said softly. "I prayed so hard, and I loved him just as hard… I wanted to make up for not being there. But when I saw Sue and Ted again, and when she told me how they'd stayed up with him around the clock to make sure he didn't feel alone in those first few days… Casey, *they* were the answer to my prayers!"

"That's beautiful," he said quietly. "I like that."

"And I know it doesn't change anything else, Casey, but it does change whether or not I could be a mom again. I didn't want to betray my son on some level, but I realized that he has a mom now—and it's Sue."

"Wait—" Casey's voice lowered, and he put his hands on her shoulders. "Are you saying you've changed your mind about that?"

"Wyatt and Will *had* a mom," Ember tried to explain. "If she were able, I'm sure her very last prayer would have been for her boys, too. Sue was the answer to *my* prayers, and if all things were equal, I think I'd like to be the answer to that mom's prayers." She blinked back tears. "But I know it doesn't change the rest. I know that. I shouldn't even have brought it up."

Casey stepped closer again and ran a tendril of her hair through his fingers. "I've had a good talk with Bert, too."

"His job—" she started.

"No, not about his job. He's happy to retire, apparently. This was about me. He had a whole lot to say, and it all made sense. Thing is, I've been so focused on owning my own land for so long that I counted my own faith in God's ability to give me my desires as if God had promised me that land. But what if God wants something different for me? What if—" Casey smiled hesitantly. "What if God had brought me the woman He'd created for me instead of giving me a ranch?"

Ember's heart sped up in her chest, and she stared at Casey, dumbstruck.

"Thing is," Casey went on, "I've wanted to teach the boys the perseverance and steadfastness you learn on a ranch—very important character traits, might I add. But Bert pointed out that flexibility will give them happy marriages." He smiled regretfully. "And that's important, too."

"What are you saying, exactly?" Ember asked, shaking her head. "Because you're going to have to spell this out for me—"

"I'm saying I love you," Casey said, his voice cracking with emotion. "I'm saying that if you could love Wyatt and Will and raise them with me, then I can be flexible on the ranching issue. I can help you run your therapy center, and keep your clients alive long enough to sort out their family issues."

Ember's eyes welled with tears. "You'd do that?"

"Like Bert says—there will be other ranches. But a woman like you? That's once in a lifetime, Ember."

Casey stepped closer again, this time closing the distance between them as he wrapped his arms around her once more. "I love you."

"I love you, too," she whispered.

"Then marry me…"

Ember stared at him, then twined her arms around his neck and pulled that tall cowboy down to her level, where she kissed him with all the love pent up in her heart. He wrapped his arms around her waist and stood up straight, plucking her straight off the ground. Ember laughed, looking into those dark, tender eyes.

"Maybe there's a way to combine a working ranch with a therapy center," Ember said as her feet touched the ground again. "I'm not sure about the details, but if we put our heads together—"

"First things first," he said, a smile turning up the corners of his lips. "Say you'll marry me, Ember. Mrs. Ember Courtright. I think that sounds good."

"I think it sounds wonderful!" she said, tears glistening in her eyes. "Yes. I'll marry you, Casey."

Casey's lips covered hers once more as the screen door slammed behind them. They turned to see Mr. Vern standing on the step, a broad smile on his face.

"Is there news?" he asked with a grin.

"Let's go buy a ranch," Ember whispered, and Casey grinned.

"That sounds good to me. But keep it in your name.

I don't want you ever thinking I married you for your land."

Together they walked toward the house, and Ember's heart finally felt full to overflowing. She'd sign the papers that would set Mr. Vern free to pursue his retirement with his ailing wife, and then Ember knew exactly what she wanted to do...

She was going to pick up those baby boys and snuggle them close, and she'd be the mother they needed so badly. Sometimes God gave second chances, and as He twined hearts together, He answered prayer after prayer with the love that joined them.

Ember and Casey went inside. She looked around that ranch house, at the floors that had seen so many cowboy boots, at the kitchen that had fed so many, and she knew that she was home. But the fixture that made this house the home she wanted to settle into was the tall cowboy who stood by the kitchen table as Mr. Vern signed the last of the papers finalizing the sale. Casey Courtright was the one who filled her heart.

She loved him—with everything in her being. And somehow, in one visit to a Montana ranch, God had given Ember more than a goal realized; He'd given her a family.

# Epilogue

On a warm, sunny day in mid-September when the heat from summer had dissipated, but the warmth still clung to the earth in defiance of the coming winter, Ember and Casey got married in the Victory Country Church.

The sermon was short, but it was on a topic very close to Casey's heart—Joshua marching around the walls of Jericho. This pastor took the story a little bit further, pointing out that Rahab, the Jericho woman who helped the spies and escaped destruction, ended up married—possibly to one of the spies themselves. That was what the Biblical records pointed to in Matthew, at least—a little bit of romance in the midst of that battle story. The walls came down, and between the lines there seemed to be a wedding. A little bit like Casey and Ember's story. Sometimes walls crumbled and hearts healed at the same time.

Almost everyone was in attendance for the Courtright-Reed wedding, and the pews were packed. Ember's father didn't make it, but he did send a very generous monetary gift. Casey's father was there, as was half the population of the town. Pastor Ted Mitchell took Ember and Casey through the most important vows of their lives.

"Do you take this woman to be your lawfully wedded wife, to have and to hold, in sickness and in health, for better or for worse, for richer or for poorer, as long as you both shall live?"

"Sure do," Casey said softly, fixing Ember with a tender smile.

"And do you, Ember, take this man to be your husband…"

Ember nodded, tears misting her eyes. "I do."

"Then I now pronounce you husband and wife. Feel free to kiss your bride, Casey."

Casey didn't seem to need any encouragement there, because he stepped forward and slipped his arms around her waist, pulling her close in a kiss, as clapping and cheers rose up from the guests in attendance.

Ember smiled up into her husband's eyes, and then they faced the church of friends and family.

"I'm pleased to be the first to introduce Mr. and Mrs. Casey and Ember Courtright!" Pastor Mitchell said. Casey squeezed her hand, and they headed down the aisle together. Ember had never felt quite so happy.

After the service was over, their photographer took them to a few different spots to take photos—by the church doors, standing with family, over by the rippling waves of golden wheat at the fence…

The babies were being held by various women in the family who passed around and snuggled them close, but by the time they made it to the field for photos, Will and Wyatt had started to fuss, and Ember's heart followed them with every lusty cry.

They were bigger babies now—already seven months old and full of personality—and Ember looked up at Casey.

"Time for some Courtright family photos?" she suggested softly.

"That sounds about right," Casey agreed, and they went to fetch their boys. Will and Wyatt stopped crying as soon as they were back in their parents' arms. And as the flash went off, recording this moment when her heart was so very full, Ember looked out at a group of kids who were observing the photos being taken, and she spotted Steven. He stood a little to the side, watching them wistfully. His parents had told him who she was, and they'd talked a few times about why she'd made that difficult choice…

"Maybe we could get a picture with the minister's family, too," Ember said to the photographer. "It would mean a lot to me."

So Sue, Ted and Steven joined them in one last picture before the babies were too tired to continue. Ember stood leaning against her husband's shoulder, Wyatt in her arms, and a stray ribbon pushed into Wyatt's mouth on his fist. Casey held Will in one strong arm, and Steven stood proud and tall between Ember and Sue, a smile on his face and his rumpled curls just a little askew in the warm wind. Sue was looking down at her son with a proud smile on her face. And Ember looked into the camera, her eyes glittering with the joy that overflowed her heart.

It would be Ember's favorite family photo from the wedding—it brought them all together.

God created a family that day that would settle on the same land where the Harpers had persevered generations before. Sometimes God answered more than one prayer at once, like when He knocked down walls and brought true love to lonely hearts. Or when mothers prayed with all their strength that God would provide for their children when they couldn't do any more...

A family was God's sweetest answer to so many persevering prayers.

\* \* \* \* \*

# THE COWBOY'S
# TWIN SURPRISE

**Stephanie Dees**

For Riley. Thanks for always encouraging me to be my best self and for loving me even when I'm not. Being your mom is a privilege.

## Acknowledgments

A book is never a solitary endeavor, and so many people helped me along the way with this book. Thanks to Melissa Jeglinski and Melissa Endlich for believing in this story and helping me define it.

Thanks to my critique partner, Sierra Donovan, and best beta reader evah, Janet Sallis. And a special thanks to those people who propped me up when I needed a friend, an ear or an idea bouncer: Sarah Kate Newton, Brenda Minton, Tina Radcliffe. You're irreplaceable.

And he said unto me, My grace is sufficient for thee: for my strength is made perfect in weakness. Most gladly therefore will I rather glory in my infirmities, that the power of Christ may rest upon me.

—*2 Corinthians* 12:9

# Chapter One

Devin Cole let his truck roll to a stop at the end of the lane, just short of the driveway to the family ranch. He slid his Narcotics Anonymous newcomers coin between his fingers and back again. He was measuring his life in days and hours now...moments, maybe. One hour since his last meeting. Six days out of rehab. Thirty-six days clean. Thirty-nine days and seven hours since he'd stopped running from God.

Forty days since he'd messed things up with Lacey—the only friend he'd managed to keep on his not-so-slow slide into recklessness and addiction. It had been a long time since his Sunday school days, but in the Bible, wasn't it always forty days that people spent in the wilderness?

A warm breeze wafted through the open window, bringing with it the scent of freshly turned dirt and ribs in the smoker. The sound of calves in the field. Springtime in Alabama.

His eyes went from the farmhouse peeking through the trees to linger on the white welcome chip sliding through his fingers. Chances were pretty good he'd gotten a better welcome from NA than he'd get from his brothers.

Unfortunately, his options were limited. As in, he didn't have any. After he'd shattered his ankle, his days in the rodeo were over. He'd tried to continue, relying more and more on prescriptions and alcohol to fight through the pain. But he'd failed. Failed his corporate sponsors. Failed his friends and family. And most of all failed himself.

He'd spent the past six days and his last thousand bucks driving cross-country, trying to make amends for the wrongs he'd done. And he'd learned apologies went only so far to repair burned bridges.

He put his old truck in gear and drove the rest of the way to the house. Even in the waning daylight, the white two-story clapboard looked a little more worn than it had the last time he'd seen it, the sunny yellow porch swing peeling and faded. No cheery flowers filled the beds that lined the walkway.

The screen door opened and his older brother Tanner stepped out in his dusty boots. Right away, Devin knew from the look in Tanner's eyes this wasn't going to be a prodigal son welcome. No warm embraces. No parties thrown on his behalf. He nodded, to himself, mostly. A firm let's-get-on-with-it nod.

Devin picked up the cane he had to use now that his pain wasn't dulled by drugs. He slid off the old leather seat, relief flooding his body when his feet touched the ground.

Home.

Tanner's blue eyes searched Devin's for signs that he was using, and Devin felt a pang of regret. With a barely suppressed sigh, Tanner pulled the door open wide. "Come on in. I've got coffee on."

Devin followed his brother into the farmhouse, noting the threadbare rug on the floor and the worn leather couch, still the same one from when they were kids. Although they'd never been wealthy, they'd gotten by, but now… It almost seemed that the ranch had aged ten years in the three since he'd seen it.

With a practiced economy of movement, Tanner took two mugs from the cabinet by the sink and filled them with coffee. "What happened to the big fancy truck you were driving last time you were here?"

"Sold it to pay for rehab."

Tanner's eyes flicked to his. "And your horse?"

"Left her with Lacey."

A dark eyebrow quirked. "Another debt?"

"You could say that." A memory of a brown-eyed girl with laughter in her eyes flashed in his mind. Devin took a swig of the coffee and suppressed the wish for something stronger. Because running from uncomfortable emotions was how he got himself in this mess in the first place, or at least that was what the counselor at rehab told him.

The fatigue of the last six weeks pulled hard at him. He took off his ball cap and scrubbed a hand through hair that could use a good trim. "I'm sorry, Tanner. I don't even know where to start to say how sorry I am."

Tanner still didn't smile. "What do you want, Devin?"

"I want to come home."

At his brother's sharply expelled breath, Devin started to panic, just a little. "You sacrificed a lot for me. I know that. And I wasted the opportunities."

After their parents died, Tanner had finished the job of raising him. He'd scrimped and saved and bought Devin his first cutting horse. He'd been at every event from the first to the time Devin kicked loose of Red Hill Springs and everyone in it.

Tanner crossed his arms. "If you're wanting me to argue with you about that, you're gonna be waiting a long time."

His hat literally in his hands, Devin closed his eyes and sent a wordless prayer toward Heaven before he opened them again and looked Tanner in the eyes. "I'm an addict. I'll always be an addict, but I don't have to be a bad person. Please give me a chance to prove I can do better."

"We've been down this road before."

Devin went still. There was nothing he could say or do to change his brother's mind. Because Tanner was right. It was a familiar refrain from his teenage years— even before the drugs, Devin had struggled. They *had* been down this road before where Devin had begged and pleaded and unfailingly messed things up. So he waited and he wondered if there was anyone left who would take him in until he could find a job.

Tanner didn't tap his foot or jiggle his leg or any of the things normal people did. He simply stared into the black coffee in his cup until he reached a decision. He looked up. "I could use the help around here."

Devin let out all his anxiety in one pent-up breath.

His brother held up a finger. "But there are ground rules, Dev, and if you break them, there are no second chances."

In the past, Devin would've brushed aside the bit about the rules. Ground rules were for boring people who didn't have any fun. Now, Devin was clinging to the rules by his fingernails, just to hold on to his sobriety. He asked Tanner quietly, "What do you want me to do?"

"One. You go to meetings every day. Two. You always tell me where you're going to be. Three. There are no rock stars at Triple Creek Ranch. You pull your own weight."

It didn't sound like much but Devin knew from experience that pulling his weight around the ranch was a full-time job. Working the farm was going to be hard with his injury but it wouldn't be impossible.

He could promise Tanner that he was different, that he'd matured past the kid who'd looked for approval in all the wrong places, but promises didn't mean much. He wanted more than anything to prove to his brother that he could change. To prove to himself that he could be more than just some rodeo guy who partied a lot and nearly got himself killed. He said quietly, "Thanks, Tanner."

"Don't make me regret this, Devin." The man who'd started raising Devin when he was still practically a boy himself had a world of disappointment in his eyes. He jerked a thumb at the stairs. "You can have your old room."

Devin nodded. He pushed back from the table and limped onto the porch of the farmhouse. He'd run far and fast away from here when he'd turned eighteen, too big for these parts. Maybe it was fitting that when there was nothing left of him, he ran home. If he was lucky, maybe it was here that he'd find all the pieces of himself he'd lost along the way.

*Two months later*

Lacey Jenkins checked her GPS one last time as she drove through Red Hill Springs, Alabama. The flower boxes that lined the street were filled with geraniums, and American flags on the lampposts fluttered in the wind. All decked out for the upcoming Memorial Day holiday, the town was adorable, but she wasn't having it. She'd been stewing for three and a half months now, ever since she'd woken up alone in a hotel room in Vegas, ink barely dry on a quickie marriage certificate proclaiming her married to rodeo superstar Devin Cole.

She should've listened to the voice of warning in her head—the one that sounded strangely like her dad, coaching her around the barrels when she was a kid. "Ride from here, Lacey-girl," he'd say, as he tapped his forehead under the brim of his cowboy hat. "Not from here" as he tapped his heart. "The heart will betray you. The head will lead you." But she'd been caught up in the adventure of it all. The romance. She and Devin had been friends—best friends—for years, even as he seemed to get more and more reckless. That weekend in Vegas after the rodeo competition ended, he'd seemed more like his old self. Sweeter and more thoughtful than he'd been in a while.

Until he'd disappeared the morning after they'd gotten married. And then, a month later, he'd had the nerve to drop off his horse for her like some kind of consolation prize.

So yeah, if she'd been mad before, now she was boiling. He'd left her *and* he'd left his horse.

Her GPS calmly announced that she'd arrived at her destination. Nerves fluttered in her stomach, a fact she noted with some irritation. She was a world champion barrel racer. She was supposed to be immune to nerves.

Turning into the drive at the farmhouse, she slowed to look around. She had the right address, but this didn't look anything like the bustling ranch she'd imagined as Devin had talked about it back when they were still friends. But still, there was a sunny yellow swing on the front porch with a fresh coat of paint and brightly colored zinnias filling the flower beds in front of the house.

She eased her truck to a stop so Reggie wouldn't be jostled. The big horse had been patient for the duration of the long trip, but he had to be as antsy as she was to get out of the truck after days on the road. She stepped out onto the gravel drive, pressing a hand into her lower back and leaning into a stretch.

It had taken her a full two days to get here, and once she set a few things straight with Devin, she'd be turning right around to go back.

Lacey reached for a file of papers she'd left on the passenger side of the truck, and when she turned back around she was eye level with three sets of well-worn boots. Her gaze skimmed the length of long denim-clad legs and stalled out at the world champion rodeo buckle at the waist of the jeans on the right before continuing upward to meet three identical sets of dark brown eyes.

She gulped. The Cole brothers were unilaterally staring at her, and to be honest, it was a little bit intimidating. But at least she knew she was in the right place.

Lacey flicked a glance at the one standing on the left side of Devin—the oldest brother, Tanner, she thought—and saw his unsmiling eyes travel from her to Devin and back again. Dark hair curled underneath a faded red ball cap. He settled it a little farther on his head and continued to stare at her.

She swallowed hard as her vision grayed around the edges. Wow. She must be more tired than she thought she was.

"Lacey? What are you doing here?" Devin's words sliced through her exhaustion and, despite girding herself with all that anger, they still had the power to hurt her.

She looked Devin Cole right in the eyes and said, "I want a divorce."

The color drained from Devin's face, and she felt a perverse pleasure that she'd managed to shock him.

"Divorce?" The other brother's head snapped straight. "You're *married*?"

Devin remained unnaturally still.

"I'll just unload Reggie, then." Tanner shifted away as if the tension strung between Lacey and Devin would snap under the pressure. He clambered down from the porch and lowered the back of the trailer. She could hear his voice as he spoke softly to Devin's cutting horse, backing him gently down the ramp.

Devin's gaze never broke with Lacey's, but he said, "Garrett, feel free to move along anytime."

The middle brother, with a mop of unruly dark curls and studious-looking glasses, shook his head. "Nope. Uh-uh. Sounds like you need legal representation. I'm not going anywhere." He grinned. "Plus, I wouldn't miss this for anything."

Lacey refused to be the first one to look away. But her head was spinning again, her husband's handsome, serious face swimming before her eyes. She groped blindly behind her for the side of the truck, her file of papers slipping from her fingers to scatter on the ground.

The last thing she saw before she crumpled was the fear on Devin's face as he dropped his cane and leaped down the stairs, his strong arms scooping her up just before she hit the ground.

Devin lifted Lacey into his arms, concern for her blocking out all other thoughts. "Garrett, get a doctor out here."

"Want me to call an ambulance?"

"No, she's terrified of hospitals. Just call someone. Please?" Devin carried Lacey up the porch steps. He managed to pull the screen door slightly ajar and kick it open. Her face was pale—too pale—against the dark shine of her hair.

He laid her gently on the wide leather couch, heart thudding in his chest. "Lace? Come on, girl, you gotta wake up. You're scaring me."

Just when he thought he'd made peace with the things he'd done when he was using, she showed up with this gem. *Married?*

He didn't really question what he'd been thinking, but what had *she* been thinking marrying him? The last thing Lacey needed was to be married to a washed-up rodeo cowboy with a drug-addiction problem.

Especially one who didn't even remember their wedding even happened.

Of all the stupid things he'd done that he didn't remember, destroying his relationship with Lacey was the worst. She was the best thing that ever happened to him and he'd screwed it up, along with the rest of his life.

But marriage? He couldn't even fathom it.

"Come on, Lacey, wake up. I know you still have a few things to say to me."

Garrett stepped quietly in the door, his cell phone and a bunch of papers in his hand. "Ash Sheehan is on his way."

Devin stabbed his fingers into his hair, worry settling into his shoulders like thousand-pound weights. "Isn't he a kids' doctor?"

"Yeah. He's also the only doctor in town. We can take her to the hospital, Dev. It's probably what Ash is going to tell us to do anyway."

"I can't." Devin dropped on the coffee table in front of the couch, his ruined ankle aching now that the adrenaline had faded. He studied Lacey's still form on the couch. Color was slowly returning to her face. "She'd kill me."

"She dropped these when she fainted." Garrett slid the papers onto the table beside Devin and placed his cane within easy reach. "Tanner's getting Reggie settled. I'm gonna go make some coffee. I have a feeling we're going to need it."

Garrett disappeared into the kitchen, and Devin glanced down at the papers.

There was a legal-looking stack, which he assumed was the divorce papers she wanted him to sign. He picked them up and glanced at the first paragraph before tossing them aside. As he did, another piece of paper fluttered to the ground. He leaned over and picked up the flimsy grainy black-and-white photo.

His skin went clammy.

He knew what this was. It was a still from an ultrasound. And this one had two arrows pointing at two tiny peanut-shaped blobs. He dropped the photo like it was on fire.

Was Lacey *pregnant*?

# Chapter Two

Devin scratched his head, his mind trying to make sense of what he'd just seen. Could Lacey really be expecting? *Twins?*

He glanced at her stomach, but it didn't look any different to him from how it always had. Maybe a little rounder. He studied her face. Maybe it was a little fuller? Her long dark hair curled past her shoulders, framing a peaches-and-cream complexion.

She was so beautiful. Always had been.

And in that second he imagined her holding two babies. Their babies. A tsunami of longing washed over him. It was a dream that seemed so far out of reach for someone like him.

He picked the photo up again. Sure enough, her name was written at the top of the image. *Lacey Cole.* Seeing it in print was a punch to the gut.

Lacey really was pregnant.

Devin scrubbed his hands over his face. He remembered waking up in Vegas and seeing Lacey lying in his bed. Realizing that, with one monumentally horrible decision in a string of really bad decisions, he'd managed to mess up the one thing he still really cared about.

That moment had changed his life.

Her eyes fluttered open and slowly focused. Devin saw the instant she remembered what happened. She tried to sit up, arms flailing, pupils dilating in panic.

He grabbed her shoulders, forcing her to focus on him. "Lacey, you're at Triple Creek Ranch."

When she looked confused, he said, "You brought Reggie home and you told me you want a divorce."

Her voice was a little hoarse and husky when she said, "Well, at least we got that out of the way."

The corner of his mouth twitched up. The bone-deep fear faded a little bit, but he was left with so many questions and no answers to speak of. "Seems like a pretty good call. I mean, honestly, what were you thinking, marrying someone like me in the first place?"

Hurt flared in her eyes, but she blinked it away. Tension still vibrated in her muscles, but she'd stopped trying to get away from him. "Clearly, I wasn't thinking at all. Did you call anyone?"

He shook his head, knowing immediately what she wanted to know. "No EMTs. I know the rules. No hospital unless you're gushing blood from an artery or some other equally dire circumstance."

Her shoulders relaxed under his fingers and she let out the breath she'd been holding. "Thank you."

"You're welcome." He dropped his hands, clenching his fingers slowly into fists. He wanted to grab the ultrasound photo, shove it in her face and demand she talk to him. *Is this yours?*

*Are they mine?*

Instead, he uncoiled his fingers one by one until

he felt in control again. "You gave us a scare. Are you feeling okay?"

Well, that was a dumb question. Of course she wasn't feeling okay. She'd just passed out in his front yard.

He was saved by a knock at the door. He jumped to his feet and nearly fell over as his stupid ankle gave out on him. Lacey didn't say anything but he could feel her curiosity as he hobbled to the door.

Ash Sheehan entered the room with an old-fashioned black doctor's satchel. He shook Devin's hand and crossed immediately to the couch. "I'm Dr. Sheehan. Garrett called me."

"I'm Lacey… Jenkins." Her eyes cut to Devin but quickly flitted back to the doctor, who didn't look anything like the octogenarian Devin had been expecting to see at the door. "Thank you for coming."

"Most of the time I see patients under the age of eighteen, so you'll have to be patient with me." Ash pulled a blood pressure cuff out of his bag and smiled, his blue eyes warming on Lacey's.

He looked like something out of a fashion ad. Devin wanted to punch him in the face.

Wrapping the cuff around her arm and tucking the stethoscope earpieces into his ears, Ash said, "So Garrett told me on the phone that you fainted a little while ago. Is this the first time something like this has happened?"

Lacey's gaze drifted to Devin again. He sighed. "I'll just be in the kitchen."

He glanced at his cane, leaning on the coffee table. He wanted more than anything to ignore it and stride into the kitchen like a man who wasn't hanging on to ninety-four days of sobriety minute by minute.

Lacey deserved better. But Devin owed it to her—and himself—not to hide anymore.

Lacey watched Devin limp into the kitchen, leaning heavily on a cane. She knew he'd shattered his ankle. Everyone knew that. It had happened on live TV. But he hadn't been using a cane the last time she'd seen him. He'd only been slightly favoring one ankle, if at all.

He'd seemed so shocked when she said she wanted a divorce. And suddenly she'd felt cold and hot and her head was spinning and she'd wondered for the first time if he even remembered they got married.

She wondered the same thing now. He hadn't seemed high that weekend in Vegas, but once she heard from mutual friends that he'd spent a month in rehab, she'd started to understand just how good he'd become at hiding it.

Well, whether he remembered their wedding or not, he'd left her without a word. That was the part she'd found unbearable. And now? It wasn't just her own heart she had to protect.

Dr. Sheehan pulled the earpieces of his stethoscope out of his ears and unstrapped her arm from the blood pressure cuff. "So I assume from your reaction earlier that this isn't the first time you've passed out?"

She sighed, her hand creeping to her stomach. "No. It's happened a couple of other times but it's been a few weeks. I thought it had passed."

"Your blood pressure's pretty low. Any history of that being an issue?"

She glanced at the kitchen and lowered her voice. "Only since I've been pregnant. I'm fourteen weeks pregnant with twins."

"Congratulations." The handsome doctor smiled. "I have a new baby myself. So, Garrett said you just drove in from Oklahoma? You were obviously sitting a lot on the trip. Did you sleep?"

She looked away. "A little, here and there."

"Okay." The doctor coiled his stethoscope around his palm and placed it back in his bag. "Are you having any pain?"

"Mild cramps. My OB in Oklahoma said it was normal, especially with twins."

Dr. Sheehan nodded. "It can be. Anything else going on? Fever? Any other aches and pains?"

She shook her head.

"I think between the low blood pressure, the demands on your body of early pregnancy and your long trip, you've just hit your limit. I also think you should see an obstetrician as soon as possible."

"When I get home, I promise I'll see my regular doctor and then I'll put my feet up for the next six months."

"Yeah, about that…" He didn't smile, which was her first inkling that she wasn't going to like what he had to say. "My medical advice would be not to plan to go anywhere for a while. You're carrying twins, which makes this a higher-risk pregnancy. If you were my wife or sister, I'd suggest you plan to stay here for at least a month, for your sake and the health of the babies. I'll refer you to an OB in Mobile and you can get a thorough workup before you try to make that trip cross-country again."

His face was kind as he shattered her plans, so at least there was that. Her eyes filled with tears anyway. "Thanks, Dr. Sheehan."

"Please call me Ash. This wasn't an official visit, just a favor for a friend." His eyes crinkled as he smiled. "If you decide to stick around for a few weeks, you should meet my wife, Jordan. She doesn't ride at your level, but horses and kids are kind of her passion."

"I'd love to." She swung her feet around to the floor as Dr. Sheehan made his way to the front door, the quick movement making her head swim again. She rested her forehead on her hand.

"I'll call tomorrow with the name of a doctor. In the meantime, take it easy."

"I will."

As the door closed behind the doctor, Devin appeared in the kitchen door with a glass of water. He crossed the room and handed it to her. "All good?"

"Yeah, he said I probably passed out because I was overwhelmed by the sight of the three fine-looking Cole brothers."

"Ha-ha, you're hilarious. What did he really say?"

Lacey took a deep breath. She'd wanted to gauge how things were with Devin before she had this conversation with him, but it looked like it wasn't going to happen on her timetable. "Can we take a walk? I've been sitting for days."

"Sure, if you feel up to it. I'd like to go out and see Reggie anyway." He held his hand out to her and, after a moment's hesitation, she slid her fingers into it, trying not to think about the way his skin warmed to hers and how right it seemed to link her hand with his.

He felt strong as he pulled her to her feet, and when she looked into his eyes, she realized how clear they were, how focused and steady. She hadn't seen him like that in a long time. It made her hopeful, a feeling she didn't have the luxury of allowing herself, not anymore. "There's something I want to talk to you about."

"Me, too." He opened the door for her, and she walked through it, taking a deep breath of the fresh country air.

Devin put his free hand in the small of her back, and she shifted away from him. They walked in silence for a few seconds as she looked around the property. "It's really beautiful here with the pastures and the fields. It's not exactly what I expected, but I like it."

"Yeah. The place looked pretty run-down when I got home a couple of months ago. Apparently, there have been some cash flow problems. Tanner's doing everything he can to shift gears and make it profitable again. It's just taking some time."

"He didn't tell you?"

"Maybe, or maybe I just didn't listen. I'm not sure which. Not sure it matters, really. It's easy for me to say now that I'd have come if I'd known, but the truth is, I probably wouldn't have."

"You should cut yourself a little slack, Devin. You love your brother. You love this ranch. That hasn't changed."

"Not as much as I should have. I'm not selling myself short, but I have to be honest with myself. It's one of the pillars of recovery. *Hi, my name's Devin and I'm an addict.*"

Hearing him say it so matter-of-factly was shocking. She'd known that he had the tendency to indulge a little too much and party a little too hard, but she hadn't realized how bad it had gotten until she'd seen the difference in him today.

He stopped by the fence to the pasture and whistled. Reggie lifted his head from the grass but he didn't move. Devin leaned his cane on the wood rail, dug a couple of carrot pieces out of his pocket and held them out. Reggie's nostrils flared and he took a few hesitant steps toward Devin and stalled, giving his owner the side-eye.

Lacey smothered a smile. Devin's horse seemed almost as mad at him as she was. She clicked her tongue. "C'mere, Reggie."

The big horse ambled to the fence and nudged Lacey's hand so she would scratch behind his ears. She obliged, murmuring to him that he was a good boy.

After getting his scratch from Lacey, Reggie gently nuzzled the carrot pieces from Devin's hand before shoving his nose into Devin's hair.

Devin laughed, his eyes lighting as he ran a hand down Reggie's neck. "I missed you, you crazy horse."

Lacey looked away. She wanted to remember the Devin who left her alone in a hotel room in Vegas. To remember the anger that fueled her as she drove from Oklahoma to Alabama. She couldn't afford to get distracted.

She came here to get him to sign divorce papers. And that was exactly what she was going to do.

Devin glanced at Lacey, who was leaning on the fence, her chin on her arms.

"I'm so sorry, Lacey." The words were out before Devin knew he was going to say them.

Her eyebrows shot to her hairline. "For what, exactly?"

"There are so many things to apologize for, I'm not sure where to start. But I think I should start with not taking responsibility that morning in Vegas. And not having enough guts to apologize face-to-face and depending on my horse to get the job done."

"Is that what leaving Reggie with me was about? An apology?"

"It seemed like a good idea at the time." His face went warm and he turned his head away from her too-knowing eyes, focusing on some trees in the distance. The tops were blowing in the late-afternoon breeze, the leaves flipping to reveal the silver underside.

A storm was coming, which seemed a fitting metaphor for the changes raining down on him if Lacey's babies were his. "I didn't know what to say to you. That morning, all I could think was that I'd finally done it. I'd done the thing that would finally drive you away, too."

"You mean, telling me you'd loved me for years and you wanted to marry me, so much that you couldn't wait another day?" There was an edge of bitterness to her tone, and he didn't blame her.

Because he felt like a total jerk, he pulled his ninety-day chip from the pocket of his jeans and held it in his fist, so he could remember that who he was now was not who he was then. He was a person who owned up to his responsibility. He was a person who found his strength in a higher power.

He was a person who told the truth, no matter how hard it was. "I was high that whole weekend. I don't have any memory of getting married. I don't remember anything about the weekend until I woke up in the bed and you were there."

Angry tears glittered on the edge of her lashes. "It was all a lie?"

He let out a frustrated sigh. "That morning—I was ashamed, knowing I'd done something so huge and couldn't remember. I let you down. There's nothing I can say to make that better."

When she looked back at him, her dark eyes were inscrutable. "I want a divorce. I mean it, Devin."

He let the words hang in the air for a minute. They shouldn't hurt, but somehow that didn't stop the sting. "I'd do just about anything for you, Lace, but I need some time to think about it."

"Why?" He could hear the exasperation in her voice as she paced away from him down the fence line. "You said yourself you don't even remember getting married. You sure don't remember why."

Devin had hoped she would tell him about her pregnancy, tell him about the babies, but since she didn't, he would have to press the point. It was too important not to. "I have two very good reasons to take my time making a decision about it."

She whirled around. "What do you mean?"

His fist was clenched so tightly around his NA coin, he could feel it slicing into his skin. "I saw the ultrasound photo. I know about the babies."

"I see." Anger sparked in Lacey's eyes. "So, what, you think that gives you the right to dictate what I do?"

He walked closer to her and reached for her hand. She snatched it back. He sighed. "I think we don't have to figure everything out today."

She visibly took a deep breath. "I came here to tell you about them. To tell you that I'm prepared to raise them on my own. You made it pretty clear when you disappeared that you weren't interested in a long-term relationship."

One of the tenets of recovery was that you didn't make any huge life changes in the first year. In the space of one afternoon, he'd blown that to smithereens. "Give me a chance, Lace, please?"

Lacey rubbed her forehead. "Look, when I get checked into a hotel, I'll text you my contact info and maybe we can talk tomorrow."

"The nearest hotel is forty minutes away." Devin paused. "But we have plenty of room, if you want to stay. Tanner and I sleep upstairs. You can have the master bedroom downstairs."

Lacey hesitated, hanging back as Devin started for the house. When he turned back to look for her, she sighed. "Fine. I'll stay, but just until we get things figured out."

He grinned and she held up a hand. "To be clear, my staying doesn't change things. I'm still mad and I still want a divorce."

At least she was talking to him, so that was something, right? Devin spread his free hand wide. "I hear you."

He hadn't let himself think about what it meant yet, that they had babies on the way, and he knew they had a lot of talking to do. But he wasn't walking away. He'd done that and it hadn't gone so well.

This time, he was sticking around, no matter what that meant.

## Chapter Three

Devin disappeared after he showed Lacey to her room, leaving her to look around the tidy space. She'd stuck to her guns with Devin but she wished she felt steadier, more sure she was doing the right thing.

When she'd been driving out here, she'd been fueled by so much anger that she didn't have space for questions. Now she'd seen Devin. All the feelings she'd had for him were trying to crowd out the anger, and she couldn't have that. Anger could be the only thing that was keeping her from falling apart.

She needed to remember he'd left her.

Maybe he'd gone to rehab, but he'd been out for months and hadn't bothered to get in touch with her. Not even a text.

She didn't want to think about the fact that he hadn't been himself, that he'd been freaked out and scared. She didn't want to think about the friendly room he'd put her in, with the large windows and painstakingly hand-stitched quilt on the bed.

She picked up one of the family photos that lined the dresser, her hand inadvertently going to her stomach.

She definitely didn't want to think about her babies and wonder if one of them would grow into a little boy with a head full of sun-kissed curls.

This situation was such a mess. She'd been so angry—was still so angry—but cutting Devin out of her life wasn't going to be as simple as a signature on some papers.

She'd known it the moment she'd seen him.

With a big sigh, she opened the door to the hall. It was still early evening but maybe she could make her excuses and just go to bed. She followed the scent of something incredible into the kitchen. She stopped short when she realized that it was Devin's brother Tanner alone, flipping burgers on the stove.

He looked up, not really with a smile, more just a deepening of the lines around his mouth. "Hi there. You hungry?"

"Yes, actually." She hadn't realized it until she'd smelled the food cooking but she was starving. "Really hungry."

She looked around the room. Like the rest of the house, it had a fresh coat of paint, the cabinets a glossy bright white. A wire basket of multicolored chicken eggs sat in the center of a round oak table.

Tanner slid a burger onto a plate and piled caramelized onions on top of it. "There are some freshly washed greens in the fridge if you want a salad. We're trying to do better with the vegetables, now that we're growing them."

She found the colander of lettuce in the fridge and added some to her plate. "We're not waiting on the others?"

"Devin will eat when he gets back. Garrett lives in town and he went home."

Lacey sat down as Tanner slid a glass of tea in front of her.

"It's decaf, in case you're wondering."

"That's fine, thanks." As he joined her at the table, she tried to figure out a diplomatic way of asking where Devin was. As the silence stretched, she gave up and went for simplicity. "So, where's Devin?"

"He's at a meeting. Sticking to a routine is really important for him right now."

She put her fork down on the table. "The doctor told me to take it easy for a few weeks before driving back, but if you think my being here is going to jeopardize Devin's recovery, I can move to a hotel room tomorrow."

Tanner glanced up from his plate. "You're welcome to stay as long as you like. You're family."

Tears pricked in her eyes, and she blinked them away, horrified. More took their place until she was sniffling and swiping at her eyes. "This is so embarrassing. I'm sorry."

Tanner wordlessly stood, walked to the counter, picked up a napkin and handed it to her, his eyes kind. "Take a bite of your burger. I bet you'll feel better after you eat."

"Thanks." She sniffed again but took a bite, followed by another and another. And he was right. She did feel a little better. She licked her fingers before she remembered the napkin. "This is so good."

"Raised right here," he said, then winced. "It's been a while since we had mixed company. Probably shouldn't have mentioned that at the dinner table."

Lacey let out a genuinely surprised bark of laughter.

"I was raised on a ranch, too. Trust me when I say I'm not squeamish. And this is delicious."

He almost smiled, and she felt an absurd sense of accomplishment. "We've made a shift from raising cattle the traditional way to grass-fed beef and free-range chickens. Organic vegetables. Got a ways to go to make a profit."

He was a man of few words—until you got him going on a topic that interested him. She tucked that away to remember about her new brother-in-law. "You're trying for a specific clientele."

He nodded, his mouth full.

Devin had said that Tanner was changing gears. It made sense in a market where farm-to-table was the hottest thing going. "Very smart. I'd love to see the whole operation tomorrow."

Tanner nodded. "I'll get Devin to show you around." He paused again and she realized that it was a habit of his, thinking before he spoke. "He's trying really hard, Lacey. I had my doubts, but that weekend in Vegas changed everything for Devin."

Suddenly, she lost her appetite. She put the burger down.

That weekend in Vegas had changed her life, too. Permanently, irrevocably changed her life. She'd tried living in the moment for one crazy, romantic weekend.

And she'd changed her future forever.

The sun was just coming up the next morning when Devin heard Lacey come into the kitchen. Without looking, he pulled a second mug down from the cabinet and filled it with coffee for her, but when he turned around, he hesitated. "Can you… I mean, is it okay for you to have coffee?"

"Yep, I'm allowed one cup, which is good for everyone's health and well-being." She was dressed in jeans and boots and a loose T-shirt, her long dark hair in a ponytail. He tried to get a surreptitious glance at her stomach to see if there was any evidence at all of the babies growing there, but if there was, he couldn't see it.

She blew on the surface of the coffee and took a small test sip, her eyes closing as she swallowed.

He wasn't sure what to say to her or how to interact with her while sober and after…all that had happened between them. Which was one of the reasons he'd stayed away. How did you have a normal conversation with someone after… There was a reason that kind of stuff was saved for marriage. Of course, they *were* actually married, an event that Devin wished with all his heart that he could remember.

Bringing the mug to his lips, he washed down the last of his sausage biscuit. "Tanner's already out in the field, but he said you wanted a tour of the farm?"

She nodded with just a flicker of a smile, but he was taken back. A flash of a memory, of Lacey smiling up at him, secret laughter in her eyes. Now, at best, those eyes were wary.

"Grab a biscuit. Reggie's the only horse here now, otherwise, we could ride, but you can see a lot walking." He finished his coffee and swiveled to put his mug in the dishwasher before picking up his cane.

Lacey looked at the biscuits loaded with sausage and turned a shade of green Devin wasn't sure he'd seen before.

"Ah… Maybe wait on the biscuit. I'll make some plain ones tomorrow."

"You made those?"

"I did. I had to pick up some skills to make myself useful around here. Not much call for washed-up bronc riders." The words were getting easier, but letting go of the dream was still hard. He'd wanted to rodeo as long as he could remember. "I can make you something else?"

"Coffee's fine for now. And I'd love to see the farm." She stepped through the door, coffee in hand.

Devin pulled the front door shut behind them and stepped out into early-morning not-yet-stifling humidity. The birds were singing and he could hear the cows shuffling in the pasture. It was his favorite time of day.

"Are you okay to walk all over the farm?"

He shot her a grin. "Thanks for asking, but yeah, I make do."

She hesitated. Then asked, "What happened to you, Devin? You were favoring the good ankle, but you were competing. You were walking without a cane."

He went a few paces without speaking. There wasn't a simple answer. "It might be easier if I start at the beginning."

They ambled together down the dirt road toward the back of the property, one of Tanner's dogs, a Rottweiler-shepherd mix named Sadie keeping pace beside them. "I'm not blaming anyone, okay? Because I take responsibility for all the stuff I did. But, if you want to know how it started, I came off a horse training in Colorado and landed funny on my shoulder."

She narrowed her eyes. "I vaguely remember that."

"It wasn't dislocated, but I think maybe I strained a

ligament or something. I went to the medical room to have it checked out and they gave me some painkillers so I could ride that night."

"For a strained shoulder?" She looked a little dubious.

"Yeah. I'm not saying they did the wrong thing, but the next time I had a little injury, I went back. More painkillers. And before I knew it, I needed pills to get through the day. I started riding broncs, instead of sticking to cutting, which I knew. And every day I got a little more reckless with my safety. Every day, I'd get a little more hurt. And the whole thing was a giant messed-up circle."

Lacey walked in silence beside him for a few feet until they broke through the trees. In front of them was a field of sunflowers. Their happy yellow faces were turned toward the east, where the sun was just breaking over the trees.

She caught her breath. "Oh, this is gorgeous."

"We'll cut these starting tomorrow. We sell them to people who sell flowers at area farmers markets." He pointed through the trees. "Back that way, in the woods, Tanner's got some pigs. Not many right now because we're just learning, but the sausage in our biscuits this morning... Uh, never mind."

She looked away, but there was a curve to her lips when she looked back. "It sounds like you guys have a plan."

"Yeah. It's slow, but as word gets out, a few people are starting to place orders and stuff."

They walked another trail and came out on the far side of the pond. It was visible from the house but just a hint of a gleam in the distance. Years ago, his mother had put two Adirondack chairs in a clearing under a big oak tree. He'd painted them a bright cheerful yellow to match the swing on the front porch the first week he'd been home.

"Want to sit for a few minutes?" When Lacey nodded, he dropped into one of the chairs, stretching his leg out in front of him, resting his hand on the head of the dog, who settled beside him.

Lacey sat quietly in the chair next to him. He pointed up in the tree. "See that scraggly end of a rope tied around that branch up there? Garrett and I used to swing out over the pond and drop. Tanner, too, but he was older. My mom would sit here. She'd always squeal when the cold water splashed her."

A smile tugged at his lips. Thoughts of his mom were always a little bittersweet. Even all these years later he missed her.

"I bet you found lots of ways to make the water splash her."

Lacey's voice broke into his thoughts and he glanced at her, forcing the easy smile. "How'd you guess? Garrett would never splash Mom on purpose. He was always the people pleaser. Middle-child thing, maybe."

"And you were the baby, the boundary pusher."

Black sheep. That's how he always thought of himself. The troublemaker of the family, the one who didn't quite fit. "Yeah, not much has changed, I guess."

"I knew you were partying and I knew you were taking crazy risks, but I didn't know why. Devin, why didn't you ask someone for help? Why didn't you ask me?"

He'd wondered when she would circle back to that. He looked out over the pond, sparkling in the morning light, and let the peace seep into him. God knew he needed it. "I didn't want you to know how bad things had gotten. I didn't want anyone to know, but especially you."

He blew out a frustrated breath, lifting one shoulder and letting it drop. "You can see how well that turned out. But I also didn't want to quit competing, and the drugs dulled the pain."

When he glanced back at her, her brown eyes were wide and serious. "So that's why you use a cane now. Because you're in pain all the time and now there are no drugs?"

"I kept riding broncs with an ankle that was held together with pins and screws and luck. So yeah, that's why I need a cane." He stood and helped Lacey to her feet, holding her hand just a second too long, wishing for something he couldn't even name. "Come on, we've got more to see."

He led her down the trail that wound around the pond and to the backside of the cow pasture. The cows followed them along the fence, pets as much as they were product. But that was kind of the point, according to Tanner. A low-stress environment was good for the animals.

She walked slowly beside him, matching her pace to his. "Cows are peaceful, I think, especially when they're just grazing in a field."

"I think so, too. I like hearing them." He glanced over at her, hardly believing that she was here beside him when he'd thought he might never see her again.

He opened the gate to the backyard. "I'll get in trouble if I don't do my chores, so I'm going to check the nesting boxes for eggs. You can wait on the porch or I'll meet you inside if you're ready for something to eat."

"Oh, that sounds like a good plan. I'll see you inside."

Devin opened the back of the chicken coop and removed over a dozen eggs, but his mind was in the house, where Lacey was waiting. They'd talked about a lot of things this morning, but the one topic they'd studiously avoided was what happened next.

It was tempting to continue avoiding it, to hang on to that small bit of peace they'd managed to scrape together this morning, but he didn't choose comfort over the more difficult option anymore. He couldn't run from hard things.

Back in the kitchen, he waited until the eggs were safely put away before washing his hands and sitting down beside her. "You like the farm?"

"Love it. Tanner's done such a careful job planning. It's amazing."

"Good. I have a proposition for you."

She went still. "Am I going to like this proposition?"

"Probably...not. But in the end, you get what you want."

"Okay," she said slowly. "Tell me what you have in mind."

"I'll sign the divorce papers on one condition."

Lacey closed her eyes. When she opened them, the wariness that had disappeared during their walk this morning was back. For a little while, it had almost been like old times. And he was holding out hope that she'd felt it, too.

"What's the condition?"

He took a deep breath. "You stay here at the ranch until the babies are born. We'll still have to work out custody and all that, but after they're born, if you still want me to, I'll sign the papers."

"Devin, I have a life—a family—in Oklahoma. I'm staying for a few weeks if the OB says I need to, but I have to go home." She placed both hands on the table and pushed to her feet. "It's a crazy idea."

"It probably is, but that's the deal." He was so nervous, but he forced himself to keep a relaxed position in the chair.

"You know I could take you to court anyway."

"I know, but I'm really hoping you won't. Give me a chance to show you that I can be a better person. That I can be a man who'll show up for his family. If you don't stay, you'll never know."

There were twin spots of color high on her cheekbones. "I need some time to think about this, Devin."

"You can have all the time you need." A fragment of a memory flashed in his mind, the two of them outside a hotel room door, her hand on his cheek and love in her eyes. It took his breath away.

He prayed that once she gave it some thought, she would want to stay.

And he would have a second chance.

## Chapter Four

Lacey was 100 percent sure she'd lost her mind. She'd spent the previous day, including the last eight hours when she should've been asleep, trying to decide if she should stay in Red Hill Springs.

She didn't even want to go into the kitchen for breakfast and she was *starving*. It would be a long six months if she spent the whole time avoiding Devin.

The reasons she'd come here for a divorce hadn't changed. Devin was a risk-taker, the life of the party, a crowd-thrilling rodeo standout. He said he'd changed, but desperation had gotten him to this point. What would happen to her when he wasn't desperate anymore?

He'd left her.

He'd lied to her.

Her hand spread across the barely visible rise in her abdomen where their babies were growing. She leaned her head against the door to the bedroom, praying for guidance, for wisdom…for backbone, even.

The back door slammed and she jumped away from the bedroom door, her heart pounding in her chest until she realized it was the guys going out to work. She cracked the door, slowly letting out a breath. Sadie lifted her head and gave a soft woof.

Otherwise, silence.

Feeling like she should be on tiptoe, she eased down the hall, through the living room and into the kitchen with Sadie shadowing her. Fluffy white biscuits were waiting for her on top of the stove and for a second she stared at them. Devin had remembered to make them plain. It was a small thing, but she tucked it away in her mind. She picked one up from the pan, slathered it with butter and took a big bite, her eyes nearly crossing. It was so good.

The back door banged open and she dropped her biscuit, which was quickly gobbled up by the dog.

"Well, hey." Devin, all six feet three inches of him, stepped into the kitchen.

She swallowed hard, wishing she'd started with coffee, or juice or something that would make her mouth just a little less dry. "Mmm."

"That good, huh?" His face split into a grin, and her pulse gave a traitorous leap.

"Delicious." She swallowed again. "What's up on the farm today?"

"Cutting sunflowers and loading them into buckets to sell at some of the farmers markets around here. Come on down later if you want. We can pull a chair up under a shade tree. Garrett will be around this afternoon to help, too." He lifted a large orange drink cooler off the counter. "Forgot the water. See you later?"

She nodded. "Sure."

Her eyes lingered on the door as it closed behind him. He looked good. He looked happy. Healthy.

She picked up another biscuit and dropped into a kitchen chair, giving the dog a warning look. "You're not getting this one, so you can stop it with the pitiful sad eyes."

It was a darn good biscuit, but suddenly she wasn't that hungry. The shock of their conversation yesterday afternoon still hadn't faded. Devin's story of how he got addicted to painkillers was so raw and real. And he'd been so good at hiding it that she'd witnessed it happening and hadn't even realized it.

How could that even happen? How had he gotten so low and she hadn't noticed? That was on her.

She sighed and got up to pour herself a glass of orange juice. Whether she was hungry or not, the babies needed calories and so did she if she didn't want a repeat of the fainting incident.

It didn't seem real that she was carrying twins. That she was a *mother* and in six months' time she'd be holding them in her arms. She couldn't afford to take chances. In the arena, sure, she'd pushed limits—hers and her horse's. But even then, the risks had been calculated.

Marrying Devin had been the biggest risk of her life. She'd been afraid she couldn't trust him, and guess what? She'd been right.

But he'd said he loved her. With tears in his eyes and the ring of truth in his voice, he'd said the words she'd wanted to hear.

And the truth—the real truth—the dirty little secret she'd been hiding, even from herself, was that she'd been in love with Devin for years. She'd fallen hard from the moment she'd met him. And that was the most dangerous secret of all. She wanted to stay here. She wanted to know Devin, the real Devin who didn't hide behind success, alcohol and that shiny gold rodeo buckle. She wanted to know if she'd fallen in love with the real Devin or if everything she'd thought about him was just an illusion.

The glass trembled in her hand. What was she thinking? She needed to hang on to her anger. She'd waited for him for over three months. She'd given him the power to hurt her... *And he had.*

She couldn't forget that. Falling in love with him again was not an option. Devin was all flash and glory. Babies were bottles and dirty diapers and not the fun kind of sleepless nights.

No. A marriage needed a stronger foundation than a drug-induced fantasy. In the daylight, she could see reality and reality said she couldn't trust him. Not yet. Maybe not ever. She had to protect herself.

Because, just like in an airplane cabin losing pressure, she had to put her oxygen mask on first so she could be there to protect her babies. And no matter what, they had to be her first priority.

So she would go to the sunflower field and she would build a friendship with Devin for her babies' sake. She would search for the answers to her questions about who Devin really was. But she absolutely would not, under any circumstances, fall in love with him again.

In the distance, Devin heard the dog's joyful bark and squinted toward the house. Lacey was walking down the dirt lane between pastures, throwing a ball for Sadie, who would chase it down, return it and bark her head off until Lacey threw the ball again. Lacey laughed, her head thrown back, long dark hair trailing in loose waves down her back.

And watching her, Devin could barely breathe. All morning long his mind had been on their conversation last night, wondering if she'd give him a chance. Wondering if she still had feelings for him at all and if she'd made a decision.

Sadie caught sight of him and streaked down the road, cutting across the field when she saw Tanner instead. "Ah. I see who's really loved here."

Lacey started across the field toward him, her crisp citrus scent reaching him before she did, the sweet aroma mingling with the green scent of the sunflowers. He drew in a deep breath as she lingered beside him.

"What are you doing?"

"Getting these ready to be sold." He glanced up at her, but his hands kept moving, prepping the flowers for transport—sliding netting over the sunflower blossom and a wide straw over the stem. He placed the flower in a five-gallon bucket at his feet and glanced up at her. "Sunflowers seem like they would be hardy, but they break easily. Underneath they're a lot more fragile than people think."

"Huh." She raised her eyebrows and looked down at her hands, where thin silver and turquoise rings shimmered on her fingers.

He narrowed his eyes. "What's that supposed to mean?"

"Oh, nothing."

Devin leaned against the table where he was working and studied her. He was self-aware enough—now—to get what she was saying. But he didn't want to talk about how mushy he was on the inside or how brittle he was on the outside. "Well, if you're gonna stand here, the least you can do is help."

Lacey shot him a look but picked up a sunflower, slid a straw over the stem and handed it to him.

In turn, Devin pulled the protective netting over the

bloom and stuck it in the bucket. He turned to her, holding his hand up for a high five.

When she gave it to him with only a slight eye roll, he grinned. Progress. They made a good team.

The thought came with a little pang. He and Lacey had been a team in lots of ways for a long time. He'd lost track of the appearances they'd made together promoting the rodeo. There'd been questions for years about whether they were a couple, and the two of them had always laughed it off.

"Best friends," they'd said. "We know way too much about each other for a relationship."

It seemed pretty ironic now that what stood between them was the terrible secret he'd been hiding and the wall Lacey had put up to protect herself. For all of their sakes, especially two little babies he had yet to meet, he prayed they could get beyond it.

Pushing the envelope had been his MO. He was always good for a gasp from the crowd. And he'd loved the approval and the admiration of an audience. But the proposition he'd made to Lacey seemed like the biggest risk he'd ever taken. He wasn't just risking his heart, he was risking the peace he'd found here. In a real way, risking his future.

It didn't make sense—not in a practical way—what he was asking, but when he thought about their babies, it made all the sense in the world. His security and peace were nothing compared with theirs.

His fingers brushed against Lacey's as he took the flower, and she jerked her hand back like she'd been burned.

He sighed as he slid the netting over the deep yellow

bloom. "So have you had a chance to think about our conversation yesterday morning?"

She breathed, the words flowing out of her with her exhalation. "I haven't been able to think about anything else."

His fingers stilled for a moment, but then he took the next flower, torn between wanting to hear what she had to say and wanting to be able to imagine he had a chance with her.

He opened his mouth to ask, just as his brother Tanner strode out of the field of sunflowers with two five-gallon buckets of flowers, Sadie ambling along beside him. *Perfect* timing.

"Devin put you to work?" Tanner nodded to Lacey, who shot him a breezy smile.

"Got to earn my keep. These sunflowers are gorgeous."

Devin scowled as he tugged another net over the head of a sunflower. "We were right in the middle of something, Tanner."

Tanner took one look at Devin's face and a single quirk of a smile flitted across his face. He pulled one of the newly cut stems out of the bucket and handed it to Lacey. "For you. The only payment you're likely to get out of a day's work at Triple Creek Ranch."

"And well worth it."

Devin rolled his eyes. "If you two are done, can we please get back to work?"

Lacey shrugged at Tanner and turned back to the table, carefully sliding a straw over one of the stems they would be selling.

Tanner gestured at the buckets on the ground beside Lacey. "Make sure Devin's the one picking these up when it's time for the next batch of flowers. They're really heavy."

"I've got it, Tanner." Devin tried to keep the edge out of his voice.

With a shrug, Tanner lifted a trio of empty buckets and disappeared between the rows of sunflowers.

"He seems sweet."

Devin sighed as he lifted the next bucket of flowers to the table.

"Why doesn't he have a wife and a couple of kids by now?"

The bucket slammed onto the table, water sloshing over the side. Devin steadied himself against the unexpected wave of grief.

Lacey looked up in alarm. "What's wrong? Did you hurt your ankle?"

He should be able to handle an innocent question by now. The accident was simply a part of his story, something that happened in the past. He just wasn't prepared for her to ask it. "Nothing's wrong. It's... Look, don't bring this up with Tanner, okay? He lost his wife and baby in the same accident that killed our parents."

Tears formed in her eyes. She looked away. "I'm sorry. I didn't know. I never should've made that kind of assumption."

"It's okay. It is. It just…creeps up on you from time to time. You think you've gotten used to the idea that it happened and you've moved on and then, well, you're not okay. And that stinks. I don't think Tanner's been okay for a really long time."

"He must've been so devastated." She laid her hand over his and laced their fingers together. "You were both so young."

He turned toward her, bringing her hand to his chest. He didn't want to wait anymore. "What do you say, Lace? Are we going to give this thing a chance?"

She shook her head and his heart plummeted to his feet. "What we're doing seems so backward. You don't get married, pregnant and *then* decide whether or not to stay together. I mean, who does that?"

"Maybe we do." He tucked one long dark curl behind her ear. "I mean, so *what*? We're married. We're pregnant. The pressure's off. Now we have a real chance to see what it's like to be together. Without the press, without the cameras. Without all the other stuff. Just—us."

Her gaze locked on his. She whispered, "I feel like I barely know you."

"That's exactly why you should stay." Devin kissed her fingers, still laced with his. "Give us a chance, Lacey. That's all I'm asking for."

"I gave us a chance, Devin. And we both saw how that turned out." She pulled her hand away. "But I'll stay. Because our babies need a dad. And because one way or another, I want to be free of this hold you have over me. I care about you but I'm not along for the roller coaster anymore. I've had enough adventure."

She backed away from the table. "I'll see you at dinner. I need some space right now."

Devin watched her walk away, a knot that felt like a boulder in the pit of his stomach. It was too much to expect her to trust him so soon after what he'd done. But she was staying and he had six months to prove to her that he was a different person. That he was a man who knew how to be responsible, who would step up when things got hard and take care of his family.

He had six months to win her heart.

## Chapter Five

As Lacey finished her dinner that night, she noticed that conversation had suddenly stopped. She glanced up. Devin was staring at her intensely, one finger touching his nose. She looked at Garrett, who had his hand nonchalantly over his mouth, with one of his fingers touching *his* nose. Tanner, oblivious, was taking his last bite of the simple spaghetti casserole she'd put together when they came in from the sunflower field.

She glanced back at Devin and he pointedly tapped his nose. She hesitantly raised her finger to her nose. "Not...it?"

Tanner's head jerked up, his shoulders falling as he noted the position of each of their fingers. He pushed back from the table with his plate in his hand. "You guys are so immature. Lacey, I expected better from you."

She laughed. "Sorry, Tanner. I love cooking but I hate doing dishes."

"I have never once won 'not it,'" Tanner grumbled. "Not cool."

Deadpan, Garrett handed Tanner his plate. "Thanks, bro. You're the best."

Lacey covered the little bit that remained of the spaghetti casserole and started to clear the table for Tanner, who took the plates from her and shooed her from the room.

In the living room, Garrett fiddled around on the piano, playing an old Beatles song. She hummed along as she walked out the door onto the porch. Taking a deep breath of the clean country air, she leaned on the rail, letting the cool breeze ruffle her hair.

The song changed to a familiar James Taylor song, a cowboy lullaby she'd heard her dad play often over the years. She heard the murmur of voices, and a guitar joined the piano. Devin's pure, clear tenor rose with the melody. A lump formed in her throat.

She liked things in categories and when things were murky in her mind, she felt out of focus. Devin defied category. When she first met him, she'd thought he was sweet and fun, if a little reckless. Later, after they'd been friends for a while, she'd thought she had figured out all his layers.

She'd been wrong about that.

For the last few months, she'd thought he was a total jerk. She'd been wrong about that, too. But now? She had no idea what to think about this person. She didn't know him at all. And she didn't know if what she was seeing now was the real Devin or a new Devin.

She looked up, whispering a prayer for discernment to the stars in the dark night sky. The stakes were so high. She needed God to guide her—trying to figure it out on her own wasn't working.

Devin's voice startled her. She'd been so far away in her thoughts that she hadn't even realized the music had stopped. "That was my mother's favorite song when she was pregnant with me. She wanted to name me James, but my dad wouldn't let her. He said she'd be calling me Sweet Baby James until I was thirty and he wasn't having it."

"Your dad had a point." She turned toward Devin with a smile. His face was half in the shadows and it occurred to her that her understanding of him was so much like that, only half in the light. He'd talked about the farm. His love for the land. He'd even told some stories about him and Garrett when they'd been little. But he'd never really talked about his mom and dad.

Now that they were facing the prospect of being a mom and dad, it was meaningful to her that Devin would share something about them. He'd been loved by his mom from before she even knew his face—that much was clear.

She hadn't had that same experience with her own mother. It had been just her and her dad since she was a little girl. She rubbed her belly idly. It didn't matter that she'd never seen the faces of her twins. She loved them already.

Devin held the guitar by the neck and leaned a hip on the porch railing, his eyes on hers. He swung it up, settled it under his arm and began to pick the tune of a familiar hymn.

She took a deep breath, letting her thoughts—and if she were honest, doubts—fly to the stars along with her prayers. "I learned how to play the recorder in the fifth grade."

"Oh yeah? Maybe we can start a band."

She snorted a laugh. "Now, that would be something to tell our kids about. I never knew you played the guitar."

"I got my first guitar for my birthday when I was nine and taught myself how to play. I bought this one later. Garrett brought it over after I got out of rehab." He shrugged. "I think playing it now makes me feel more connected to who I was before."

"Before rehab?"

"No." He paused and glanced out to the pasture where his horse was nibbling on grass in the moonlight, his eyes narrowing against his memory. "Before the accident. I stopped playing after that. My mom was always singing along to something, but after she died, I don't know, it just didn't seem right to have music in the house." He looked at her then, his fingers stilling the vibration of the strings before he picked up the melody again. "Seems silly, saying it out loud now. My mom wouldn't have wanted that."

"You were so young. Maybe it was your way of acknowledging what a huge loss it was." The more she got to know the Cole brothers, the more she realized how much life had changed for all of them the day of the accident. Devin was the youngest and Lacey had to wonder if all the reckless adventures Devin chased had been an attempt to keep from actually feeling the grief of losing his parents.

But he was playing the guitar again and he was talking.

He was trying.

She took a deep breath, feeling like she was standing at the edge of a diving board, her toes over the edge, her balance wobbling. "I'm going to the doctor in the morning. You can come…if you want."

He stopped playing. "You're serious?"

"You want to?"

A grin split his face. "Yes! Yes, I want to!"

"The appointment is tomorrow morning at ten."

"Ten. Got it." He glanced at his watch and started for the house. "I gotta get out of here or I'm gonna miss my meeting."

"I'll be here when you get back."

He paused with the door half-open, looked back and shot her a smile. "I'm really glad."

"Me, too." She said it without thinking, but it was true. And the thought scared her.

Because it meant she had something to lose.

Lacey had a death grip on Devin's hand as they walked into the obstetrician's office. He waited beside her, trying not to intervene as the receptionist tried to tell her that Dr. Lescale wasn't taking new patients and Lacey patiently corrected her. When Devin saw Lacey's fingers tremble as she finally picked up the pen to sign in, his hand landed at the small of her back and didn't move until she was seated in the comfiest chair in the room.

He took the chair next to Lacey, his knees sticking out at an awkward angle, his cane leaning against the table next to him. He felt conspicuous. And like a giant. Like a giant conspicuous guy who didn't belong here.

The urge to reach in his pocket for his NA chip was almost irresistible. It wasn't a talisman, he knew that, but it was an object that grounded him. He reminded himself he belonged here. He was Lacey's husband and the father of the babies she was carrying. Maybe their relationship hadn't happened in the conventional way, but it was a fact: they were married.

He took a deep breath and looked around the room.

Really looked. He scratched his neck and caught the eye of a guy a few chairs down who was sitting next to an extremely pregnant woman who was periodically crying into a tissue. He looked away quickly.

"Are you nervous?" Lacey's voice interrupted his thoughts.

"Me?" He waved away the concern. "Not at all. You?"

Her brows drew together. "Not really. I guess I'll be glad to know everything's okay, though."

The door opened. "Lacey Cole?"

Lacey stood, and Devin grabbed his cane, halfway out of his chair before the nurse held up her hand. "She'll be right back. We're just getting some info right now."

Another woman in baby blue scrubs came out and called a name, and the crying lady left. Her partner took a deep breath and stabbed his fingers through his hair. Devin gave the guy what he hoped was an empathetic look.

"Pregnancy is nuts, you know?"

Devin looked around for someone—anyone—else. Was the guy talking to him or talking to himself? To be safe, Devin nodded slightly.

"That your wife?" The guy hooked a thumb toward the door to the back.

So he was definitely talking to Devin. "Oh…uh… yeah. You?"

"Yeah. We'd only been married a year when we found out she was pregnant. Goodbye, honeymoon, am I right?"

Devin guessed that depended on your point of view but didn't say anything.

It didn't seem to matter. The man kept talking. "I mean, she's been literally crying for months. Sometimes I think I'm gonna need a life jacket in my own house. I don't even know what she's crying about. For real, I don't think she knows what she's crying about."

Devin closed his eyes and imagined that he was on a beach in Florida. Soft white sand, the warm sun and a cool breeze, the sound of the waves smoothing the shore.

No one oversharing.

"Right, man?"

Devin opened his eyes. "Oh, uh, sure."

The door opened and the nurse looked at the hot pink sticky note attached to her finger. "Devin Cole? We've got a room available for your wife."

Devin was hobbling across the room before the nurse finished her sentence. He couldn't get the image of that woman crying into a tissue out of his head. Was Lacey going to be like that? Had she just not hit that stage?

He'd never seen a pregnant woman cry like that. Granted, he hadn't been around that many.

Or any.

Walking through the door to the back room felt kind of like stepping into Narnia. It was freezing back here for one thing. And it was definitely a foreign land.

The nurse stopped in front of a door, knocked slightly, then opened it without waiting. Lacey was sitting on the exam table in a paper gown, fingers gripping the edge and bare feet dangling. Her eyes were wide and shiny. A sheet covered her upper legs.

She shrugged, with a sheepish sort of look on her face. "Here we are."

"Yep. Here we are." Hot prickles formed on the back

of Devin's neck, beads of sweat forming on his fore-head. He was not supposed to be here. Mortals were not supposed to be in Narnia.

"You look a little grim," Lacey said.

"No, it's fine. This is great. Really."

Lacey laughed. "Whatever you say."

He scrunched his nose at her.

The door flew wide. A petite woman wearing scrubs and a white coat strode in, stuck her hand under the sanitizer dispenser and turned to Lacey with a smile as she rubbed the gel on the surface of her hands. "I'm Dr. Lescale. Here's what I know—you're pregnant with twins, history of low blood pressure and fainting. And my friend Ash referred you to me."

"Right." Lacey held out a hand. "Lacey Cole. And this is Devin."

The sound of his name with hers never failed to jar him. He leaned back against the wall, taking the weight off his ankle and trying to be invisible.

The doctor looked at the computer monitor, scrolling and clicking. "Your vitals look good. Feeling okay?" At Lacey's nod, she picked up what looked like a remote control and raised the table while simultaneously slid-ing out a footrest for Lacey. "Let's see if we can hear those babies."

Devin shifted on his feet. He felt awkward but he knew it had to be nothing compared with how vulnera-ble Lacey was feeling. At least he had all his clothes on.

When Dr. Lescale had Lacey settled, she pulled out a little machine with a wand at the end of it. After squirt-ing some gel onto the end of it, she ran it over Lacey's stomach.

"You're almost sixteen weeks along? You're going to be really showing soon."

Dr. Lescale looked up at Devin. "Come here, Dad."

With a gulp he hoped wasn't audible, he moved over to the doctor, who placed the wand in his hand and guided it into place.

The doctor narrowed her eyes, listening. "Just… there."

With that, a whooshing sound, almost like the sound of a washing machine, filled the room. A big smile spread across Lacey's face and her eyes filled.

Dr. Lescale smiled, too. "Good strong heartbeat for Baby A. Now let's find Baby B."

With a sure hand, the doctor guided the wand to just the right spot and the sound of another heartbeat filled the room.

Without warning, a tear spilled down Devin's cheek. He lifted his shoulder and rubbed it away. But as the sound continued, so did the tears, and the fact that he was going to be someone's daddy became not some nebulous fact that he knew, but a genuine reality, right there under his hand.

A tear splashed onto the paper cover of the exam table, and Dr. Lescale looked up with surprise. She immediately removed the wand and handed Lacey a tissue. "I'm just going to give you two a minute while I get some prenatal vitamins together for Lacey."

The door closed behind the doctor and Devin remained where he was, his hands spread wide on the exam table, letting it take his weight, his head bowed. He took a shuddering breath, dragging air into his lungs.

The first touch of her hand was so soft he almost

missed it. But again he felt it, the featherlight touch in his hair. He should open his eyes, say something funny, brush off the seriousness of the moment, but he couldn't do it.

He couldn't pretend that his tightly leashed control hadn't shattered the moment the first beat of his baby's heart sounded in the room. He couldn't pretend at all.

Slowly he raised his head. Her fingers were still in his hair. Her eyes on his. "Dev," she said hesitantly.

He forced a smile. "I'm okay. I'm fine. Sorry I got emotional."

"Don't do that."

"What?"

"Pull away from me. They're your babies, Devin. It's okay to be a little overwhelmed when you hear their hearts beating for the first time."

He swallowed hard and tried to smile again and make a joke, but the smile was a quirk of one corner of his mouth, the laugh a choking swallow.

Devin took a deep breath and straightened as the door to the hall opened and the doctor stuck her head in. Lacey's hand fell back to her side.

"I'll meet you at the car." Devin felt her sigh, but he couldn't stay in that tiny room with the walls closing in. And he couldn't put a name to the emotion, but it felt more threatening than the most dangerous bronc he'd ever faced in the arena.

# Chapter Six

Lacey opened the passenger-side door and slid into the seat. Devin handed her a white paper bag that smelled suspiciously like french fries. She sent him a look out of the corner of her eye and opened the bag. Pulling out a few and shoving them in her mouth, she asked, "How did you know I was starving?"

"I'm the one who cooks breakfast, remember? I know you didn't eat." He handed her a milkshake. "I also seem to remember you once told me that fries without a milkshake are 'just another root vegetable.'"

"Oh, you are the best." She took the lid off the milkshake, grabbed another handful of fries and dipped them, closing her eyes as she savored her favorite post-rodeo indulgence. "Whoever built a fast-food place next to an OB's office was a genius."

Devin put the truck in gear and drove toward the farm. She finished her fries in silence, brushed the salt from her fingers and crumpled up the bag. "So. Are we going to talk about what happened in there?"

He didn't take his eyes off the road. "Nope."

Lacey thought for a minute and then shrugged. "Okay."

He looked at her then—an incredulous, disbelieving look.

"I mean it, Devin. You can have your feelings without talking about them. I have feelings all the time that I keep to myself."

His eyebrows slammed together. "Like what?"

She sat back against the seat and looked out the window so he wouldn't see her smile. "Like I'm not going to tell you."

He sighed and stared out the windshield as he drove, both hands on the steering wheel. Three long minutes ticked by in silence before he said, "I was distracted when I came into the exam room, wondering when you were going to start with the nonstop crying, and then I heard the heartbeat and it was…" His voice choked again. "It was so real, you know? That there's a baby— our baby—two of them. It was a little overwhelming is all."

Lacey considered being smug that she'd gotten him to talk about his feelings, but what he'd said was so right on target that she just smiled.

He growled. "Happy?"

"Yeah." She laughed.

A few seconds later, she said quietly, "When I first found out I was pregnant, I was kind of mad about it, like, of *course* that would happen to me, but then I heard their heartbeats… And all of a sudden, I was their mother. And it didn't matter how it happened. They were mine." She glanced over at him. "It rocked my world."

He didn't say anything, didn't even take his eyes

off the road, but he reached over and laced his fingers with hers.

She stared at their hands, wanting to deny that her stoic facade was cracking. She didn't *want* to feel anything for him. He'd broken her heart.

They'd spent so much time together in the past. Hours in barns at various arenas around the country. Hours on the road. She'd told him everything. And apparently he'd remembered it, like he remembered that she only really liked french fries dipped in chocolate milkshake.

How could she not have noticed that in all the time they'd spent together, he'd told her almost nothing? She drew in a breath and bolstered her resolve. He'd skipped out when things had gotten serious in the exam room because that was what Devin did. And despite his tears, despite the fact that they were tied together by their babies, she wasn't going to fall for him. She couldn't… Because if she couldn't trust her own heart, what could she trust?

In her mind, she heard her daddy's voice and could almost feel his finger tapping her forehead. "You trust your head, punkin'. Not your heart. Your heart will go after that brass ring every time. Your head will tell you if you have what it takes to make it."

She had to trust her brain and approach her relationship with Devin the same way she would the barrels, with mental toughness. In the ring, if she let emotion—or nerves, or fear, or worry—ruin her concentration, she lost her edge. Her horse, Magpie, was sensitive to Lacey's tiniest change in attitude and she depended on Lacey to be relaxed and focused and confident.

She'd learned that lesson from the time she was old

enough to get on a horse and trot around the practice ring. Mind over matter.

In the back of Lacey's mind, though, she knew that no matter how much her dad told her to use her brain, it wasn't intellect that kept her chasing cans. It was passion. And instinct…and heart.

The truck bounced over a rut. Devin winced. "Sorry."

When Lacey looked up, she realized she had no idea where they were. She'd been so deep in thought that she hadn't noticed Devin had passed Triple Creek Ranch.

"Where are we?"

"Red Hill Farm. There's an equine therapy program here. The lady who runs it has a horse she wants me to take a look at." He pulled to a stop by a huge white antebellum house. A handful of little children were playing in a fenced area in the backyard. A woman with one long red braid over her shoulder and a baby in a sling across her chest walked out of the barn.

She met them mid-driveway, one hand holding the baby in place, the other outstretched to shake Devin's hand. Her eyes widened as a particularly shrill shriek split the air. "Sorry about the noise. Preschool is out for the week, so they're all here."

"No worries." His hand on Lacey's back, Devin introduced her to Jordan Sheehan, whose face lit up.

"Lacey Jenkins. Wow, it's a pleasure. I've seen you ride—you're amazing."

"Thanks." Lacey smiled. "So let me see if I've got this right… You're married to the pediatrician and you have…a lot of kids."

Jordan looked confused for a moment before she cracked up laughing. "We have two kids. Levi—the one sliding like a maniac over there—is almost five.

And this little peanut here is Essie. She's two months old. The rest of the kids are my sister's. She and her husband are foster parents."

"Oh, wow. I'm only having two and it seems overwhelming. I can't imagine."

"Congratulations!" Jordan grinned. "I get it. But trust me, you get used to the noise level."

Devin walked toward the covered arena where a beautiful red-and-white paint mare was circling. He rested his arms on the top of the fence. "So what's her story?"

Jordan sighed. "She's a one-owner horse. Sweet as buttercream frosting. Her elderly owner was put into a nursing home recently and the children thought it would be great to donate Dolly to our program."

"Seems reasonable."

"She's so gentle. We all thought she would be a good fit...until we got her near the kids. She's terrified of them."

Devin dug a sugar cube out of his pocket, stuck his fingers in his mouth and whistled. The mare's head came up and she trotted closer, drawn to the sugar. As she approached the fence, one of the kids on the playground yelled. Dolly wheeled immediately, speeding to the opposite end of the arena, ears pinned back.

"Yeah. That pretty much sums it up." The baby whimpered, and Jordan jiggled her.

"I hate that it's not going to work out for you to use her in therapy." Devin picked up his cane from where he'd leaned it against the fence. "Mind if I take a closer look, ride her a little bit?"

"Not at all. Let me just take the baby over to the nanny."

"I'll hold her," Lacey volunteered.

"If you're sure, that would be great. Mrs. Matthews has her hands full today." A few seconds later, Jordan placed her baby girl in Lacey's arms. "Just yell if you need anything. Ready, Devin?"

With her heart in her throat, Lacey looked into the little-bitty face. Essie's skin was almost translucent, auburn lashes fanning out over her cheek. Her tiny little rosebud mouth worked in her sleep, as if she were dreaming of her next meal.

Lacey drew in a shaky breath and walked across the yard, easing into a swing under the wide branches of an oak tree. She thought she'd understood what it meant that she was about to have a baby—two babies—but holding this sweet girl made her realize… She had no idea what she was getting into.

Rocking gently, baby Essie tucked safely in her arms, she glanced at the gate as Devin rode out on Dolly. He took her into a simple figure eight, concentrating on the shape, letting her know he was leading. Every time she'd get a little distracted by the noise of the kids, he'd redirect her to the pattern they were walking.

He was so sensitive to every flick of the horse's ears, every twitch of her shoulder. And he calmed her effortlessly. Lacey had seen him do it a thousand times.

She admired him so much. She was also confused by him, her emotions all over the place when it came to their relationship. And the little bundle in her arms reminded her just how high the stakes were.

Hours later, finally back at Triple Creek, Devin had Dolly firmly ensconced in a stall in the barn nearest the pasture where Reggie was spending his retirement.

She'd be able to hear the other horse and smell him but not see him. He suspected that part of the problem with Dolly's behavior was that she'd been the only horse her owner had. She was spoiled... And she was sad.

He shook a few extra oats into her bucket and scratched her neck just under her mane. "There you go, sweet girl. I'll see you in the morning."

His body ached with exertion as he limped his way up the stairs and into the house. He hadn't ridden in a long while and his ankle was in revolt. Since he didn't take painkillers anymore, he was hoping a couple of acetaminophen and a hot bath would at least take the edge off.

He'd taken only a couple of steps into the room when he heard the yelling coming from behind a closed door. He stopped, staring at nothing while he sucked in a long breath...and opened the door to the office.

Tanner was standing over the desk, his hands braced on either side of some kind of ledger. Devin could only imagine that it was the ranch finances.

Garrett was sprawled in a leather chair, a bored expression on his face, as if he'd heard this lecture a thousand times before. And Devin was sure that he had, because without a doubt, the lecture was about Devin. He just wasn't sure exactly what he'd done to deserve it. This time.

Devin leaned against the door frame. "What is it, Tanner? Did I forget to unload the dishwasher? Miss an egg in the henhouse? Leave wet clothes in the dryer? What?"

Garrett sat up a little straighter, his voice a warning. "Dev..."

Devin stopped Garrett with a hand held up against

the words. "No, Garrett. I've never in my life been able to do anything good enough for Tanner."

Garrett stood up, putting himself between the two brothers, oldest and youngest. "That's not exactly fair, Dev."

Devin was tired, in pain and just so over the chip on his brother's shoulder. "What did I do wrong this time, Tanner?"

"The horse."

At the words, Devin advanced. "Since when do I need permission to bring a horse home? It's a ranch, still. Right?"

Tanner's eyes were emotionless. "Since we don't have the money to feed it."

Devin recoiled, his mind struggling to make sense of what Tanner said. "What?"

Tanner closed his eyes and stretched his neck, rubbing the side of it with his hand. When he opened his eyes, he said, "We're barely staying afloat."

A coughing noise interrupted them. The three of them turned in tandem to find Lacey standing in the door. She tried a hesitant smile. "Dinner's ready?"

Tanner stalked toward the kitchen. "There's no sense in talking about this anyway."

Devin looked at Garrett, who shrugged.

When they were all seated around the table and grace had been said, Devin cut into his baked chicken. Without lifting his eyes, he said, "So let's talk about what we can do to make some money."

Tanner slammed his fork down and put his hands on the edge of the table, ready to push himself back. "This is not the time to discuss this."

Garrett put his hand on Tanner's shoulder. "Devin's

right. You've been carrying this a long time. The ranch belongs to all of us. All of us need to figure out how to fix it."

"I can go into the other room so you guys can work this out." Lacey stood, but Tanner waved her back into her seat.

"You want to talk… Let's talk. I've done everything I can do to get this place back on its feet. And it's working. It's just not working fast enough."

"What's the bottom line, Tanner?" Garrett took a bite of his chicken and stabbed a piece of their home-grown asparagus.

Tanner's cheeks were ruddy. "When we inherited the farm, there was already substantial debt. I've paid it down but we're just not bringing in enough yet to get it paid off in time. We're gaining ground but…"

"…we need to brainstorm ideas for bringing in more cash." Devin picked up his sweet tea. "So who has ideas?"

Garrett raised his hand. "How about goats? You can drink the milk and make cheese and soap to sell."

Tanner got up and scrounged in the drawer under the microwave, coming up with a half-used pad and a pen. He sat down and scribbled a word. "Okay, goats. Anything else?"

Devin gave Garrett a skeptical look. "I mean, don't get me wrong, I love goats, but we don't know how to make goat cheese or soap. What about bees? We could sell the honey at farmers markets, like we do the sunflowers."

Tanner wrote it down, but this time he made a face. "I think that's a great idea, but doesn't it take time for bees to make honey? We don't have a lot of time."

"True. Maybe we could rent space to a beekeeper. That would bring in a little money and bees are good on the farm, anyway." Devin looked down at the table. Garrett looked out the window, Tanner at the pad in front of him.

Lacey drew in a breath and all three of them focused on her. She glanced from one to the other. "No, I mean, I was just taking a breath."

"Oh." Devin slumped to the side.

"But…"

Tanner looked up at Lacey. "It couldn't be worse than goats or bees. No offense," he said to his brothers.

Garrett shrugged. "None taken."

"What's your idea, Lacey?" Devin was exhausted. His ankle ached and tension knotted his shoulders. He was ticked that Tanner hadn't told him and Garrett how bad things were. But they were in this together. All of them.

Lacey winced. "It seems silly… But in Oklahoma, a lot of farmers have roadside stands. Tanner has already been working at growing organic vegetables. We have zucchini out the ears. I saw the blueberry bushes in the field behind the pond and they're about to be ripe. We have eggs for days. Maybe we could…build a farm stand?"

Devin looked at Garrett and Tanner. He wasn't sure what the two of them were thinking but he was pretty sure his wife was brilliant.

Tanner wrote it down on the pad and then looked up. "We'll have to get a permit. But I have wood in the barn and, you're right, we have more vegetables than we know what to do with. I think it's a viable plan provided we think it through."

"Yes! Up top." Devin held up a hand for a high five. Her gaze softened on his. "I'm already there."

Devin's grin slowly faded. He'd said that to her once at a competition after a ride. She'd held up a hand for a high five and he'd pointed to the leader board and sent her a cocky smile. *I'm already there.*

He'd missed her. It just hit him how badly he'd missed his friend. She'd been there beside him, willing to stay, and he'd locked her out.

He didn't want to lock her out anymore.

Tanner cleared his throat, and Lacey looked away. His brother tapped the pad with his pen. "So I've got some researching to do."

Devin looked at his watch. "I've got to get to a meeting."

"Guess that means I've got the dishes." Garrett pushed back from the table.

Devin grabbed his cane. Lacey followed him through the living room to the front door and he turned back to her. "You're brilliant. In the morning, let's sit down and make sure we're tracking together. Okay?"

She nodded, and he wanted so badly to just drop a kiss on her lips, the way a husband would. But he knew she wasn't ready. They weren't ready.

Instead he smiled. "It's a date, then."

He'd seen his mom walk his dad to that same door a million times. He'd never realized that he wanted that. The admiration of the crowd was something. He'd never forget what it felt like to have them chanting his name.

But he would trade it all for the admiration of one woman. And he prayed that he could be the kind of man she could trust.

The kind of man she could love.

## Chapter Seven

With country music playing softly in the background, Lacey hummed to herself as she rinsed her mixing bowls and spoons in the sink. Her fourth batch of zucchini brownies was in the oven. The first three batches had been, in order, too crumbly, too gooey, too zucchini-y. Way too zucchini-y. Even though that wasn't really a word.

Her goal was to perfect a few simple recipes so they could sell baked goods made with their own produce at the farm stand. So far, she hadn't been successful. But she wasn't a quitter. The guys might be quitting her brownies, though, if she couldn't come up with a decent recipe.

Baking gave her time to think, and even with the sound of the guys' hammers competing with her music, the farm was peaceful. It was strange, really. She'd always thought that racing barrels was the height of happiness for her. And maybe it *was* the ultimate in happiness, but she hadn't been content—not when she was always chasing the *next* win.

She loved the feeling of the wind in her hair, the exhilaration of the competition and the thrill of winning. She loved the competition and pushing herself, but contentment? Contentment was what she felt being a part of life on the ranch, working with Devin and Garrett and Tanner to make plans and create something new.

The timer beeped, and Lacey pulled open the oven to check on the zucchini brownies. They were slightly underbaked but she was hoping that they would be just the right amount of chewy when they cooled.

She heard the front door open as she slid the pan onto the top of the stove. With her quilted oven mitts still on her hands, she walked into the living room just as Devin placed a laundry basket full of clothes on the coffee table. "What's this?"

"Jordan brought over some maternity clothes."

"Aw, that's sweet. And the flowers?"

"They just reminded me of you." The last few weeks had blown by in a blur of discarded farm stand designs, permit paperwork and paint chips. And Devin had taken to picking whatever wildflowers were blooming and putting them in a blue-and-white splatterware pitcher in the kitchen—just because she liked them.

Last night he'd made lasagna from scratch because it was her favorite. He'd underestimated how long it would take to make by about two hours and his brothers had been ruthless, but she thought it was sweet.

"These are so pretty." Lacey added the flowers to the ones already on the table and turned around to see Devin leaning over the pan of brownies. She smacked him with the rooster side of the oven mitt. "I can't believe you! Sneaking a brownie when my back was turned."

He pointed to his mouth and let his eyes roll back in

his head, and as much as she tried to act annoyed with him, she couldn't do it. "Good? Really good?"

"So good. What did you do?"

"The Triple Creek Ranch Triple Chocolate Brownie recipe is top secret." She pretended to lock her lips and throw the key out the window.

He very slowly put his fork down, and she felt the giggle rise in her chest. She took a step back, putting one oven-mitted hand up between them. "Uh-uh. Don't start with me, Devin. Go hammer something."

Devin advanced slowly, his eyes on hers. She turned to run, the laugh breaking free as he grabbed the oven mitt, tugging her back to him.

She laughed. "You have chocolate on your chin."

When she wiped it with a quick scrub of the hot pad, his smile faded. "You're so beautiful."

With his arms wrapped around her, she went still. She'd been very careful about touching him. But now, in his arms, she let herself imagine just for a minute that their wedding had been planned, their marriage for real…their love the forever kind.

She could paint a fantasy of herself right here in the kitchen, laughing at something Devin said, their babies in high chairs at the kitchen table. And it felt right.

"Lace…" His voice was husky in her ear.

She looked up and found his dark brown eyes intent on hers, and so close. When he leaned forward, she moved closer. She knew he was going to kiss her, and she wanted him to.

It was *so* tempting to let all her worries about the future go and just ride with the feeling, but she couldn't.

She wanted to cry at the injustice of it, but pretending things were different wasn't fair—to either of them.

With her hand still in the oven mitt on his chest, she said, "Wait, Devin."

He immediately let her go and stepped back, the realization of what almost happened all over his face. "I'm sorry. I didn't mean to assume anything..."

"No, it's not that, it's...oh." She blinked. "Hold on a sec."

"You okay?" His voice was concerned and he reached for her, his hand hovering somewhere around her elbow.

"Yeah, I'm fine." She laughed, slid the oven mitts off and took his hand. She placed it on the swell of her stomach. "There. Wait, no. *There.*"

Lacey rested her hand over his and watched his face, waiting for him to realize what he was feeling. Wonder spread across his face as he let out an awestruck sigh. "He's kicking?"

She nodded. "I wasn't sure at first, but yeah. He—or she—is *definitely* kicking. I think maybe all the chocolate experiments I've been eating woke them up."

"It's our babies." His voice hitched on the words, and her heart ached. He cupped her face with both his hands and let his forehead gently touch hers. "I know our relationship is anything but normal, but the babies—I'm just blown away, Lacey."

And he was right. They were in a mess and everything was wrong. Everything was wrong except for the amazing rightness of their twins.

This time when he tilted her chin up, she didn't resist. When he brushed his lips across hers, she closed her eyes and leaned in, letting all her thoughts drift away and the feelings wash over her.

Until he lifted his head and gazed into her eyes with a soft, indulgent look and she froze.

He didn't say anything, just stood there with his heart in his eyes.

"I'm sorry, Devin." She took a step back, wishing they were still friends so she could give him a hug and tell him everything would be okay. But she didn't know that. What she did know was that they'd been down this road before. The only thing that was different was there was more on the line.

She took another step back, her chest tight. "I'm so sorry, but we can't do this, Devin. *I* can't do this."

"I know. Really, it's fine." He dropped his hands. His phone rang. He pulled it out of his pocket and looked at the readout. "I'll get this outside."

He was back a minute later, his hand over the receiver, his face gray tinged under his tan. "It's the mayor's assistant. The marshal of the Fourth of July parade got the stomach flu and they'd love 'a couple of former rodeo stars' to fill in."

"We can't do that," she whispered.

"I don't know how to get out of it. It's this afternoon." Even his whisper was miserable.

She rubbed her temples, wishing she could rub away the headache forming behind her eyes. She shrugged. "I mean…okay, sure. Whatever."

His eyes on hers, he took his hand off the mouthpiece and put the phone back to his ear. "Okay, yeah, we can do that." To Lacey, he mouthed, "I'm sorry."

Lacey sighed, every fiber of her being rebelling against acting the happy couple. She tossed the oven mitts onto the counter. "Yeah. Me, too."

Staging took place on the circular drive of the Red Hill Springs Middle School. Devin and Lacey were assigned the back of a candy-apple-red 1988 Corvette convertible that spent most of each year in Harvey Haney's barn. Someone had glitter-glued Marshal onto poster board and stuck it to each side of the car.

Lacey, in bright red boots, jeans and a cowboy hat, looked the part of a Memorial Day parade marshal. She was all smiles as one of the members of the marching band stuck his trumpet under his arm to help her into the back of the car. Her nearly waist-length hair bounced in loopy curls that made Devin's fingers itch to touch it.

The chaos on the middle school lawn was barely leashed, not even close to being controlled, when a woman in jeans and a navy blazer stopped next to him. "Devin Cole? I'm Wynn Grant… Mayor Grant. Thanks so much for filling in at the last minute. When I heard from Garrett that you and Lacey were in town, I just knew you'd be perfect to fill in."

"Glad I know who to blame. Nice to meet you." Familiar reflexes kicked in and he flashed a grin, tipping his hat forward over his eyes. Behind him, he heard Lacey smother a laugh with a cough. "Have you met Lacey yet?"

Wynn Grant turned to Lacey with a smile. "Thank you so much for letting us talk you into this. You're a champ."

"So, are there any instructions?" Devin asked.

"Just smile and wave. If you want to throw candy, there are a couple of buckets of fireballs on the seat."

"Yes, ma'am." About that time, Devin heard three sharp whistles. The marching band began to play and the volunteer firefighters started up the sirens.

The mayor was gesticulating and her lips were moving but he had no idea what she was saying. Finally, a pickup truck pulled up beside her with a similarly glit-tered sign that said Mayor stuck to the side doors and at least a dozen kids in the truck bed.

Mayor Grant said goodbye, or at least Devin as-sumed that was what she said, and Devin climbed into the back of the red Corvette beside Lacey. Mr. Haney, in his ever-present overalls, slid into the driver's seat, adjusted the rearview mirror and gave them a small salute.

The line ahead of them started to move, and just outside the gates to the school stood their first parade spectators. They looked so happy, sitting in lawn chairs, decked out in their red, white and blue. Flags fluttered on the lampposts all down Main Street. And for the first time since Mom and Dad died, Devin felt connected to his hometown.

His mom had loved all the little celebrations they had in Red Hill Springs. He'd grouse and complain when she made him put on a Santa hat or a patriotic shirt and hauled him down to Main Street, but he'd loved the festivities, too. Mostly he loved hanging out with his friends and gathering up enough candy to fill a pil-lowcase. But that memory led to his mom, too, with her cool hand on his forehead later when he moaned and groaned with a stomachache.

Lacey nudged him with her elbow. "Where's that signature move? Your fans are waiting."

He shot her a grin from under the brim of his hat, a move he'd made hundreds of times for the cameras, and she laughed.

"There it is. Give the people what they want." She picked up her hat by the crown and waved it as they passed a few people sitting in their front yard with what looked like a bag of boiled peanuts.

He snickered. "Talk about a signature move."

She gave him a saucy shrug as she placed her hat back on her head. "Just how does this thing end?"

Devin waved to a few kids who were shouting his name and then leaned close to her ear so she could hear him. "At the town square for a barbecue."

As the parade passed, people would walk behind it, or get in their cars and drive to the square. There were inflatables and games for the kids and a band playing music for dancing.

The sun was starting to set as they pulled into the parking lot. The string lights had been turned on over the dance floor and Mayor Grant was there to meet them. She helped Lacey out of the car and said, "You guys are almost off the hook. I'm just going to introduce y'all and then we'll have the opening dance and you'll be released to eat as much barbecue as you like—on the house.

"Wait...dance?" Lacey's feet stalled out and she shot him a get-me-out-of-this look.

"Mayor, I think you and your husband should open the dance floor, as the 'first couple' of Red Hill Springs." Devin looked down at his cane. He wasn't sure exactly how he was going to be able to pull this off.

"It's tradition that the marshal opens the dance floor." Wynn Grant glanced down as she followed his gaze to his cane and her words trailed off. "I mean, unless you don't think you can?"

He had no idea if he could, really, and that fact was galling. "No, I'm fine. Of course we'll do it."

Devin limped onto the stage with Lacey beside

him as the remainder of the parade stragglers gathered around. The screams and laughter of kids jumping in the bouncy houses filtered through the band's soft country music.

Wynn tapped the mic and cleared her throat. "Now, some of y'all know that we asked these rodeo sweethearts to be the marshals of the parade at the very last minute and they were nice enough to agree. So, I'd like to introduce four-time world champion barrel racer Lacey Jenkins and three-time world champion saddle bronc rider Devin Cole."

There were some whistles and cheers. Devin took off his hat and gave a little head bow. He held his hand out to Lacey, who curtsied to the crowd.

Mayor Grant said, "I've just learned that Devin and Lacey are newlyweds, so how awesome is it that they'll be opening the dance floor for us tonight?" She half turned to the band. "Take it away, boys."

As the band started to play, Devin wanted to fall straight through the dance floor. He was pretty sure that if there were an award for World Champion of Awkward Moments, he would be sporting a brand-new belt buckle. He painstakingly made his way down the stairs and leaned his cane against the stage.

As he held his hands out to Lacey, he knew she was thinking he'd never turn away from a challenge, even when it was the right thing to do. She had every right to be mad, but she didn't leave him standing there. Instead, she stepped into his arms as the band sang about forever.

He looked into her eyes and smiled, shaken as his memory transported him back to Vegas. The same song was playing, but Lacey'd had a very different look in her eyes then. Instead of wariness, there was trust. Instead of careful conversation, there'd been laughter. Devin had twirled her out and when she spun back into his arms, she'd fit like she belonged there.

He'd blacked out almost everything that happened that night—the night they got married—but this moment he remembered. Because from the time he entered rehab, that dance became his anchor.

The moment *before* he hit rock bottom.

How was it that marrying Lacey was both the best and worst thing he'd ever done? His heart ached, his chest tight with emotion. She was his forever person. He knew it. But he also knew that back then he hadn't owned what it took to stick around.

She knew it, too. And that's why he couldn't be offended that she looked like she'd rather be in a pit of snakes than dance with him in front of the whole town. Or kiss him in the kitchen.

Of course she didn't want to be with him. Because he was definitely the worst decision she'd ever made.

He led her into a twirl under his arm and brought her back in, lacing his fingers with hers with a smile just for her. When she laid her head on his shoulder, he slid his hand up the small of her back and just held her.

Devin didn't know what the future held. But he loved her. That much, at least, he knew.

A firecracker popped a few feet away and as Devin jerked his head around his feet stumbled. Without missing a beat, Lacey caught him, balancing the both of them. And in that second, his resolve stumbled, too.

He could stay sober, but he couldn't fix what was broken. His grandpa used to say, "Devin, you can't make a silk purse out of a sow's ear." As a kid, he'd thought that was ridiculous. Because who wanted a silk purse anyway?

But Devin wanted Lacey to have the silk purse. He wanted her to have everything she needed, the best of everything. As much as he wanted to deny it, he couldn't. He wasn't the best. At anything.

And Lacey deserved so much more.

# Chapter Eight

Lacey arranged small bunches of daisies in the buckets lining the bed of the old red Chevy truck. She finished the scene off with a chalkboard sign that indicated two dollars. The weather was warm and humid but the breeze kept it from being oppressive.

Devin was being uncharacteristically quiet. Perched precariously on a step stool, he leaned forward to hang her handmade-quilt-square bunting from the edges of the tin roof.

He wobbled as he reached out with the staple gun, and she flinched. "Maybe we should wait for Garrett to put that up."

"I don't need you to baby me, Lacey. I can put up the bunting without you hovering every second."

She pressed her lips together to keep from saying what she wanted to say, which was that he was an idiot. Instead, she took a deep breath and tried another tack. "What I mean is that with two sets of hands, it would be easier."

Not to mention safer.

"No."

Okay, then. She mentally raised her hands in defeat as she backed away from the building, but she didn't exhale until Devin had the bunting secured without killing himself.

She gave it a critical eye. "The bunting is really cute. It gives the place the feeling that it's been here awhile. I think the truck needs to come back about a foot, but other than that, once the vegetables are in the bins, we're ready to go."

He got off the step stool, hopping on his good foot until he had his balance. He was so stubborn. "I'll push the truck back."

"Devin, wait. Let Tanner help you." She bit her bottom lip, waiting for the response. She knew her comment wasn't going to go over well.

He shot her a glaring look. "No."

Lacey put herself between Devin and the truck. "Look. I don't know what you're trying to prove, but what you're about to prove is that your ankle can't handle the pressure and you're going to be in so much pain that you won't be able to walk at all."

She gave him the look she'd gotten from her dad a million and one times. The look that said, *you better think before you argue.*

He held her gaze another ten seconds before he dropped his head with a sigh. "I'm sorry. I'm just so… frustrated. I almost fell at the dance last night. I would have if you hadn't caught me."

Hands on hips, she said, "And?"

He shrugged. "I guess I wanted to prove to you that I can do what you need me to do. And I know I can't. I work around the farm all day and do what has to be done, but by the time I get home from my meeting I'm exhausted. My ankle hurts. And I can't sleep."

"Why didn't you say something before now?"

He looked so miserable. "Because I don't know how I'm going to do this."

"What, Dev?" She was so afraid he was going to say be sober. She couldn't imagine how much pain he was in, but she felt like she was seeing the real Devin for the first time and it would kill her to lose him now.

And that thought itself was something she needed to put away for later. Right now Devin needed her to focus.

"We're about to have two babies. How am I going to help you? I can barely move by nine o'clock at night. And how will I walk a baby? If I have one hand on my cane, I can't pat a baby or even hold it right."

"Devin, no." She shook her head, reaching for him, but he stepped away.

"I'm serious, Lacey. What if I stumble or, God forbid, fall while I'm holding one of them and you're not there to catch me?"

She could think of only one way to allay his fears. Show him that he could do it. "Come in the house with me right now."

"I don't want to go in the house. I'm moving the truck because that's what you said you wanted. So that's what I'm doing." He scowled. "I don't want to talk about this anymore."

"Come in the house. This is more important than the truck." She started for the house without looking back and after a minute she could hear his uneven gait as he followed her across the lawn, grumbling under his breath.

When they got into the house, she went into the

kitchen and poured a glass of milk and picked up a cookie from the ones she'd made this morning. She handed him the cookie. "Here. Eat this. I think maybe your blood sugar is low. You're acting kind of hangry."

He narrowed his eyes at her as she started digging through the basket of clothes that Jordan had brought over, but he took a bite.

"I know that thing's in here somewhere." She dumped out the basket. "Ah. Here it is."

She held up a limp loop of fabric. "This is how you hold a baby when you don't have any hands."

"I'm…not sure I'm following you."

"Just give me a second, Devin." He huffed out a breath and she had to smother a giggle. He sounded exactly like his pouty horse when Reggie was miffed about something. "Hold your arms out."

"I thought you wanted me to eat the cookie."

She stopped and raised one eyebrow.

He shoved the whole thing in his mouth.

"That's mature. Now hold your arms out."

This time he did as she asked, one corner of his mouth pulling into an unwilling smile.

She held up the wrap. "I watched a video. It's not as hard as it seems." She talked out the steps as she acted them out. "Put the tag in the middle of your stomach. Flip the ends around your back and over the opposite shoulders."

He stared at a spot on the wall behind her. "It would be great if I knew what you were doing."

Muttering to herself, she shoved the ends under the first strap she'd made, crossed them around his back again and tied them in the front, all the while trying not to breathe, as his familiar woodsy scent came up to tickle her nose.

She stepped back and looked. Now that she'd done it, she was kind of skeptical that it would work at all. "I think that's right."

Devin opened his mouth and she put up a finger. "Wait. Just let me try it."

Lacey grabbed a couple of shirts and wadded them up into approximately the size of a newborn baby. She made a pouch from the straps across his front and shoved the baby-shaped figure inside. When she secured the "baby" with the original layer of fabric, his mouth dropped open.

Her gaze went to his.

"Look, Ma, no hands," she whispered.

His eyes were dark pools, his lips tight with emotion.

"You're going to be a great dad, Devin. Having a cane isn't going to change that."

He sucked in a shaky breath, took the wrap off over his head and tossed it onto the couch. When he spoke, his voice was husky. "What if they're sad that I'm not like other dads? That I can't shag balls for them or run plays in the front yard?"

"Well, first of all, our kids are not doing anything as dangerous as football…" When he snorted a laugh, she felt vindicated. "You're right. You might not be able to do those things… But you can teach them how to fish. You can tell stories about the rodeo and show them how to ride. How to play guitar. Things only you can teach them."

She faced him, holding him by both arms. "Have you ever seen a kid happier than when their daddy's truck pulls up in the driveway? Babies love their mamas but they lose their minds with joy when daddy gets home. That's not about what you do, it's about who you are."

He looked away, his throat working.

Lacey reached down, picked up the glass of milk from the coffee table and handed it to him. "We have a lot to work through, Dev, but I'm not worried about the kind of dad you're going to be. I know you're going to be amazing."

Devin stood still, the glass in his lax fingers, until he heard the door close behind him. His mind had been buzzing with all the ways he was going to stink as a dad, and she'd answered every one of them with flawless logic.

He was still scared. But maybe he wasn't going to be an utter failure. Maybe he just had to be a little creative.

When he opened the door again, Lacey was sitting in the swing on the front porch with a book. He sat down beside her and toed the swing into motion.

He wanted to say thank you for what she'd said—and done—to help quiet his fears. Instead what came out was, "Your cookies are good."

She gave him a quizzical look, but she smiled. "That makes me happy. Even the colored frosting is all organic, like our produce. I've been thinking we could do flags in July, apples for back to school, pumpkins in the fall, you know, seasonal stuff."

"You're so talented and so creative. Is there anything you've ever done that you're not good at?"

Lacey looked down at her book. She took a quick breath, then paused again before meeting his eyes with a direct, serious look. "I don't think I was a very good friend."

"No, you were a good friend. I was just a really good liar." He sat back and rocked them in silence for a minute, all the tension draining out of his body. "I don't want to lie anymore, Lacey. I don't want to pretend to be something I'm not."

"You don't have to."

He tapped the armrest of the wooden swing with his thumb before saying, "Buck Williams from *Rodeo Roundup* magazine called a few days ago. He wants to do a feature on me and come here to do the interview. I said yes."

Her face flushed and she pushed out of the swing, launching herself to her feet, leaving the pages of her book to flutter in the wind.

"What are you thinking?" he asked.

"I'm not even sure. I want to be happy for you but I'm worried. I'm afraid you haven't given yourself enough time to heal emotionally. And, to be honest, I'm not thrilled about what it means for us when the entire rodeo universe is gossiping about us."

When she turned around, he nodded. "I understand your concern. And I'm not going to talk about us, I promise. I want—need, really—to share about rehab."

"I'd like some time to process this."

The regaining of his feet wasn't as graceful as hers, but he did it, grabbing his cane from the wall for balance. He walked to the other end of the porch and stood beside her, looking out over the grassy pasture where Reggie casually grazed. "Look, Lacey, I'm not ashamed about this."

He paused. "That's not right. I am, but shame is what keeps people from seeking help. Getting addicted to painkillers after an injury happens a lot. People hide the fact that they're addicted because they think it's a personal failing. In reality, it's much more complicated than that."

Her eyebrows drew together in thought, but still she didn't say anything. And suddenly, he was doubting himself all over again. Doubting *them*. How could it possibly work out with Lacey? She'd acted like she understood him, but maybe she was just waiting for him to fail. Or maybe she'd never had any intention of trying to make things work.

But that was the fear talking again. He remembered the way she'd wrapped the baby sling around him a few minutes ago and released the breath he'd been holding. "I promise you this. Doing the interview is not about fame and it's not about getting back in the game. It's about letting other people like me know they're not alone."

Her hand was on her stomach, where their babies were growing, and tears gathered in her eyes. "Okay. If this is important to you, then I support you. When is he coming?"

"Tomorrow."

Devin paced the floor inside the farmhouse as he waited for the reporter to arrive. He'd done hundreds of interviews, but none of them had been as important, or as tricky, as this one would be.

He hadn't seen Lacey this morning. He wasn't surprised. Being with him came with a whole lot of baggage that she didn't want to unpack in public. And honestly, he didn't blame her.

In his mind, he ran over the points he wanted to make as he answered questions about his time in rehab.

Even though he'd been waiting for it, the knock surprised him.

He took a deep breath, said his millionth prayer and pulled open the door.

"Buck! Man, I've missed you." Devin gave his friend a one-armed hug.

"I've missed you, too. I don't have nearly as much fun now that you're retired. That is, if you're retired?" Buck gave him a speculative look.

"There's no such thing as small talk with you. I forgot about that." Devin laughed. He and Buck had become good friends before one too many concussions had taken Buck out of the competition and into the press. "I thought maybe we could sit outside. You want something to drink?"

"No thanks, I'm good." Buck followed Devin to a small grouping of chairs with a small table between them. As they got seated, he gave the landscape an appreciative look. "It's beautiful here. I can see why you want to be home."

"I'm partial to it." Buck was right. It was a gorgeous summer day. The sky was so wide and so blue, with huge, fluffy white clouds. The trees and the grass brilliant green, not yet faded by the harsh summer sun.

"Thanks for agreeing to do the interview."

Nerves twisted up in Devin's stomach again but he refused to back away from this. The cost of pretending to be something that he wasn't was too high. So he nodded.

Buck pulled out a tape recorder and laid it on the table. "Okay?"

Devin nodded again. "I'm ready."

The door opened and Lacey walked out onto the

porch. She dressed casually in faded jeans and a T-shirt and not a lot of makeup. But her hair tumbled in loose waves around her shoulders and her pregnancy was undeniable.

He appreciated what she was trying to do, but once their relationship was out?

There was no going back.

# *Chapter Nine*

Lacey stood in the open doorway. Joining Devin's interview had seemed like a good idea when she'd thought of it before she went to sleep last night. As she stood here, about to blow their lives wide-open, it didn't seem so smart.

But then she got a look at Devin's flabbergasted face and she knew she was doing the right thing. Because they might have the weirdest marriage in history—and she doubted that—but she'd been his friend first. From here on out, she was going to remember that.

He stood as she stepped onto the porch and closed the door behind her, intercepting her before she could get to Buck. "What are you doing?"

Her gaze locked on his. "Joining your interview."

"Are you sure you want to do this?"

"One hundred percent." So, the number was actually hovering around 40 percent, but Devin didn't need to know that.

Buck's gaze bounced from one of them to the other. "Uh, hey, Lacey."

She gave him a warm hug. "Surprised to see me?"

Buck was still obviously reeling because he was having trouble finding words. "Yeah, I mean, I'd heard rumors that the two of you were together in Vegas, but no one had any evidence of that being true. Until now... I guess?"

"That's outside the scope of this interview. I'm sorry, Buck, but my relationship with Lacey has to be off the record. I want to be transparent about what I'm going through, but Lacey isn't a part of that."

She laid her hand over his, threading her fingers through his. "It's okay, Devin. I'm not trying to hide our relationship."

"So," the reporter said slowly. "You two are..."

"Married." Lacey squeezed Devin's hand. "And pregnant. With twins."

Buck burst out laughing. "I have to hand it to you. You two never do anything halfway." He paused, then looked at Devin, a question in his eyes. "So, she's the reason you went to rehab."

At the same moment Lacey said no, Devin said a firm *yes*.

The word hit her like a blow. "Yes?"

"Yes." He draped his arm across the back of the seat. "She's the reason I went. But she's not the reason I stayed."

Buck smiled and made a note on his pad. "What did make you stay?"

"I knew there were things in my life I didn't deal with. A lot of things, actually. I'd stuffed it down for years, and riding broncs and partying helped with that. But it got bad enough that what I was going to lose was more painful than just dealing with it."

"And did you deal with it?" Buck's question, true to form, was direct.

"Yeah. It's ongoing." Devin's smile tipped up. "Staying sober is a little harder. It means making that choice every day. Every minute sometimes."

"And are you planning a return to rodeo?"

Devin paused. Following his gaze, Lacey knew he was looking at Reggie out in the pasture. The two of them had been an indomitable team. It had to be painful to know you'd never experience that again.

The silence stretched. Finally, Devin looked Buck square in the eyes. "No. I won't be back. I'm grateful for all the fans and everyone who made this part of my life so amazing." He glanced at Lacey. "But my ankle injury took me out of contention and, to be honest, my priorities are a little different now."

A half an hour later, Buck closed his pad and stuck his pencil through the wire closure. "Frankly, I'm glad to see the two of you finally together. Mind if we walk around a little? I'd love to get some photos of you guys before it gets too hot."

So Devin showed Buck around the farm, Lacey's hand firmly in his grip. And for just a while, it felt like old times, like maybe they didn't have so many unresolved questions between them. It gave her a glimpse of how it could be between them on the other side.

She was still so confused about what she wanted. She knew Devin should be involved in the lives of the twins—she'd grown up without a mom and she'd missed that. She wouldn't do that to her babies. But beyond that, she just didn't know.

Being with Devin was so confusing. Despite her anger and hurt, she'd never stopped having feelings for him. She just didn't know what those feelings were, exactly. And she definitely didn't know where she wanted to go with them. Or even if she wanted to go somewhere with them. Loving Devin and trusting him were two very different things.

Buck stopped them by the pasture where Reggie was spending his retirement. "Let's take one right here by the fence. Face each other so the people can see that baby belly, Lacey."

Warmth rushed into her cheeks, but she did as he asked.

"Now, I want to see a kiss."

"Nope." Devin's response was quick and firm. But his arm snaked out and he pulled her toward him. She laughed as her balance shifted. He put his hand over hers on her belly to help her stay upright and he kissed her on the forehead.

Her throat tight, she took a step back, but she left her hand on his. For years, she'd dreamed that one day Devin would look at her like that, with his heart in his eyes. She wished she could be sure that it was real and not just Devin still hiding what really was instead of sharing the truth.

As Buck packed up his camera, they walked him back to his rental car. Devin paused, his arm around Lacey. She was aware—too aware—of the warmth of his fingers curled around her waist.

Devin picked up the conversation. "I just want to say this before you go, Buck. I did this interview because addiction is something a lot of people try to keep in the dark. That's twenty-one million Americans trying to hide their substance abuse problem."

Buck nodded. "What do you want to say to people who might be struggling?"

"It's time to bring it to the light. Having to ask for help is not something to be ashamed of. It's not a weakness." He glanced at the barn, where it seemed he could see his dad in the entrance. Boots on. Sleeves rolled up. Dusty hat.

A lump formed in Devin's throat and he swallowed hard. "My dad used to say strength doesn't come from doing what you already know you can do. Real strength comes from overcoming things you never thought you could."

"That's the wisdom of experience right there. And it's a good word." Buck shook Devin's hand. "Thanks, man. Lacey, anything you want to add?"

Her shoulders trembled and Devin pulled her tighter against his side. She looked up at him as she spoke. "Just that... I'm proud of Devin. What he's doing is hard, and instead of trying to pretend his life is perfect, he's sharing what he's been through so other people don't have to feel so alone."

Devin cleared his throat as Buck pinched the bridge of his nose between his fingers. "Now y'all have gone and made me cry. Thanks a lot. I hope I'll be able to do this justice, Dev. It was really great to see y'all. Now I've got to go so I don't miss my plane." Buck got in his car and slammed the door, sending them a little wave as he drove down the driveway.

For a moment, they just stood and watched Buck drive away. They'd done hundreds of interviews together, but this felt different—was different.

Devin sighed. "Well, that's done. Nowhere left to hide. I feel both relieved and nauseous."

She nudged him with her shoulder. "That sounds about right to me. And I meant it when I said I was proud of you."

"You being there made it easier. Better." He waved a hand, as if he could wave away the emotion that all the talking had dredged up. "Come on, let's go find a cup of coffee."

Lacey turned back to the house, Devin's arm still around her waist. She should step away—she knew she should—but the peace between them at this moment was too good to let go of just yet.

A gust of wind came out of nowhere, her hair whipping around her face. When she could finally see again, she realized Devin was focused on something over her shoulder.

She turned around to look. The clouds were dark and building, their color ranging from charcoal to ashy gray. "That doesn't look good."

"I don't know which way that's going but it looks like the bottom's about to fall out."

Tanner came roaring down the lane in the all-terrain vehicle they used for farm work. He stopped beside them and jumped out. "There's a whole line of storms moving in from the gulf and the fence is down in the back field. Half the cows are out and one of them just dropped twins. I have to get the cows in and fix the fence before we lose our stock in this storm."

As he spoke, he walked into the barn, Devin right behind him. Lacey squinted toward the south just as a lightning bolt streaked across the sky.

"I'm going with you." Devin grabbed rain gear from the tack room and shrugged into it.

"I'll take care of it." Tanner grabbed the toolbox and went right back out the door.

Devin followed him. "I can help."

Tanner slid into the seat of the ATV and cranked it up. "I have enough to worry about out there. I can't be responsible for you, too."

He didn't wait for an answer, just whipped the vehicle into a turn and drove off.

Devin walked through the barn to the door that led to the pasture. He stuck his finger and thumb into his mouth and let out a piercing whistle, calling Reggie.

Lacey didn't try to stop Devin. She knew if she wasn't pregnant she'd be saddling up, too. Tanner needed help whether he wanted to accept it or not. And while Devin was injured, Tanner couldn't ask for a better team than Devin and Reggie to have his back.

With Reggie tacked up and ready to go, Devin stuck his good foot in the stirrup and swung his other leg over the saddle. Reggie sidestepped as Devin settled in the saddle, and Lacey wasn't sure if the big horse was excited to be going out or nervous because of the storm.

"You'll get inside?" Devin pulled his hat down over his eyes as thunder crashed. "I've got to go."

Rain pelted the tin roof of the barn. She raised her voice over the noise. "I'll be fine. Go."

She watched him ride out of the barn into the storm, lowering his head against the wind and the rain, and looking like some kind of hero out of an old-timey cowboy movie.

Lightning streaked the sky, splitting into multiple veins and racing to the ground. She picked up his cane and sprinted for the house, completely drenched by the time she reached the porch. She shook the water out of her hair and opened the door, pausing to look back, down the road.

Devin was out of sight, but he wouldn't be out of her mind. She'd be praying nonstop until he and Tanner returned to the house safe and sound.

Devin couldn't see through the driving rain. He wound through the woods behind the field. He'd caught sight of Tanner trying to bolster the fence as he'd passed the field. The cows were strewn from here to the property line.

He understood why Tanner said what he did. Devin wasn't mad. He just knew that if he was going to stay here on the farm, things weren't going to work that way. Devin may be injured but he had to be useful. If he wasn't, he may as well give up.

Besides, all discussion about his skills aside, Reggie was the best cow horse Devin had ever seen. It would be criminal not to let him use his talents.

Reggie didn't hesitate. He knew exactly what to do to get the cows to move the direction Devin wanted them to go. And when one cow started moving, others noticed and started to tag along. The new mama with her calf was under a tree near the fence line and Devin turned her back toward the other cow. "Come on, Mama, you know you want to go home."

Thunder rumbled in the distance. He couldn't tell if the storm was coming or going. But the rain had slacked off, leaving the farm in a kind of quasi dusk, just enough light that he could see another cow with one of the older spring calves wandering off. He nudged Reggie to go after the cow, running just even with her until she saw him.

She was stubborn and took a few more steps the other way, but Devin moved Reggie slowly forward until the cow acknowledged she wasn't going on a walkabout tonight and slowly turned back to join the rest of the small herd.

Their stock was valuable. They couldn't afford to lose even one. He rode the back of the herd until they found Tanner finishing up the repairs on the fence. Devin sidled up to Tanner as the cattle turned into the pasture, moseying in their no-hurry way. Tanner, his hands encased in yellow leather gloves, used the pliers to attach the wire fencing to the post. He'd have to come back out tomorrow to make sure it held and that it was secure. But for tonight, it would keep the cows where they belonged.

Tanner made a final twist with the pliers and looked up at Devin. Raindrops were hitting his face and clinging to his lashes but he didn't seem to notice. "I could've done it without you."

"You're welcome." Devin tamped down his annoyance. Tanner was on his own path.

Tanner took his hat off and rubbed his sleeve across his eyes. "We're missing one of the new calves. He's a twin and Mom was rejecting him. He doesn't stand a chance out there alone. Want to help me look?"

"What color is he?"

"Chocolate brown, some white on the face." Tanner looked into the field where the cows were acting like they'd never left. "There's another storm right behind this one. We're not gonna have long."

"Let's go." Devin clucked to Reggie and wheeled around, heading back into the rangy pines while Tanner cranked up the ATV. Visibility was terrible, rain still dripping from the sky and the trees, the clouds dark and ominous.

They split up, Tanner starting on one end of the pasture in the ATV, Devin on the other on horseback, searching to the property line until they met in the middle. He yelled to Tanner, "Anything?"

"No sign. You up for another pass?"

"We're not leaving him out here, so yeah."

This time they worked out from the center, and about five minutes into the second search, Devin heard Tanner yell. He turned Reggie and met Tanner coming back toward him, carrying the calf in his arms. He was tiny and limp. Devin wasn't even sure he was breathing. "Is he alive?"

"I think so. Barely. We need to get him warm and dry and fed. Can you take him in while I check the rest of the fence?"

"Of course."

Tanner handed the little cow up to Devin, who laid him gently across his lap. "I'll take care of him."

He nudged Reggie with his heels. "Let's go, bud."

As Reggie picked up the pace, the little calf didn't move. Devin rubbed his neck with one hand. "Come on, baby, you can make it. You're tough."

Devin was exhilarated and exhausted by the time he wheeled Reggie into the barn. He slid off the horse and onto his good foot, hopping a little until he could stand. The calf slid right off and into his arms. Devin laid him gently onto a blanket and then quickly untacked Reggie, lifting the saddle off last and putting it over the saddle stand in the tack room.

Lacey had clearly been back in the barn because there was fresh hay and feed in the largest stall. She was always thinking about the other person. He was torn between wanting to yell at her for going back out in the storm and wanting to kiss her for knowing he would be exhausted.

He led Reggie into the stall and gave him a good rub before closing the door. "You've still got it, old man."

Lifting the calf into his arms, he struggled to his feet. Every step was agony on his wrecked ankle. Since he didn't have a choice, he just kept taking steps, one at a time, until he was at the door to the house.

Lacey was there opening it before he could even try to figure out how he was going to knock. She pulled him into the house, getting her shoulder underneath his and wrapping her arm around his waist for support. "Is he okay?"

"Don't know." Devin was out of breath. "Mama rejected him and he's wet and cold. Dehydrated, too, probably."

He laid the calf on the rug in the living room and rubbed the small face between his palms.

Lacey ran to the laundry room and came back with an armful of towels, warm from the dryer. She knelt beside Devin, handing him a towel. She used another as a blanket and a third to begin drying the baby's hindquarters. "Do you have colostrum?"

He glanced up at her. "Yeah. There's a cabinet in the laundry room where Tanner keeps all the meds. We've got a couple of bottles and the milk replacer on the bottom shelf."

"I know what to do. I've raised at least a dozen bottle babies in my time. You go get dry before you get sick, too."

Devin looked up ruefully. "Do you know where my cane is?"

Asking her for it was hard enough, and to her credit, she made no comment, just handed him his cane from the corner of the room. With the cane taking his weight, he slowly gained his feet. "Thanks, Lacey."

At his side, she turned her face to his. "When you get through changing, I made some taco soup. It's warming on the stove."

He stared into her brown eyes, so clear and expressive. If things had been different, he would have pulled her close and kissed her until those beautiful eyes melted on his.

She put a hand to her hair. "What? Do I have something on my face?"

Devin shook his head. "No. I just like being with you. That's all."

A silence hung in the living room, except for the sound of the rain on the roof and the soup simmering on the stove. Lacey put her hand to his cheek, caressing it with her thumb. She hesitated, maybe afraid to say something she would regret. Finally, she said, "I like being with you, too."

*If wishes were fishes*, his mother used to say. She would never finish her sentence. If wishes were fishes… *what*? He'd said that often enough to her as he was growing up. She would shrug with a smile and tell him one day he would understand. She was right. Now he knew. Fish were plentiful. Wishes coming true, not so much.

With his slow, halting gait, he started up the stairs. If he was blessed enough that one of those wishes came true, it would be that Lacey would trust him with her heart.

Because if he had another chance, he would guard it with his life.

# Chapter Ten

Lacey roused slowly, feeling like she was climbing out of a deep hole and someone was bumping her legs as she tried to climb. She squinched her eyes tightly closed, waving the person away with a grumble. "Stop it—I'm tired."

She started climbing again but the nudges to her legs continued. Struggling to a seated position on the couch, she opened her eyes and looked down. Big dark brown eyes with the longest lashes she'd ever seen blinked at her before a smooth, wet tongue streaked out and wrapped around her wrist.

"Hi, baby." Laughing, she leaned forward and scratched the calf between the ears and under the chin. He reminded her of a puppy—a really, really big puppy—wanting to play. "Oh, you are cute. You remind me of Sadie."

Hearing her name, the dog lifted her head, then laid it back down with a subtle groan. Yeah, it had been a long night, but the little calf was standing on wobbly legs and bumping her knees with his head, trying to get her to feed him. Thank goodness. One more thump from the calf's nose and Lacey began the process of heaving her off-balance body to stand up. "Okay, okay. I'm getting up."

Thunder rumbled in the distance and, through the half-closed blinds, Lacey caught a glimpse of the pearl-gray sky. So, the storms were still rolling through. Neither she nor Devin had gotten much sleep. They'd put the little calf on one of Sadie's dog beds. He'd been so weak he couldn't lift his head, much less have the strength to drink from a bottle. It had been so rushed and so touch-and-go that they hadn't even wanted to name him.

She and Devin had taken turns giving him "doses" of colostrum with a turkey baster and Sadie had mothered him, too, licking his face and cleaning him up. Lacey had taken a deep breath and girded herself for the heartbreak of his not making it through the night. She was so happy she'd been wrong.

He'd apparently gotten enough calories for a jump start because he was now trying to munch her fingers, looking for one that would feed him.

Lacey pushed to her feet as Devin stepped out of the kitchen, carrying tongs and wearing a bright red apron. "I thought I heard some noise out here. Well, how about that? Nemo is up."

"Nemo?"

"We were bonding in the middle of the night and I had to call him something. He was lost and we had to find him? Get it?" He pointed the tongs at her. "You wanna try to do better?"

"Nope. I'm good with it. But just so you know, I'm naming the babies." The calf butted her in the backside. "We better get Nemo a bottle before he has a meltdown."

He grinned. "Already got one made. I was feeling hopeful."

"I'll check on breakfast while you try the bottle. I don't want him to decide he needs to head-butt the babies."

"Oh, good thought. The spoon for the grits is by the stove."

"Got it." She lifted the lid to the pot and backed away from the steam before giving it a stir. "I've never had a calf in the house, but I'm an expert at bottle-feeding. My dad doesn't believe in feeders, so we always had at least a few bottle babies each season."

Tanner stepped into the kitchen from the back porch, taking off his wet hat. "Hand-feeding is better. It doesn't last long and the calves are healthier. He looks like he's getting his strength back."

Devin held the bottle where Nemo could reach it and turned to the side so he wouldn't get head-butted in a sensitive area. She grinned. Seemed like Devin had some experience with bottle-feeding calves, as well.

Tanner knelt down and when Nemo grabbed hold of the teat, he steadied the calf's head so he could stay latched on. Nemo sucked down the bottle in about two minutes flat and knocked into Devin's hip, wanting more.

"So here's a question—where are we going to put him now that he's on his feet?" Tanner looked up from where he knelt on the floor. "Any thoughts?"

"He needs a bib."

"That's your thought?" Tanner blinked seriously.

Lacey tossed him a dishrag, which he used to wipe the little cow's slobbery mouth. When Tanner thought she wasn't looking, he gave Nemo a rub behind the ears before standing up. Lacey smiled to herself. *I see you, tough guy.*

"These are almost ready." She took the lid off the pot of grits and stirred it again from the bottom, fixing her gaze on Devin. "What if we put him in the ring next to the barn?"

Devin shrugged. "It could work. We're going to have to get the calf a buddy of some kind or he's going to be lonely…and loud."

"No more animals." Tanner pointed to himself. "Not Noah," he said, then gestured to the barn. "Not an ark. I mean it, Devin. He can have Sadie."

The dog, who'd moved her sleeping position from the living room to under the kitchen table, huffed softly as she heard her name. Tanner patted her head. "See, she's already looking forward to it."

He grabbed a biscuit with ham from the pan where they were warming. "Put the calf in the laundry room on the dog bed until we're sure he's stable and then we'll move him outside."

"When it stops raining," Lacey interjected into the conversation, then immediately felt like she should turn around and see who gave that order to Devin's brother.

Tanner stopped and stared at her for a few seconds. Long enough for Devin to notice and look up, his eyes traveling from Tanner to Lacey and back again.

"When it stops raining," Tanner conceded.

She smiled. "Perfect. No grits for you?"

"No, I'm going to take the opportunity since it's raining to pay some bills." He grimaced. "Or open some bills, anyway. Which reminds me, Devin, there's a stack of mail that's been piling up on my desk for you. Can you come and get it?"

"Coming." Devin picked up his cane, leaned toward Lacey and stage-whispered. "I want grits."

She elbowed him. "I know. Can one of you take the calf to the laundry room on your way out, please?"

Tanner picked up the calf with a grunt. "He's going outside as soon as it stops raining." In answer, Nemo laid his head on Tanner's shoulder.

Lacey pressed her lips together. Tanner was toast. He didn't even have a chance against those long brown eyelashes. And the calf? She was pretty sure it already thought it was a dog. With quick, efficient motions, she loaded their bowls with grits and sprinkled cheese over the top. She put a ham biscuit on the plate with some of the melon she'd cut up last night while the guys had been out searching for the calf.

Devin came back with a stack of mail that he tossed on the table. "I'm starving. That looks delicious, thank you."

They ate quietly, Devin tucking into the grits like he'd never seen food before. Lacey ate her grits and biscuit and sat back, sipping her single cup of coffee.

Devin picked up his mug and leaned back in his chair, shoulders slumping. "I'm exhausted. How much do you think we were up last night?"

"I don't know. We were both awake until around four, I think. I passed out on the couch after that. Did you sleep at all?"

"About an hour, I think, maybe two, if you count dozing in between trying to feed Nemo."

"I'm so tired." Lacey stared blankly at a spot on the wall. "This is what the next year of our life is going to be like."

"At least. What about when they're teenagers? We can't sleep then."

She turned wide eyes on him. "I didn't know night

before last was the last time I'd get to sleep for eighteen years. I should've enjoyed it more."

Devin laughed. "I have an idea... We'll take turns sleeping."

Lacey looked down into her mug. Joking with Devin reminded her of how things used to be. As much as she loved it, she couldn't take things for granted anymore. He was trying, but they had a long way to go before she would trust that he would stay if things got hard. And things would get hard.

He'd been the life of the party and the darling of the rodeo circuit for the last five years. She'd been in love with him longer than that. But when he left her in that hotel room alone, it broke something between them. Something she wasn't sure she could get back.

She took a deep breath, drained her remaining coffee and pushed away from the table. Sitting here, laughing with Devin... It was a little too much like actually being married. And that realization just made things hurt worse.

Devin's smile slowly faded. He didn't know what happened. One second they'd been commiserating about the state of their sleep for the next eighteen years, and the next she was contemplating the bottom of her coffee mug as if it held the secrets of the universe.

But that wasn't exactly true. He did know what happened. She was scared. And it was because of him. He just wished it didn't cause an ache in his heart every time she pulled away from him.

He grabbed the pile of mail and tried to focus. If he didn't sort through it, Tanner would be disappointed in him. And he was doing everything possible to make sure that didn't happen.

He flipped through the envelopes.

There were a few small outstanding bills he needed to pay. A request from an acquaintance—someone who hadn't been notified of Devin's change in circumstances—for a donation to charity.

And a flier from the hospital. "Hey, what's this?"

He pulled the sticker loose and unfolded the paper. "Magnificent Multiples class. Cool. It says here they cover must-know topics such as crib safety, choosing a car seat, scheduling—do babies really have schedules?" When she didn't answer, he went on. "Also what to expect in labor and delivery and a tour of the hospital. It says here, not mandatory but strongly recommended. Do you want me to sign us up?"

Devin glanced up. Lacey's face had gone white. "Lacey?"

She blinked, shuddered and focused her eyes on him. "I can't go to that."

Devin studied her face. He knew she was not a fan of hospitals, to say the least, but this was just a class. "They're just gonna teach us how to make a bottle and change a diaper. No big deal."

"The class is at the hospital."

He frowned at the paper. "Well, yeah, but looking at the map here, it's barely in the door."

"I'm not doing it." She stood, picked up their plates and dumped them in the sink.

"I don't think they're gonna tell you the delivery is off if we don't go, but it says here that they strongly encourage participation."

She didn't say anything to that, just turned on the water and started washing the dishes to load them in the dishwasher.

Devin stood up, grabbed his cane and walked over behind her, putting his hands on her shoulders. Her muscles were concrete. "Lacey, talk to me."

Instead of answering him, she spun, walking away from him, out of the kitchen and straight out the front door.

He braced himself with both hands on the counter. Lacey was one of the most self-confident people he'd ever met. She never hesitated to reach for the brass ring. And she should know this class was necessary.

With a sigh, he flipped on the electric kettle and picked up where she left off rinsing the dishes in the sink. Okay, so she was freaked out by hospitals. He knew that. He'd sworn often enough not to let the EMTs take her to one unless her life was hanging in the balance. He just didn't know why.

Putting the last dish in the dishwasher, he closed it up and turned it on. No matter what was motivating Lacey's fear, he knew her and he had to believe she was afraid of the hospital for a good reason.

The only problem he could see—and it was a big one—was that she was going to have to give birth at some point.

With his cane in one hand and a mug of herbal tea in the other, he made his way to the front porch. Rain dripped from the eaves, dark clouds still swirling in the sky.

Lacey was sitting in the chair at the far end of the porch, where they'd had their interview with Buck. Was that just yesterday?

It seemed like a lifetime ago.

"Hey." He approached her slowly and held out the mug. "Sorry it's not coffee."

"Thanks." She took the mug. "Wanna sit?"

He eased down next to her on the love seat, put his arm across her shoulders and studied the rain. "I'm not going to pretend that I understand what's going on in your head right now."

Lacey's head dropped back against his arm and she sighed. "Probably for the best."

"So, I'm not trying to state the obvious, but sooner or later, we're most likely going to have to go to the hospital at some point."

"I know." Her voice was small and quiet, so unlike her that he looked down at her again.

"What if I make the reservations? Going for the class might be a good way to test the waters. And when you're ready to talk about it, *if* you're ready to talk about it, I'll be here."

"I don't think the waters are going to be very inviting, but we can try."

"Yeah?" When she nodded, he hugged her closer to him. "I say we stop talking about the bad place and discuss what we're going to name our little team ropers, since the big ultrasound is coming up this week and apparently you don't think I'm good at naming things."

"You're not." She didn't even try to hide her laugh. "Do you think they're boys or girls?"

"Well, they can be team ropers either way, but I'm calling boys."

She shook her head. "Nah, I'm pretty sure they're girls."

Devin scoffed at that. "Have you seen me and my brothers? We don't have girls in our family."

"Guess we'll see."

"Guess we will."

She tapped his knee. "If you're right, I'll make breakfast every day for a week."

He raised an eyebrow, his eyes narrowing into a speculative squint. "I get to sleep in?"

"If you're right. Which you're not."

"Okay, so say I'm wrong…"

She grinned. "You have to rub my feet every day for a week."

"Deal. But full disclosure… I'd rub your feet anyway."

"You would?"

"Of course." That she didn't know he would do absolutely anything for her made him feel like a heel. The silence between them stretched. He'd been so focused on "winning" her back that he really hadn't stopped to think about how she actually felt.

Not the part about being mad at him, but the part where she was pregnant and married and nothing was normal for her. At all. "You know, Lace, I've never been where you are, but I bet you feel alone in all this and I do know what that feels like."

She looked up at him and gave her head a small shake. "It's silly to feel alone when I'm here with you and Tanner."

"You can be in the middle of a crowd of people and still feel alone. I know because I lived it. And when you have secrets, you feel like there's a wall between you and the rest of the world."

Her eyes were huge and dark and tears gathered. "I do feel like that sometimes. I want to share this—all of this—with you, Devin. It's why I stayed. I'm just not fully there yet. I'm trying."

"I know you are. I'm trying, too." There was a hot

knot of emotion in his chest and he swallowed hard. "If you need anything—sheesh, this sounds cheesy— but if you need *anything*, I'd be honored if you'd let me help you."

She giggled and rubbed the tears from under her eyes with her thumb and finger. "It does sound cheesy, but thanks. I'm already huge. I have a feeling I'm going to need a lot of help in the next few months."

"I'm here for it."

"I know." She turned her gaze to the pasture, where the grass was glistening in the rain. "How about Prudence for a girl? My first horse's name was Prudence. I really loved that horse."

Devin closed his eyes, rapidly running the scenarios through his mind. One, she was joking and he should laugh. Two, she wasn't joking and if he laughed, her feelings would be hurt. Three... Wait a minute. Her shoulders were shaking. He grinned. "I love Prudence. And it's precious that you would name our baby after your first horse. I'm thinking Elmo for a boy."

She stopped laughing. "Like the fast-food joint or the fuzzy red puppet with the annoying voice?"

"Well, I was thinking of the hamburger place, but now that you mention it, that puppet is downright adorable."

She sat up and glanced back at him from under her lashes. "I'm so glad I know you're kidding. I'm going in to check on Nemo and then, if you don't mind, I'm going to take a nap."

"I don't mind at all. I'll wake you up when lunch is ready."

"Thanks, Devin." She took a few steps toward the

door before turning back. "And thanks for not pressuring me to talk and just being with me. I appreciate it."

"Anytime." When the door closed behind her, he laid his head back against the chair. Their relationship was so tricky. And he was sure he was messing it up every day.

But God had brought him through the worst of his addiction and was with him every single day. He knew God was with him and with Lacey and their babies, too, even through all the confusion.

He wanted everything to be okay with Lacey. He would say he wanted to have the relationship they had before, but that wasn't it. He wanted this relationship. The one they had right now. The one they were building on mutual trust and respect.

And he trusted that God could take what they offered and build them into a family.

His phone rang in his pocket and he looked at the readout. It was Lacey. "Hello?"

"I'm thinking Gomer, like Gomer Pyle, for a boy. I bet he'd be the only Gomer in his kindergarten class."

"I think you are sleep deprived and you need a nap." The last thing he heard before the phone went dead in his ear was her laughing. He chuckled to himself, shaking his head.

His wife was resilient and spunky and beautiful. She was going to be an amazing mother to their babies.

Baby boys… He was sure of it.

He couldn't wait for the ultrasound—not because he wanted to sleep in, but because every step in this wacky journey they were taking brought him closer to his babies and closer to Lacey. And that was exactly where he wanted to be.

## Chapter Eleven

The lights were dim in the exam room. The only sound was the tapping of the technician's fingers on the keys of the computer. Lacey'd had an ultrasound when the doctor first suspected she was carrying twins, of course, but this one was different.

This time Devin sat at her shoulder, wide eyes glued to the monitor, mouth slightly open. He was so into it and she loved seeing his excitement.

The tech moved the wand across her stomach. "So we're almost finished with measurements for Baby A. Oh, here's the little face."

It was a blur of light and shadow, but Lacey could make out eyes and a nose and a mouth. As they watched, the baby rubbed its hand across its cheek. Devin didn't speak, but he slid his hand down her arm and linked his fingers with hers.

"And you want to know the gender?"

"Yes." Lacey glanced up at Devin. He had a twinkle in his eye. She knew he was thinking about the little game they had going.

Once again, the tech moved the wand around, zooming in and out until she stopped and pointed to the screen. "Well, guys, congratulations, Baby A is a boy."

"Yes!" Devin grinned and did a little I-was-right boogie. "I knew it. You're cooking breakfast every day for a week."

Lacey shook her head. He was so predictable. And so ridiculously cute. How was she supposed to use her brain and make wise decisions when he looked at her like that?

"And let's go to Baby B…" The ultrasound technician guided the wand into position. "Baby B is definitely *not* a boy."

"It's a girl?" Lacey's hand crept up to cover her mouth. She looked up at Devin. "One of each okay with you, cowboy?"

"It's one of each." His voice was delighted, his eyes tender as he looked down at her. "I don't know why we never considered that combination."

"Ah, there's Baby B's face. She looks like she's sucking her thumb." The tech pointed to the screen. "And I could be wrong but it looks like she has a dimple."

Devin laughed. "Perfect."

Lacey watched as the technician took the measurements for Baby B, shadows and light stretching and fading on the screen, but she didn't really know what she was seeing. Boy or girl… It was fun to joke and guess, but she really just wanted to know they looked healthy. "They're okay?"

The tech shot her a distracted smile as she continued the scan until finally, with a few more spins of the roller ball on the ultrasound machine and clicking of measurements, they were finished.

The tech handed her a cloth to wipe her stomach.

"Dr. Lescale's going to look over the video and she'll be in to visit with you. You can get dressed."

She left the room, turning the light on as she closed the door behind her.

That wasn't quite an answer.

While Devin waited outside, Lacey dressed quickly, nerves overtaking her stomach. Was the tech not supposed to tell them anything? What if something was wrong?

Dr. Lescale entered the room, laughing at something Devin had said. Surely she wouldn't be laughing if something were wrong with their babies.

Lacey sat in the chair next to Devin, her hands twisted in her lap, as the doctor sanitized and pulled the computer monitor toward her, sliding on her glasses.

After a moment, Dr. Lescale glanced up, looking at them over the top of her reading glasses. "Babies look great. Tracking just right size-wise for their gestational age of twenty weeks. Baby A is a little bit smaller, but that's not unusual. Any questions?"

"They're okay?" Lacey's eyes filled, and she blinked back the tears. "I don't know why, I just all of a sudden got worried."

The doctor picked up a tissue and handed it to her. "Completely normal to have some nerves, especially on a big day like today. But I don't see anything that concerns me. All the signs I look for are good. One thing to be aware of is that it's very rare for twins to go to forty weeks. That's nothing to worry about. Babies born beyond thirty-two weeks normally do very well."

Lacey blinked, suddenly feeling like there was an anvil on her chest. She could possibly have only twelve more weeks of pregnancy to go?

The doctor looked between the two of them. "Any questions so far?"

Lacey looked at Devin. "You have any questions?"

He hesitated. "Yeah. I just want to know… When is the crying going to start?"

Lacey and Dr. Lescale both swung around to stare at him. "Crying?"

Devin shifted uneasily in his chair.

Lacey wanted to be supportive, but inside she was still reeling from the timeline bombshell. She just kept thinking twelve weeks…twelve weeks…twelve weeks. How was that even possible?

"When we were here last time, in the waiting room there was a pregnant lady and she just cried nonstop. Her husband said she'd been crying for weeks."

To Dr. Lescale's credit, she didn't even snicker, just reached across and patted Devin on the hand. "I think you're in the clear on that one. Crying without ceasing is not a normal part of being pregnant."

"Oh, what a relief. I mean, I'm here for it, Lacey. Whatever it is. Even crying."

Lacey shared a look with the doctor, who smiled and made a notation on a sheet of paper and handed it to Lacey.

"I'll see you in one month, before that if you have any concerns."

The door closed behind the doctor and Lacey slumped in the chair. The babies could be here in as little as twelve weeks.

And she still didn't have the foggiest idea what happened after that.

Devin cranked up the truck, shooting Lacey a sideways glance. She'd been so quiet on the walk to the parking lot. "Talk to me. What's going on in your head?"

"I don't want to talk right now, Devin. I just need to figure stuff out."

He started to put the car into gear and then stopped. "No. You don't. Or, to be more exact, you don't have to figure it out on your own. Talk to me."

"Fine. You want me to talk, here goes. If things were different, we wouldn't have to hurry this. We could take our time and we would know if… We would know if this could work out."

"You mean, we would know if I'm going to stay sober."

She lifted her chin. "Yes, partly."

"What's the other part?"

"We don't know *anything*, Devin. We're not just pregnant. There are *actual* twins in here. Actual babies. And in twelve weeks, they could be here and I'm going to be responsible for them." Her voice broke on a sob and she buried her face in her hands.

Devin froze. So, Dr. Lescale had apparently been wrong about the crying. He put his hand on Lacey's shoulder and gave her an awkward pat. "It's gonna be okay, Lace."

She turned on him, her face flushed, eyes flashing angrily. "How can you say that? We don't have anything ready. Nothing. We don't even have names picked out. We're living with your brother!"

Her voice was rising, and he realized he hadn't seen her get upset since she'd come to Alabama. She'd been furious with him then, no doubt, but since then she'd seemed to take everything in stride.

Maybe she was due a freak-out. He felt like freaking out.

They'd been rocking along like everything was fine and like there was no time limit on their relationship, but they'd come face-to-face with that time limit today. When the babies were born, that's when they made the decision. They had to, for all their sakes.

Lacey sniffed and rubbed the tears from under her eyes. "I'm sorry—I'm fine. I want to talk to my dad. I'm just gonna call my dad and tell him that we're having a boy and a girl."

"Of course." Devin put the car in gear and drove out of the parking lot as Lacey placed the call, his head reeling. Emotional whiplash was a real thing. He felt shell-shocked.

He'd been so happy looking at the images of the ultrasound, so overwhelmed with love for those tiny little babies. They had fingers and toes and little faces and they were a part of him and a part of Lacey and, no matter what else happened, they were an amazing gift from God.

And now to realize that Lacey still had so many doubts about their ability to be a family and do what was right… So, she wasn't wrong. They did have a lot of things to settle and they didn't have a lot of time left to do it. But every day they grew closer and knew each other a little better. That had to count for something. Unless it just wasn't enough?

He knew she had family in Oklahoma—he'd met her dad a bunch of times. But hearing her excited voice on the phone talking about the babies terrified him. Before she brought his horse home, she'd planned to have the babies without him. And if they didn't get their relationship figured out soon, she really might leave.

When she did, she'd be taking their babies with her, a thousand miles away from him.

She hung up the phone. "My dad's excited. He's already bought a couple of toddler saddles. I keep telling him he's got a little while before they'll be ready to ride."

Devin guessed maybe it was his turn to be quiet. He didn't know what to say because he knew that, to Lacey, his words had little value. He'd made promises to her that he hadn't kept.

He'd left her. And when she was scared about the future, that was what she remembered. Not all the times they'd come through for each other.

She remembered that he'd left.

Pulling over to the side of the road, he turned to her. "I just want to say right now that if you go back to Oklahoma with our babies…" His voice broke and he had to stop for a minute and get his emotions under control before he could go on. He cleared his throat. "If you go back to Oklahoma with Prudence and Elmo, I'm going with you. Our babies will have a dad."

She stared at him, her expression unchanging. "Prudence and Elmo. What about Gomer?"

Saying their names, she started to laugh again, which frustrated him. He didn't want to hear laughing.

He wanted to hear that they were in this together.

But when her giggles finally quieted, she put her hand on his. "I don't know what I'm doing. I'm a total mess. When the doctor said we could have the babies in twelve weeks, I freaked out. I'm the girl who always has a five-year plan. There are so many questions about our future and we don't have any answers."

"I know." He brushed the hair away from her face with a gentle hand and wished that he could hold her close and tell her everything would be okay and that she would believe it. "I'm scared, too. But we'll figure it out. Just promise me we'll figure it out together."

She drew in a deep breath, her eyes searching his. She raised her shoulders and let them drop. "Okay. I promise."

He put the car in gear and pulled back onto the road. They still had a lot more questions than they had answers, but for this minute at least, they were committed to figuring out the answers together.

"What in the world?"

Lacey looked up at the sound of Devin's voice. There were cars going every which way in front of their farm stand. People were milling about. One couple was taking a selfie by the old red truck filled with flowers.

Devin pulled over. "I guess we better see what's up."

She got out of the car just as Tanner strode out of the crowd with an empty barrel. He had a wide grin on his face. "I just had to refill the corn and the okra. The zucchini brownies and the cookies are *gone*. Wiped out in the first hour."

"I guess I better make some more."

Devin looked dazed. "How did this happen?"

Tanner shrugged. "All I did was a little ten-minute interview with the local paper. They ran it as a feature today. I had no idea so many people would want to come and check it out."

Jordan Sheehan pulled up next to them with her window rolled down, red hair in a high ponytail on her head. "Did you make these cookies, Lacey?"

Lacey nodded.

"The color's really all natural? Levi can't have anything artificial."

"No artificial anything. Unbleached flour, organic sugar, natural coloring, pure vanilla."

Jordan laughed. "Do you know how hard it is to find a cookie that kid can eat? I'm so excited. I'm going to bring him by after school tomorrow."

Lacey flicked her thumb toward the house. "I'm going to make more cookies."

"Hey, you okay? You look a little shell-shocked."

"Yeah. I'm fine. We just had an ultrasound. It's a boy and a girl."

"Aw! Congrats! It's all feeling pretty real about now, isn't it?" Jordan's eyes were kind and Lacey felt tears well up again.

"So real."

"Let's get some lunch soon and I'll tell you the story of how my oldest joined our family. It's a doozy. Let's just say I can relate to how you're feeling right now."

"Lunch sounds great. Text me the details and I'll be there." Lacey waved as Jordan pulled away. She looked around for Devin, who seemed to be deep in conversation with someone, so she started for the house. Apparently, she was going to have to make more brownies and cookies.

She smiled to herself. She'd had her doubts about whether the roadside farm stand would work or not, even though it was her idea. She was so thankful that something, at least, was going according to plan.

A frantic moo detoured her to the round pen, where

she stopped to rub Nemo's head. He was so soft and so sweet. So loud. Devin was right. He needed a buddy.

In the kitchen, she laid all her ingredients out before starting the food processor to shred the zucchini. She had to admit that slamming the vegetable into the processor and whizzing it to shreds was kind of therapeutic.

So the dream of her future wasn't turning out the way she imagined it and she had feelings about it. Big deal. She was about to be a mother. She didn't have time for unresolved feelings. It was time to get rid of them.

The first zucchini she named anger. She jammed it into the processor and turned it on. *Anger, you are shredded.*

She felt a little silly, but oddly enough it really did help.

Next came fear. She held up the zucchini and shook it. *Fear, you do not have a hold over me.* She shredded it.

Sadness, shredded. Disappointment, shredded.

A tear ran down her cheek. She always tried so hard to find the joy in the moments, to look for the good in things. In people. And usually, she was successful.

In this situation, she was just so out of her depth.

She knew she couldn't do it alone. She could shred all those bad feelings and let them go, but she needed something in their place.

She needed Devin. She needed her family.

And she needed Jesus.

She let her eyes drift closed and took a deep breath, just acknowledging the letting go and the filling up. *I need you, Jesus. I need you to fill all the empty spaces I'm feeling right now.*

"Hey." Devin spoke softly from the doorway. "You good?"

She opened her eyes and smiled. And for the first time in a long time, she really did feel better. "I'm okay. Taking out my feelings on the zucchini. Talking to Jesus about it."

Devin's smile deepened. "I know we talked about this a little bit in the car, but I just wanted to tell you that I understand having doubts and being scared. I'm scared every single day. But that doesn't mean that we can't figure out what to do and be good parents. You're gonna be a great mom."

"Thank you." She lifted her shoulders. "You're right. I am scared. I want to be able to take it all in stride but I can't. I need help."

"I've just gotta tell you, when I looked at those babies on the ultrasound today, I thought my heart was gonna explode. I've never loved anything more than I love them. I'd never do anything to jeopardize their safety."

His words were exactly what she wanted to hear. What she needed to hear. She had no doubt that he meant them, just like she'd meant it when she'd said she was letting go of her fear. Somehow she had to stop being afraid that everything Devin said would disappear like dust in the arena.

Somehow she had to learn to believe him again.

# Chapter Twelve

Devin paced in the living room and looked at his watch for the fourteenth time. "We're gonna miss the class if she doesn't hurry. What is she doing in there?"

Tanner looked up from the book he was reading. "Trust me. That's not a question you want to ask."

Devin sucked in a breath, willed himself to be patient and started pacing again. He'd made the reservations for the class two weeks ago when they'd gotten the flier in the mail. She'd agreed to try.

"You're gonna make a hole in the rug with all that tromping back and forth." This time Tanner didn't even look up from his book.

Devin didn't bother answering, just "tromped" back to the opening where the hallway led to the bedroom. "Lacey? We've got to leave or we're going to be late."

The bedroom door opened and she stepped out wearing cropped jeans, a flowy shirt and flip-flops. "You try getting dressed with a beach ball for a belly and then we'll talk."

He wasn't going to give her a chance to back out now. "Makes sense to me. Come on, let's go."

Her steps slowed. "I just want to get something to eat before we leave."

"I packed you a sandwich. It's right here." He scooped up a brown bag that held a sandwich and a bag of chips.

"Oh." She frowned. "I'm going to need…"

"Water?" He picked up an insulated mug. "Right here. Ready to go now?"

"I guess so." Picking up her bag, she followed him out the door.

Devin made the drive to the hospital in a record twenty-four minutes, which he figured was a good practice run for their actual drive to the hospital when Lacey went into labor.

Whipping into the parking lot, he slid into a parking spot. His hand was on the door handle when he looked over at Lacey. "Awesome. We made it with a minute to spare. Let's go…"

The words died on his lips as he looked—really looked—at her. Her hand was clenched around the seat belt, her knuckles white with tension. "Lace? You okay?"

She didn't look at him, just stared straight ahead, giving a quick shake of the head, so small he might've missed it if he hadn't been watching closely.

As her breaths came in quick harsh gasps, he realized she was having a panic attack. Stretching until he could reach the lunch he'd made for her, he dumped the sandwich and chips onto the floor of the truck and handed the empty bag to her. "Breathe into this. Okay?"

Lacey still didn't answer him, but she took the bag and placed it around her lips, closing her eyes.

He'd messed up. He should've believed her when she

said she couldn't do this. This wasn't just regular nerves. Her fear was a living, breathing thing, and whether he knew the reason or not, he knew there was one. He put the keys back into the ignition and started the car, pulling out of the parking lot as quickly as he'd pulled in.

For ten minutes or so, he just drove, letting her fear ebb away and her breathing settle. When she removed the bag and let her head drop against the headrest, he knew she'd gotten through the worst of it.

He spotted an ice cream shop up ahead in a small strip of stores and he pulled up out front. "Let's get some ice cream."

Lacey opened her eyes. "I really just want to go back to the farm."

"So, hear me out and if you still want to go back, I promise I will listen."

She lifted her hands in surrender. "Okay, fine."

"We haven't been on a date. Like, ever, honestly. I want to buy you some ice cream and walk around the park across the street. No agenda, just you and me."

She didn't exactly smile, but her mouth tilted up a smidge. "That actually sounds kind of nice."

"Cool. I could really go for some rocky road. But only if it has actual marshmallows in it. None of that fake marshmallow-ribbon trash."

"I forgot how opinionated you are about ice cream. Maybe I need to rethink this."

"Don't you dare." He grinned and opened the door, grabbing his cane, wishing like crazy he didn't have to.

"I want a double scoop of strawberry."

When he raised an eyebrow, she nudged him with her elbow, laughing when he had to hop to maintain his balance. "You deserved that. Two babies, two scoops. The end."

A few minutes later, they were back on the sidewalk with dripping cones. They didn't talk much, just walked along, eating their ice cream, looking in the windows of the little shops. Devin pointed to a birdhouse in one of the stores. "I bet we could make something like that to sell at the farm stand."

When they passed a jewelry shop, he stopped again, his attention caught by a display of shiny hand-stamped bangles in the window. "Want to go in?"

"I've got to finish my ice cream, but if you want to, go ahead. I'll come in a minute."

He pushed open the door to the store, glancing back to make sure Lacey was still occupied.

"Can I help you?" A woman with long straight blond hair walked toward him.

"Yes. I want one of those bangles with the letters. Like the ones in the window." When she pointed out a display by the register, he picked up the bracelet that had caught his eye. "This one."

He handed her the bracelet and his debit card. A few minutes later, Devin opened the door and stepped outside just as Lacey was finishing up her ice cream and dabbing at her shirt with a napkin. She looked up with a laugh. "I think I got more *onto* my stomach than I got into my stomach. What did you get?"

"You feel like sitting in the park for a minute?"

"Sure." It was so normal—to grab her hand as they crossed the street. He wanted more moments like this when they were just a couple out on a date, when they could relax and just be together.

Devin led Lacey to a bench. Laughter and squeals—

and the occasional wail—filtered through from the playground. Parents stood around, some of them still in suits and work clothes, watching as their kids ran out some energy.

"I saw something in the window and thought of you." He handed her the bag, feeling butterflies in his stomach like maybe he'd crossed a line that they weren't ready to cross.

She pulled out the bracelet he'd bought. Her eyes darted to his. She pressed her lips together and once again he worried that he'd made a mistake.

It wasn't anything fancy, just shiny gold-tone brass, but it had the letters *MAMA* stamped on it. She held it in her fingers, just looking at the word. A tear splashed onto the tissue paper it had been wrapped in.

His eyes widened. "It's okay if you don't want to wear it. It was just an impulse buy."

She lunged toward him, wrapping her arms around his neck, their babies between them. With a sigh, he closed his arms around her.

Lacey buried her face in Devin's shoulder. He was just so sweet. In all the anger and angst and absurdity of their situation, she'd forgotten how thoughtful he could be. She sat back, sliding the bracelet on her wrist.

"You're gonna be a great mom, Lacey."

"I love it, Devin." When she looked down at it, she wanted to cry all over again. "I know you don't understand my deal with the hospital."

"No, but I'm not judging. I know you. You're one of the bravest people I know. If you're scared of something, I know you have a good reason."

"It's hard to talk about. I've—I've never told anyone."

"You can tell me when you're ready, Lacey. It doesn't have to be now."

"I know. And that you trust me without knowing the story just makes me want to tell you more." She smiled, but her stomach turned with anxiety. "Did you know I broke my arm when I was five? The day I turned five, actually."

He shook his head and she went on. "My parents had gotten me roller skates for my birthday. They gave them to me that morning before my dad went out to work on the ranch. I begged my mom all day to let me try them out, but she wanted to wait until my dad got back. She said her back was hurting."

"That seems like it would be hard for a five-year-old to understand."

"Oh, it was. I was so upset. I begged and cried and pleaded. Finally, she told me if I could get them on, I could go out to the garage and skate out there."

Devin's arm slid around her shoulders. "I don't like where this story is going."

He had no idea. Really no idea.

In her mind, she could see her feet with the shiny white skates and the tangled-up laces. Her five-year-old self had imagined that she would skim across the floor like one of the ice skaters she'd watched on TV. "You know how stubborn I am?"

He nodded. "I'm acquainted with that side of you."

"I didn't know how to tie shoes but I smushed them around and wadded them up and convinced myself that it was just as good as being tied. And when I pushed off the step, thinking I was going to glide on my new skates, what really happened is that the laces got tangled around the wheel and I went down hard on the concrete floor. I broke my arm in two places. It was terrible."

She looked up to find his eyes, filled with distress and concern, on hers.

"My mom was really mad. It was what she'd been warning me about all day, but she took me to the emergency room and waited with me until they put me in a room." She swallowed hard, the ache in her throat making it hard to talk. "By that time, I was in shock and I was scared. I begged her to stay with me, but she said she wanted some coffee. She told me she was going to the cafeteria and… She left."

"You must have been terrified. You were so little."

She ran her fingers across the letters that spelled *mama* on her bracelet. "That was the last time I saw my mom."

*"What?"* His eyes went wide with shock.

With a little shrug, she told him the rest of it before she could chicken out. "I waited for hours but she never came back. They wouldn't fix my arm without someone there to sign the papers. It seemed like forever before they finally got my dad on the phone."

"That's a horrible thing to do to a little kid." He shook his head. "I'm so sorry, Lacey."

His words loosened something for that little five-year-old who had been so scared and sad. "I thought it was my fault because I wouldn't leave her alone about the skates. Now I know there was nothing I could have done to stop her. If it hadn't been the skates, it would've been something else."

"It was *not* your fault." He said it so vehemently that she had to laugh a little.

"I don't know where she is now. My dad got divorce papers in the mail a few months later. Sometimes I would look for her face in the stands when I was racing. It's silly. I don't really even remember what she looked like."

"It's not silly. She was your mom and she should've been there. That's on her."

"I do know that much." She shrugged. "And I know rationally that I shouldn't be afraid of the hospital. I've tried so many times to just walk through that door without a thought, but every time I freeze up. Or worse, have a panic attack like I did tonight."

"I'm so sorry I didn't know. I wouldn't have pressured you to take that ridiculous class."

"I want to take the class. That's the part that makes me so frustrated."

"You do?" He went quiet for a minute, watching as the parents on the playground called their kids to go. The sun was sinking in the sky and, even on a summer evening, it was time for them to head home for baths and bedtime. "What if we try again? No pressure, we'll just see how far we get."

She had her doubts, but he seemed so hopeful. "Maybe."

"I'll set it up. We'll try to go and if we don't, we don't. No big thing. At least we'll be together. Deal?"

She studied his face with a million thoughts running through her mind, mostly about how it was a terrible idea to put herself through that over and over again. But she had to try because as much as she'd like to imagine that the babies would just appear when the time came, the fact was she would be giving birth in a hospital. She had to face it at some point.

She sighed, shaking her head. "Deal."

They stood up together. Devin pulled her in for a sideways hug. "I'm so sorry I left you in Vegas. It must have felt like being abandoned all over again."

"Yeah, it did, kind of. It brought up a lot of feelings I thought I'd gotten over."

"I don't deserve a second chance."

She shook her head. "Nope. But our babies deserved a chance at a dad. And maybe I wasn't ready to give up on us, either. I don't know what's going to happen, Devin. I do know that I'm glad I've had the chance to get to know you again."

As they turned back toward the car, she slid her fingers into his. "How do *you* feel? I don't want to pry, but I'm curious. Does being sober feel like a relief? Is it stressful? Do you ever stop thinking about it?"

They walked along in silence for a few minutes, and the sounds around them soaked into her consciousness. Cars whizzed by. Bells jingled as people entered the little shops. Live music filtered in from a nearby restaurant. But it was his hand clasping hers that felt real and present.

"It's hard to put in words, but to answer your question, being sober is a relief. Having my addiction out in the open is a relief. The stressful part—for me anyway, but it's probably different for everyone—is that I feel like I have so much to make up for. I broke trust with you and with my family. With my corporate sponsors. And some of that I'll never get back."

"Do you ever stop thinking about it?"

"My ankle reminds me. But every once in a while I forget. I go to meetings because I need to be reminded that I'm an addict and because being with other people who continue to be sober is helpful."

"Do you think you'll ever do drugs or drink again?" It was a loaded question, and one she desperately needed an answer to.

He was quiet. "I don't think so. But I can only be responsible for these twenty-four hours right now. I know I'm not going to drink or take painkillers today. I'll go to a meeting later tonight because it helps me stay sober tomorrow. Does that seem weird?"

"A little bit, but only because I haven't experienced it."

They got to the car and he beeped the locks open, but he didn't say anything else. They drove home in silence. She wasn't sure where his mind was, but she knew her mind was spinning with all the things they'd talked about tonight.

She was almost grateful for her panic attack because she felt like Devin had opened up to her in a way he never had before.

When they pulled in the driveway at the house, he put the truck in Park but he didn't turn it off or get out. The light from the porch glinted off her bracelet. She cleared her throat. "You said I'm brave, Devin, but I need you to know that I think you're the brave one. You live with pain every day, and despite that, you're doing what it takes to be the person your family needs you to be. I respect that. I'm not impressed by how hot you are or how long you can stick on a bucking bronc. I'm not impressed by your gold buckle. I am impressed by how you're trying to do what's best for you and your family."

His breath was shaky. He looked away, but he reached for her hand again. "I don't think I'm worthy of your respect, Lacey. I've got my demons to face down, just like you."

She nodded. "You told me I didn't have to face mine alone. Well, neither do you."

The surprising thing was, she meant it. She'd been thinking of his battle with addiction as something he had to conquer alone. But this wasn't some goal he'd set for himself, like sticking to the saddle longer, or pushing himself in the ring just a little further. This was real-life important.

That didn't mean that she'd forgotten what he did or that everything was okay between them forever. But he'd been there beside her today as she'd fought her battle.

And she could be beside him as he fought his.

## Chapter Thirteen

Lacey stumbled into the kitchen for her daily cup of coffee. It was getting difficult for her to sleep between the twins deciding that her sleep time was their playtime and the random contractions she assumed were Braxton Hicks.

She'd heard the guys as they got up for breakfast, but she stayed in her room. After sharing her childhood trauma with Devin last night, she felt a little tender. A little crowded, almost—not by Devin, but by her overly large emotions. *Thanks, pregnancy.*

When Tanner and Devin had left to do their chores, she'd drifted back to sleep and slept way longer than she intended. She had lots to bake today. But coffee came first.

After dumping enough cream in the leftover coffee to make it palatable, she slid her feet into flip-flops and walked out the front door onto the porch. The ceiling fans were on, creating a breeze, which was good because even at 10:00 a.m., the temperature was already soaring.

Nemo was standing at the edge of the ring facing the

pasture, mooing for all he was worth. Then she realized Devin was up on Dolly, working her in the field as Nemo bellowed. He could get about halfway across the field toward the loud little calf before the horse would slow down. Each time Devin would gently guide her back toward the round pen.

He was striking on horseback, always had been. It was no wonder she'd had such a crush on him from the first time he'd stepped into the arena. But really, she knew. He was meant for her. In so many ways, he was meant for her. There was a mountain range of problems between them, but she hoped and prayed they were steadily making progress through them.

Lacey walked, mug in hand, across the driveway to lean on the fence, so she could see Devin at work. He was so patient and so calm with Dolly. From her new vantage point, she realized that Sadie was in the pasture, too. When Dolly would start to shy, Devin would give Sadie a command and she would take the lead, showing Dolly that there was nothing to fear ahead.

It was beautiful to watch the rapport between the animals and Devin. He was in his element. Almost as if he'd heard her thoughts, he glanced up, smiling when he saw her standing by the fence. She wondered if he was thinking of last night, too. Her cheeks heated again and she looked down, suddenly feeling shy.

Tires crunched on the gravel driveway behind her. She turned around as Garrett got out of his SUV, slammed the door and waved. "Hey, it looks like there's a good crowd at the farm stand today. You hired a teenager to work it?"

"When she can. We check in on things, replacing the produce and baked goods when we have them."

"I want to get some of those zucchini brownies before I go."

"Sure." Lacey heard a noise from the back of Garrett's SUV. "What was that? Is there an animal in there?"

Garrett's face went ruddy. "Uh, yeah. I did some legal work for a farmer I know. He offered to pay me with a couple of kids he was planning to bottle raise."

Her mouth dropped open. "Oh… Tanner's gonna kill you."

"Yeah, I know." Garrett laughed, but he walked over to the SUV and opened the back, pulling out a big dog crate and placing it on the ground. When he opened it up, two of the tiniest goats she'd ever seen bounded out. They tilted their heads and let out the sweetest little bleats.

Fuzzy and white with black markings and little black hooves, they were adorable. One of them kind of toddled over to her and pulled on the leg of her pants with his soft goat lips. If she'd been able to get back up, she would've dropped to her knees immediately to cuddle him.

"Oh, Garrett. They're so cute."

"Right? How could I refuse?"

From the fence, Devin said, "You say no. That's how."

"You're one to talk while you're riding a horse someone gave you." Garrett grinned. "Tanner'll get over it. He's just a little slow to adjust to change."

"They're really cute. I bet Nemo will like having friends." Lacey leaned over and scratched the littlest one on the head. "What are you naming them?"

"Thelma and Louise."

"Perfect." She laughed. "I hope they don't get in quite that much trouble."

Dolly was snacking on some grass while Devin chatted, and Sadie, recognizing a chance to nap, came under the fence to lie down at Lacey's feet.

"We're going to have to make a pen in part of the north pasture for these guys. The round pen is fine while they're bottle-feeding, but they're going to need grass soon." Devin patted Dolly's neck.

His brother nodded. "I'll look at my calendar for next week and see when I can do it."

"And you're going to drive out here four times a day to feed them?" Devin tightened up on the reins as one of the little goats got closer to Dolly. The horse shied away, but she acted more curious than afraid. "She's doing better. Did you see that?"

"She's doing great." Lacey laughed as one of the goat babies tried to jump on Sadie's back and fell off. "I would help feed if I could."

Garrett shoved his hands in his jeans pockets. "I thought maybe I'd stay in the cabin by the creek for a few weeks until they're settled in and can go longer between bottles."

Devin nodded slowly. "Works for me. The place is a dump, though."

"It needs some maintenance, so it'll be a good time for me to do it after work. We can't afford to let the roof fall in."

"All right, sounds fine to me, but you have to tell Tanner." Devin looked toward the house. "Confound it, Garrett, they're eating my daisies."

Garrett ran for the house as Lacey laughed. "Those

goats are going to give him a run for his money. He has no idea."

Devin shook his head. "No idea."

Walking back with one goat under each arm, his tie flapping over his shoulder, Garrett said, "I don't know what to do with them."

"Put them in the round pen with Nemo. We've been leaving the door open to the barn." Devin clucked to Dolly. "We're going around a few more times and then I'm putting her in the pasture next to Reggie for the rest of the day."

As Devin rode away, Lacey turned to Garrett. "Are the bottles in the trunk? I'll get today's ready for you, if you want me to."

"That would be so awesome, Lacey. There's a shopping bag with a bunch of stuff in the back of the SUV."

"I'll get them. You get Thelma and Louise settled with Nemo. You might want to check the hay in the open stall and make sure it's fresh." She walked around to the back of the SUV and retrieved the bag of goat supplies. There were two small bottles and a gallon container of goat's milk that the farmer must've given Garrett.

She hated to tell him, but that wasn't going to go very far. He was going to have to figure out what to feed these guys and fast.

They had babies coming out their ears here at Triple Creek Ranch. Prudence—or Elmo—gave her a big kick in the ribs as an exclamation point to her thought. She rubbed her belly. "Hey, watch it, there, little one."

There was another kick in response. Lacey chuckled. "I think you get that behavior from your dad."

She dumped the calf bottles and the goat bottles into

the sink to wash them out and put some water on to boil to make Nemo's formula.

Her eye caught on the flier from the hospital for the Magnificent Multiples class. It was only a couple of weeks before she'd promised to try again.

This time, at least, she knew what she was up against and Devin was aware of her fears. It was for the babies.

This time she would handle it.

Devin flipped over in bed and kicked the covers off. The clock said 3:24 and he hadn't been to sleep yet. His ankle was aching from his time up on Dolly today, the muscles in his leg spasming from trying to compensate.

He stared at the ceiling for another minute before deciding to get up and try some chamomile tea. Sometimes it would relax his muscles enough to sleep.

Rolling out of bed, he stumbled into the kitchen, stopping short when he saw Lacey sitting at the kitchen table, a tray of cookies in front of her and a bag of frosting in her hand. "Hey, what are you doing up? It's three in the morning."

She jumped and frosting squirted out of the bag in a long stream. "You scared me! Give a girl some warning next time you sneak up on her in the middle of the night."

"Sorry." He limped to the stove, slid the kettle onto the burner and started it up. "I'm making some chamomile tea. Want some?"

"Sure." She filled in the frosting on a cookie that looked like a flip-flop and laid down her piping bag. "So why are you awake?"

"Ankle hurting. You?"

"Couldn't get comfortable with this big ole belly.

And apparently, the twins find my sleeping time to be the ideal playtime. It's like they're doing karate in there."

"Don't take this the wrong way, but is it weird? It seems like it would be."

"Yeah, it's kind of weird when you think about four arms and four legs and two heads." She laughed. "I just freaked myself out a little bit. I'm sorry you're hurting."

"It's okay." He poured the steaming water over the tea bags he'd placed in the mugs. "I've learned to make peace with it, for the most part."

"What do you mean?" She slid a cookie over to him.

"You asked me if I thought I'd ever drink or take pills again. I know I had the reputation of always being up for a party. But for me, the drinking and the drugs weren't about the partying. Or really even about the high. It was about…stopping the pain." He broke the cookie in half and took a bite.

"Oh, Devin. And you're still dealing with the pain."

"Yes." He very carefully dunked the tea bag in his mug. It was easier to talk when he wasn't looking at her. He was so much more comfortable making her laugh than he was with serious conversations. "I can frame it differently now, though."

She picked the piping bag back up and began the process of frosting another cookie, but her brow furrowed. She still didn't know what he meant.

"I try to remember something I learned in therapy." He took a sip of his tea. It was too hot and he burned his mouth. He set the cup down. "The pain in my body reminds me that I'm alive. If I dull the pain with drugs or alcohol, I dull everything else too…joy and laughter, even the ability to make a decision that's both sorrowful and sweet."

Her eyes on the cookie in front of her, she asked the question he always dreaded to answer. "Was it only physical pain you were trying to dull?"

Devin looked away. He didn't want to talk about his parents. It was one thing to share memories about his mom or dad, but talking about how he felt about their dying was different. His feelings about his parents' death were complicated. A toxic mix of sadness and guilt and grief.

"My parents' death…" His voice thickened and he stopped to clear his throat. "It's been so long. I don't understand why it's so hard to talk about. Or why it affects how I live my life now. Why it still…hurts so much."

"You don't have to talk about it, Devin. Of all people, I understand that."

But he had a choice to make. Either he was all in with Lacey or he wasn't. Either she knew everything about him or he'd always wonder if things would've been different.

Their pasts had such an effect on their present—who they were and the decisions they made. That was never clearer than when he'd tried to get Lacey to go into the hospital for that class.

In the wee hours of the morning, the kitchen felt cozy, a small cone of light in a dark, silent house. It felt safe, as if they were the only two people awake in the world right now. The words came without his bidding. "I was in middle school, at football practice. I was supposed to get a ride home from practice with my friend Sam, but I messed around and by the time I realized I needed to leave, Sam's mom had already come and gone. I, um, borrowed the coach's phone to call my mom. My parents had already passed the school on their way home from picking Tanner's wife and baby up from the airport, but she said they would come and get me. I heard my mom tell my dad they needed to turn around. My dad was grumbling, but he did it. A few seconds later, I heard the crash."

Tears were pooling in her eyes when he looked up. She blinked and twin tears streaked her cheeks. "Oh, Devin."

He swallowed over the ache in his throat. The next part was the hardest to get through. "I screamed into the phone. Begged my mom to answer me. For a few minutes, I heard crying and then just…nothing. We found out later that the man who hit them had been distracted by a bird hitting his windshield. He hit them broadside as they turned back onto the road. His air bags worked. He survived. Tanner's baby, my nephew, was the only one alive when they pulled them out of the car. He died the next day."

She didn't say anything. He didn't expect her to. What could you say to a story like that?

He stared into the amber tea, his eyes following a lone bubble on the surface until it popped. And he said the words that had haunted his mind since the day of the accident. The real reason he'd pushed himself so hard. The real reason he'd nearly destroyed himself. The pain didn't come from his ruined ankle.

The pain came from inside him. "It was my fault."

Her head jerked up. "No. Devin, *no*. It wasn't your fault. You didn't cause the accident."

"If I'd just done what my mom told me to do, I'd have been home waiting when they got there. I've relived that afternoon a million times. More. If I'd just gotten in the car with Sam, they'd be alive right now. All of them."

"You don't know that." She reached across the table to touch him and he grabbed her hand like a lifeline. "Devin, you don't know that. They could've stopped to let a dog pass in front of them, or gotten held up in a traffic jam, or had to stop to pick up milk. Anything could've been the variable that had them right there at that exact moment."

He shook his head. "Any of those things could have happened but I know I was the reason they were turning around to come back to the school. I have to live with that."

"Okay. I understand that. I believe it was an accident but I understand you feeling the way you do." Her eyes were huge in her face, and Devin suddenly felt like he should be comforting her instead of the other way around.

With a sigh, he admitted the truth that he was finally facing about his addiction. "I was reckless and stupid, trying to numb the pain with drugs and alcohol and adrenaline. And I was too selfish to see that I wasn't just hurting myself. I was hurting you. Tanner and Garrett. And my mom wouldn't want me to live my life like that. She'd want me to take care of my brothers. And she'd want me to be happy."

She swiped at the tears on her cheeks, and the knowledge slammed him in the gut. He loved her so much.

He'd known it forever. He just didn't think he was worthy of love in return. And now things were so complicated between them... He just had to pray that God could work things out where Devin couldn't.

He reached over and gently rubbed a tear away with

his thumb. "That morning in Vegas, I didn't know we'd gotten married, but I knew I needed to get help. Because hurting you was the last thing I wanted to do."

Lacey scrubbed her hands over her face. "How did we manage to mess things up so badly?"

"I seem to have a talent for it." He picked up his mug and drained the rest of his ice-cold tea. "Are you ready to get back to bed yet?"

"I'm gonna finish these cookies before I go back so you can take them out to the stand in the morning. I'm not sleepy and the babies are still in the mood to rumble, apparently."

"I'll head up, then." He grabbed his cane and walked to the door before he stopped. "I just want to say one thing before I go. This thing between us, it's not about responsibility to me."

Lacey pushed to her feet and walked over to him, stopping about a foot away, her eyes locked on his.

He shifted his weight. "I know I don't deserve—"

She grabbed his shirt, dragged him to her and kissed him. He sighed. Finally.

*Finally.*

His arms closed around her, the sweetness of sugar and vanilla permeating his senses.

She took a step back, her cheeks a little rosy. "It's not about responsibility for me, either. I just wanted to make that clear."

Looking down, he laughed. "Okay, then. I'll see you in the morning."

"See you in the morning."

## Chapter Fourteen

Lacey closed her eyes as Devin pulled into the parking lot at the hospital. They were trying an afternoon class this time, and despite his running description of every bronc he'd ever gotten thrown off and her own determination to breathe through her anxiety, she wasn't sure she could get through it.

"Lacey?"

"I've survived way worse than a class in a hospital. I can do this." He'd barely pulled into the parking space when she opened the door to the car and slid out.

"Lacey…"

He sounded unsure, and she glanced back at him. "It's only for an hour."

The words were firm in her mind but her voice sounded weak and breathy to her ears. She focused on the door to the hospital. *It's like any other door.* She took one step. Two. And despite all her efforts, she felt it as her brain took over and her fight-or-flight response kicked in.

Heart rate jacked. Breathing shallow. Muscles tensing. Vision narrowing.

She faltered to a stop, her body swaying as her vision swam.

Devin's arm, strong and steady, moved around her waist, bolstering her, turning her back toward the car. "Come on. We're leaving. We can try again in two weeks."

He opened the door to the truck and she slid in, her body feeling boneless. Why was this so hard? She knew it was irrational. She just didn't know how to fight it.

"I'm sorry," she whispered when he got in on the other side and cranked the truck up with a roar.

"No worries, babe. We'll try again. Right now, I say we go shopping."

"Shopping?"

"Yep. I got my last check from my corporate sponsor about a week ago and I tucked it away for baby stuff."

"I don't know, Devin…" She knew they had to shop for all the things they needed. And she wasn't in denial that they were about to have twins. It was that shopping for all the stuff together seemed a lot like planning for her to be here after the babies were born.

It was intimate, too, a thing couples did together. The last thing she wanted was an awkward hour in a baby store with Devin, but considering the kiss she laid on him last night, she should probably get over that. Her cheeks heated as she thought about it now.

Yeah, she passed awkward a long time ago.

Devin kept driving. "It'll be fun. We can get a big *P* to go over Prudence's bed and a big *E* to go over Elmo's."

Lacey shot him a look. "That was a *joke*."

Pulling into the parking lot at a store called Heaven Sent, Devin said, "When the owners named their store, do you think they were thinking about the babies being 'Heaven sent' or were they thinking about all the new parents who were going to spend all their money here?"

"The second one, for sure. I definitely think they're most interested in your credit card." She unbuckled and got out of the car. When he held the door open for her, she walked in and immediately melted. Pale pastels, luxurious textures. Precious prints. Everything seemed so soft and sweet. So perfect for tiny fragile humans.

Devin walked past her with a cart, stopped where the aisle turned and looked back. "You coming?"

She wanted to say yes. She wanted to dive right into the fun of picking out all the things for the twins. But she stopped herself. Staying in Alabama had been about giving herself time to come to a decision.

This was a big step.

She'd trusted Devin in Vegas and he'd left her. Now it wasn't even as much about trusting him as trusting her own judgment. She'd been so wrong about him before. She was falling for him again, but what if she was wrong now?

This shopping trip, as wonderful as the idea was, felt like losing her power to make the best decision, the safest decision, for her and the babies.

She shook her head. "Devin, I'm not sure if this is a good idea. You've been trying so hard. And I… really appreciate that. But it's only been a few months. What if you buy a ton of stuff and I don't…it doesn't work out for us?"

"Do you think it's not going to work out for us?"

She didn't answer him. "Why don't we just get one of those portable crib things? I saw one online that had twin bassinets in the top."

His face hardened into stubborn lines. "It's important to me that the babies have actual cribs and an actual nursery. I know we still have decisions to make, but I don't want them to feel like they're negotiable in my life."

"Where are we even going to put them? There's no room for baby beds in the master bedroom."

"I have some thoughts on that. My mom's sitting room is right next to the master bedroom where you're sleeping. No one has used it since… Well, no one has used it. I thought we could make that the nursery."

The fact that he'd been thinking about where the babies would sleep and planning this shopping trip was a good sign. But at the same time, the fact that he'd made some big decisions without talking them over with her made her uncomfortable.

Devin dug a piece of paper out of his pocket. "I made a list. Want to start with the cribs? Come on, this will be fun. Do we need two?"

Reluctantly, Lacey followed him across the store. "I guess? Or maybe we could just get one. I think sometimes people let twins share until they get a little bit bigger."

She wandered into one of the mock-up nurseries, sliding her finger along the soft white wood railing on one of the cribs. "I like this one."

"I like it, too. It's low to the ground and I think it's small enough to fit two in that sitting room. How about the gray ones?"

She scowled, finding herself annoyed that he wanted to choose the color of the crib. "White would go with everything. We can leave the walls white, too, and use different colors for their bedding."

"Okay, white's kind of predictable, but they're babies. I don't think they'll care." He picked up two of the tags from the display attached to the rail, looked at his list and laughed. "We have so much stuff on this list."

They walked through the store, Devin pushing the cart, Lacey lagging behind. She'd come to Alabama for a divorce, and instead she'd gotten options. But now? With every baby item he tossed into the cart, it felt like her options were getting more and more limited. Like she was racing closer to a life with Devin and their babies at Triple Creek. Preparing for the twins to arrive and planning a nursery was another set of roots growing deep, anchoring her to Red Hill Springs.

A faint echo of the panic she'd felt at the hospital began in her chest. She stopped walking, took some deep breaths and tried to think logically. Her stress made sense. She'd had no control over her life when her mother decided to abandon her. No control when Devin had left her in Vegas.

In coming to Red Hill Springs to confront Devin, she'd taken the reins back for herself—or so she thought.

Now she wasn't so sure.

She'd learned so much about him since coming here. But the sting—no, that word didn't begin to touch how she'd felt that night—the *devastation* of being left by Devin on their wedding night was still there. Even worse was the realization that she hadn't known him at all—she'd only thought she had.

Things were different now. With every confidence offered, every late-night secret shared, they grew closer to a real relationship, an honest one. But she was a long way from being able to trust him with her life, with the babies' lives. Trusting his sweet-talking promises hadn't gotten her anywhere before but married, pregnant and alone.

"How about stars for the bedding? Blue for P and yellow for E?" His voice broke into her thoughts. She looked up to see Devin holding up two packages of crib sheets.

She took another deep breath and tried to concentrate. "I love the colors. I was planning to color-code the babies. If you like blue and yellow, we could use those colors for everything."

"It's a brilliant idea. Let's go pick out bottles."

Within an hour, they had a cart full. Two sets of everything: bottles, pacifiers, swaddling blankets, bedding, baby swings and bouncy seats. And Devin had arranged for the cribs and a rocker to be delivered the next day.

She consulted his list. "Okay, the only thing left here is a baby monitor and infant car seats. We have to decide if we want a separate stroller or a whole-system thingy."

Devin stopped the cart. "I saw a video monitor back there with the sound machines, so we can get that. But maybe we need to do a little more research on the car seats."

"We have time, but that's one thing we really do need. We won't be able to leave the hospital without them."

"Noted. We'll get the car seats as soon as possible. I'm going to check out. Why don't you go to the truck so you can get off your feet?"

He was directing her without consulting her again, but her lower back and hips ached from the strain of two babies. "Fine. I'm exhausted. And starving."

After checking out, Devin loaded everything into the back of his truck and slid into the seat beside her. "Whew. I'm tired. How about a burger?"

She *did* want a burger. But she also really, really wanted to be the one to make the decision, even if it was only what they had for dinner. "I want pizza. And I'm ready to go back to the house."

"Okay, pizza sounds good. Pepperoni?"

"Cheese."

"Cheese it is."

She watched him as he carefully backed out of the parking spot. She knew he was working hard to stay sober, working hard at the farm and just in general trying to do right by the people he cared about.

He'd been happy and excited today in the baby store, patient and kind with her at the hospital. She could see him as a dad one day, showing their kids how to bottle-feed a calf or patiently guide a horse.

They'd been making slow and steady progress, but with the kiss last night and the whirlwind shopping trip today, things suddenly felt like they were out of her control. A big reminder that she was living in Devin's world.

Back at the ranch, Devin grabbed the still-warm box of pizza they'd picked up in town. "We can unload all the stuff later if you want to eat first."

"That would be great." Lacey didn't look at him, just made her way to the porch with Sadie dancing a welcome around her legs. She dropped into a chair. "I'm so tired."

He slid the box onto the table between them and flipped the lid open. She grabbed a piece and bit into it with a sigh.

"I'm sorry it was such a long afternoon," he said, "but I'm glad we got some stuff for the babies. I guess we'll need to get some baby clothes next." He glanced at her as he took his first bite, trying to read her face. He knew something wasn't right. He just couldn't put his finger on what. Or why. In the few months Lacey had been in Red Hill Springs, they had carefully stayed away from making any plans for the future, but he was ready to take some cautious steps forward. Unfortunately, he wasn't sure Lacey had the same feeling.

She'd gone along with his plan for the afternoon but she hadn't seemed very happy about it. Not unhappy, exactly, just not committed to the idea of building a nursery.

But he'd meant what he said to her in the store. He didn't want to feel like the babies were visiting. He didn't want her to feel that way, either. The thought struck him. *Oh.*

Maybe that was part of the problem. The room that was Lacey's was a room his mother had decorated. It didn't have anything of Lacey in it. For as much as Lacey had made this old farmhouse feel like a home again for him, he didn't think she'd say the same.

It was something to think about. He picked up another slice just as Lacey finished her second piece.

She leaned back in the chair. "I want another piece but there's no room."

"Oh, man. That's a complication of pregnancy I never considered." Devin finished up the crust on his, closed the lid and picked up the box. "I'll take this inside and stick it in the fridge so you'll have some later if you get hungry."

When he came back out with his guitar, she was sitting on the porch steps, her legs stretched out in front of her. He sat down on the step beside her and started picking a little tune.

The stars shone bright and clear out here in the country, away from city lights. Devin could hear the animals shuffling in the barn, the cows in the pasture down the dirt road. The night was peaceful and he prayed that he could claim that peace for himself.

He prayed that Lacey would feel it, too, that she would know how much he cared about her. That was what the shopping trip was about today. As much as he wanted things to be settled, he knew she was still scared. He'd left her and she was afraid if she trusted him again that he would break her heart. But how did you prove that something *wouldn't* happen in the future?

All he could do was show her every day that he had grown. That his priorities had changed. Taking a risk with his life seemed to come naturally to him. Taking a risk with his heart, a lot less so, but he was willing to try.

He looked down at his fingers on the guitar and began, hesitantly, to play a tune he'd written a few weeks ago. He looked at Lacey and sang, *"I'll be your sunshine when it rains. You'll be my antidote to pain. I'll be your sweater when you get cold. You'll be my soul mate when I grow old."*

With her eyes full of some unnamed emotion, she watched his fingers on the strings. He had no idea what she was thinking, but he sang the chorus straight to her. *"We may be mismatched like your cowgirl socks, but I'm yours for life, Lacey, you're my rock."*

He smiled as the words repeated. *"Bah-bah-duh,*

*may be mismatched like your cowgirl socks, but I'm
yours for life, Lacey, you're my rock."*

As his fingers plucked the last couple of chords, he
chuckled into the self-conscious silence that followed.
He waited for Lacey to respond with a joke like she so
often did, and when she didn't, he supplied one himself.
"I don't think I'm going to have a career writing music."

A tear slid down her cheek. Lacey looked away from
him as she whispered, "I don't want to love you again."

At her words, his fingers paused on the strings, but
he picked it up again. "I know. It's okay."

"I'm sorry I was so out of sorts today. I wish I could
blame pregnancy hormones, but I'm pretty sure it's just
me. I love all the stuff we picked out. And I love the
song." She let her head drop in her hands. The words
that followed were halting, her voice husky with pent-
up emotion. "Everything feels like it's spinning out of
control."

Devin laid his guitar to the side and put his arm
around her. He'd caused her pain and he couldn't fix
it. He didn't know how. So, he just sat there with her
while she cried.

After a few minutes, he said, "I remember the first
time I saw you. I think you might've been eighteen."

"Nineteen," she corrected without looking up.

"You swaggered into the barn with your big brown
eyes and your cowboy hat. You had on jeans and boots
and a shirt that said Get Up, Show Up, Never Give Up.
I walked over to talk to you and you said—"

"Excuse me, I don't have time for you to hit on me.
I'm taking care of my horse right now." She interrupted
him with the words she'd said when she first met him
six years ago, and her eyes met his. "I was such a jerk."

He laughed. "I think my heart fell right out of my chest onto the floor of the barn. Even though you blew me off, it was the beginning of our friendship. And even though it may not feel like it right now, this is a different kind of beginning, Lace. We're still finding our way, but we're gonna be okay."

He didn't know for sure that what he said was true. Her fears were big and they were justified.

*Get up, show up, never give up.*

He could beg her to stay, but in the end, the choice was hers. It had always been hers.

# Chapter Fifteen

Devin opened the door to the future nursery. It was a light and bright room, which had been his mom's hiding place when the testosterone in her household got to be a bit too much. No leather or random sports equipment in this room... The space had been filled with flowers and ruffles and girly-scented candles.

Garrett let out a low whistle. "I haven't been in here in years. It looks exactly the same, like she should be sitting on the couch and yelling at us for interrupting her prayer time."

"I know, right?" Devin and his brothers hadn't been allowed in there without knocking. Even then, admittance was dicey. Being the youngest, he remembered often sitting on the floor with a basket of crayons and a coloring book until he started school.

Mom had used the room for her quiet time. He had so many memories of opening the door to find her leaned over her Bible, tracing the words with her finger, or listening to a sermon while she crocheted.

None of them had any reason to go into her sitting room since the accident. It had been dusted from time to time, but otherwise it had remained exactly the same, none of them wanting to be the one to clean out their mother's stuff. It was still hard, even with so much distance.

But it was time. The last thing Mom would've wanted would be for this room to sit unused. She'd taken so much pleasure in it.

"Mom would be happy that we're doing this." Garrett picked up a stack of magazines from a decade ago and tossed them into a trash bag. "She'd be mad that we let it go so long."

Devin nodded. "I can just hear her now. *You boys—*"

"*—I shouldn't have to ask you to do something that clearly needs doing.*" Garrett completed the sentence they'd heard their mother say at least a thousand times. "She could really be bossy."

With a laugh, Devin grabbed a garbage bag and started shoving the throw pillows from the couch in there. "She really could, but then, she had three rowdy boys that would just as soon wrestle as listen."

Tanner stuck his head in the door. "I wasn't rowdy."

Garrett rolled his eyes. "*Pfffft.* I beg to differ. You just didn't get caught as often."

"I've got a few minutes if you want me to start on the closet."

Devin grimaced. "It pains me to say this, but we could use your help with the furniture. We're planning to load up the back of the truck and take it all over to the cabin."

With Garrett and Tanner hefting the couch, Devin grabbed the cushions he could carry and followed them outside to toss them in with the sofa.

Lacey came out the front door right after him with

the last two cushions. "It looks so much bigger in there without the couch. Are you moving the rest of the furniture, too?"

"Yes, except for the dresser that Mom used as a TV stand. I thought we could wait on that and you can decide if you want it in there or not. Do you think anything else should stay?" He wasn't going to stop trying to move them forward, even if they were taking baby steps. But after yesterday's conversation with Lacey about how out of control she felt, he hoped maybe it would help if she were making the decisions.

"Y'all should go ahead and move the furniture. I'm headed over to Jordan's for lunch. But when I come back, we can take a look and talk about the rest of it?"

"Sounds good." Devin stumbled backward as his brother nailed him with a big black bag.

Garrett laughed as he bounded down the stairs. "They're throw pillows, get it?"

"Oh, I get it." Devin grinned and slowly reached into the bag.

Lacey made a T with her hands. "Time out, children. Wait till the pregnant lady is out of the way." To Devin she said, "I'll see you later."

Devin watched as she got into the truck and started it up. Surprisingly, he wasn't too disheartened by their conversation the night before. Instead, he actually felt like they were getting somewhere. She cared about him, and that wasn't any baby step, either, even if she was unhappy about it.

A throw pillow drilled him in the side of the head. "Stop mooning and let's get this done."

Devin whirled around to see Garrett doubled over. "Who's mooning?"

Tanner shook his head. "You are. Most definitely. Mooning."

Not even taking offense because it was true, Devin smiled. "Come on, let's get this furniture to the cabin. I've got a nursery to clean up."

Lacey passed the driveway to Jordan's house twice before she finally saw the teensy-weensy sign that said Sheehan beside a small opening in the trees. She pulled up to a home that looked like it had been built last century and lovingly restored.

She could hear a baby crying from inside the house when she stepped onto the porch. She knocked on the door and waited. With her hand raised to knock again, she heard footsteps.

Jordan opened the door, a very small baby in her arms. Essie, whom Lacey had held the day at Red Hill Farm, was on a blanket on the floor screaming her head off. Jordan raised her voice. "Hey, come on in. Sorry about the noise. Everyone was in a great mood until about five minutes ago when Amos had a poopy diaper at the same time Essie decided she was ready for a nap."

She held the tiny baby out to Lacey. "You mind?"

"Oh. Um. Okay." Lacey took the baby from Jordan, who immediately went to pick Essie up from the floor. "Who is this again?"

Jordan laughed as she settled in an oversize rocker-recliner with Essie, tossed a muslin blanket over her shoulder and began to feed her. "My sister and her husband are Amos's foster parents, but on the day he was supposed to come home from the hospital, two of the other kids came down with strep throat. Amos was a preemie, and since Ash and I are still licensed to foster, we said he could stay here with us until they've been clear for a few days."

"That makes sense. I think." As she eased onto the love seat, Lacey looked down at Amos snuggling in her arms. He blinked up at her with eyes so dark blue they were almost black. If he weighed five pounds, she would be surprised. It was hard to imagine, but her babies would probably not be much bigger than this when they were born. They could be smaller, if they came earlier. "Is he pretty low maintenance at this stage?"

"In a way. He sleeps a lot, but because he's so small, we have to be sure to feed him every couple of hours. He gets tired fast so he doesn't take much at one time." Jordan paused, apparently thinking. "The last preemie we had was on an apnea monitor. That thing was a pain."

"That sounds a little…daunting." Especially since Lacey would have two at the same time. Even more daunting if she was doing it alone. But if she stayed with Devin, she would be staying because it was the right thing for all of them, not because she was desperate for help with twins. "Are you planning to keep fostering?"

"We're staying licensed for now, but we're taking a break until Essie turns a year old…at least. We stay busy enough just doing respite for Claire and Joe." She sighed. "I'm not a very good hostess these days. Sorry not to have lunch waiting when you got here. I do have some chicken salad and fruit in the refrigerator."

"Oh, it's fine. Trust me. I'm just glad to get out of the house for a little while. I haven't had a lot of time to make friends here, so it's nice to get to visit."

"How are things over at Triple Creek? It looked like the farm stand was going really well."

"I think it's going okay. I'm making zucchini brownies and those cookies you liked almost every day."

Jordan said, "They're so good. Hang on. Let me put Essie in her bed before we both die of hunger."

Her new friend disappeared into a door leading from the kitchen and returned just a couple of minutes later. Tugging open the refrigerator door, she looked back at Lacey. "I bet your kids are up on horseback before they're walking. You and Devin seem like such a good match."

To Lacey's horror, her eyes filled. Jordan stopped in the middle of the kitchen with an armful of food from the refrigerator. "Oh, no, I said the wrong thing. Hang on."

Jordan walked over to the farm table in the middle of their big open living area. She laid out chicken salad, a package of fresh fruit chunks and some crackers, returning to the kitchen for forks and paper plates. "I'm so not a hostess. I'm looking at this thinking it would all look better on some china."

Lacey sniffed and smiled, relieved that—for the moment, at least—Jordan had changed the subject. "I know you're kidding. I've been on the rodeo circuit for so many years. I wouldn't know what to do if someone put china in front of me."

With a laugh, Jordan pulled a couple of bottles of water from the refrigerator. "You knew just the right thing to say."

Putting a spoonful of chicken salad on her plate, Lacey said, "How did you and Ash get together?"

"You mean because we seem so mismatched? Trust me, no one was more surprised than I was. Levi was adopted from foster care and when he first came to me, he had some special medical needs. Ash was right there with me the whole time."

"That sounds amazing." Lacey took a bite of her chicken salad but her appetite disappeared as she thought about what a polar opposite her experience with Devin had been from Jordan's with Ash.

Jordan lifted a chunk of cantaloupe. "So, I'm just going to warn you that I'm nosy and opinionated, so stop me if I overstep. But I get the feeling that maybe you're not feeling so great right now?"

With a big sigh, Lacey considered her options. She needed a friend desperately, someone who could be objective about all the things. "Can I share with you in confidence?"

Jordan lifted a hand. "Wait here. I'll be right back." She went into the kitchen, pulled a container of chocolate ice cream from the freezer and grabbed two spoons from the drawer. "Here's the deal. My sisters and I have this rule. What is said when the ice cream is on the table is secret. Period."

How did Lacey share something so personal when she barely understood it herself? "So, Devin and I have been friends forever and that was all it was for a long time…until we had kind of a whirlwind romantic night. Devin proposed and we were in Vegas so we got married. Which I thought was great, until I woke up the next morning alone. And pregnant, as I found out a few weeks later."

Jordan pushed away her plate of chicken salad and pulled the ice cream container into the center of the table. "I think we're going to need this. I heard Devin went to rehab."

"He did and he's been sober for months now. I came

to ask him for a divorce and found out that he didn't even remember the wedding. Since he found out about the babies coming, he's been great. I honestly can't tell you why I'm so terrified. But I am. Terrified."

Jordan took a spoonful of the ice cream. "I was reading about trauma recently—it's a big part of fostering—and I learned that the brain remembers things even when we don't have a conscious memory of them. Like, this thing happened and this is how I felt so I'm going to do everything I can to avoid that feeling again ever. The kids don't know why they're acting the way they are. It's mostly unconscious."

With her own spoon halfway to her mouth, Lacey narrowed her eyes. "So you're saying even if I think I want to trust Devin, my brain is telling me I should run because I was hurt before?"

"That's exactly it. When I was dating Ash, I was literally petrified that things were going to end badly and I was going to get my heart broken. And I was a new mom to Levi and I was afraid Levi would get *his* heart broken. I was a mess. I was so scared that I broke up with him."

*"What?"*

"I'm serious." The baby in the living room started to whimper. Jordan dug through a diaper bag hanging on the chair next to her and pulled out a tiny bottle, breaking the seal and screwing a nipple onto the top. "Do you want to feed him?"

"If it's okay." Lacey watched Jordan, bottle in hand, as she picked Amos up from the bouncy seat. She seemed so confident in her skills, so at ease, even with this super tiny baby.

"Hey, little buddy, are you hungry? I bet you are."

The baby was squirming, his face getting red when Jordan handed him to Lacey. She stuck the bottle in his mouth and he was soon eating happily.

Holding the baby gave her something to do, something to think about besides how insecure she felt right now. "So what changed that made you able to take a chance with Ash?"

Jordan drew her shoulders up with her breath and dug the spoon into the carton of ice cream one more time. "You're not going to like this—but, there's a tipping point, when the pain of being away from someone hurts worse than the heartbreak would if it even happened. I mean, if it's going to hurt anyway, you might as well be happy in the meantime, right?"

Lacey stared into her new friend's face. "I never thought about it that way. You're right."

The baby's bottle hissed as he sucked the last bit of milk out of it. Lacey looked up in panic.

Jordan said, "Just sit him up on your lap. Hold his head up with his chin between your thumb and pointy finger—there you go. Now pat his back. He's so new, he's still really limp."

Lacey patted Amos's back until he let out a little burp.

"See, you're a natural. So, are you in love with him?"

The question jerked her back to the conversation. She sighed. "I don't want to be in love with him."

Jordan smiled. "Yeah, that's not what I asked. I said I was nosy and opinionated, so here comes the opinion. If you love him, you have to tell him."

Her eyes on the baby's precious little face, Lacey said, "I don't know if I can do that."

With a shrug, Jordan said, "If it's gonna hurt any-

page 379 of 414

way, what do you have to lose? Don't answer that. Just think about it."

"Thanks, Jordan. It helps to have your perspective." Honestly, it seemed like she had a lot to lose, but if she didn't try, she'd be depriving her babies of their dad without even giving him a real shot. She'd be depriving herself of her husband and Devin of his wife. "It's so hard to sort out."

"Your feelings are justified." When Lacey looked up, Jordan said, "They are. Without question. But if you want a future with him, you're going to have to forgive him. I'll be praying for you, my sweet friend. I know this isn't easy."

Those words lingered in Lacey's mind long after she handed the baby back to Jordan, gave her a hug and thanked her for the time together. She pulled into the driveway at Triple Creek Ranch and put the car in Park.

She'd been praying for wisdom and clarity. She'd prayed for relief from the fear that had plagued her ever since she found out she was pregnant.

He left her in Vegas, yes. And yes, she felt abandoned. But Devin wasn't her mom. It was a completely different situation with a completely different outcome. It was time for her to stop punishing Devin for what her mom had done.

So now, she prayed for the courage to trust him. If it was going to hurt anyway, what did she have to lose?

## Chapter Sixteen

With his arm around Lacey's waist, Devin held his breath as they walked toward the hospital door. Lacey was whispering something under her breath and he didn't dare interrupt her as they inched forward. The last four weeks had been peaceful, idyllic almost, the routine of the long farm days calming in a strange way. Lacey had seemed content to simply be together, often joining him as he'd done his chores, pestering him to share stories about his childhood. He obliged her with the adventures of Tanner, Garrett and Devin. And they'd both managed to ignore the fact that the date of their babies' birth and their self-imposed deadline for a decision was coming soon.

He hadn't even wanted to mention the parenting class, but with a determined set to her chin, Lacey reminded him it was their last chance. She'd never backed away from a challenge as long as he'd known her and his admiration only grew as he watched her battle her fear and win. When they reached the door, she didn't look up. He opened the door and she walked through it.

A wall of cold air hit them in the face when they entered the building and her steps faltered, but he just kept going and her lips started moving again. A few seconds later, he opened the door to the classroom and they were inside. When he eased her into a chair close to the door, she looked up and took a deep breath.

He was so proud of her for not giving up. They weren't home free yet—they had the hospital tour to get through after class but, for the first time, he felt hopeful that they'd be able to do it. "You okay?"

Her face was still a little white, her hand a little clammy in his, but she nodded. "Now it's just any other classroom."

The teacher walked to the front of the room with a big toothy smile on her face. "Welcome to Magnificent Multiples! If you'll look in your complimentary diaper bag, you'll find that we've put together a notebook for you with lots of ideas for how to manage your multiples, whether you have two or three or more!"

Devin turned to Lacey with wide eyes and mouthed, "More?"

She shook her head and murmured, "I think I'm good with two, thanks."

The teacher walked them through the notebook, filling his head with all kinds of advice he didn't know he needed. Feeding schedule. Sleep schedule. Gender-neutral clothing because who wants to be figuring out if a onesie is pink or blue in the middle of the night? Not a lot of snaps because they take too long. And the best news of all… They could expect for their twins to go through six *thousand* diapers in the first year.

When Lacey squeezed his hand and said, "Breathe," he realized he'd been muttering out loud.

He didn't hear a lot after that. For his own sanity, it

was probably better that he think about other things. He was planning to be involved in the care of the babies and he knew it was probably going to be hard, but some things? It was probably better to just not know.

"So, we're going to take a small break before we walk through the labor and delivery wing in the hospital." The teacher's bright, cheerful voice cut into his thoughts. He scowled. She could afford to be cheerful. She wasn't going to be buying six thousand diapers this year. "In your bag, you'll find some peanut butter crackers and a couple of small bottles of water. For a busy parent of multiples, it's just as important to keep your own energy up when you're out and about with your babies."

As Lacey handed him a package of crackers, she grinned. "Don't forget to pack your snacks, cowboy."

"I'll just add that to the long list of things I need to remember. My brain is tired." He pulled the plastic wrap apart and took out a cracker. "She didn't answer any of my questions."

"Like what?" Lacey looked amused, but he knew for a fact she'd been chasing that barrel-racing championship buckle when other girls were babysitting. She had little to no baby experience, just like him.

"Like what do you do if you're by yourself and both of them are crying at the same time? What if one of them's hungry and one of them's wet? Or one needs to burp and the other needs a nap? She didn't cover any of that stuff."

Her expression went from amused to concerned, her bottle of water halfway to her mouth. "You're right, she didn't. Those are very good questions."

He shrugged as he crunched on a cracker. "I guess

we'll figure it out. In the meantime, we got some coupons and a diaper bag full of samples."

She put the bottle of water down and said firmly, "It's going to be fine."

He shot her a look. "Are you saying that to yourself or to me?"

"Both." She laughed as their facilitator cleared her throat in the doorway to the classroom.

"Okay, everyone, we're going on a little tour. We'll be visiting an empty L&D suite but there are people in the other ones, so remember to be respectfully quiet."

Lacey's expression turned wary. She sucked in a breath, and Devin remembered they weren't out of the woods yet.

He took her hand in his and helped her to her feet. "Don't overthink it. We're just going for a walk."

Lacey nodded, but her throat worked as she swallowed.

Waiting until the other expectant parents left the room to move into line behind them, he said, "Have you thought any more about names?"

She followed him into the hall, her eyes straight ahead, her hand wrapped around his in a painful grip. "You mean other than Elmo and Prudence?"

He smiled. "Yeah. But to be honest, I do kind of like those now that we've been calling them that."

"Not a chance are we naming our kids Elmo and Prudence. We could keep the initials, though, if we can think of something to go with them."

"Like Penelope or Patience?" He raised an eyebrow.

"Or Paul or Patrick for boys."

"Okay." He hung back as their leader scanned her badge across the reader mounted beside the double doors and the group entered the OB wing. "I see where you're going with this." He thought for a minute. "I like the name Phoebe. It's old-fashioned but feminine. It would sound good over the loudspeaker at the rodeo. Riding next is… Phoebe… Cole."

Lacey let out a shaky laugh as he dragged the syllables out like the announcer would. "You're right. It's cute. I say yes to Phoebe. Can we use Rose as a middle name? It's my grandmother's name and she helped raise me after my mom left."

"Phoebe Rose." He tried it out to see how it sounded together. "It sounds classy. It has meaning. I like it."

They stopped outside a glass window where a nurse in pink scrubs was wrapping a baby in a white blanket with pink and blue stripes. When she saw them in the window, she smiled and held up the baby, who looked like a burrito with fat baby cheeks.

"Oh, how precious." Lacey put her hand on the glass. "It's so hard to believe that we'll be seeing our babies very soon. In some ways, I'm so not ready. In others, that day can't get here fast enough."

"I feel the same way." He realized they were the only ones still loitering by the nursery window and reached for her arm. When she startled at his touch, he realized that while she was handling this better than he'd expected, she was still strung tight with anxiety. "You're doing great. We're going to make happy memories here."

Her eyes met his and she nodded. "You're right. I can do this. Let's go."

As they followed the group toward the other end of the hall, Devin said, "Do you have any thoughts about an E name for a boy? The only one I can think of is Elvis, but I think maybe that's a no?"

"Definite no on Elvis." As they waited to enter the maternity suite, her fingers tightened on his and she visibly focused on breathing.

"Let's go see where our babies are going to be born." As the group filed out, he stepped into the maternity suite with Lacey. He wasn't sure what he expected, but it was nice, set up kind of like a living room with warm wood tones and a sofa and chairs. The medical equipment was there but as unobtrusive as possible.

Lacey's grip on his hand loosened slightly as she looked around the room. "It looks pretty nice in here. We could bring one of the quilts from home and it would be even better."

*Home.* The word wound through his consciousness and came to rest somewhere in the vicinity of his heart, the feeling even more pronounced because he felt it, too. The farmhouse hadn't been home since his family died, but now, with Lacey there, it was home again.

She made it feel like home.

Devin grinned. "I agree. A quilt would be perfect. And maybe we could bring in some wildflowers and one of the cows, a few piglets…"

She elbowed him. "You are so annoying."

With a grin, he slung his arm around her shoulders. "Yeah, I know."

As they walked out to the car, she said, "What about Eli? It has a good solid sound. James Eli Cole?"

"James Eli? It's perfect. My mom would be tickled that we'll have a Sweet Baby James." He chuckled as he unlocked the truck and pulled open the door for her, holding her arm as she awkwardly got in. "Eli and Phoebe. It sounds right."

When she was fully in the truck, she turned to look at him. "Did we just name our babies?"

"I think we did. We are *such* good parents."

She was laughing when he closed the door. He paused for just a second to acknowledge the enormity of what they'd just accomplished. He closed his eyes, winging a quick prayer of thanks to God because after two months of false starts, they'd finally attended a class at the hospital.

And they had rocked it.

Turning the key in the ignition and starting the air-conditioning blowing, he realized he hadn't asked her... "So what exactly were you saying to yourself as you walked into the building?"

A bemused smile crossed her face. "I spent last night reading stories about women who've done incredible things—hard things—and telling myself that if those women could do those amazing things, I could do this. So as I was walking in, I was saying their names to myself. *Mother Teresa. Malala. Elizabeth Blackwell. Eleanor Roosevelt.* Like that."

Devin leaned over the armrest and kissed her temple. "They can't hold a candle to you. Let's go home."

And he smiled. Finally things were starting to go right.

Lacey was still smiling when Devin pulled up to the farm. She hadn't realized how alone she'd felt in her fear, but his easy acceptance had lifted that weight and made it possible for her to face it.

Tonight, walking in the doors of the hospital had

been uncomfortable, but she'd known she could do it. And when they'd walked through the hospital to the labor and delivery, she'd been nervous, but he'd kept her mind occupied talking about the babies' names.

She rubbed her belly with both hands. Phoebe and Eli. She loved them so much.

"Why's the house dark?" Devin's eyes were on the farmhouse as he held his hands out and helped her slide out of the truck to the ground.

"I don't know." At almost thirty weeks pregnant, she was feeling so unwieldy, more and more off balance as the twins grew heavier. Devin's hand at her elbow steadied her as they started toward the house. "Did Tanner mention he had something to do tonight?"

"He didn't say anything to me." Devin walked up the steps and stuck his key in the lock, but the doorknob turned easily, the door pushing open. "Tanner? You here?"

Devin flipped on the lights. Tanner sat in the recliner, a pile of unread mail on the table beside him, an open letter in his lap, his face carved into lines that hadn't been there when they'd left for the hospital. Sadie lay at his feet.

Lacey didn't know what was going on but it couldn't be good. Tanner was not one for dramatics. He was the quiet, capable, *reasonable* one. If he was sitting in the dark, it had to be bad.

Devin sat down in the chair beside him, leaning forward, his elbows on his knees.

"I'll go make some coffee." Lacey started for the door.

"Stay. This affects you, too." Tanner's voice was raspy and strained.

She slowly turned around. "What's going on, Tanner?"

Devin's brother lifted the piece of paper from his lap and let it flutter to the ground. "The bank is foreclosing on the farm. They've given us thirty days to come up with the full amount of the loan or they're taking it."

"What! Why? We've been making payments!" Devin grabbed the paper from the floor and stared at it. "They can't do this."

"Yeah, they can. They started sending notices about six months ago that they were calling in the loan because the payments had been erratic. I was hoping they'd give us some more time since we're turning a small profit now, but they're not. We've lost the farm. *I* lost the farm."

"No, Tanner, that's not true. The farm is all of our responsibility. We let you down."

Devin's brother stood, his face expressionless. "You didn't let me down. Tomorrow I'll go to the bank and try to talk to them one more time, but I'm afraid we're out of chances unless we can somehow come up with ninety-seven thousand dollars."

"I have some money put aside and I can ask my dad if he could loan us the rest until the farm is profitable," Lacey offered hesitantly.

"No." Tanner and Devin said it at the same time, turning identical brown eyes to her.

"I figured that's what you would say, but if you change your mind, say the word and I'll make the call." At Devin's side, Lacey slid her hand into his.

He cleared his throat. "I think we need to pray. I know we're not really into talking about our faith— and that's okay, I'm not knocking it. But this… It seems important to me."

Tanner shook his head. "I'm not sure prayers are gonna do a lot of good now, Dev."

"Humor me." Devin held out a hand to his brother, who reluctantly took it. Lacey held hers out, and Tanner gripped it with his work-worn hand. She couldn't imagine how he felt. He'd worked so hard.

Devin bowed his head and took a deep breath. "Dear God, I'm not good at this kind of stuff. But this is about family. It's about home. It's about a foundation for our future. We need You, God, and we pray if it's Your will that You would help us find a way to save the farm. Help us to trust You no matter what the answer is. Amen."

There was a sheen in Tanner's eyes when they looked up. He cleared his throat. "Thanks, Devin. I'm going up to bed now."

His footsteps heavy, Tanner climbed the stairs, leaving Devin and Lacey still holding hands in the middle of the living room.

"Hey." Lacey wrapped her arms around Devin's waist, holding on as he pulled her closer, looking into his steady brown eyes. "I just want you to know I love you. I've always loved you. I know I haven't been fair to you, but I'm trying."

She wasn't sure when things had shifted—it had happened so gradually—but she knew that he could do it. He wasn't just acting like a victim of something that had happened to him. He'd consistently chosen the path that had brought him closer to the man that she had always known he could be.

He reached up and brushed her hair away from her face with a gentle hand. "You can have as long as you need. I'm not going anywhere. I want to be a husband and a dad. I love you."

Up to this point, their lives had been spent waiting for that eight seconds or fourteen seconds in the arena, and their lives weren't better when they did that. They were always looking for that next record-breaking ride, the next high point. And yeah, they'd accomplished some amazing things, but they'd missed so many moments, looking into the future, just waiting.

She didn't want to miss the moments anymore.

They were too precious.

"Your prayer was perfect. It was the right thing to do." She didn't want to move from his arms. His hand rested on her belly where their babies were growing and she suddenly wanted her children to grow up in this house. To run in the fields and swing on a rope swing into the spring-fed pond.

He sighed again, his arms tightening around her. "It's all I know to do. We've worked as hard as we can work. We're out of options. Now we have to believe that if God wants us to be here, He'll provide a way."

# *Chapter Seventeen*

The sky was deep purple, with just a hint of orange in the west, when Devin headed to the barn with a bottle for Nemo. He found Garrett already in the barn feeding ravenous baby goats.

Garrett looked up without a smile, eliciting an angry butt from one of the babies when the nipple slipped out of its mouth. "How're you doing?"

"Not good. You?"

"Not good. Not since I talked to Tanner this morning. I put my house in town on the market a few hours ago but I doubt it'll sell in time to make a difference. It's worth a shot, I guess, but even then, it's not going to bring in the kind of money we need to stave off the bank."

"I don't have anything left to sell." Devin paused, earning a firm nudge from Nemo for his inattention. "Unless maybe I could sell Reggie."

"No. We don't sell family members."

"Without a farm, he won't have a place to live anyway." Devin paused, grief at the thought of losing their home settling like a weight on his shoulders. He'd imagined raising his kids here. Growing old with his brothers. It wasn't just a house. Their future was on the line. "We could sell off the cattle, but it would take years to recover from the loss of the herd, which wouldn't solve anything."

"We don't need ways to make income now. We need an influx of capital. I knew money was tight, but this is bad. I can't believe we didn't know." Garrett held the bottles up higher so the baby goats could get to the last little bit. "Okay, okay, here you go, you little beggars."

"I guess Tanner wanted to fix it so we didn't have to worry about it. He's always been that way. He tried to get me to come home after I hurt my ankle so he could take care of me. He was right, but I wasn't having it."

Garrett sighed. "Well, you have to be ready to make a big change like that. And now you're married to Lacey and about to have twins, so what would you do different anyway?"

Devin turned incredulous eyes on Garrett. "Dude. So many things I would do different."

"Fair point." The kids sucked the bottles dry and Garrett pulled them away, eliciting bleats from the little goats.

Nemo was a slow drinker compared with the goats. One of them tried to jump up and steal the calf's bottle. Devin nudged it away with one leg, amused at its tenacity when it immediately tried again.

Devin was pretty sure he already knew what Garrett would say about his proposal, but he was going to talk to him about it anyway because they were all in this together.

Still, he hesitated. He'd come so far in repairing

the relationship with his brothers and the last thing he wanted to do was damage it again. "So…"

Garrett looked up.

"I got an email last night around midnight. There's an invitational rodeo in Colorado Springs this weekend. The purse is a hundred thousand dollars." He kept his eyes on the hungry calf, not quite able to make eye contact with Garrett.

His brother sat back on his heels. "That sounds like a terrible idea if you're thinking about it. You're well past the deadline to enter anyway."

Nemo finished his bottle and Devin pulled the towel scrap from where it rested over his shoulder and wiped the foamy milk residue from the little calf's face. "That's the thing. It's been booked for weeks, but one of the riders broke his shoulder blade in training yesterday and they want a full roster. They emailed me to see if I was interested."

"It's not worth it."

"What's not worth it?" Tanner's voice broke into their conversation. He stood in the doorway to the stall, the keys to the ATV in one hand, a travel mug of coffee in the other.

Devin shot Garrett a look. He wasn't ready to talk about this with Tanner. Not yet.

Garrett shook his head. "Devin's thinking about riding in the invitational this weekend."

"That's about the dumbest thing I've ever heard." Tanner walked closer. "You could lose your foot. You have a wife and two babies to think about. I suggest you put them first."

"How do I put them first if we lose the farm and I

can't support them?" He'd been trying to shove it down all day but the panic rose like bile in Devin's throat.

He did have a wife and two babies counting on him. How could he turn down a chance to save their livelihood? The livelihood of his older brother and the family home for all of them?

"I've got to get out of here." Devin gave Nemo a final scratch behind the ears, grabbed his cane and started for the house, Garrett right in step with him. Devin cocked a glance at his brother. "Where do you think you're going?"

"I'm going in the kitchen with you because I'm hungry and because I want to make sure you tell your wife about this craziness."

"I'll tell her, but I'll tell her when I'm ready. Now get out of my way. I'm going to cook some supper."

When he entered the living room, Lacey was just coming out of the kitchen. She had her hair in one of those loose bun things. Tendrils fell around her face, which was pink from the warmth of the stove. His heart filled to overflowing with love for her. It stopped him in his tracks—the inexplicable, overwhelming feelings he had for this woman.

"I just stuck some corn bread in the oven and I got the greens Tanner picked simmering. I have cookies to make tonight, so I thought I'd put my feet up for a few minutes while the corn bread is in the oven. What are you guys up to? Feeding time?"

Garrett gave Devin a pointed look. "What's going on, Devin?"

"Devin?" Lacey turned toward him, concern in her eyes. "Are you okay?"

"I'm fine. I got an email asking me to compete in

the invitational in Colorado Springs this weekend. They had a late withdrawal and they want to fill the roster."

"You're not going to do it, though, right?" She'd gone very still, one arm curving around her belly in a protective gesture.

"I…"

Garrett interjected. "Why are you even considering this? The only sane answer is 'No, I'm not going to do it.'"

"Devin?" Lacey's eyes were steady on his. "Why would you risk it? You've come so far."

Garrett turned his gaze to Devin, as well. "Why would you risk it, Devin?"

Devin closed his eyes and sucked in a breath, counting to ten so he wouldn't yell at his brother. He gave up before he reached six. "Garrett, get out. Go fix yourself a sandwich at your own house and let me talk to my wife."

"There's no food at my house." With a scowl, Garrett turned and stalked toward the front door.

"You should've thought of that before you tried to pick a fight between me and Lacey."

The door closed behind Garrett, who was still muttering. "Try to do the right thing by your brother and what do you get? Nothing. Not even a crumb of corn bread."

"Sometimes I wonder how I have the same DNA as those two. We couldn't be more different." He walked into the kitchen. "Do you want to have some tea and talk?"

She nodded and he pulled two glasses out of the cabinet and poured sweet tea over ice. He set her glass in front of the chair she'd settled into at the kitchen table and got the lemon out of the refrigerator for her.

Hashing out the offer with Lacey about competing in the invitational was not high on his list of things he wanted to do. In fact, he couldn't think of many things he wanted to do less, but he was learning. Hiding from issues and problems didn't mean they didn't exist. It just meant putting off the pain until later. And sometimes waiting meant the pain was going to be a whole lot worse than it would've been if he'd just dealt with it in the first place.

"So tell me about the offer." She looked down to where her hands cupped the cold glass, her lashes hiding her eyes.

"Any other time, I wouldn't consider it. I know you've had your doubts, but I've made my peace with retiring. I'll leave that to you and our kids, if they want to rodeo, but... This invitational has a grand prize of one hundred thousand dollars."

She nodded slowly. "That money would save the farm."

"It would."

"If you won."

"Yeah." That outcome was far from a given. He hadn't been on a bucking horse in months. He was the current titleholder and he could assume with some degree of certainty that he had the muscle memory to pull it off, but even in top shape, sometimes the best riders still got thrown. "There's no guarantee."

"I don't want you to do it. I'm scared. And it's not just me being scared for you. I'm scared for what it means for our kids."

He nodded, hoping Lacey didn't notice his fingers clenching around his glass. "I know."

"I understand if you feel you have to, but I'm begging you not to do it, Devin. Please don't take that chance. There has to be another way to save the farm."

"If there is I haven't thought of it yet."

"You will." Lacey's eyes were so dark, he could barely see her pupils, but he could see the storm of turmoil in them. He reached for her hand and pulled her to her feet and into his arms, feeling the tension in her as she battled for control.

"Can I say one thing?"

She nodded and he took her hand, placing it over his heart. "I know it's tempting to be reminded of how you've been hurt before. Maybe when you feel that doubt creeping in, just remember you're the one this heart beats for. I'll always come back, Lacey, I promise. Can you just promise you'll trust me? Please?"

She hesitated but lifted one shoulder and let it drop. "I can promise I'll try."

"Let's eat supper and then you've got to get some rest and so do I. No one got any sleep last night. But no matter what happens, we're going to have a lot of work to do around here." He tipped her face toward his and pressed a kiss to her lips, almost losing it when he felt them tremble under his. "I love you."

"I love you, too."

*Trust me.*

He prayed that he would be trustworthy, that she would see him that way. The words were easy to say and so hard to live up to. But somehow he had to find a solution to what they were facing as a family.

Somehow he had to find a way.

\* \* \*

Lacey lumbered out of bed at four forty-five the next morning. Sleep was getting more and more impossible the bigger the babies got. In the adjoining bathroom, she splashed cold water on her face and looped her long brown hair into a loose bun on her head. She was almost positive she'd heard Devin in the kitchen making breakfast. He wasn't sleeping either, apparently.

And no wonder. It was hard to imagine a worse scenario for a ranch family than losing the ranch. They'd had some hard times on their ranch growing up, but she didn't think they'd ever come close to losing it.

She didn't blame them for being tied up in knots about it. Suddenly not knowing where she'd be taking her babies home from the hospital was a little disconcerting, to say the least.

Following the scent of coffee into the kitchen, she went straight to the pot. She poured herself a cup and grabbed a biscuit from the stove, taking a bite as she turned toward the table. Her motions slowed as she saw a familiar stack of papers.

It was the divorce papers she'd brought with her, the ones that Devin had said he wouldn't sign unless she stayed until the babies were born.

Her first reaction was a flash of anger. She'd been abandoned before… Why should she expect him to be any different? He'd wanted to prove to her that he could change. That he could be a better person.

She picked up the papers and turned to the back page, even though she had a feeling she knew what she was going to find.

And she did find it. His dark scrawl on the very last page.

She sank down into the kitchen chair and stared at the signatures on the page that meant they were divorced. She felt the acid rise in her throat as fear bloomed in her heart.

She saw just the corner of a small yellow sticky note between the pages and pulled it out. In the same dark scrawl it said, *Please trust me, Lacey.*

Had he just been pretending to be content with being a family man? Or had she been the one pretending… pretending to give him another chance?

Holding the note in her hand, she realized the anger and fear had drained away, leaving her numb. She had no idea how she felt. She needed air.

Picking up her coffee, she started out to the front porch as Tanner came down the stairs. "Is he gone?"

"Yes."

"I thought I heard the truck start up. I'm so sorry, Lacey. I don't know what to say."

"He signed the divorce papers." She had to swallow hard, but the words still barely rasped out. "And he left a note that said to trust him."

Tanner didn't say anything, just shook his head and went into the kitchen. A few seconds later, she heard the chink of a ceramic mug hitting the countertop and coffee splashing in it.

She continued to the porch with her own mug of coffee, walking out into the pre-sunrise quiet. A rooster crowed from the backyard and she wondered if he was confused by the humans being awake already.

Her feelings were so confused, her heart literally aching in her chest. She didn't know what to believe. Devin had shown her again and again over the course of the last few months that he'd changed. That he *was* a person she could trust. Still, she couldn't help but feel abandoned once again. Hurt and confused again. And once again, he'd gone without a word, leaving a document behind.

Just over seven months ago it had been their marriage certificate. This morning it was their divorce papers. And what did that even mean? Had he signed them because he was breaking their agreement and planning to do something he knew she wouldn't approve of?

*Please trust me*, he'd said. How did she trust him when he had all the power? But did he? From the beginning, she'd been the one who wanted to end things. He'd been the one holding on to a marriage that seven months ago hadn't even existed except on paper.

Maybe by signing the divorce papers, he was giving her the power to rewrite the script. Giving her the power to be the one who walked away. Giving her the choice.

She closed her eyes, her mind drifting back to the moment in the kitchen when he'd placed her hand on his chest. That strong, steady heartbeat under her hand.

Walking to the porch swing, she sat down, letting her feet lift off the floor as it swung back with her weight. Out of the corner of her eye, she saw something on the far end of the swing and she reached for it. It was Devin's Bible. She'd seen him reading it just yesterday.

She ran her hand over the smooth surface, the pages curling in the summer humidity. It was getting ragged, the color of the leather worn from use. She opened it and realized that the inside pages were filled with notes and tabs and bookmarks in Devin's handwriting.

She turned to the first one. Psalm 139. *I praise you for I am fearfully and wonderfully made.*

Her throat began to ache as she turned to the next tab. 2 Corinthians. *For when I am weak, then I am strong.*

Tears gathered in her eyes as she turned to the next marker in Titus 3. *He saved us not because of works done by us in righteousness but according to his own mercy... So that being justified by his grace we might become heirs...*

Faster now, she turned to Ephesians 2, tears streaming down her face. *For we are his workmanship.*

Galatians 3:26. *You are all children of God through faith...* And in Devin's hand in the margin, she saw that he'd written *It's not who I think I am, it's who God says I am. God says I am His.*

*God says I am His.*

Slowly, she closed the book. As she lifted her coffee and took a trembling sip, she watched pink dawn spread slowly up the darkness, the stars winking out one by one as light filled the sky. How did she trust that the sun would come up each morning? Because it had for all the days of her life?

How did she trust a God she couldn't see? Because even in her darkest moments, she knew that there was hope. Day after day, she was reminded of His goodness and faithfulness. Even when she didn't understand her circumstances.

The front door opened and Tanner stepped outside. He walked to the porch rail and leaned on it, his mug of coffee in his hand. "I tried to call him. He didn't pick up. What do you want to do?"

She wasn't confused anymore. She wasn't numb. She knew. "What I really want to do...is believe him when he says trust me."

He shot her a look. "Past experience says that's a horrible idea."

She sighed and wiped her face of the tears that had fallen as she'd read the verses in Devin's Bible. "I know."

Tanner sighed, his eyes still on hers. "Are you going to call him?"

"No." She hesitated. "For some reason he needs time and I...need to give it to him. If we're really going to make our relationship work, I have to be able to trust him. I do trust him."

It was a terrifying feeling, like wading into the deep water and not knowing if the undertow would sweep you away or if the waves would gently nudge you back to shore where the warm sand and the safety waited.

But Devin had fought hard. She knew he hadn't made this decision lightly. She wanted to trust him. And she believed in him. So she did.

# Chapter Eighteen

Five days after Devin left in the middle of the night, Lacey heard the television come on in the living room and her heart rate immediately skyrocketed. The invitational rodeo was tonight.

Tanner had repeatedly tried to reach Devin with no response other than a short text that said, I'm fine. Trust me.

He'd checked in with her by text twice a day, morning and evening, to make sure she was doing okay. She wanted to ask where he was and what he was doing, but she didn't. He'd asked for her trust.

She was trying to give it to him. But the longer she waited, the more worried she got. She prayed that he was attending meetings, that he was getting enough sleep. He'd been under so much stress. Was he sticking with the lifestyle changes that had helped him on the path to wellness or was he back in that old environment and tempted to give in to the lure of old habits?

He'd signed the divorce papers. And she couldn't help but ask herself what he was planning for her, for their unborn babies. But every time she wondered if he'd somehow changed his mind about wanting to build a family together, she remembered him placing her hand on his heart and promising he would always come back.

Tanner had placed a plate of cold cuts, fruit and vegetables on the coffee table in front of the couch, but the idea of eating right now made her feel sick.

Even so, when the rodeo started with the national anthem, she felt a wave of nostalgia. She'd been competing since she was a preteen and the rodeo, in many ways, was home to her.

On television, the announcer said, "We were sad to hear that Travis Montrose won't be competing tonight due to a broken shoulder blade during practice earlier this week. The latest report from his family is that he's recuperating well after surgery and promises to be here next year."

There was no mention of Devin filling in.

A band of muscles tightened across her stomach, a quick rush of pain catching her off guard and stealing her breath. She closed her eyes, waiting it out. Obviously, sitting here was doing her no good. She pushed to her feet. "I need to get some air. Call me if you see Devin."

Grabbing a handful of carrots from the kitchen, she walked outside into the balmy Southern night. The cicadas were singing and a soft breeze was blowing. She focused on the sound of the animals in the field. It felt so peaceful compared with the turmoil brewing inside her.

She walked to the edge of the pasture, and Dolly took a few timid steps toward her. A carrot held out in Lacey's flat hand was the deciding factor and the sweet mare stuck her head over the fence for a treat. "Hey, girl. Are you feeling a little lonely?"

Dolly looked at her with big velvet brown eyes.

"Yeah, me, too." Walking toward the barn, Lacey pressed a hand into her back where it ached. She was carrying so much weight in the front that her back had been killing her all day. She focused on breathing, on the random flicker of the fireflies across the pasture. One. Two...

Despite Devin's absence, despite everything, she could take in the beauty of a quiet country night. She could appreciate that she belonged here. He belonged here, too. She whispered the words. "Protect him, please, God. Bring him home safely."

As if He had heard her pleas, the rattle of a horse trailer and the growly engine of a truck reached her ears as it turned into the drive. She barely dared to hope that it was Devin, even as an expectant feeling rose in her chest. Her hands went to her stomach where their twins were kicking. *Please, God, let it be Devin.*

His old truck pulled to a stop near the barn. She let out the breath she'd been holding—it was him.

Lacey rushed toward the truck, meeting him as he slid out of the cab and onto the ground. He took a step and caught her up in his arms, burying his face in her hair. "You stayed."

"Of course I stayed."

"You didn't call me." He put his arm around her as they walked toward the porch. "I was afraid you were mad."

"I knew you needed space to do what you needed to do."

"What did I do to deserve you?" He stopped walking when they reached the glow of the porch light and turned to look at her. She studied his face. He looked tired, his beard a little stubbly, his eyes weary but clear, and she was so happy to see him.

She laughed, the sound winging into the wind and with it her worries about Devin. She still had no idea where they would be living in a month, but he was safe at home. "Clearly, you don't deserve me. I've been a wreck since you left."

"I'm sorry, Lacey. I felt like I had to do something to help save the farm. And I wanted you to have the space to walk away, if you wanted to. I hoped you wouldn't."

He turned to face her, holding her two hands in his. "I want to get the words right but I don't know if I can. I'm so—um—emotional. I've been practicing."

With another laugh, she leaned forward and kissed him. He dropped one of her hands and cupped her face, his whole body relaxing into hers, bringing her into the curve of his embrace. He sighed.

"That is not helping me clear my thoughts." He took a step back, pressing his hands together as if he were praying, and took a deep bolstering breath.

He released it, holding his hands out, palms open to her as if he couldn't do anything else. "You have my heart, Lacey. From the moment I saw you standing in the driveway with those awful divorce papers, I knew that you and I could have the greatest adventure together. I don't need the spotlight. I don't need the risk and the thrill. I need you. Just you."

Lacey's eyes filled, her vision blurring.

"I had a lot of time to think on the drive. I realized I was afraid of losing hold of who I was, but it's past time to let go of all that old shame I felt, all the things I tried to push down and hide. And I have to put away old dreams that don't fit me anymore."

She placed her hands in his and he held them tightly, looking down at her with the most tender expression. "I trust that we're going to build new dreams. Together."

As they stood in the warm circle of light from the porch, he let go of her hand and dug in his pocket. She gasped as he pulled out a ring. She recognized her grandma Rose's diamond ring immediately. "Devin, how...?"

"Your dad gave it to me. I went to ask his permission to ask you for your hand in marriage. I want to do it right this time." He looked down with a smile and tossed her words from months ago back to her. "In the right order."

Kneeling down, he held one of her hands and held the ring up with the other. "Lacey Elizabeth Jenkins, I love you and I promise to love you for the rest of my life. Through everything. Mountaintops and valleys, kids and dogs, rain and sunshine. I promise I will never give up on our love."

Containing her tears was not even a possibility as he said, "Will you do me the honor of becoming my wife? Officially?"

Lacey held out her hand and he slid the ring onto her finger. She looked down at the old ring and back to Devin's eyes, her gaze catching on his and holding it. "I was so afraid of being hurt again. But I realized after you left the other day that if I had to choose between safety and love, there was no contest. I choose love. A safe life without you is not a life I want. I trust you and I will always love you. Now, please, come here?"

"So that's a yes?" He stood with a laugh as she grabbed his head and pulled his lips to meet hers.

"Yes!" She dropped her head to his shoulder and

stood in his embrace, letting happiness and hope for their future wash over her, his solid strength reminding her that together they could face anything. "Yes. Yes. Yes."

A throat cleared behind them. Devin lifted his head with a smile. His brother stood on the porch, a wary expression on his face.

Devin sighed. "Well, I guess you know I didn't win a hundred thousand dollars."

"I figured that when I didn't see you ride tonight." Tanner took the steps in his slow, steady way. "It's all right. We'll figure something out. I'll go let Reggie into the pasture."

Devin put a hand out to stop Tanner. "Actually that's not Reggie."

His brother turned slowly around, his eyes narrowing. "Where's Reggie?"

Devin took a few steps toward the trailer. "Being asked to participate in the invitational shook something loose in my brain that I should've thought about a long time ago. Sure, I'm a rodeo champ, but Reggie's a rodeo champ in his own right." He shrugged, with a half smile. "Lacey's dad helped me line up five ranchers who are willing to pay a steep price to have Reggie sire a foal. It's not a hundred thousand dollars, but maybe it's enough to negotiate more time with the bank."

Unemotional, practical Tanner had tears standing in his eyes. He cleared his throat again, a perplexed expression on his face as he tried to figure out what to do with all the stuff he must be feeling.

Devin hugged his brother, who'd been the one to give him another chance, and he was so grateful that he could be the one to give Tanner one. "I know you aren't sure you can count on me yet. It's okay. I'll be right here, pulling my weight. It's about time."

Tanner gave a short nod and looked away, his fist pressed to his lips. When he looked back, his voice was thick with emotion. "If that's not Reggie, who is it?"

Devin walked to the end of the trailer and opened it. He walked into the trailer, speaking softly to the patient horse inside. "Come on, beautiful girl. Someone's waiting to see you."

As he backed her out of the trailer, Lacey gasped. She dug one of the carrots from her pocket and held it out for her horse as Devin led her forward. "It's Magpie. Oh, sweet girl, I'm so glad to see you."

"Your dad and I thought Magpie might be a good pasture buddy for Dolly." His heart was so full—the expression on Lacey's face more than worth the trouble it had been to bring her horse to Alabama.

Lacey gasped, grabbing her belly, leaning forward with a low groan.

Devin was at her side in an instant, his arm around her, holding her steady. "Babe? What's going on?"

"It's okay." Her eyes still closed, she ground the words through her teeth. "This has been going on all day. I'm fine."

Tanner took Magpie's lead rope and guided her toward the barn as Lacey grabbed Devin's hand, her grip nearly cutting the circulation off.

She looked up with panic on her face. "It's too early. We're barely even thirty weeks yet. We can't have the babies. I won't do it."

Devin looked up and nodded at Tanner as he came out of the barn. "We need to go. Now."

His brother dug his keys out of his pocket and ran to his truck, turning it quickly and pulling up next to them.

Devin helped Lacey into the back seat of the truck and jumped in beside her as Tanner sped out of the driveway toward the hospital.

His heart was racing, thoughts throbbing in his head like an ache that wouldn't go away. He'd just figured it all out. They were just getting started. He loved Lacey and he loved their babies and there was absolutely nothing he could do at this point to help them. He wanted to cry, but there were no tears. Nothing except Lacey and their babies.

Devin slid his hands across her belly, shocked to feel how tight it was, and he knew he would give anything to switch places with her.

*Please let them be okay, Lord. Let all of them be okay.*

He murmured into her ear, "I'm gonna be right there with you every step of the way. I love you, Lacey. I'm not going to leave you. I promise. We're doing this together."

Lacey opened her eyes slowly, wincing as she pushed up in the bed. The last five weeks had gone so slowly as she'd remained in the hospital on bed rest, doing everything possible to keep the twins inside and growing. But last night they'd delivered two healthy babies who were breathing without oxygen and holding their own.

She looked to the left and chuckled as she saw Devin asleep in the very uncomfortable recliner he'd been in almost constantly since she'd arrived five weeks ago. But they'd made it. Thirty-five weeks and one day.

A whimper came from a bassinet by the window. Devin shot to his feet. "What? Which baby is it?"

"That's Eli. Phoebe's in the corner."

Devin walked to the bassinet and looked down. "Hey, buddy. Did you kick out of your swaddle? Let's see what we can do about that."

Like a pro—because he'd been practicing with the nurses for five weeks now—he snuggled Eli back into his burrito wrap and lifted him gingerly into his arms. "I can't get over how tiny he is. How much did he weigh again?"

"Five-one. Right? And Phoebe Rose was five-four?"

As if she'd heard her name, Phoebe started stirring in her bassinet. Devin passed the little baby bundle that was Eli to Lacey and crossed the room to Phoebe. He rewrapped her and picked her up, tucking a pacifier that covered nearly her whole face into her mouth. He walked to the bed, swaying gently and crooning to the baby.

Lacey laughed. "You are in so much trouble with that one."

"Why do you say that? I haven't been shopping for a pony yet…okay, I made a few calls, but that's all." He grinned at her. "I know I'm probably going to regret saying this because now that they're here, it isn't going to get easier. They're going to be yelling at us frequently and vehemently at least through their teenage years… But I'm just so glad to meet them."

She looked down into the tiny face of her baby boy, who she imagined would look exactly like Devin when he grew up. He had thick curly brown hair and dark lashes, and he already had her heart, just like his daddy did.

Meeting Devin's gaze, she said, "I love you."

Devin eased down to the side of the bed. "I love you, too. These last few months have been…" He stopped, cleared his throat. "These last few months have been more than I could ever deserve. I'm grateful for every minute, even the awful ones."

The door pushed open with a soft knock, and Tanner stuck his head in. "Y'all up for visitors?"

He had a plate wrapped in tinfoil, and Lacey's eyes snagged on it immediately. "What's that?"

"Just some zucchini brownies, if you're not sick of them. I used your recipe."

"They're good, too," Garrett interjected, as he came into the room, followed by Lacey's dad, Logan Jenkins.

"Hey, Dad, come meet your grandbabies."

Logan crossed to where his daughter reclined in the bed and rubbed her head. "Can't wait."

"Eli, this is Grandpop." She held Eli up for a kiss and her dad obliged, lifting him from her hands and kissing the tiny, fuzzy head.

The rancher's eyes were suspiciously damp. "Pleased to meet you, Eli."

Logan passed the baby to Garrett, who looked down in awe. "Wow, he's so little. He does kind of look like you, though, Devin. I think it's that scrunched-up expression. Or maybe the pointy head."

"You're so funny." Devin scowled. "I hope all you people used the hand sanitizer before you came in here."

Garrett raised an eyebrow at Logan. "I told you he was going to be giving orders."

"They're beautiful babies. Congratulations, guys." Tanner laid the plate of brownies on the counter and slid out the door.

Lacey looked up, meeting Devin's eyes. He shook his head slightly. "It's just gonna take time."

Her dad held his hands out for Phoebe Rose, and as he looked into her face, his eyes filled with tears again. "Your great-grandma Rose would be so proud to know you."

Drawing in a shaky breath, Lacey was almost relieved when the nurse came in to shoo out the visitors so they could do her vitals check. "We'll see you guys a little later."

After Garrett and Logan handed the babies back to their parents and left the room, the nurse turned back and winked at Lacey. "I'll be back in a few. Catch your breath."

Devin put a sleeping Phoebe in her bassinet, reached for Eli and tucked him back into place, before settling on the bed beside Lacey. "You holding up okay?"

"I'm tired but I feel good. I think it'll probably take some time to get my stamina up again."

"We're going to be tired for a long time." He looked down at her with a twinkle in his eye. "Worth it."

"Every second." She lifted her hand into the air for a high five, the diamond ring he'd given her sparkling on her finger. "Up top?"

A fleeting smile crossed his face as tenderness filled his gaze and he leaned forward, giving her a gentle kiss on the lips. "Already there, Lace. I'm already there."

# Epilogue

*Two months later*

Lacey held Devin's hand as they slowly rocked on the porch swing, the baby monitor beside them. It was a warm night for November, still in the sixties, and Lacey was barefoot, one foot sticking out from under the quilt he'd tossed over them when they'd sunk to the swing in exhaustion.

"Do you have any regrets?" Her voice was soft and sleepy.

He looked down at her in surprise. "In general? Sure."

She nudged him with her elbow. "That is not what I'm talking about."

"I definitely have some regrets about inviting a hundred people out here for a wedding this afternoon. I thought they were never going to leave when the dancing started."

Lacey laughed. "That's not what I mean, either."

"My only regret is not realizing sooner that the night